UNFORTUNATELY

Francine

Joan Vassar

To my daughters: Angelique, Ja'Nair, and Mariah, thank you for test reading the work. Your support means much to me. To my BFF Marty' thank you for the great feedback. To my editor Felicia Murrell, thank you for understanding my quirks and rolling with me. To my readers, thank you for embracing my work and me.

PROLOGUE

ATLANTA, GEORGIA
APRIL 1995

She sat across the table from him in a trendy restaurant, downtown Atlanta, unable to believe they were together. He had finally asked her out to her great shock. Frankie was a plain Jane compared to Jalal, but her sister had convinced her that opposites attract. She kept her hands folded under the table, so he wouldn't see them shake. Frankie was jumpy in his company, but even a girl as green as she wouldn't have refused a date with him. He was too striking.

Jalal ordered for them while offering no response to the attractive waitress who treated her as though she were invisible. After speaking with the server, he turned his undivided attention back to her. Frankie wasn't sure if this action pleased or added to her anxiety. She could barely hold eye contact with him, and she was positive she couldn't eat. The longer she engaged with him, the clearer it became that she was out of her league with Jalal Dorsey. She regretted allowing her sister to fill her head with the possibilities.

Jalal stood six feet easy with smooth chocolate skin, deep brown eyes and beautiful lips. His dark hair was cut close with a bit extra on top. The crisp, white dress shirt he wore was open at the throat with the sleeves rolled up past powerful forearms. On his hips and hanging right were a pair of black trousers. Frankie was glad they were seated; the cream-colored table-cloth hid the plainness of her outdated blue dress.

"How long have you and your sister been living in Georgia?" Jalal asked.

Frankie's voice squeaked embarrassingly before she recovered. "We been here about three months."

His eyes narrowed. "You nervous being here with me, Frankie?"

"N-No."

She lowered her gaze to break the intensity of his stare and heard him chuckle. The sound caressed her like velvet.

"Eyes on me, Princess, not the table. I want even the smallest intimacy from you." The smile on his face reached his expressive eyes.

Frankie took a fortifying breath before she brought her eyes back to his. She smiled weakly and nodded her head, slightly acknowledging his request.

"You look pained, Princess, what can I do to make you relax?" Despite her discomfort, he leaned in. "I won't let you get away from me. I want you, woman."

His words made her gasp as she gazed into his beautiful face. Francine wanted to look away—set down his intense stare. But she couldn't back away from his powerful presence. He didn't appear to warrant a response, and she was thankful because she could think of none.

A loud commotion started to the left of the restaurant and seemed to grow closer. Frankie turned as a tall, shapely, caramel skinned woman came barreling toward their table. She had thick, black hair that was parted in the middle and hung about her shoulders. The woman wore a burnt orange dress that clung to her curves and stopped well above her knees. Natural brown leather heels laced up her legs, adding to her appeal, while making Frankie feel even more plain.

"What the fuck, Jalal, you out on a damn date?" the woman shrieked.

Jalal sighed and directed his words to her instead of the woman.

"Frankie, this is not what you think."

The woman also directed her words to Frankie. "Oh, bitch, this is exactly what you think."

Thrown by the chaos, Frankie glanced about the restaurant noticing the shocked and curious faces of the people watching the drama unfold.

She looked to the front door trying to gauge her escape when Jalal's voice brought her back to the matter at hand.

"Tonya, ya know where we stand."

"Where the fuck do we stand, Jalal? What you tryna say?" the woman in the sexy dress continued to yell.

"Frankie, let me take you home." Jalal offered in a dismissive tone.

"I don't think so." Frankie held her hands up as if to ward him off.

Tonya, as Jalal called her, turned her despising gaze on Frankie. "So, you going for the homely type nowadays."

Frankie's spine stiffened as she reached for her purse. She brought her eyes back to meet Jalal's and took a steadying breath. "I don't do drama, and I hate ghetto shit."

Jalal actually laughed when Tonya gasped at the insult, but Frankie didn't waste any time getting the hell on. She turned from the table and marched past the impolite stares of the other patrons toward the entrance. Behind her, she could hear Jalal calling her name, but she ignored him. She pushed at the glass door in a rush and when she stepped into the Georgia night air, she groaned from embarrassment.

She could hear the chaos following her; she wanted to be away from Jalal and his bitch. Frankie made a left on Peachtree Street NE and picked up her pace. She would hail a cab when she was free of the foolishness happening. Jalal yelled her name again as she rounded the corner. There was no need to look back, she'd had enough.

* * *

Troy was seated in his black Mercedes Benz–the tinted windows rolled down. He was people watching as he pursed his lips blowing smoke from the side of his mouth. It had been a rough day and people watching in Atlanta relaxed him. He was flicking the butt of his cigarette out the driver's side window when he felt, rather than saw, a burst of energy to his right. Focusing on the sidewalk in front of Joe's Steakhouse, he saw a young woman step from the restaurant–her demeanor uneasy.

She wore a dark dress that understated her beauty even from this distance. Her hair was pulled up in a neat bun accentuating her slender neck. She cast her eyes around frantically, before turning to the left of the entrance and hurrying away. He was about to get out and offer his assistance when he remembered that he never engaged. Troy almost hooted at the notion. Suddenly, a man and a woman spilled from the restaurant.

"Frankie! Frankie, don't leave!" The guy called after the young woman scurrying away.

"Let that bitch go. Why are you doing this, Jalal?" the woman standing in front of the guy demanded.

Troy watched as the guy turned and yelled in the woman's face. "Tonya, we done here. I don't wanna see yo' ass again. This is the second time ya done this, but I like her. I'm not gonna let you ruin shit."

"Where you meet her, Jalal?" the Tonya woman yelled back in dude's face.

Troy chuckled as he watched the drama unfold. Chick shit—he didn't know any man that handled it well. He also hadn't seen it handled so poorly, but he was thankful to Jalal. If nothing else, the brother was amusing. Troy hadn't chuckled in weeks. The Jalal cat liked crazy women and once upon a time when he was younger, Troy did too. It appeared Jalal was trying to make a change, but old girl in the tight dress wasn't having it. He couldn't help it, Troy leaned back in the plush leather seat and laughed out loud.

Jalal turned toward the car, as if sensing his presence. He turned back to the woman in front of him and slowly bit out. "Stay. The fuck. Outta my way, Tonya."

Troy watched as the younger man strode away in the opposite direction. He decided to follow the Frankie woman. Maybe he *would* interact, it had been *too* long. He would allow himself a reprieve from the darkness that had become his life. Turning the key in the ignition, the headlights came to life as the car drifted into Sunday evening traffic in downtown Atlanta. The night air was mild. Along the sidewalk, lovers intimately held hands, strolling and speaking with one another.

There weren't many people about, a sign that the weekend was coming to a close. He could see the Fox Theatre on the left. On the right, patrons spilled out the door of an Italian restaurant laughing and conversing. Troy found the woman, Frankie, in the middle of the second block. She looked over her shoulder twice as if to ward off trouble; he grimaced. He knew the look and wondered if she detected his presence. Troy didn't consider the thought farfetched because he was indeed trouble.

Traffic moved at a snail's pace, and he was becoming anxious. His plan was to ride up ahead of her, park and get out of his car. He would wait for her to pass and strike up conversation. But there was a jeep in front of him and the light was red. Frankie made it to the corner and turned. When he caught up with her, she was in the middle of the next block approaching the intersection. It was more of a side street, but shorter and darker. The light at the end of the thoroughfare was red.

Troy weighed the disturbing thoughts tumbling over in his head. He was a hazard to the innocent young woman in his sights. He feared his intentions, his anger and his thirst for violence. Mostly, he dreaded his needs and his inability to control them. Still, he was a man and his need to fuck eclipsed all reason at times. This was shaping up to be one of those moments; most alarmingly, he did not wish to reel himself in. It had simply been *too* long.

He allowed his car to crawl down the street behind Frankie. She appeared so engrossed in trying to get away from her date, she didn't even notice him openly following her. When she reached the corner, he considered letting her go, but it was a feeble attempt at regaining control of his person. He blew out a shaky breath and slammed his large fist against the dashboard. Closing his eyes, he tried to steady himself before refocusing on Frankie. He needed to get his mind back on track and then he could go home–jerk off and fall asleep.

At the corner, the girl stopped looking both ways as the light turned green. There was a lamppost illuminating the intersection but not well. Troy had talked himself into backing away when a windowless van screeched to a halt in front of Frankie. The door slid open and a tall dark figure got out, causing Frankie to step back in fear. She screamed as the man grabbed and dragged her into the van before speeding off.

Troy's first mind told him to make a left at the light and head in the opposite direction. Instead, he followed for a few blocks and watched the van blend seamlessly back into traffic. They kept straight on Ponce De Leon until some of the streets had no identifying signs. It was as if the markers had been removed on purpose. As was the way in Atlanta, one could be downtown enjoying the city and excitement, but travel ten minutes in any direction, and one could end up in a run-down area, filled with trees and dilapidated structures. He followed the van to such a place, having turned off his headlights a few blocks back.

The vehicle approached an abandoned automotive shop and drove around back. Troy pulled over to the side of the road, a half block back. What the hell was he doing? She was probably dead already and they had come here to dump the body. He knew he should make a U-turn and leave, but he didn't. Troy rolled his car slowly up the narrow drive, praying he didn't get a nail in one of his tires. He did not need to be caught in a place like this; he couldn't go back to jail. He would take his own life before succumbing to captivity again.

In front of the building, a lone streetlight flickered. Troy reached into the glove box and retrieved his gun. He checked the weapon, then got out of the car. The stench of rotted trash assailed him. Closing the car door quietly, he stepped in something soft and his shoe sank into the squishy matter when he added his weight. He turned his head as the trees around him began moving on an easy breeze that carried more foul air. The bushes shook, and small squeaks could be heard under the noise of the insects. He turned his mind from rodents and the unpleasantness of the situation.

Drawing his gun, he approached the van. His educated guess—there were at least two men; one to drive and one to subdue the girl. Still, there could be more than two, so he advanced cautiously. Once on the side of the vehicle, he looked guardedly inside—empty. Behind him, Troy heard a gut-wrenching scream. She was still alive. Stealth like, he moved toward the building, observing from the dirty window two bright floodlights hanging over a pipe from the ceiling. Frankie was cuffed to a hook dangling from above and she was on her tiptoes.

A dark-skinned man stepped forward and slapped her. "Shut up, bitch!"

Another man came forward, his complexion light brown. He cut Frankie's dress and bra open, leaving her exposed.

"Please don't do this!" she pleaded, her words falling on deaf ears.

The first man spoke nervously. "We gotta shut her the fuck up."

"Relax, man, can't nobody hear." The second man answered.

Troy backed away from the window and moved toward a door about five feet away. The door was made of heavy metal and slightly ajar. He stared at it for moments, wondering if the hinges would squeal. Troy was hoping for the element of surprise but given the condition of the place, he doubted the door wouldn't announce his arrival. His fate decided, he yanked the door open and it did indeed squeal. He instantly heard footsteps moving toward him. The shorter man appeared to the left of the entrance.

Troy pointed his weapon and yelled, "Don't move." The man dipped back hastily before he turned and ran.

"Help me... help me, please!" he heard Frankie screaming.

Troy gave chase. He rounded the curve in the small hall and let off two shots, tapping the first man in the middle of his back twice. The man dropped to the ground, and Troy stepped to him shooting him in the back of the head. Quickly, he checked the felled man's pockets and found nothing. The other man took off running to the back of the shop. Troy ignored Frankie and her pleas for help. He continued past her in pursuit of the second man. Before the man could reach the back door and slip out, Troy shot him twice in the leg. His prey went down cursing and yelping in pain.

The man attempted to crawl away, but Troy was on him with the quickness dragging him back to where Frankie was chained up.

"Please get me down. Let me go..." she sobbed.

While holding the man by the collar, Troy took in the sight of Frankie cuffed and chained to the hook overhead. The dress she wore hung haphazardly from her person to reveal small firm breasts and a flat stomach. One of her eyes had begun to swell and her top lip was busted. The bun in her hair had come loose but not completely. The groan coming from his victim brought Troy from his musings.

"Let me go... I'm bleeding. You shot me!" the man wailed.

Turning his attention back to his victim, Troy spoke in a calm voice. "Where is the key to the cuffs?"

Frankie started screaming again, and Troy lost his patience. "Quiet, woman!" She began to shake and sniffle, but she stopped hollering.

"The key?" he asked again.

When the man didn't answer, Troy took aim and shot him in the other leg. Frankie whimpered before stifling her cries as the man yelled out in pain.

His quarry grunted, sweating profusely. "My pocket...the key is in my pocket."

Troy reached down none to gently and extracted the small key from the man's pocket.

"What's your name?" Troy asked.

"Sammy."

"Your partner's name?"

"Harold," he grunted.

"Well, Sammy, what was you and yo' homey planning for the girl? And don't lie to me. I have no tolerance for bullshit."

"We was finna take her money and have a little fun."

"Fun? Get up!" Troy barked.

"I can't, man… my legs. I can't." Sammy cried out.

"What were you two geniuses going to do with her after you finished having fun?"

Sammy was shaking and crying, unable to meet his glare. "Tell me." Troy demanded softly.

"Harold was gonna kill 'er."

He heard Frankie breathe in sharply at Sammy's words. Still, he didn't acknowledge her as he raised the gun to the side of Sammy's head and pulled the trigger. Reaching down, he dragged the dead man toward a door at the back of the shop.

* * *

Frankie could hear the man with the gun moving around on the other side of the wall at the back of the shop. She heard the heavy door scrape the floor and then everything grew quiet. The blood on the ground left a path to the back of the room where she could see the lifeless hand and foot of one of the dead men. She thought of Sammy's words. He had said, they were going to rob, rape and kill her. They were dead now, but she still did not feel safe.

Frantically, she twisted about, her eyes scanning her surroundings looking for chance and opportunity. Along three of the walls were empty, metal shelves that went from the ceiling to the floor. Two battery operated floodlights hung from above, and both were positioned on her, leaving the edges of the room shadowed. She was stretched out like a slab of meat at a butcher. Her arms and feet ached, but she didn't dare scream.

Frankie believed the man with the gun left, never to return. She looked to the back of the shop for any sign of him—there was none. It felt like hours had passed since he dragged Sammy away, but in reality, it had only been minutes. Feelings of hopelessness assaulted her and she wept. She had been about to succumb to her fear and scream for help when she heard the door scrape. After a few moments, the man with the gun stepped from the shadows directly in front of her.

He stood so close that she had to lean her head back. He was a big man, and this made her circumstance that much more uncomfortable. The man before her wasn't dark of skin but neither would he be considered light. His face was the color of black coffee with a drip of cream; he wore his hair cut close and his goatee meticulously trimmed. On the right side of his chin was a patch of gray hair. Frankie avoided his eyes, for in them she knew she would not find safety.

He wore a white tank top, tucked neatly into blue jeans that were held up by a black leather belt. A blue shirt was thrown haphazardly over his left shoulder. His hands were fisted at his sides, a definite sign of tension. When she could no longer hide from his scrutiny, she brought her eyes up to his. Upon contact, she knew he would kill her. This was no rescue. Silence clung to them as tears slid down her cheeks. She shuddered before him, powerless to stop it. His eyes were huge in his face, their color so brown they appeared black as he regarded her. The expression on his face confirmed the terror she felt. Anger and a need for violence rolled off him in waves. *So, this is the last person I will encounter in life,* she thought.

He abruptly reached out and touched her, allowing the backs of his fingers to gently stroke her nipple. She attempted to move away, but the trembling in her body intensified and her precarious position swung her right back into his touch.

"Please... don't," she sobbed softly.

"Quiet." He snapped, the word razor sharp.

He dropped his hand and frowned at her. Frankie pursed her lips to stifle her cries. Was this man going to finish what the others started? The thought made clear her only course of action. She let her head fall back and let loose a blood chilling scream. His large hands went around her throat... And everything went black.

1

CALHOUN, GEORGIA
APRIL 1995

Frankie woke terrified and disoriented. Her brain reached for a coherent thought, but none came. She gathered her strength and tried to sit up but found that her right hand had been restrained. Panic filled her as events and images came flooding back to her in a rush. The room was dark save for a splash of light coming from a door that sat ajar on the left. As she became more aware of her environment, she noticed the strong smell of cigarette smoke. Frankie wasn't sure how long she had been out, but she was sure of one thing–she wasn't alone.

Nothing about the atmosphere felt familiar, starting with the smells. Different scents layered the room, playing with her senses. The smell of freshly laundered sheets, Egyptian Musk oil, male and cigarette smoke coexisted. Frankie continued to feign sleep as his face flashed before her mind's eye. She saw the man who had saved her, so he could kill her. If she were going to survive, she would have to face him. While she mentally prepared herself, a deep voice floated from the left of the room.

"I know you're awake."

A lamp next to the bed illuminated the room with a soft *"snick"*. Frankie didn't respond, instead she took self-inventory. Naked, except for her underwear, she lay on top of a fluffy comforter. There was nowhere to hide, so she slowly opened her eyes. The room was larger than she thought. Out in front of her was a wooden door leading to a hall–she surmised. On the right side of the chamber was a big cherry oak dresser with no mirror. Deep in the corner and next to the dresser was a huge black leather chair; behind the chair sat a reading lamp that would drape over the person seated.

Frankie took a deep breath before turning her head to the left, and it was as she had feared. He stood there naked, watching her–arms folded over his massive chest. Seeing him in his state of undress only brought home the need to shield herself. When she attempted to cover her breasts with the arm not cuffed to the headboard, his rusty voice startled her.

"The key is on the nightstand next to you."

She didn't answer him but reached for the key. And though she fumbled a bit, she managed to free her wrist. Frankie retreated under the covers, clutching the fabric to her chest. She felt something move on the edge of the bed and changed her focus. The contents of her purse were spilled out, and the small deodorant she kept for emergencies rolled between the footboard and the mattress. Scanning her personal effects, she noticed her house keys missing along with the letter she promised her sister she would mail to their mother.

"Are you going to let me go?" She already knew his answer.

"No."

She hated the weak tremble of her words. "Are you going to kill me?"

"I haven't decided yet. But if yo' ass gets to screamin' again, I will."

His words could have been comedic, but his deadly tone made the danger unmistakable. She felt her eyes water and the tears began to flow, still she made not a sound. His face held no readable expression, causing her dread to mount. She tried to look away, but his eyes held her prisoner and coupled with their nudity. He controlled the situation, and his next words confirmed her thoughts.

"I won't try to stop you from running, but understand, my house is twenty miles away from the nearest town. There are snakes, bears, and coyotes. If you run, I won't chase yo' ass. I'll leave you to the elements. Do you grasp what I am saying?"

"Y-yes."

Frankie was defeated by his description of her circumstance. She was from New York, and at twenty-four, she didn't even drive. A person didn't need to drive to navigate New York City. Hell, there were about two trees in her old neighborhood of Jamaica, Queens. *Twenty miles,* she thought, in her heels and underwear. Why had she thought Atlanta was safer?

"This will be your room for now," he said as if she were a welcomed guest. "You are free to move about the house."

"I don't have any clothes."

He didn't answer right away and while his face remained impassive, his eyes lit up. The space between them began to pulse. She pulled her gaze away, unable to handle the apprehension she felt. Her eyes fell to the floral pattern that dressed the bed.

"You'll dress when I tell you."

At his barbed reply, she dragged her focus back to him. Alongside her unease, Frankie actually felt indignation. She wiped the dampness from her face before the words popped out, unfiltered.

"This ain't my fault. I'm the victim here, remember? Why save me to steal me away from my family? Why spare my life to treat me this way?"

"This *is* your damn fault. Why would you wander down a dark street without regard for your welfare? I won't go back to jail–not for you or any fuckin' body else." His voice boomed into the quiet.

"How can you go to jail for saving my life? They were going to rape and kill me," she countered, hoping to get him to see reason.

"Are you kidding me," he yelled. "Who would believe me? I killed two men because of you."

He gestured with his hands as he spoke, the muscles in his chest and arms flexed with his every move. His words were filled with accusation as hostility emitted from him, stealing the life from the room. He grabbed at the back of his neck, letting his head drop. Her eyes ventured below his waist, then bounced back to the bed out of embarrassment. She was living a series of unfortunate events, and she was unclear how to help herself.

"The police would believe me when I tell them you saved me." She said softly.

"Are you really that damn naïve?" He growled. "You will dress when I say, Francine."

The use of her real name made her flinch, and she was sure it was a tactic to showcase his authority. Curtly, he turned away, dismissing her.

Frankie couldn't help herself. As his hand touched the knob, she whispered, "A real hero."

"Watch it, Francine. I don't like sharp tongued women." He left her alone with that statement and the implied threat. She didn't even know his name.

* * *

Troy stood in the darkness of the hallway trying to gather himself. It had been a long night. He hadn't long come in from the woods at the back of the house. They buried the men who abducted her on his property. Butch mixed the acid and poured it into the hole with the bodies. The van remained at the auto shop, but they wiped it down of all prints. The old man was methodical when it came to shit like this. Troy had missed it, but Butch found an earring and two hairpins. They went through the shop inch by inch making certain there was no evidence of Francine left behind.

Butch didn't question him when he told the story of Francine and the men he shot. The old man only asked if he'd cleaned up properly. Troy had been strangely calm when he responded that he hadn't cleaned up at all. The girl hindered his first mind. Removing her hollering ass from the scene had been his only thought. Jewel stayed with the girl while he and Butch removed all traces of himself and her from the shop. It was four in the morning, and he was wound too tight for sleep.

He showered in the master bath before donning jeans in the smaller bedroom at the end of the hall. The room consisted of a cot with a white sheet and a blue hospital blanket. Next to the bed was a little brown table that held a lamp, a digital clock, and a glass of water. Beyond the table sat a box, and inside that box were several cans of sardines, five packs of cookies and ramen noodles in all flavors. He spent most of his time in this room. He didn't need or want too much space, it made him feel bare.

Troy paced the perimeter of the room, stopping periodically at the window to stare into the receding darkness. He left the door open so he could see when she ventured out into the rest of the house. There was no getting around it, he had risked much following this woman. He was now immersed in a kind of trouble from which he didn't think he could untangle himself. The carelessness of his actions could compromise more lives than his own. The fact that Butch hadn't called him on it only deepened his guilt.

When he replayed the events of the last evening, it all came back to him in images that both excited and frightened him. The recollections of her were so vivid, he could almost reach out and touch. He could see her in a collage of moments that connected them to this space in time. There was Francine when she first burst from the restaurant. Next was the sway in her hips as she attempted to flee her date and his chick-drama. But the picture in his head that brought his dick to life–Francine with her hands cuffed above her head; her dress and bra slit open to reveal flawless, cocoa brown skin with dark, plump, berry-like nipples that were erect from the coolness of the shop.

The girl was exquisite and to his shame, he found even her fear of him titillating. He could still see her standing before him in the abandoned shop, shaking from the effort to quiet her sobs. The distress radiating from her tasted deliciously of subjugation, making it impossible for him to back away from the situation. Incarceration equated to the simplest details of his life being dictated by another and it fueled his need for control. The path now held two choices–intimidation with the ability to carry out every threat or homicide.

The sun was starting to spill through the window when Troy headed for his office. He would set up the necessary meetings and call in a few favors. Once he weighed the matter, he would decide the best course of action.

* * *

Frankie never found sleep after he left the bedroom. When day broke, the view from the picturesque window was disheartening. Stretched across the back of the house was a large patio of naturally colored, decorative stones. At the edge of the stone, stood a red brick oven for grilling. After the patio and grill was a dense grouping of trees. The woodland was so thick, it was as if the sun never rose. The trees went on for as far as the eye could see and while Frankie measured her chances, a deer skirted by. She hung her head in despair.

Backing away from the window, she began the process of going through the bedroom. It was an exercise to promote sanity and foster hope. She would bide her time, for an opportunity would surely present itself. Until then, she would remain alert. The key was to recognize a chance at escape and be ready to capitalize on it. Frankie would start by ignoring him while exploring her surroundings.

In the light of day, the walls were painted a rich wine color with white trim. The dresser had five drawers, in the first two were neatly folded men's sweaters. In the next two drawers lay t-shirts and dress shirts. The last drawer was filled with men's socks and underwear. On the left of the room, she found a small bathroom with a bathtub and shower combination. The color scheme was a buttercup yellow, making the shower curtain almost see through. The shelf between the toilet and sink was occupied by fluffy white towels perfectly stacked. On the lower shelf sat soaps and lotions, along with a comb and brush pushed intimately together for the sake of space. The sink stood on a white pedestal with huge knobs marked H and C.

She quickly took advantage of the bathroom and shower. Before stepping from the tub, she scrubbed her underwear by hand and hung them over the curtain rod to dry. He hadn't told her she could dress, but she would rather try his patience on the matter than go about naked. She knew he would be angry, still it was a way to practice getting a hold of herself in his company. Managing her dread when dealing with him was important because he seemed to enjoy it. She figured this out not from his actions but through his intense scrutiny.

After dressing in one of his t-shirts, she settled on a pair of his underwear–gray boxer briefs. He was such a large man that she had to cut the underwear down the side with scissors from the nightstand. She smiled with satisfaction when she tied a knot in the fabric to keep the boxers from sliding down her legs. Once dressed, Frankie brushed her hair back in a ponytail before tackling the walk-in closet. There were several men's suits hanging neatly to one side with dress shoes placed against the opposite wall. The shelf that wrapped around the overhead space was bare.

She sat ramrod straight at the foot of the bed planning her next move, the clock on the top of the dresser read 9:45 a.m. Getting up her nerve, Frankie stood and opened the bedroom door, but she did not venture over the threshold. Instead, she backtracked to the leather chair in the corner and seated herself. Listening to the sounds of the house, she tried to squelch her fears. Frankie realized one thing for sure—for all her bravado, she was scared out of her mind.

Moments after the door was swung wide, the smell of coffee wafted into the room. And though she was starving, she didn't follow her nose. She heard clanking noises and knew the kitchen was down the hall to the right. As the day pressed on, the sounds grew louder and then softened at times, but no one came to her room. It was after nine p.m., and the darkness that surrounded the house became complete. Coming from New York, night-time in Georgia seemed like a living, breathing thing. After dark in Queens was tamed by light, but here it was suffocating.

The clock read 10:30 p.m. when she heard at least three men conversing. She panicked at the thought of two more men. Her mind wandered back to the van and being snatched from the corner as she tried to cross the street. The man, Sammy hit her several times while the other man drove. The swelling of her lip and eye did not represent what was going on up in her head. Even with her first two abductors dead and gone, her circumstance had not improved.

She had not left the room for two reasons—she had dressed against his wishes and facing him made her want to scream. He had been deadpan when he told her that he would kill her if she got to hollering again. This line of thinking pushed her toward emotional exhaustion—add to it the fact that she had not eaten since before her date with Jalal. Throughout the day, she drank water from the bathroom sink to sustain herself.

Frankie had not thought of her sister or mother, who without a doubt were looking for her. They knew she would never stay away and leave them to worry. She was also positive that Jalal, the last person she was seen with, was catching hell. Her sister Jennifer could be mean as hell when she thought someone was trying to harm their little family. Yet even knowing all her sister's strengths, she didn't think Jennifer could handle this man. If it could be helped, Frankie never wanted her sister to encounter him.

It was late, she laid in the bed, but wouldn't sleep. The door had no lock, still she closed it. If she made it through the night, she would leave the room tomorrow. She was weak from lack of food; her eyelids grew heavy. Frankie's last thoughts before she reluctantly fell asleep were of him. Where did he come from? Who was he? What was his name? Would he kill her? Would he share her with his friends?

* * *

Troy stood facing Butch and Levi. The old man didn't speak. Levi, on the other hand, questioned him and Troy hated it. The tension in his office was high, because unlike Butch, Levi was calling him on his shit.

"You want the woman, that's why she's still alive. Ain't we too old to be thinking with our dicks?" Levi asked.

"Do you even hear yourself?" Troy replied with a coolness he did not feel.

"There are plenty of women in our circle you could have. Why follow some bitch on the street and jeopardize everything? Based on what ya said, you had time to back away. Do you want out—is that it?" Levi continued to badger him.

Troy stared at Levi, offering nothing in the way of a response. Prison life left him ill-equipped to deal with everyday issues, let alone high stress. He saw other men as adversaries, making it difficult to shelve his aggression. The small act of a disagreement set him to violence. Butch must have sensed where this was going because he stepped in.

"Easy, Levi, sometimes shit happens before a man can get a handle on it."

Levi took a breath before answering Butch, but his gaze never left Troy. "I get it, old man, but Troy and I know this ain't one of them times. Shit, under better circumstances, you or I would have to save the girl *from* Troy. The women in our circle don't ask questions and they expect nothing. Let's call a spade a spade—he fucked us all with this move."

"I'll help Troy get this under control." Butch said.

"You gonna help him kill the woman? Anything less ain't help." Levi countered.

"We all need sleep," Butch said. "Let's talk tomorrow."

Levi chuckled. "I know bullshit when I hear it."

"You owe me." Troy said flatly.

He stepped forward closing the gap between Levi and himself. They had escalated to a silent standoff, and Levi didn't retreat. He was taller and broader than Troy, but they had brawled before and they could do it again if necessary. In fact, he was sure Levi would try to push him to a fight.

"Fo' sho' I owe you. You calling in a marker and I'm good for it. Show me the woman. I wanna see the shit I'm stepping in." Levi demanded.

He thought of Francine's nudity and answered a little sharper than intended. "Fuck you, Levi."

"Troy." Butch said his name like a plea.

He didn't look at the old man when he walked away. Instead, Troy replied, "Wait here."

Troy stood in the kitchen, hands braced on the countertop trying to cool his temper. He knew Levi didn't care about seeing Francine. What Levi was concerned about was whether he had gone rogue over some ass. If he had, they could do nothing about it. He was the boss, which meant–*he was the money*. He wouldn't bow out, but he would pick his own poison and he would fuck who he wanted. The organization would not become his new prison.

When he gathered himself, he headed for her room. Francine was asleep when he turned on the lamp beside the bed and spoke her name. She opened her eyes slowly at the sound of his voice. Troy realized instantly that something wasn't right. Her tone was weak when she put her question to him.

"Are you going to share me with your friends?"

"I don't share."

He watched her relaxed at his words, and then stepped back from the bed. "Come with me."

"No."

Troy glared at her, "There are two types of people in this world, Francine, those who give orders and those who take orders. In which category do you think you fall?"

She sat up in the bed and the covers fell away. He saw that she wore one of his t-shirts. She stepped over his question. "Were you following the men who took me or me?"

"You," he answered without hesitation.

"Why?"

He had time to think on why he followed her and gave her the truth. "I wanted to fuck you."

Her voice wobbled. "And after, were you going to kill me?"

"I hadn't decided." Troy's voice was bland.

"I'm a victim in this mess and you're a predator."

"So, you agree that you will take orders and I will give them," he countered, unmoved by her clever change of the categories.

"My family will be worried about me. Please—"

"You dressed without my permission and you refuse me." He didn't want her to plead for something he wouldn't grant. "I can think of two other categories we fit in."

She attempted to look unfazed. "I thought there were only two types of people in this world."

"I guess if you really look at it–it's all the same."

She quieted, and he knew she recognized the menace in his words. Still, she did not inquire about the new groups that identified them, so he volunteered the information.

"I think we fall into the categories of the punisher and the punished."

He met her gaze and there was no bluff in him. Francine pushed back the covers and climbed from the bed. She stood before him staring at his chest, her body trembling. When he spoke, it was to offer his list of demands.

"You will eat at least twice daily, and you will drink plenty of water. When I am home you will come to me twice a day–after breakfast and at 3:00 p.m. Do you understand?"

She nodded, but never looked up.

"I can't hear you."

"I understand," she whispered.

"Good." Turning, he headed for the door without checking to see if she followed. When they reached the kitchen, he waved her over to the refrigerator. "Find something to eat."

He leaned back against the counter and crossed his arms over his chest. She stared at him before moving toward the refrigerator and pulling the door open. Troy studied her as she found the jelly. "Peanut butter?" she asked.

Using his chin, he pointed to the pantry. Francine disappeared into the closet and reappeared with the bread and peanut butter. His t-shirt came to her knees, until she got on her tiptoes to get the milk. It was then that he saw his gray underwear tied in a knot at her waist. He had to fight to remain expressionless, she was too damn lovely.

Francine was placing the carton of milk on the table when he heard Butch and Levi in the hall off the kitchen. He had gotten so lost in her that he forgot about them. She stopped moving at the sound of their feet on the wood floor. Her eyes widened when Levi stepped into the kitchen followed by Butch. She looked back at him briefly, and he saw the alarm in her eyes. He could understand her fear of all three of them.

She turned back to face them but didn't speak. The old man and Levi stood to his right while Francine stood in front of the table to his left. He kept his gaze on her, even as Levi attempted to provoke.

"I can see why you followed her, Troy." Levi stepped closer to Francine, causing her to take a self-preserving step back. "Give her to me, I'll handle this shit for free."

Her gaze bounced up to meet his and she wasn't breathing. She was waiting for his decision to either keep her or give her to Levi. The fact that had Levi moved into her personal space left Troy with no choice but to acknowledge him. He turned his attention on the other man and glared, but Troy didn't respond to the offer.

Levi pushed some more. Smiling, he reached out to grab Francine's arm. "Sweetheart, come with me."

Troy stood to his full height of six feet, dropped his arms and fisted his hands. "Shit about to get basic in here. Measure twice, my man—cut once."

Frozen where she stood, Francine was overwrought. Levi chuckled before he dropped the hand that hovered a hair from touching her. She was cornered by him and let out a shaky breath when he backed away. Troy was about to dismiss them when Francine ran to him and collapses against his chest, wrapping her arms about him. Showing his weakness, his arms went around her quivering frame with one hand stroking the nape of her neck. She was crying, but she did so silently. Levi's eyes lost their amusement when he offered food for thought.

"Bind her to you. The commission of the murders happened before you married her, so spousal privilege may not apply. But..." Levi lingered in thought for a moment. "But the marriage will discredit her and make her duplicitous. Since you ain't gonna kill her, marry her, fuck her and knock her up. I will leave for New York in the morning to follow her mother. Butch will follow her sister. It's your job to make clear the art of blackmail."

Francine flinched at Levi's every word, but she didn't let go. As Troy scowled at Levi, his mounting anger was laced with an unhealthy dose of jealousy. The simple truth was Francine would be safer with Levi than himself. He hadn't understood the dynamics of this conversation until seconds ago—Butch called Levi and dimed on his ass. Levi was handling him and Francine while leaving him the hero in the situation. Troy then turned his angry glare on Butch, who lent no reaction in his return gaze.

"I'll report back when I touch down in NYC." Levi said over his shoulder as he exited the kitchen.

Butch turned and left, leaving Troy with the chore of making her understand that Levi's words weren't idle threats. Her mother and sister really would be killed if she didn't comply. As if on cue, she whispered against his chest.

"I don't want to marry you."

Francine backed away and looked up at him. Her eyes were swollen, her nose runny and her lips puffy. She grabbed the collar of the t-shirt she wore and swiped at her nose. The woman moved him, but he stuck with the task.

"You don't have to want to marry me. You have to weigh your dislike for me against your love for your mother and sister."

"I can't be a wife to you," she said softly, her voice faltering.

Troy crossed his arms and leaned back against the counter, studying her. She was telling him she didn't want to fuck him. He had been with several women since his release, but it had been about the sex, not the woman. It had also been a long time since he wanted a woman, and he wanted Francine. She would obey because he would command it. He didn't threaten, as was his way, instead he asked a telling question.

"You on birth control?"

"Yes," she answered.

Her answer sparked the unfamiliar feeling of jealousy for the second time in minutes. "The dude you were with at the restaurant, did you fuck him?"

"You were in the restaurant?"

Troy thought back on the argument between the guy and girl at the front of the restaurant. The Jalal dude wanted Francine, and he told the other woman so. His anger was boiling below the surface.

"Answer me, Francine."

"No."

He pushed her no further. "Go eat."

2

AIN'T NO SUNSHINE

Three days had passed since Francine was abducted. The scene in the kitchen the night before brought home a new type of terror. They wouldn't just kill her, they would kill her mother and sister. The thought of harm coming to her family because of her actions made her belly roll. Life as she knew it was forever changed. She was in a prison with no bars.

She was amazed she hadn't fainted when the man Levi asked if he could have her. He was larger than Troy, both in height and muscle. She worried Troy would let him take her. Levi was a brown skinned man with big eyes and a crooked nose that thickened around the nostrils. He had mockingly fat lips. His hair was cut close, and he sported no facial hair. Menace dripped from his person, still he backed off when Troy spoke.

The older man with him was a blur that she couldn't recall. Her focus had been on Levi who wanted her dead. It appeared he was angry that Troy had decided not to kill her. He had spoken about her as though she wasn't even there. She could still hear the chill in his words when he said, *"Since you ain't gonna kill her, marry her, fuck her and knock her up."*

She finished dressing in a gray t-shirt and a pair of his blue boxer briefs and made her way to the kitchen. Francine hadn't encountered anyone other than Troy in the last few hours, but she was sure someone else came and went from the house. She just hadn't run into that person yet. Starting with the kitchen, she explored her surroundings.

If the situation weren't so dire, Francine might have been able to appreciate the beauty of his home. The kitchen had a color scheme of brown, beige and chrome. In the wall to the left of the sink was a three-part chrome oven that boasted of digital settings. The lighting hood over the sink matched the chrome oven and the faucet. In front of the sink and in between the oak cabinets was a huge bay window that allowed for sunshine in ample amounts. The cabinets had black wrought iron handles that added to the character of the setting. The granite countertops were beige with hints of black and brown. On the right of the sink was a large two door, chrome refrigerator. Lastly, there was an island in the middle of the kitchen that made the room appear bigger and the floors were tiled to match the counters.

Francine didn't overindulge. She sat at a big, brown table with six matching chairs eating a peanut butter and jelly sandwich with a glass of apple juice. The kitchen had two entrances on either side and the position of the table allowed the person seated to observe both. The walls and door frames were painted a glossy white, lending to the immaculate feel of the space. Still, she felt trapped.

When she finished eating, she went to find Troy, per his demands. The house was shaped like a "U", causing her to have to backtrack past her bedroom. Along the corridor, there were two doors on one side and three on the other, each left open to reveal beautifully furnished bedrooms. The master bedroom had a huge, black, four poster bed with a matching armoire and dresser. The entire ceiling was mirrored and to the right of the bed was a fireplace. The drapes were drawn back, showing off a picturesque woodsy scene and in the far corner of the room was an open door leading to the bathroom. Francine did not dare step over the threshold.

The other two bedrooms bragged of sleigh beds with blue and burgundy bedding. Each room felt hotel-like and cold, yet both were clean. The last door on the left was a powder room for guests with only a sink and toilet. As she rounded the turn in the hall, there were two more doors. One was an office and the other a small room that was sparsely furnished with a cot. Next to the bed was a little table that held a lamp, a digital clock, and an empty glass. On the floor next to the night table was a box filled with food.

Afraid of what she might find, Francine did not venture into any of the rooms. The curve in the hall spilled out into an enormous living room with a black leather sectional and matching ottoman. The area rug was checkered in watercolors giving the room a spring like feel. In front of the couch was a big sixty-inch television. On the walls hung new age art that was angled and sharp but not colorful. In the far corner, there were plants of all sizes. And with the green drapes tied back with thick decorative stays, the sun danced wistfully over the leaves. There was a tiny alcove leading to the front door that was made of distorted glass inside the wooden frame, allowing for more light—but not prying eyes.

Sidetracked from exploring the house, she had overlooked her purpose—Troy. Francine felt him before he spoke. His presence made the hairs on her body stand on end. She wondered if there would ever come a time when she no longer felt shaken in his company. He stood quietly behind her waiting for her to acknowledge him. When she could gather herself, she turned to find him dressed in a dark pair of jeans, no shirt and bare feet. The button of his jeans was undone, revealing the destination of hair under his navel. She looked up into his eyes.

"Good morning, Francine." His voice unnerved her.

"Good morning, Troy."

His eyebrows popped, and she was sure it was her use of his name. He never told her his name, but the man Levi had called him Troy.

He studied her fixedly. "So, you *are* paying attention."

"I prefer to be called Frankie—not Francine."

"I won't call you Frankie. You're too beautiful to be called by a guy's name. I don't like it."

"Is Troy your real name?"

"No."

They stood staring at each other, seconds past before she got up the nerve to ask, "So, what's your real name?"

He crossed his muscled arms over his chest and did something she hadn't expected, he smiled. But she was leery of him, so she did not reciprocate.

"Ernest Stephen Bryant."

"Where does Troy come from?"

"It sounds cool—cooler than Ernest."

"I see." She held back her laughter. He wasn't her friend.

He must have read her mind because he switched subjects. "You plan on shredding all my underwear?"

"I want to go home, Troy. I want my life back."

Nonchalant, he said, "This is home, Francine. I have answered this question, don't ask me again."

His warning could not be missed, still she asked, "Do you plan on never letting me out of this house? Why marry me? Why not keep me chained to the bed?"

Her words were out before she could stop herself. She didn't want to give him any ideas, but she did want him to see reason. He became frighteningly quiet, yet his eyes blazed. She took a step back, but he reached out and grabbed her by the neck, stopping her retreat. He pressed the palm of his hand against her throat causing her to have to swallow. The pressure wasn't painful, but the implication was there.

"You will control your fucking anger, and I will do the same. Am I clear?"

"Yes," she whispered.

"Because if I get angry, shit won't go well for you."

She tried to look away, but he released her neck and grabbed her firmly by the chin, forcing eye contact. "You will be allowed to leave the house and see your family. There will be no need to chain you, Francine. I'm serious when I say I will kill your mother and sister. Levi has already located and followed your mother, Doris Adams to the elementary school where she works in the cafeteria. Butch has followed your sister, Jennifer Adams on a job interview. Should the police have any reason to focus on me—outside of the shit they already hound me about—your mother and sister will disappear without a trace. You understand me?"

"I understand, Troy."

"Try not to piss me off, Francine."

"What if I make you mad by mistake?"

"Try not to piss me off, Francine." He repeated before releasing her chin and stepping back. "We will try this again later when my ass has calmed down."

He was about to turn and walk away, but he stopped short as if he remembered something important. "You will marry me tomorrow."

Francine watched as he turned and exited the living room, the strength in his physique evident with every step.

* * *

It was after midnight before he finally stopped pacing the house. Troy smiled when he relived the exchange between himself and Francine from the previous morning. He hadn't been upset at all–quite the opposite. Francine both thrilled and aroused him. When she was near, the hairs on his body stood on end and he wondered if the sensation would ever cease. He found himself craving their interactions, still he would do violence to subdue and possess her. There would be no misunderstanding between them because he meant every threat issued, and he was prepared to back up his words with action.

Jewel, Butch's woman had come to him once Francine had settled for the night. She set up the master bedroom with the necessities of a woman in mind. And with Butch's brawn, they moved the clothing he purchased for Francine into the closet and drawers. Troy had given Jewel the week off with her coming to do certain chores for him at night. He was trying to give Francine a chance to become accustomed to her new life without an audience. This also gave him time to enjoy her. When he was able to quiet his brain, he laid down on the cot. He drifted in and out of sleep until quarter to six in the morning.

In the master bedroom, Jewel laid out the white backless dress he picked for Francine, along with dark blue trousers and a white dress shirt for him. He shaved and showered, before pulling on a pair of sweatpants. Jewel had offered to help Francine get ready, but he refused. He wanted this time with her before the ceremony, so they could communicate. She would have questions, and he would provide the answers. He wanted the intimacy of helping her dress and getting to know her.

Troy could hardly contain himself as he made his way down the hall to her room. Francine was seated in the chair staring at the door–she was expecting him. She was again dressed in one his t-shirts, orange this time, and her hair was pulled back in a ponytail. Her brown eyes were wide with apprehension and unease. She looked like she wanted to scream, and he had to rein himself in. His body was moving toward an erection with her fear fueling his need to overpower her.

He took a breath and without preamble said, "Come with me."

Troy thought she would reject his request. Instead, she moved to stand in front of him and engaged in eye contact without him having to ask for it. He noticed the swelling in her eye and lip had gone down. There was still a slight discoloration of the skin below her eye, but Francine was so incredibly lovely, he almost couldn't think. She surprised him when she asked, "When you decide you don't want me anymore, will you kill my mother and sister?"

"That won't happen."

"You don't want me to piss you off." Her voice shook with the effort of conversing with him, still he was impressed.

"No, I don't want you to piss me off."

"But I will piss you off and this will cause you to kill my family."

"You pissin' me off will cause me to punish you. You discussin' the murders *with anyone* will cause harm to your family."

He could see her brain working, but she responded with a question he didn't expect. "What did you go to jail for?"

"Double homicide." She didn't recoil, and he figured it was because she had witnessed him in action. Before she could say more, he said, "Come with me, Francine."

He reached out and she placed her hand in his, allowing him to lead her to the master bedroom. Once inside, he closed the door, giving them some privacy. In a few hours, the pastor of his mother's old church would arrive with his wife. Pastor Simmons and his wife Grace would preside over and witness their nuptials. The good pastor had also eulogized his sweet mother. Jewel and Butch would also be in attendance–minus Levi.

She stood with her back against the door, and he stepped away to give her space. He sat in a kitchen chair that must have been brought into the bedroom by Butch or Jewel the night before. The goal was not to tower over her, still he would coerce–just a little bit.

"This…" he gestured with his hands, "This is our bedroom. You will sleep in here with me from now on."

"I'm not ready to sleep with you." She answered softly.

"You will never be ready if I allow you to be separate from me, Francine. We will be husband and wife. You will not ignore me."

"So, everything about us will be forced–everything between us will be against my will?"

"Do you plan to reject me at every turn?"

"I will never speak on the murders, Troy. You don't have to marry me to keep me quiet. Your threat against my family does that without the extra pain of marriage. I don't want sex with you–you frighten me," she finished on a whisper.

You frighten me. Her words gave him a hard on, and he was thankful he was seated. His heart slammed into his chest. "I want sex with you, Francine."

She looked to the floor, breaking eye contact and he immediately felt the loss. He was desperate, so he tried enticement. "As my wife, I will take care of you and the things that concern you. Your mother could retire and move to Georgia. I will purchase a home for her and your sister. You will be allowed to visit them when you please and they will be welcome here."

"I don't want you to meet my mother and sister."

Leaning forward and placing his elbows on his knees, he sighed. The room became crowded with the presence of his frustration, and he knew she felt it. He laced and unlaced his fingers as he tried to lay out the rules. His speech was pressured, but he wanted her to understand his position.

"You may not fully appreciate what's going on but trust me when I say that marrying me will provide protection for you and your family. There are people who are fanatical about my well-being. These people see my downfall as their own. You represent a threat, simply because I risked much to save you. My attraction to you is viewed as a weakness, but they are willing to let me handle you. If I fail in dealing with you, they will attempt to handle you, and this would cause more bloodshed. Francine, you will learn to compromise with me, comply with my orders and you *will* fuck me. You will be my damn wife in private and in public. Are we on the same page?"

"Why should I trust you, Troy?"

"You should trust me because you are still alive. If I had not come along when I did, you would have been robbed, raped and murdered."

He watched as tears spilled from her eyes, the realization of his words hitting their mark. She pulled the collar of the t-shirt up to wipe away the tears and switched subjects. Though he wasn't prepared, he answered.

"You spent time in jail, do you have AIDS?"

"No, I have recently been tested. I'm clean."

"Have you ever had sex with a man?"

"No, I have never had sex with a man and contrary to popular belief, every man in jail is not engaging in man on man. Every man in jail is not in danger of being raped and some inmates participate in man on man willingly."

"How old are you?" she asked.

"Thirty-four."

"Do you have family? Where are they?"

"My mother died years ago. I have one sister; she and I are not close. Monica is sweet, but I'm not the same brother she grew up with. She lives in New Jersey."

"I'm not ready for you, Troy."

He sat back in the chair. "Compromise with me. Let me help you dress for today—let me touch you."

She wasn't breathing as she gazed at him. Francine offered no definitive answer, so he tested the reins of his control.

"Come to me, Francine."

She pushed away from the door but didn't move for seconds. Finally, she crossed the room to stand before him. His hands shook when he reached out and pulled her to straddle his lap. She gasped when her weight settled on his erection. He groaned when he palmed her ass, grinding her down on him. She placed her hands on his shoulders as she looked into his eyes. Her facial expression registered surprise as her lips slightly parted. He knew she felt the sparks too.

Troy leaned in and pushed his tongue into her mouth, tasting her briefly before pulling back. He was engulfed by her sweetness. His voice was strained when against her lips he whispered, "Shit, Francine."

"Easy, Troy." Her voice was breathless.

He relaxed his body but not his grip on her ass. When he could trust himself, he spoke. "You will shower and dress with me present. It's the beginning of acceptance between us."

"You're not going to like having me as a wife. I'm bossy, my mother and sister tell me so all the time."

Francine's face was serious, and he understood her concern was real. She spoke as if she were confessing some great sin. He chuckled, unable to stop himself.

"I will help you work on being bossy."

Francine's body stiffened with anxiety, causing his dick to pulse. "I don't want to be punished."

"We talked enough, we both need to start getting dressed."

Reluctantly, he released his hold on her, but she didn't move. "Being afraid of you is exhausting."

"Go shower." He whispered in her ear.

* * *

As Francine walked into the bathroom, she could feel him at her back. Their interactions were intense, leaving her with even more questions. How is he not still locked up for a double homicide? What does he do for a living? Are there more people than Levi who wanted her dead? Who are these people who want his safety at the cost of her life? What did he mean by more bloodshed?

She was deep in thought and didn't hear him behind her. "You need help turning the shower on?"

His question made her focus on the bathroom. The tiles on the walls and the floor were a dark chocolate. Against the far wall, the shower took up the entire space. The glass barrier was perfect, almost invisible if not for the chrome handle. On the right was a large step up tub, just shy of being a small pool. There was a double sink opposite the shower with a vanity on the end, complete with a dainty chair. The bathroom was bigger than the apartment she shared with her mother and sister in Queens.

She looked at the dials that controlled the water pressure and temperature and realized she did need his help. "I guess I do need some assistance getting all this space age shit to work."

He threw his head back and laughed at her frustration before opening the glass door and turning on the water. When he turned back to face her, his silence told her to undress. She hesitated for the briefest of moments.

"This is privacy, Francine–this is our new normal. I won't say it again."

There was an edge to his voice that wasn't present seconds ago, an indicator that he was becoming irritated. Francine resisted the urge to turn her back on him before removing the t-shirt she wore. When the shirt floated to the floor, she pushed her underwear off her hips and stepped out of them. She stood still while holding his gaze.

"I have only been with one guy when I was twenty. It wasn't …"

"Did he hurt you?" His voice became deep–gravelly.

"No, neither of us were experienced. But he wasn't…"

"Like me." He finished for her.

"He didn't scare me." She attempted to explain.

"He didn't interest you either." He said with a grin. "Ya probably bossed his ass around–then dumped him.

"I did," she admitted, watching his eyes widen.

He laughed out loud and to her shock, so did she. Troy stepped back and opened the shower door, so she could get in. She stepped into the water and was about to ask for a washcloth, when he stepped in after her. His big body blocked the steady stream of water as he reached for the bottle of soap on one of the shelves. Squeezing some in his hands, he rubbed them together until they became frothy. She wanted to back away from him, but it would get her nowhere.

Troy placed his hands about her neck, applying enough pressure to control her movements, and massaged the soap into her skin. The action made her swallow. His hands moved out to her shoulders and down to her collarbone, until he palmed her breasts. Involuntarily, she moaned, but he didn't linger. He lathered her belly before allowing his fingers to drift between her legs.

"Troy…" she breathed.

He leaned in and whispered over the sound of the rushing water. "You have a bald pussy. I fuckin' love it."

Francine's body tingled from his touch and his words. Abruptly, he pulled her against him and lathered her back and rear end. He spun them until she was in the stream, and when her body was soap free, he turned off the water. Stepping from the stall, he wrapped a towel about his waist for which she was thankful, then handed one to her. She didn't dry herself, instead she quickly wrapped it about her.

"Come," he demanded as he reached out for her.

He bent and picked her up. Blindsided, the sudden action made her squeal but not in delight. Troy carried her back into the bedroom and laid her across the bed horizontally. He undid her towel, laying her bare to his scrutiny. Francine was overwhelmed and looked away, but there would be no respite. She forgot the ceiling was completely mirrored, giving her an even more intimate view of her situation. He undid his own towel, letting it drop to the floor and his erection bobbed free. She watched as he reached down and fisted himself. His head fell back, and his eyes locked on her in the mirror. She felt pinned to the bed by his gaze. He was immense.

Troy kneed her legs apart and climbed onto the bed. He hovered over her with his hands on either side of her head. Francine had no choice but to give him her attention. He was all consuming and though she tried to control her unsteady breaths, he was aware of every little thing. When he spoke, his voice was tight and thick. He stole the air from her lungs.

"Breathe, Francine. I don't want to hurt you. I want to make you feel good."

Since she struggled with the simple act of breathing, she didn't try to respond. He leaned down and pushed his tongue into her mouth. There was an urgency in his kiss, and she was surprised to feel him shaking too. He pulled away, pressing his lips to her neck and breastbone. The hairs on his chin heightened her awareness of him. He licked between her breasts and the feel of his tongue made her pant. Her eyes rolled up in her head when he began to place soft kisses all around her nipples without touching them.

When he finally pulled her right nipple into his hot mouth, she cried out. He sucked hard, pulling the nipple against the roof of his mouth. Shamelessly, she moaned when he offered the same treatment to her other breast. She wanted more, but he backed away to trail kisses down her belly.

"Open for me," he commanded.

Francine was so enthralled by his touch, she opened to him without hesitation. Her gaze floated back to the mirrored ceiling. The image above was everything she didn't know she could be. Abstractly, she took inventory of their reflection and almost came from the beauty of it. Troy rubbed his cheek against her inner thigh, and she opened her legs a little wider. She watched as he used the flat of his tongue to lick her entire slit.

"Ohhh." She moaned.

She tried to focus on her reflection to keep from drowning in sensation, but it did no good. The light sheen of perspiration on her skin, the roughness of his tongue and the way he fixated on her clit brought her to orgasm–repeatedly. He climbed back over her with the essence of her clinging to his goatee. Leaning down, he kissed her deeply, allowing her a literal taste of passion.

Troy stretched out on his side next to her and pulled her to face him. His jutting manhood fell between her thighs, rubbing deliciously against her. He didn't try to enter her, and Francine was unsure if she was relieved or disappointed. He whispered against her ear.

"I won't go up in you–you rubbin' your pussy on me is enough to get me there."

Francine began to glide her clit and wet folds along his rigid member with no extra persuading from him. She cupped his face accepting the eye contact before kissing him. It was the feel of his tongue against her own, the friction of his manhood against her core and the feel of his hands clutching her ass that brought about two types of release. Emotionally overwhelmed by the events of the last few days, she had been abducted and damn near murdered–only to be rescued and then stolen from her life. She had been manhandled by Troy, which frightened, confused and titillated her.

A violent current of pleasure overtook her, and Francine burst out crying. The emotional release sharpened her physical nirvana and she stiffened as her empty sex clinched and spasmed. She was foggily aware of him groaning her name, before feeling spurts of warmth between her now sticky thighs. He broke the kiss, and she pushed her face between his neck and shoulder. She was hiding from him. Everything about Troy was overpowering, but she wasn't ready to back away from him. He drew her to him, while rubbing her back tenderly. She wept.

"Francine."

"Y-yes." She sniffled.

"I won't ever get tired of you."

* * *

Troy stood staring down at the top of Francine's head. She was wearing the white backless dress he had chosen. The soft material looped around the nape of her neck, adding to her loveliness. On her feet were a swanky pair of black heels that made her chocolate legs–divine. She had been shy and awkward with him since he had taken her with his mouth. Oh, how she damn pleased him. He hadn't experienced innocence in a woman–ever.

He wanted to bury himself in her tight body, but her honesty stopped him. She had only been with one man and it had not been good. Troy would go slow while teaching her body to crave his touch. He would employ the tactic of delayed satisfaction in hopes of deepening the intimacy they would achieve. She must have sensed his mood because she finally looked up at him. Francine's eyes were bright with unshed tears, and he instantly felt vexed.

"I'm nervous, Troy. Please don't be angry."

"You don't have a choice."

"No need to bully me, I'm not trying to back out of marrying you. I understand the rules."

"Tell me, Francine, what *are* the rules?"

"If I piss you off–I will be punished. If I speak of the murders, my family will be killed. I am to compromise, comply and …"

She trailed off, and he pushed her to continue. "And–what Francine?"

"I am to compromise with you, comply with your demands and fuck you. This will keep me and my family safe."

"If you follow the rules, you might enjoy yourself."

"You're a bad man, Troy, so enjoying myself isn't high on my list. I understand my place."

"And what's your place, Francine?" The edge was back in his tone.

"My place is to remember who you really are."

He was about to ask who she thought him to be, but she wasn't finished. "I understand my mother and sister will meet you. Please limit your interactions with my family. I won't invite them here–I don't want them around you. When can I let them know that I'm all right?"

"You're breaking rule number one." He warned.

"I know."

Troy's temper was burning so hot, he had to work at restraining his impulsiveness. They stared at each other until he said, "We have guests."

"I have one other favor to ask. Please don't hit me in the face or break any bones when you punish me. This will help me keep my family from worrying."

Troy stared at her, clear about what she thought of him. He would not offer comfort to her because she was giving him attitude. She was attempting to shame him, but that would do no good. He left her words hanging.

"We have guests, Francine."

She nodded, acknowledging their talk was over. Troy stepped back and pulled the door to the bedroom open.

"After you," he said.

Francine stepped into the dimly lit corridor and waited for him to lead the way. He moved forward with her walking slowly beside him. When they entered the living room, he felt Francine at his back. She was hiding. Troy looked about, getting a feel for the situation before he introduced Francine. Pastor Simmons stood in the corner conversing with Butch while Jewel and the pastor's wife fussed over an inviting table of appetizers. As he glanced about, Troy understood what added to Francine's discomfort. Levi stood in front of the large window, looking tense.

When their gazes clashed, Troy knew Levi had business to discuss. He nodded, acknowledging that they would speak later, and then turned to address Francine. "You ready?"

"Levi…"

Troy cut her off, speaking for her ears only. "You are mine, Francine—you need never fear the next man."

She met his gaze, and he watched as she struggled to close herself off from him. If he were being honest, he didn't have to marry her. He could get her silence and cooperation without this drastic move. But when he turned the issue of Francine over in his mind—the matter was clear. He wanted her in every way a man could want a woman. Troy wanted her to be his wife, and he would take all choices from her, so she would have to surrender.

Francine was correct, he was a bully.

*** * ***

When Troy took her by the hand and led her into the living room, she felt faint. Still, she had managed to dam up the excess feelings flowing within her. The old man had unnerved her with his silence in the kitchen, but Levi wanted her dead and he had been vocal about it. She lent her focus to the artwork on the wall as she allowed Troy to drag her along. Once they stood in the center of the room, Francine had no choice but to engage.

"Good afternoon, everyone. I'm glad you all could make it." Troy said.

"Ernest, good to see you. Ya looking well." An older man greeted, using Troy's real name.

"Pastor Simmons, I'm especially happy you could make it. There wouldn't be a show without you."

The pastor chuckled, and Francine gave him the once over. The brown skinned man stood before her dressed in a black suit with a white shirt and black shoes. Several moles clustered along his cheeks and he had no hair on the top of his head, though the sides were picked out in an uneven afro. His shoulders were slightly stooped as he moved in to hug Troy and clap him on the back with fondness.

When he stepped back and focused on her, Francine noticed his brown eyes were wet. Troy ignored the older man's expressive state and continued with the introductions. "Pastor, this is my Francine. Sweetheart, this is Pastor Simmons."

"Nice to meet you, sir." Her voice shook.

"Nice to meet you, Francine. Ernest, she is a beauty," the pastor said, before yelling, "Gracie, come meet Ernest's love."

An elderly woman came forward, hugging and kissing Troy. "Hello, Ms. Gracie, you are looking lovely as ever."

"Oh, you rascal–you. Still tryna charm me. Ernest, you ain't changed one bit."

Troy laughed as the older woman turned to Francine. She wore a black wig that swooped down over her forehead like a bad hat. Ms. Gracie had small eyes and a wide nose. Her lips were a bright red that was too loud for her dark complexion, and her perfume did not distract from the smell of moth balls. She wore a blue dress with little shiny stars on the lapel and matching slippers.

Francine was uncomfortable because the woman stared at her for moments before turning and directing her words to Troy. "Where you steal this lovely girl from, Ernest?"

"Right off the streets of Atlanta." Troy responded without hesitation.

Turning back to Francine, the older woman said, "Ernest is a good one. But he'll work yo' nerve, be patient wit' 'im."

"Yes, ma'am, I'll try. It's nice to meet you."

She pulled Francine into a motherly hug before stepping aside. It was then that she noticed another woman standing behind the pastor's wife. Troy spoke as if reading her mind.

"Francine, this is Jewel, Butch's wife."

"Nice to finally meet you, Francine," Jewel said.

The woman before her was older but not elderly. She was light of skin, which made the scar around her right eye prevalent. Her left eye was larger, causing her features to be imbalanced. Jewel had soft wavy hair that was combed in a mushroom to hide her scars. She stood about five feet, two inches and was thin of frame. She wore a sky blue shirt with navy blue dress pants and black square heels. Seeing the old man next to his wife, he actually looked younger than she did. Francine thought him old because he was older than Troy–not because he was old.

She had not known the old man's name before this moment. Butch stood about six feet with broad shoulders and a muscular frame. He had dark smooth skin with thick black and gray hair. His eyes were dark in color with an awareness that made Francine feel as though he could see her thoughts. The bridge of his nose was straight, and his lips were full. The couple before her looked hard and dangerous; she did not like them. When she could gather herself, she spoke.

"Nice to meet you both."

Butch nodded his acknowledgement but did not speak, rattling her even more with his silence. He wore black dress pants with a white shirt. She never dropped her eyes to his feet, she couldn't look away. It didn't feel safe. When they moved to stand to the left of her, Levi walked up. Francine would have stepped back, but Troy firmly placed his hand on the back of her neck, stopping her retreat. She was being forced to face him as Troy did the talking.

"Levi, this is *my* Francine."

Francine was certain she did not know a man bigger than Levi. She had to tilt her head back to look in his face. He wore a dark pair of jeans and a white dress shirt with the sleeves rolled up over his powerful forearms. There was a smirk on his face.

"Nice to finally meet you, Francine."

She heard the sarcasm that he did not try to conceal. Francine stared at him, but she couldn't bring herself to speak. His smirk turned into a full-fledged smile as he flashed straight, white teeth. When she could take no more, she gave her attention to the decorations that hung around the room in celebration of a marriage and a man she didn't want.

White streamers dangled from the ceiling with big, white paper bells on the end. There were roses in five different vases scattered about the room. Two of the vases held a dozen red roses, another held lavender roses and still another held white roses. It was the vase full of yellow roses with red tips that made her breath catch. The flowers were beautiful.

Troy had released her neck, and she felt the heat of his hand against the small of her back. Leaning down, he asked, "Do you like the flowers?"

Levi had walked away, seating himself on the couch. Mentally, she was keeping track of him and Butch—involuntary self-preservation. The first time she met them in the kitchen, she had been overwhelmed and cataloging Butch had been impossible. Now, she would be cautious where those two were concerned.

"Yes, Troy, the flowers are lovely."

"Which ones do you like best?"

"I have never seen lavender roses or yellow roses with the red tips."

"Did you know the color of a rose has a specific meaning?"

Francine didn't know, but it made sense. He turned her to face him and now both his hands were on her bare back. Strangely, Troy's embrace made her feel safe from the undertow of peril that saturated the air.

"No, I didn't know the color of a rose had a specific meaning."

He smiled down at her, and Francine was taken aback by the quivering in her belly. Troy radiated authority, masculinity and sex. She couldn't deny his appeal as she obsessed over the shape of his mouth. Francine tried to disrupt the spell by breaking the visual contact between them, but Troy commanded otherwise.

"Don't look away." When she did as he directed, he continued, "You were mean to me in the bedroom before we came out to greet everyone. Why?"

"I didn't think I was mean to you."

His smile didn't falter. "I'm going to punish you for being mean and then lying about it."

Francine was overstimulated by Troy and the atmosphere in the room. She tried to back out of his hold, but he stopped her.

"So, you will start punishing me today?" her voice was weak and contrite.

"You were angry with me because you orgasmed in my arms and you wanted more. This is confusing to you, so you were mean. You tried to close yourself off to me, and you pretended not to be clear about it when asked. I was going to give you time to adjust to me before I fucked you. But now, I see no sense in waiting. You will not shut me out, and you will come to our bed ready to please me."

"Troy…" she was breathless.

"That's it, Francine, get used to saying my name." he chuckled. They stared at each other before he continued. "Lavender roses represent love at first sight. The yellow roses with the red tips represent falling in love."

"I was trying to understand how to exist with you." She whispered.

"No, Francine, you were trying to give me orders about interacting with your family and you. Your bossy ass was trying to set limits for me. I ain't havin' that shit."

He didn't look mad—what he looked was amused. She was ready to end the conversation, when he asked, "Did you like the way I made you feel, Francine?"

She hesitated, and his eyebrow popped, daring her to lie. "Yes, Troy, I liked the way you made me feel."

He leaned down and kissed her so deeply, she moaned from the electricity she felt when their tongues touched. Behind her, she heard the pastor say, "We better get started, so the young couple won't have to live in sin."

"Don't I know it, Pastor," Gracie said.

"You ready, my Francine?"

"Yes, Troy."

The next twenty minutes were a blur for Francine. She and Troy moved to the center of the living room with the pastor standing in front of them. Next to Troy stood Butch and Levi. Gracie and Jewel stood next to her, but Francine didn't acknowledge them. In her hand was one white rose, one yellow rose and one lavender rose.

When Pastor Simmons spoke, she felt frail. Their joining was a collage of half phrases and promises that mentally she couldn't follow. "Do you, Francine Marie Adams, take Ernest Stephen Bryant to be your lawfully wedded husband?"

"I do."

Do you, Ernest Stephen Bryant, take Francine Marie Adams to be your lawfully wedded wife?"

"I do."

As the words floated between them, Francine felt life as she knew it slipping from her grasp. Butch handed Troy two rings. The smaller ring was a gold band encrusted with diamonds all the way around. Troy then handed her a wider gold band with no diamonds. She pushed it onto his finger with ease and that simple act changed everything.

"I now pronounce you husband and wife, by the power... You may now kiss the bride. Ladies and gentlemen, I'm proud to present Mr. and Mrs. Ernest Stephen Bryant."

Troy spun her around and kissed her full on the lips. The pastor and his wife clapped as Butch came forward to shake Troy's hand. Francine looked to the floor to keep from having to deal with Butch, but he stepped up and nodded his approval while offering nothing verbal. Next, Jewel came forward and hugged Troy.

"Congratulations, Francine." Jewel said, but they didn't embrace.

Pastor Simmons and his wife stepped forward, hugging them both. They were genuine in their feelings for Troy. Gracie was choked up. "Ya mama would have been so happy today. I'm so thankful you outta jail–glad ya got yo' life back."

Francine was curious about the exchange between Gracie and Troy, though he only smiled. She could see his mood changed with the mention of his mother, but he worked to hide it. As Gracie was moving to the side, Levi came forward. Francine moved in closer to Troy, and he placed his arm around her. She looked down, so she wouldn't be part of the interaction.

"Congrats, man," she heard Levi say.

"Thanks."

The air between them was charged, and Francine wanted to disappear. Troy's next words made her tremble, but she never looked up.

"I didn't invite you, so what bad news are you here to tell me?"

"It's time to start cleaning this shit up." Levi replied.

There was a long pause before Troy said, "Francine and I need to meet with the pastor and then we'll talk."

"Aight."

When Levi walked away, Troy waved the pastor over and invited him to the office. Once inside, Pastor Simmons was all business. He produced several documents that required attention from both her and Troy. It was strange signing her new name next to his. Troy's signature was bolder and neater than her own. The pastor left some of the paperwork and took some of it with him before heading for the door.

"Ernest, Gracie and I will be in Atlanta for two more days if you need us. We'll head back to New Jersey on Friday." The pastor smiled warmly at them. "I know you have business to handle, so we'll get out of your way. Thank you again for the wonderful accommodations, Gracie is excited about sightseeing and the play."

"Thank you, Pastor. I'll be in touch." Troy answered.

Francine watched as the pastor quietly left the office, and Troy began to pace. His agitation palpable, he stopped in front of the window, and she gave herself a moment to look around. There was a large oak desk to the left of the door with a huge black leather chair behind it. In front of the desk were two uncomfortable looking chairs that added to the coldness of the room. Turning her attention back to Troy, she noted his ramrod straight posture and understood that the iciness she felt was coming from him.

"Can I go back to our room until you finish with your business?"

"No."

She didn't want to experience Troy and Levi at the same time. Being with them in a closed off space was more than she could handle. But Francine couldn't say she was afraid of Levi because it seemed to set Troy off. It popped in her head to beg for a reprieve, but the office door opened before she could think of what to say. She was forced to reassess the immediate danger–Levi stood between her and Troy, blocking her from safety. The chill in the room grew even more tangible.

With Troy's back to the room, he didn't seem to realize the stress she was feeling. Francine retreated until she felt the wall at her back. Levi eyed her, and she was positive that he had intentionally positioned himself to cut her off from Troy. He spread his feet and crossed his large arms, stealing the life from the room. She held his gaze because she was frozen in place–not because she was brave. The office was so quiet, when Levi spoke, she jumped. He never took his attention from her.

"There's a contusion under her eye and her lip was busted."

"Yeah." Troy answered, his attitude apparent.

"What happened to cause the bruising?"

"One of the men tried to stop her screams." Troy replied.

Her new husband still wasn't facing them, and Levi continued to study her. "Butch said there was two of them."

Troy's voice was tight. "Yeah, Butch helped me sort shit out."

"Did they pose a threat?"

"No," Troy said.

"Did you feel—"

Troy cut him off. "I ran them down and let off six shots. Imminent danger doesn't apply here."

"You ran them down? Aight, man." Levi stepped back so he could look between her and Troy.

It was then that Troy turned to look at her. "Yeah, I ran them the fuck down. I couldn't let them go. They would have done it again. Fo' sho' this wasn't their first time, and their other victims ain't fare so well. The elderly, women and children are better off. But this ain't the shit we gon speak on, so what difference does it make?"

"The difference is we can't save the damn world, Troy." Levi snapped. "She's too weak for the life we lead. If she says the wrong thing…"

Troy's nostrils flared as he stepped closer to Levi. "I will explain myself for Francine's sake because the truth is I don't give a shit what you think. She's mine and if anyone tries to separate her from me, I'll kill them."

"Does she even know who you are?"

The ice in Troy's next words made Francine quake. "She is learning who I am. But you, Levi, you know who and what I am. There will be bloodshed if anyone tries to harm her or take her from me. And since we're sharing, Francine's fear of you tests my control—back the fuck off."

The air in the room went stale when Levi turned to her. "He's threatening me for you."

She dropped her gaze just as he asked, "How well did you know Jalal Dorsey?"

Francine's head snapped up and her eyes went to Troy. He nodded. "I was a waitress where Jalal ate lunch. It was our first date."

Levi took another step back, leaving her path to Troy open and she took it. She went to him and wrapped her arms about his waist. His hands on her bare back meant she was safe. Troy's recollection of the incident, the stand-off between him and Levi, and being asked about Jalal pushed her toward a silent hysteria. Francine was wrung out.

"Jalal Dorsey is a person of interest in the disappearance of Francine Marie Adams. The police are holding him and sweating his ass."

"Which police station?" Troy asked.

3

THE ACCUSED
ATLANTA

Troy sat in the back seat of his silver Yukon while Butch drove. Next to the old man sat Levi, who had not spoken since they left the house. In the back seat with him, Francine had effectively succeeded in ignoring all of them. She stared out the window, never looking his way. He wanted to pull her onto his lap. But he refrained, giving her the room she would need to deal with the ensuing chaos.

Like his young wife, Troy focused on the countryside until the view became more urban. Glancing at his watch, he noted it was 4:46 and the day had turned gloomy. It hadn't rained, but the weather had changed drastically from the sunshine of earlier. The change in weather also depicted the change in his mood. He had felt lighter when she allowed him to touch her. Now, he was drowning in rage and jealousy. Troy did not want her to mingle with Jalal Dorsey.

He had given her one command. She was not allowed to answer any questions unless directed by him. When the precinct came into view, Troy went through his mental list. He had changed his clothes to a pair of faded blue jeans, work boots and a blue pullover shirt. In his possession was his driver's license and one credit card. Anytime he encountered law enforcement, he operated as though he would be detained.

Once the truck was parked, the old man and Levi got out, leaving him alone with Francine. Voice shaking, she asked. "Who are you?"

"I'm your husband." He popped the door open to stop the banter that always happened between them.

Troy unfolded his large frame from the back seat before turning back to assist Francine. His wife was dressed in dark blue jeans, a white shirt and blue sandals; her French manicured toes peeked seductively through the leather. She had brushed her hair up in a neat ponytail, which highlighted her beauty, her innocence and her appeal. He wasn't remorseful for having stolen her.

Troy noted the rows and rows of black and white squad cars before adjusting his gait to match Francine's. Butch walked in the front and Levi tailed them, both shielding Francine.

At the entrance of the building, two officers were escorting two black males in handcuffs into the station. Troy weighed the men and gauged one to be under age. He made mental notes, but he had to address his own circumstance first. As they approached the orange bricked structure, he felt Francine's fingers tighten in his. He stopped and, with some effort, smiled down at her. It was the best he could do because once they entered the precinct, she would get her first glimpse of the real him. His heart was pounding in his chest for Levi was correct in asking, *does she even know who you are?*

In the last few months, Troy had spent a lot of time in different jails, police stations and courthouses. Some were newly upgraded to reflect the times while others still had a 1970's feel. The four of them moved through the smoked, brown, glass doors into the lobby. No matter the furniture, it was the same as any town USA. The lighting was clinical and bright; white plastic chairs neatly lined the perimeter of the room. At the center of the lobby stood a large raised desk with a uniformed cop seated behind it.

The cop was a white man with salt and pepper hair, cut almost to a buzz. There were five people scattered throughout the lobby, probably waiting to speak with someone. The officer's eyes fell to Troy as if trying to place him and then to Francine. Upon recognition, he stiffened.

In his periphery, Troy noticed a slim white man with wild brown hair, moving toward them. "I'm a reporter for—" Butch stepped into his path, blocking him.

"Back off," the old man barked.

The reporter wasn't deterred. "You're Troy Bryant. Would you like to make a statement about being incarcerated for a crime you didn't commit? How are you adjusting to life on the outside? Is it true the state of Georgia paid you ten million? How do you feel about becoming a person of interest in the disappearance of your lawyer?"

Never taking his gaze from Francine, the officer behind the desk spoke up. "Roger, if you don't stop, I'll have you cleared out and the boys won't talk to you when they got something."

Troy ignored the reporter and Levi addressed the officer. "Is Jalal Dorsey being held for questioning?"

The reporter didn't back off, but he got quiet. The cop didn't answer Levi, instead, he picked up the phone and spoke briskly. "Yeah, I need you in the lobby. Important."

A minute went by before Troy heard a door open and click shut in the distance. He could hear fast paced walking coming toward them. Butch and Levi were also looking in the direction of the footsteps when a plump, brown skinned man rounded the turn. He stood just under six feet, dressed in blue slacks and a sky blue, button down shirt. On his feet were a pair of well-worn, black oxfords. The man looked to be about thirty-five to Troy.

"Dan?" The newcomer said to the cop at the desk, his eyes scanning the four of them.

"They're here about Dorsey."

Troy guessed him to be the detective on the case. Levi stepped forward and introduced himself. "My name is Sean Levi Bryant, Attorney at Law."

"Detective Wilton. How can I help you?"

"There seems to be a misunderstanding regarding Jalal Dorsey. We are here with proof that no crime has been committed."

Wilton pulled a photo from his pocket, and Troy watched as his eyes sharpened with awareness.

His attention fixed on Francine with a combination of disbelief and appreciation for her beauty. Finally, Wilton's scrutiny dropped to where

Francine held tightly to his hand before looking him in the eyes. Troy's expression remained poker-faced.

"Follow me. We can speak in private back here." Wilton said.

Butch didn't follow, but Levi answered, "After you, Detective."

They followed Wilton to a black metal door at the end of a long corridor. When they stepped through the entrance, the smell of burnt coffee and coercion was thick in the air. The walls were a dull tan and the floors–gray with several large black desks facing one another. Along the far wall was a long gray desk with six black office chairs that sat belly up to it. Each of the newfangled desks had an overhead compartment for space saving. At the far end of the room were three black doors that, in Troy's mind, led to uncomfortable interrogation rooms.

The detective led them to the third door that sat on the end of a smaller hall. Troy knew the setup, the little passageway connected to another large office that housed more desks, cages and observation rooms. The observation rooms offered one-way mirrors into each of the interrogation rooms, along with the ability to listen in. Troy tried to release Francine's hand to allow her to enter the room first, but she wouldn't let go.

Once inside the room, there was a rectangular wooden table with three gray folding chairs. As the detective spoke, he kept his hand on the door. Troy had expected this. He knew the detective would excuse himself and then attempt to spy on them. "If you all can give me a moment, I'll be right back. Can I get anyone something to drink?"

Levi shook his head, so Wilton focused on Francine. "Can I get you anything–Ms. Adams, right?"

"No, sir."

When Wilton left, Troy bent and whispered to Francine. "They are observing this room and possibly listening in."

Francine nodded, but she did not speak. She also didn't release his hand. He exchanged a look with Levi and shook his head. They both knew it was about to turn into a dog and pony show. Levi glanced at his watch and to Troy the gesture meant *prepare yourself*.

Thirteen minutes passed before Wilton returned with his partner in tow. He remained chipper as he made the introductions. "This is my partner, Detective Hill."

Hill didn't acknowledge Levi or him. He spoke directly to Francine. "Where have you been, honey? Your family was worried."

"Mrs. Bryant is an adult who is free to come and go as she pleases, Detective. As for her family, she will address the matter privately. We are here because it came to my employer's attention that Mr. Dorsey is being held and she wanted to make clear his innocence." Levi replied.

Troy gauged Hill to be about thirty-two, ex-military and physically fit. He had blond hair, cut to a buzz with intelligent blue eyes. Hill stood over six feet and though his partner was black, he looked like a nigga-caller when it was convenient for him.

Hill turned to Troy, his demeanor hostile. "Ernest Bryant, the Silent Activist, correct? How did you come to be with our victim? I'm sure you can understand our curiosity."

"Detectives, there is no victim here. Do you or do you not have Jalal Dorsey in custody?" Levi inquired, his patience now short.

Troy was trying not to lose his shit when Wilton stepped closer to Francine and asked, "May we speak with you in private, Ms. Adams? You seem afraid, we can help you."

Hill backed his partner and asked, "What happened to your eye and lip, sweetheart?"

Though Troy knew Hill was addressing Francine outside her name to set him off, it was working. His ass was hot, and it appeared Levi was too. "Detective Hill, my client's name is Mrs. Bryant. If you don't want the department to be slapped with a sexual harassment suit, I suggest you address her properly."

Francine spoke up. "I am nervous, Detectives. I'm afraid you'll hurt my husband. He's been polite, and you especially, Detective Hill—you have been nothing but rude. As for my eye and lip, I fell in the parking lot of Burger Best. Apparently, the city dug a hole due to a water main break. The hole wasn't filled back properly or tagged for caution. I called the city from my home phone on Friday afternoon to complain. Are you suggesting that Ernest hurt me? What does this have to with Mr. Dorsey?"

Troy almost laughed out loud when both detectives' eyes widened. He was smug when he locked eyes with Levi, who looked impressed. Wilton recovered first and tried to play his trump card. "Your mother and sister are in the next conference room. We wanted to hear your story before we confirmed your presence."

"My story, Detective, is boring–my family wants to control everything about me. While this will be uncomfortable for me and my actions labeled impulsive, it's not a crime to live life to the disappointment of others." Francine countered.

"Levi, my wife and I will go and speak with her family. Will you deal with Jalal Dorsey?" Troy asked.

"Of course, Mr. Bryant."

Turning to Wilton, Troy asked, "Can you direct me to my in-laws?"

* * *

Francine didn't know for which to feel regretful, meeting Jalal or encountering Troy. If she were being honest, she even felt some kind of way toward her sister. It had been Jennifer who talked her into going on a date with Jalal. Nothing had been within her control since that fateful evening. Now, the last thing she wanted was an audience when she faced her mother and sister.

Troy led her from one conference room to another. Detective Wilton stopped for a moment as if to allow for a breather before opening the door wide. He strolled in first and Troy stepped back, allowing her to enter next. The sight that greeted her was beyond painful. Her mother sat hunch shouldered while Jennifer attempted to comfort her. Apparently, they had not been told of her presence.

"Ma–Jennifer."

Her sister looked up first, eyes swollen and red. "Frankie?"

Her mother's head popped up and she was sobbing. "Francine Marie, where the hell have you been?"

Before she could form an answer, they were up and coming at her. They embraced her together with her mother hugging her tightly and her sister cuddling them both. Francine couldn't help it, she cried too.

"I'm so sorry. I didn't mean to make you worry."

It was her apology that made her sister take a step back and really look at her. Jennifer was her best friend, and nothing got by her. Troy stood behind them, alone… watching–waiting. Francine didn't even glance back at him. She needed to get through this part before they could all move on.

"Who are you? Are you a detective?" Jennifer asked, speaking to Troy. Worried he was at his limit, Francine cut Troy off from responding "No, Jen, he isn't a detective. This is Ernest Bryant, my husband."

Both her mother and sister gasped at the same time, but it was her sister who recovered first, almost shrieking, "Ya damn husband? What are you saying? You were off chasing some man while me and Mommy worried about you?"

Jennifer pulled the white, button down sweater she was wearing snuggly around her. It was as if she was trying to ward off the bullshit being handed to her rather than the chill from the air conditioner. Her mother stared at Troy as if she couldn't believe what she was hearing or seeing. Hell, Francine couldn't believe it either.

"My friends and family call me Troy."

"So, your old ass must got a thing for young girls. You ain't none of my damn friend or family." Jennifer went there, and Francine gasped.

Behind her, Francine heard Troy chuckle; the sound caused her to turn and look at him. He appeared thoroughly entertained, but her mother wasn't. "Mr. Bryant, Frankie has been missing for four days. I flew in from New York, worried that my child was dead in a ditch. Only to be told she got married and didn't tell me or her sister."

"We apologize for the trouble we caused." Troy said, and Francine was surprised to hear contrition in his tone.

Her mother turned to her. "When did you get married?"

"We got married today, around noon. I was coming home to talk to Jennifer this evening and discuss moving some of my things to Troy's house."

"Well, if you only got married today, that should be easy to undo." Jennifer said, full of authority.

"You'll come back home to New York with me." Her mother piggy-backed off Jennifer's words.

"Francine." Troy growled, the frost from his mood crowding the room. Her mother and sister must've felt it too, because the room went quiet.

Troy reached out his hand to her and she stepped back from them. When she placed her hand in his, Francine felt suffocated by the gamut of emotions emitting from him. Strangely, the most prevalent feeling radiating from his person was desperation and she was sure she was reading him incorrectly. But his voice, though full of menace and dominance, held an element of anxiety. Francine was smart enough to recognize that anxiety for Troy was akin to violence.

Another thought niggled at her and then bloomed. Her mother had come to Georgia expecting to identify her remains. Francine's mind flashed back to the auto shop–being strung up with rape and murder the only possible outcomes of such a situation. She realized in that moment, her mother and sister could be living a different conclusion had Troy not happened along. Their anger was better than their sorrow.

When she looked up into his eyes, they were ablaze with the hum of rage. Boldly, she reached up and cupped his face, pulling him down to her. She kissed him softly and against her lips he gritted. "Mine, Francine."

"Yes." She whispered back. "I promise."

Stepping back from her, Troy glared at her mother and sister. Francine almost burst out laughing as she witnessed their shock. His touch was possessive, but his temper had lessened.

"I'm done with this." He growled.

He turned for the door, but he didn't release her. The worry in her mother's voice stopped her. She hated to treat her family so shabbily after all they had been through. But she had to take a stand because they all needed to coexist. Francine knew what they did not–her mother and sister weren't visiting the morgue to view her body. She could never cross him; the goal here would always be to maintain the safety of her family.

"I made a mistake in the way I handled things and I'm sorry for the worry I caused. But Troy is my husband. I won't leave him, please try to understand."

"When did you become a selfish bitch?" Jennifer asked.

Francine felt his grip tighten, but he said nothing. "Troy and I would like to invite you both to our home. I will spend the next few weeks kissing your asses because this is my fault. Accepting him is non-negotiable. He is my husband, and this won't go away."

Her mother sighed, and Francine took it as a sign. "Troy, this is my mother Doris Adams, people call her Dot. Ma, this is my husband, Ernest Stephen Bryant. Friends and family call him Troy."

"Ms. Adams."

"Troy…" her mother replied.

"This is my sister, Jennifer–Jennifer, this is Troy."

"Nice to finally meet you, Jennifer." Troy said, but the stress was back in his tone.

"Really? Fuck both of y'all right now." Jennifer countered.

"Clearly, you thought my ass was dead. Which scenario would you prefer, me dead or you annoyed?" Francine snapped.

The sisters squared off until Troy intervened. "Come, ladies, we'll make certain you get home."

When he opened the door, Francine was suddenly weary. Jennifer, however, stormed out of the conference room and didn't look back. Her mother reached out pulling her into an embrace that made Francine's eyes water. Troy released her, so she could return the affection.

"I really am sorry, Ma. I learned my lesson," she said softly.

"Ya better never do this again." Dot countered as her voice broke.

Stepping back, Francine let her mother move through the door of the conference room first. She followed, glad for the small reprieve. Troy placed his hand on the small of her back as she heard a familiar voice call her name.

"Frankie! Baby, thank God you're safe!"

Francine looked up to find Jalal moving swiftly toward them, and he appeared as tired as she felt. She had forgotten the other reason they had come to the police station. There would be no time to think or do damage control because Jalal reached out and snatched her into his arms. His hold was crushing. Francine couldn't tell if the pounding she felt came from his heart or her own.

"Baby… baby, I told them I could never hurt a woman." Jalal crooned as he nuzzled her closer.

"I'm sorry for all you been through. I had no idea." Francine tried to untangle herself from him.

She heard Levi's voice. "Dorsey, come with me."

Jalal's grip tightened and Levi pulled him off her. In her attempt to get away from Jalal, she backed into her husband. Troy's displeasure vibrated about her causing her to lose her train of thought.

"Frankie… Sweetheart, please don't leave. I need to speak with you." Jalal's anxiety that she would disappear again was obvious.

"Troy and I came because we wanted to clear up any misunderstanding. We came as soon as we heard," Francine replied.

Jalal focused on Troy for the first time and smiled. "Thanks, man. This shit is crazy, I almost caught a case. I was about to be property of the state. I've seen you speak several times–never thought this would happen to me."

"I'm glad it worked out for you, man." Troy answered.

Jalal was overwhelmed when he reached out to shake Troy's hand. Her husband was gracious, but his vexation didn't diminish. When Jalal stepped back, it was as if he had realized that she was standing with her back to Troy's front. His eyebrows drew together as he spoke.

"Will you wait for me so we can talk, Frankie?"

"My husband and I have an appointment. I'm glad everything worked out, Jalal. Please know I would never deliberately try to hurt you."

"Husband?" Jalal countered.

She smiled. "Yes, I married Troy today."

Jalal looked back at Troy, and Francine was sure he now felt the throb of annoyance coming from her husband. There was a pregnant pause before Jalal narrowed his eyes. "Last Sunday, were you the dude in the black Benz?"

Troy chuckled, but Levi offered distraction. "Dorsey, follow me."

Detective Hill went with Levi and Jalal. Detective Wilton turned to Troy. "I'll lead you back out to the lobby."

Francine clasped hands with her mother, and Troy walked behind them. When they reached the exit, she noticed the office had become crowded with both plainclothes and uniformed cops. It seemed Troy was the attraction. The looks on their faces ran from admiration to contempt, but her husband gave no reaction.

Detective Wilton pulled the door open with the beep of a key card, allowing her and her mother into the corridor first. As they walked toward the lobby, Francine could hear a loud disturbance. Behind them the door opened again with Levi and Jalal stepping into the hall.

Levi looked pissed. "It's a shit storm out there."

Troy nodded. "It was inevitable."

Levi looked at the two detectives. "This was done out of spite."

Hill laughed, and Wilton looked to the ground. Levi glared at them before moving out in front of her and her mother. Troy brought up the rear and once in the lobby, Francine saw it was dark outside. The brown glass made it appear later than it really was. Still, she wanted to have coffee with her mother. She had been about to ask Troy when flashes of bright white light began in rapid succession. Francine was momentarily blinded, losing her thought.

She blinked several times to bring her vision back into focus. There were spots before her eyes, along with her sister, who looked panicked as she stood in the middle of the lobby. When Jennifer finally found her voice, she directed her words to Troy.

"Who the fuck are you?"

4

THE MAN

Troy watched as Levi leaned down and whispered something to his sister in-law. Jennifer looked up at Levi and though she was shaking, she nodded. Next to him, his wife whispered, "Troy, what's happening?"

He didn't exactly know how to explain the shit that was his life. Who he was and what he had become in the black community varied based on who was observing. But tonight, at this moment, he felt tired, irritated, jealous and provoked. He didn't deal with the press nor did he feel the need to explain himself to the world. There was no office he coveted, so he didn't care what the public thought. His mission was already made complicated by the miseducation of his people–he did not think the press would help bridge the gap. Especially since, in many cases, it was the press that slanted the truth, painting people of color in the worst possible light.

The police weren't even trying to control the mob of reporters out front. Butch wasn't in the lobby, but they still would have to wade through the madness to get to the truck. The detectives were sending a message... *You don't want to speak with us then speak with the press.* He had wanted to keep her to himself a while longer, but maybe it was best to claim her openly. Francine was clutching her mother's hand when he spoke.

"Levi will help your mother and sister. You will stand with me."

Francine didn't hesitate as she directed her mother over to her sister and Levi. She stepped forward and took his hand. Troy didn't engage Levi again, and even with the uncertainty of Jalal Dorsey, he turned, heading for the entrance of the police station. He pulled the door open and stepped onto the landing, his wife at his side. Levi stood on the opposite side of Francine, her mother and sister behind them. Beyond Levi, Jalal stood quiet, looking confused.

Out in front of them were two news trucks and a bevy of reporters. The flash started again, and Troy knew there would be no relief. Next came the intrusive questions.

"Troy, how did you end up with the victim?"

"Troy, when was the last time you were in contact with George Ingalls? How do you feel about being a person of interest in his disappearance?"

"Troy, did you get married? What about Karyn Battle, are you still seeing her?"

"Francine, isn't Troy too old for you? How did you end up with the Silent Activist? Where have you been for four days? Did you realize your lover, Jalal Dorsey was being held for questioning?"

The questions went on without ceasing, each ruder than the last. It was the mention of Jalal being her lover that pushed him to action. Troy raised his hand and the crowd grew hushed. They were shocked that he was going to speak.

"Good evening, ladies and gentlemen. As you all know I don't address the public through the press. It lessens the probability of being misquoted. Tonight, however, I will make a statement–I will *not* answer questions."

There were more flashes as the journalists and news cameras focused on him. When he was sure he had their complete attention, he continued. "I am honored to announce that Francine Marie Adams became Mrs. Ernest Stephen Bryant today. She has made me a happy man."

Over the heads in the crowd, Troy saw Butch pull the truck to the curb. The steps in front of the police station weren't high. They were actually standing among the reporters, their backs to the glass doors. He caught Levi's eye and nodded.

"Ladies and gentlemen, please back away so Mr. and Mrs. Bryant can make it to their vehicle. Mr. Bryant has advised me that if you all leave your contact information with me and play nice, he'll allow three of you to his next event."

The news reporters didn't back away. He and Levi had used that trick one time too many. Pissed, he stepped forward bogarting his way through the crowd with his wife in tow. Jennifer and Doris walked behind them and Levi brought up the rear. There were more questions and accusations, but they were making progress until he felt Francine stumble.

Violently yanked from his grasp, the mob got between him and his wife, and Troy pushed past two white, male reporters to find Francine sprawled out on her back. When he attempted to get closer, the taller of the two tried to block him while shoving a mic at her.

"Francine, where have you been for four days? Did you know the city was looking for you? It's been said by your husband that the police don't search for victims of color with the same vigor they use in the search for white victims. Do you feel as though you wasted taxpayer dollars?"

"How long have you been with Troy? Did you know he was photo-graphed with Karyn Battle days ago?"

At the sight of Francine on the ground, everything came to a grinding halt but his temper. Thankfully, Levi stepped between him and the reporter.

"Don't do it, man, they're trying to set you off. She's fine and handling this shit better than you," he whispered for Troy's ears only.

Levi backed the group off with threats of harassment, and Troy helped Francine to her feet. Her mother and sister looked like deer in headlights, but Francine was smiling. Butch was out of the car in seconds helping to move the crowd back.

Troy pulled her into his embrace and against her ear he asked, "You all right?"

She nodded and then offered verbally, "Yes, Troy, I'm fine. I'll do better at keeping up next time."

Troy lifted her into his arms and strode toward the truck with the threat of bodily harm to anyone who tried to impede them. Butch helped the other ladies into the truck and shut the door with a thud. Levi climbed into the front passenger seat. As the vehicle eased slowly away from the curb, Troy noticed Jalal staring into the tinted windows, seeing nothing. *Fuck him*, Troy thought, let him find his own damn way.

The car was silent while everyone tried to collect themselves. Troy sat with his arm around Francine, and he knew she could feel his rage chok-ing him. He had examined his constant state of aggression and realized he hadn't been this angry in months. The explanation was obvious, Francine made him feel like a rabid dog. The reason—he had rescued her from two men who meant to do her harm. Now, he wanted every man to understand that she belonged to him. And still, he was her new prison. There would be no letting go.

They had been riding for about fifteen minutes when Francine broke the quiet. "Troy?"

"Yes, Francine."

"Who is Karyn Battle?"

Levi burst out laughing, and he thought he saw Butch's shoulders shake. Troy didn't respond to her question, not because he was ignoring her. He was ignoring Levi, still, she had taken him by surprise. She was inquiring about Karyn and not that bastard George Ingalls. Francine wanted to know about an acquaintance and not the reporters. Troy grinned, he would punish her later for questioning him. But he did like it.

Butch pulled through the gates of the Oak Tree Apartments in Marietta and continued on until they reached Building Ten. When the car came to a stop, neither Dot nor Jennifer moved to open the door. It was Francine's mother who asked what Troy was sure his wife was thinking.

"Troy, I would like to see where my daughter is living. We realize it's your wedding night..."

"Levi will walk you both to your apartment and wait for you. You are both welcome in our home."

"Thank you." Dot's voice tight with concern. "We won't be long."

The ladies got out followed by Levi. Butch parked and got out as well, leaving Troy and Francine alone. His wife began scooting away from him to follow her mother and sister.

"No, Francine."

"Troy, I would like to get some of my things."

"Butch will see to moving your things next week."

She stopped moving and stared after her mother and sister. "Thank you for letting them come home with us."

He wanted her to himself, but he understood her mother's plight. It wasn't his goal to bully her mother, just Francine. Troy never commented on her mother, he had other questions he wanted answered.

"Do you still want Jalal Dorsey?"

Butch opened the door for the women, and she never got a chance to answer. Levi loaded their bags in the back and then they were off. They rode for an hour and twenty minutes before they reached his house and all the while, Troy pondered the fact that she never answered him. He told himself it didn't matter if she wanted Dorsey. She couldn't have him.

Troy helped Levi bring in the bags while Francine led the women to the bedroom she first stayed in. After the events and aggravations of today, he didn't think he could manage intimacy of any kind with Francine. And though he never did anything in haste, it seemed Francine incited him to impulsive behavior. Jealousy appeared to be his constant companion. The feeling had him in a headlock and the more he struggled, the tighter the chokehold became.

"We have two engagements in North Carolina, both private affairs. The headcount for the first event is sixty at five thousand a plate. The second occasion is a headcount of thirty-five at one thousand dollars a plate." Troy said once they were settled in his office.

"You had a crazy week. We'll move forward at your pace," Levi replied.

"We'll leave for Charlotte in two hours," Troy said.

If Levi thought it strange, him wanting to bounce on his wedding night, he didn't say. Troy knew what he needed, and it was to put some distance between him and the sweet thing in his home.

"We'll stop for me to get my things on the way out of Georgia," Levi stood.

"I'll drive the first half, bring the Benz around."

"That's fine with me, meet you out front in a few." Levi said, and then he was gone.

Troy found his wife and the other ladies in the living room seated on the sofa. All three looked up at his entrance, nervous at the sight of him. He had not really taken inventory of them because a lot was going on. Dot looked to be in her mid-fifties. She was a slender, brown skinned woman with small eyes, a fat nose and thick lips. Her hair was gray around the front of her head and pulled back into a ponytail. It was clear from the lines and creases in her face that she had lived hard. Jennifer, on the other hand, was a few shades lighter than his wife, but they looked alike. His sister in-law had slanted brown eyes, a straight nose with high cheekbones. Her lips weren't as plump as Francine's, but her mean ass was attractive.

When he focused on Francine, he devoured everything about her. She was shorter than both her mother and sister, which made it comical that she bossed them around. His wife was also darker than the other ladies with deep brown eyes, keen features and juicy lips. Her bottom lip was slightly fatter than her top and it made him want to kiss her.

"Francine, I need to speak with you."

His wife stood and walked over to him as Jennifer asked, "Frankie is afraid of you. She won't tell us the truth, so I'm asking you. Why is my sister scared of you?"

If he weren't in such a shitty mood, Troy might have been impressed. There was no mistaking that Jennifer was afraid of him too, still, she wanted to protect Francine. He glared at her before responding, "For the same reason you're afraid of me."

"Jennifer, please, you can't insult my husband in our home. If you don't want to stay, I can have Butch take you home."

"No, I'll stay here with you – 'cause you out yo' rabid ass mind." Jennifer replied to Francine but never took her eyes off Troy.

He took Francine by the hand and led her to their bedroom. When he shut the door, Francine immediately spoke.

"I'm sorry about my sister."

Troy didn't respond about Jennifer, it was Jalal touching her that troubled him. Still, he wouldn't repeat the question, it made him feel weak.

"I have business to tend to in North Carolina, I'll be leaving tonight. Butch and Jewel are here for you. The incident with the reporters doesn't happen often, but you are not to leave this house without Butch. He will drive you wherever you wish to go."

"Butch and Jewel give me the willies. I don't want to stay with them."

"They live on the property, and Jewel keeps our house. You will treat them with respect, do you understand?"

"Yes, Troy, I understand. They know you abducted me, and they helped you. I should fear them like I fear you, correct? Do you even know anyone who doesn't look like they've done a bid for manslaughter?"

He almost laughed, but he was still salty about earlier. "No, Francine, I don't know anyone who hasn't killed someone."

"When will you be back?" she countered, not acknowledging his statement.

"I will give you three days with your family, then Butch will bring you to me in Charlotte. You will attend two events with me. Jewel will pack for you, she knows what I want you to wear."

He tried to back away from his insecurity but failed. "You never answered me."

"About what?"

"Do you still want Jalal Dorsey?"

"What difference does it make? Me, you, Butch, Jewel and Levi are one big happy family now."

She stood with her back to the door, and he towered over her. He reached out, wrapping his right hand about her throat. Francine swallowed, then gasped as he added slight pressure to make her understand that he had the power between them. In her eyes, he saw arousal–not fear. He kissed her softly before backing away.

"While I'm gone, I'll call at 9:30 am and then again at 9:30 pm. You will take my calls in the office. Do not miss my calls, Francine." She nodded, and he went on. "Go be with your family. I'll see you in a few days."

* * *

After Troy left with Levi, her mother and sister went to bed. Francine went to bed as well, and though she was drained, sleep did not come. The two men with the van popped in her head, and she had to work to back away from all thoughts of being strung up. She felt unsafe and confused with Troy gone. But what troubled her the most, she missed him, and that revelation alone caused her to sob. It was four in the morning before she found sleep.

Francine woke to a light tapping on the door and the sun shining brightly. She was disoriented until she heard her mother's voice.

"Frankie, you up?"

"Come in," Francine invited.

The door opened and in stepped her mother dressed in blue jeans and an orange t-shirt that read, "Kiss the cook". She stared around the room but didn't comment until she spied the mirrored ceiling.

"Ya think this man might be too much for you?"

Francine was embarrassed. She and her mother didn't discuss sex, and she wanted to keep it that way. "Did you sleep well?"

Her mother was still looking up at the ceiling and snapped her gaze down. "You married a man I think is too much for you. And after yesterday, I can see you're not going to leave him. But please don't try to tell me you're not afraid of him because we are all afraid of him."

"Ma, Troy can be intense, but I want my husband." Francine said, and to her own surprise it was the truth.

"Did you know who he was when you met him?"

"No."

"You wanna tell me how you met this man and ended up missing for four days?"

"No, Ma, I don't want to talk about being picked up by an attractive stranger with you. What's important is that he is my husband, and I am fine."

"I wouldn't have recognized him if the press hadn't mobbed us. He spoke at a meeting for black teachers in New York about a year ago. The city was turned upside down because of his visit. I don't remember much else, but the female teachers at my school talked about him for months."

"I never heard of the Silent Activist. I think it says more about me than it does about him." Francine replied.

"I don't know his story. I know about the event in New York." Dot clarified.

"When Jennifer wakes, do you want to go to Atlanta?" Francine wanted to change the subject.

"No, but I would like to go to the grocery store and cook in that kitchen."

It appeared her mother wasn't going to allow herself to be distracted with sightseeing. Her mother wanted information, and Francine knew old Dot could be patient. She would have to be cautious in dealing with her family. While she was contemplating how to proceed with her mother, her sister walked into the bedroom with an attitude. Apparently, she was still angry from yesterday.

"The house is beautiful," her mother said.

Francine was uncomfortable with saying 'thank you'. It didn't really feel like her house after all, especially with Troy gone. When she climbed from the bed, her sister rolled her eyes. She was dressed in the shirt Troy wore the night before. Francine refused to examine why she wore it to bed. She was about to tell them she was going to get dressed and find Butch, but there came another knock at the door.

"Come in," Francine called out.

Jewel peeped her head around the large door and smiled. It did nothing to lessen the harshness of her scar. She looked more the thug than Butch, which was saying much because he was scary.

"Good morning, Francine."

"Good morning, Jewel. I'm glad you're here. This is my mother, Dot and my sister, Jennifer. Ladies, this is Jewel, a close friend of Troy's."

Everyone offered polite conversation, and Francine prayed Jennifer wouldn't show her ass. She created a diversion when she asked, "Jewel, I hope it's all right with you, but my mom wants to cook in the kitchen."

"It's your kitchen, Francine. Of course, it's all right with me."

"Can Butch take her to the supermarket?" Francine continued.

"Butch would be happy to drive you wherever you need."

"Can I see what's in the pantry, so I know what I'll need?" Dot asked.

"Absolutely," Jewel replied.

Jennifer was dressed in black jeans and a black t-shirt. She had black socks on her feet—no shoes. They moved toward the door with Jewel and her mother discussing baking. When they disappeared into the hall, Jewel turned back and whispered. "It's 9:25, Troy will be calling in five minutes."

"Yes, thank you." Francine said, before rushing into the closet. She found one of Troy's robes and headed to the office with two minutes to spare. The phone rang promptly at 9:30, and her stomach lurched. She picked up on the second ring and his voice flooded through the receiver.

"Good morning, Francine."

She was breathless when she answered, "Good morning, Troy."

"How are you feeling?"

Hearing his voice made Francine understand why she had cried all night. She was immediately back in the auto shop, waiting to be raped and murdered. When in Troy's and even Levi's presence, they were the threat. Staying alert with them kept her from focusing on what could have been— but now with them gone... There was nothing to do but concentrate on the fact that she had been stolen from her life. Unable to help herself, she broke down.

"I-I'm fine," she sniffled, trying for normalcy.

"You going out with your mother and sister?"

She couldn't speak right away, and he patiently waited for her to gather herself. This made her situation even worse before it got better. Finally, she replied, "No, my mother likes the kitchen. She wants to do some baking."

"Jewel will love that. Don't tell her I said so, but she can't cook."

Francine was thankful to him for allowing her time to get her shit together. "I didn't know who you were before yesterday."

"At this point, you know me better than most."

The timbre in his words was consoling to her real issue, but they would not discuss her abduction over the phone. Also present in his statement was sexual innuendo meant to alter her train of thought.

"I'm uninformed as a person of color, Troy."

She could hear his smile over the phone. "I'm uniformed as a person of color as well, Francine."

In the background, she could hear sudden conversation. "I have to go and get my day started. I will call you again, tonight at 9:30."

"All right, Troy."

The line went dead, and she was left staring at the phone. When she placed the handset back on the cradle, she realized that she wanted her family to go home. She worried she might break down again and her mother would see through to her dishonesty. And the hostility coming from her sister wasn't helping matters either. She would find a way to have Butch take them back to Marietta, she would.

* * *

As the late afternoon pressed on to evening, Francine wandered between her bedroom and the living room. She discussed with Jewel the attire required for each event and set about packing. Poor Jewel was left entertaining her family, but it was safer. Her mother and sister would get nothing from the housekeeper. When her sister came into her bedroom and saw her packing, she looked upset, but Francine ignored her concern.

Her mother had been cooking all day, and the house smelled heavenly. As a child, the aroma of good food lifted her spirits, but today it turned her stomach. Francine didn't even try to find out what they were having for dinner. It was 6:30 in the evening when her mother found her in her bedroom.

"It's time to eat."

Francine smiled. "What did you cook?"

"I made baked macaroni and cheese, collard greens and two stuffed chickens. For dessert, I baked two cakes, one chocolate and one yellow, both with chocolate frosting. I also baked an apple pie and some chocolate chip cookies."

"You cooked all that for you, me and Jennifer?"

"No, I invited Jewel and Butch," her mother said.

"Poor Butch and Jewel, the burden has fallen to them."

She followed her mother back to the kitchen where Butch, Jewel and Jennifer waited.

"Francine, come see all the good food your mother cooked." Jewel said.

Troy had been right, Jewel was excited and Butch looked pleased as well. He nodded when they made eye contact. She wondered if he spoke to her mother at all. Jennifer looked agitated, and Francine didn't think dinner would go well. But she would try for her mother's sake.

They were all seated at the kitchen table and began serving themselves. Butch looked as though he had cleaned himself up to partake in such a fine meal. Jewel looked proud of the spread, and it appeared she couldn't stop smiling. Francine managed to spoon a small amount of food on her plate before her appetite vanished.

Francine's fear of Jewel and Butch was set aside as Jennifer became the new hazard. She was weary from the constant battle of wills and needed all her strength to deal with Troy; she couldn't expend energy on foolishness.

"I see you was packing. You plan on disappearing again?" Jennifer threw down the gauntlet.

Both Butch and Jewel tried to focus on their food. Her mother stared between them, unsure what to do. "Jennifer, I made a mistake and I have apologized. What more would like me to do?"

"I would like you to tell the truth. You're afraid of that man you callin' yo' husband. Shit, you afraid of these two as well. They look like damn murderers." Jennifer gestured at Butch and Jewel. She wasn't finished either. "You know what that damn Levi told me at the police station? He told me if I didn't shut up, he would beat me with a bag of oranges."

Francine looked at Butch and Jewel who kept eating. When she caught Butch's eye, he actually smiled. She tried not to laugh, but Francine couldn't help it, she giggled. This, of course, only set Jennifer on the war path.

"I don't believe you met Troy and decided to marry him. I think you are a hostage here and these two are helping him." Jennifer sneered.

"Jennifer, stop it." Their mother was clearly exasperated by her daughter's rudeness.

Her sister then turned her nastiness on their mother. "Don't tell me you fallin' for this shit. They got a nice kitchen, so fuckin' what."

Francine didn't bother to address Jennifer, she turned to Butch. "Butch, I'm sorry to stick you with my rude ass sister. But when dinner is finished, can you please drive Jennifer back to Marietta?"

She didn't even wait for a response from Butch before she turned to Jennifer. "If you honestly thought I was in danger, you wouldn't be talking shit. You will not be allowed to be abusive to my husband or Butch and Jewel because you are angry with me."

Francine stood, allowing her gaze to bounce from person to person. When she addressed her mother, there was no question she was at the end of her rope. "Ma, you can stay or go with Jennifer. But please understand, Jennifer will not be welcomed back until she learns some respect for others. You should also know that I will be leaving to join Troy in Charlotte for two events. I will call you daily, but I don't know how long I'll be gone. I have never been to one of his speaking engagements."

Her mother looked sad. "I will be leaving for New York day after tomorrow."

"Troy has offered to move you to Georgia and purchase a place for you." Francine wanted to offer comfort to her mother.

"Why can't Mommy stay with yo' high and mighty ass? Oh, I know why–cause y'all got something to hide." Jennifer gritted out.

"I will pay my half of the rent on the apartment until the end of the lease. Mommy can't stay with me and Troy because I don't want her to hear me learning to appreciate the mirrored ceiling."

Jewel coughed, and even though Butch never stopped eating, he patted his choking wife on the back. Francine dropped her napkin and walked out of the kitchen.

* * *

It was midnight, and Francine couldn't sleep. Butch had driven her mother and sister back to Marietta. Jewel went home to the small apartment she shared with Butch over the garage. Alone in a strange house with thoughts of rape and murder, Francine paced and paced, but it did no good. She was coiled too tight. The worst part, she couldn't turn to her mother and sister for support. They could never know.

As she wandered about the house, she stumbled into a media room equipped with large, plush burgundy chairs and a huge screen. On the left of the room was a full bar and she helped herself to a stiff drink; Absolute–no chaser. She was leaving the entertainment room when she heard what sounded like water. In the corridor leading back to the kitchen, there was a door that she was sure led to the garage apartment. But when she opened it, she was greeted to the sight of an indoor pool. The glass walls were all cranked open on angles like a greenhouse but screened in. The cross ventilation moved a soft breeze, making the space refreshing instead of stifling.

Stepping back into the hall, she closed the door and headed back to the kitchen. She found Butch waiting. Francine was uneasy, but she stood quietly, spurring him to speak first. She decided that if she were going to have to live with him, she would have to manage their interactions better.

The old man actually chuckled. "Your mother and sister are home safe. Jewel will see to it that your mother makes it to the airport, since I will be driving you to Charlotte."

She stared at him for a moment taking in all that was Butch. The sound of his voice was like velvet, and Francine couldn't decide if the sound was deadly or calming. She cocked her head to the side and openly studied him.

"How long were you in jail?"

"Fifteen years."

"For what?"

"Involuntary Manslaughter."

"What time would you like for me to be ready to leave for Charlotte?"

"I'll ask Troy what time he expects us and let you know."

Francine nodded and moved past him, determined to keep pacing while she finished her drink. His words followed her.

"Best dinner I had in a long time."

She turned back and looked at Butch who was smiling. Francine offered no response before turning back on her way. In the living room, she fumbled for a while with the remote until she figured out how to turn the television on. As she sat flipping through the channels, she stopped when she saw a still frame of Troy. The caption read: Troy Bryant and his women.

The screen changed to a perky blonde adorned in a green dress. She was holding a white card and her hair moved seductively as she spoke about Troy.

"As you all know, Silent Activist, Troy Bryant spoke to the press for the first time since his release from prison almost two years ago. Ernest Stephen Bryant, also known as Troy, announced yesterday evening to the press that he has gotten married. Mr. Bryant married a local woman newly relocated from Queens, New York."

The woman's voice faded away as a clip of her and Troy hit the screen. Francine grimaced when she saw the shock on her face. After Troy made his statement, the screen cut back to the blonde anchor.

"Mr. Bryant was seen about town in Charlotte, North Carolina, with longtime flame Karyn Battle. The couple had dinner at an upscale restaurant this evening, and Ms. Battle held onto Troy's arm until they disappeared into the limo." The blonde anchor shuffled the cards in her hand. "It appears the Silent Activist forgot his own announcement."

The screen cut away again to show Troy with a tall dark-skinned woman with bouncing hair, wearing a little black dress and heels. His hand was on the small of her back. The woman was gorgeous. The last thing Francine wanted was a man who carried on publicly with other women.

She zoned out and turned the television off before the piece on Troy was done. How could she deal with her mother and sister if he behaved like this? She finished her drink, placed the glass on the coffee table and headed for their bedroom. Fuck Ernest Stephen Bryant.

* * *

Troy stood facing Karyn in the foyer of her townhouse. Dinner had been intense, and she almost fainted when they left the restaurant. He had to hold her up until they were safely in the limo. The idea of seeing her in a public setting hadn't been his best. She'd seen the news and his announcement regarding Francine and had not taken it well.

He had been honest with her from the onset about his feelings. When he first came home from prison, he'd been starved for pussy and banging everything that moved. And though he always practiced safe sex, he knew he had to get ahold of himself. Levi had introduced him to Karyn; she was better for his image.

Their setup had been perfect. Karyn claimed she wasn't looking for serious, but after six months, things changed. She had always been kind and never did she refuse him anything; still, his feelings had never moved beyond fondness. Karyn was thirty-two and beautiful, standing almost five-feet, nine-inches with dark skin and legs for days. Sexually, she was so responsive to his touch that they fucked anywhere and everywhere. The icing on the cake–Karyn was a successful pediatrician. She was a catch, she just wasn't for him.

When Troy came to understand they weren't on the same page, he backed away from the physical side of their relationship. His lust was now a beast that needed to be bound and gagged for the sake of his public image. Karyn remained his companion, but he was, once again, starved for pussy.

"Where did this girl come from?" she asked.

"Karyn."

"I love you, Troy. How could you think I wouldn't ask questions?"

"I'm not going to discuss it. Please, baby."

She covered her face and cried. Troy didn't know what to do. He pulled her into his arms and held her. When she finally stopped crying, he whispered, "I never meant to hurt you, sweetheart."

Her voice was thick with emotion. "I suspect you never gave me a thought. You looked agitated when they referred to Jalal Dorsey as her lover."

"My goal wasn't to hurt you," he reiterated.

She reached up and kissed him before stepping back from him. Dismissive, she said, "I have to get up early in the morning. Congratulations to you and Mrs. Bryant."

Troy heard her sarcasm, yet he felt nothing but relief. He didn't even look back when he took his leave. The night air was still as he stepped from Karyn's home. Once on the sidewalk, the limo moved into position, but Troy waved it off and began walking. He removed his dinner jacket, undid his tie and unbuttoned his top button. In his peripheral vison, he could see the limo as it followed slowly. He lit a cigarette and inhaled deeply.

Butch had called to inform him of the quarrel between his wife and her sister. He also reported that Francine had asked her sister to leave. When he had spoken to his wife at 9:30, she had not mentioned the matter. He wondered if she missed him. Jalal Dorsey popped into his head, and Troy could see him holding on to Francine for dear life. Karyn had been correct about his agitation with the press for thinking Dorsey, his wife's lover.

The time away from his wife had not helped his attitude, he felt even more volatile. He missed their banter and her fear. Troy missed Francine. He stopped walking and took a final drag on his cigarette when blue and red lights appeared in front of him. The squad car pulled onto the sidewalk blocking his way. Troy threw his cigarette down before raising his hands in the air–palms out.

Two white, uniformed officers got out of the car. One hung back, gun drawn. The other officer came forward with a flashlight, blinding him.

"You from around here?" the cop asked.

"No, a friend of mine lives in this subdivision."

"Can I see some I.D.?"

"Back pocket," Troy said.

"You can get it, slowly." The cop instructed.

Troy reached for his wallet and handed the cop his license. It was dark, so he couldn't see the badge number. After shining the flashlight on his I.D., the cop asked, "That your car and driver?"

"Yes."

"If you have a friend who lives in the area, why are you wandering about late at night on private property?"

Troy chuckled to release steam. This exchange could end badly if he didn't proceed with caution. Karyn was one of six black residents in the Haven Cross subdivision. She had no trouble with her neighbors until he started visiting. The HOA started sending nasty correspondence about her grass and other petty matters, but Karyn had been gracious through it all.

"My friend doesn't live in the area, she lives in this subdivision, Officer…"

"Taylor. My partner is Overgaard."

"Officer Taylor," Troy repeated, trying the name on his tongue before he continued, "the sidewalk isn't private property."

The cop stared at him before handing back his license. "I'm going to ask you to move along. We don't want to have to run you in for loitering and prowling."

"I concede that the hour is late, Officer, but I haven't taken flight or attempted to evade. I think it's clear my purpose here is not to commit a crime. I was smoking a cigarette and didn't want the interior of the car to smell stale."

Troy kept his hands palms out as he stared the cop in the face. The limo was why they hadn't beat his ass yet. They must have run his plates and figured he wasn't worth the public fallout.

"I'm asking you to move along," Taylor said.

"Thank you, Officers, have a good evening." Troy said as he turned and headed for the limo.

They stayed on the car until he was out of the subdivision. His driver was about forty and had been in and out of prison since he was sixteen. Jesse was dark in the extreme with mean eyes and rough features. He had been working for Troy for a year and was reliable. Troy liked most that he didn't speak much, and he was discreet.

Jesse drove him back to his high-rise condo in downtown Charlotte. When he moved through the lobby, the doorman greeted him.

"Mr. Bryant, good to see you."

"Same here, Charlie. How you been?"

"I'm good, sir, and you?

"I'm good."

Charlie was an older white fellow with a ready smile. He was about five feet, ten inches with gray hair and warm brown eyes. His red jacket, with the large brass buttons, was crisp as always. Troy kept moving toward the elevator as Charlie called out.

"Have a good evening, sir."

"Same to you, my friend."

A thick strip of red carpet trailed to the mirrored elevators doors. Troy caught sight of his reflection in the doors and shook his head–his anger was visible. When the doors slid open, he used his key card to push number twenty.

Once on his floor, he took a left out of the elevator. The color scheme was the same as the lobby except the entire floor was carpeted red. There were only four units on his floor, making for larger condos than the lower floors. Troy came to a stop in front of a tan door marked 2001 under the peephole. Using his key card, he stepped into the foyer and dropped his jacket and keys on the russet chair by the door.

He turned on the light in the foyer and lit another cigarette before moving to stand in front of the floor to ceiling windows. With one hand in his pocket, he exhaled smoke from his mouth and nostrils. He wanted to speak with Francine, but it was after midnight. When he finished his smoke, he laid on the oversized chocolate couch and closed his eyes.

* * *

It was 9:20 in the morning when Troy sat at the desk in his office. Behind him, the large window offered an overcast day as the city of Charlotte came to life. He picked up the receiver at 9:29 and dialed. The phone rang and rang–Francine did not answer. He hung up, then called back and still, his call went unanswered. He stood and stared out the window, collecting himself.

Finally, he called the main number and the line rang in the kitchen. Jewel picked it up on the first ring, and he had to bite back his annoyance.

"Jewel, it's 9:30. Francine didn't answer the phone."

"Oh, good morning, Troy. Hold on please, I'll go check on her for you. She was up late and may have overslept."

He didn't respond–he couldn't. His anger had gotten out in front of him, and he couldn't think. Jewel was gone for about five minutes.

"Troy, you still there?"

"I'm here. Where is Francine?"

"Uh… Francine is in her old room."

Troy's patience was gone. He snapped, "Why in the hell didn't she answer the phone?"

Jewel coughed. "Francine told me to tell you she doesn't want to speak to you."

His voice was dead calm. "Why the fuck not?"

"She saw you with Karyn Battle on the news."

"Is that *all* she said, Jewel?"

"No."

"What else did she say?" he ground out.

"Why don't you let her cool off, Troy?" Jewel coaxed.

"I'll be home this afternoon," he slammed the receiver down.

Troy looked up to find Levi standing in the doorway. He spoke, but Troy was beyond reason. "I don't know what happened, but you don't need to go back to Georgia in your frame of mind."

"You can help me manage my businesses not my fuckin' marriage."

Troy dismissed Levi and picked up the receiver. He dialed the airline.

* * *

It was quarter to five in the evening when the car service Troy hired pulled onto the long drive of his property. He didn't bring any luggage, just his I.D., cash and one credit card. Butch was standing on the small stoop between the two potted plants when the black town car came to a stop. Troy paid the driver, an older black woman with thick locks and several moles around her eyes. They hadn't conversed as she maneuvered the Atlanta traffic, and he liked it that way.

When the car pulled away, Troy stood on the stone pathway leading to the front door. There was no mistaking the message, the old man was blocking him from entering the house.

Troy was shaking with anger. "I'm gonna tell you like I told Levi! You will not manage my fuckin' marriage, old man!"

Butch was unfazed. "You and Francine been through a lot in the last week. Whether ya know it or not, what happened to her got you both

fucked up in the head. The girl being jealous of Karyn is a sign she's softening towards you. Don't ruin it by manhandling her. If you physically harm
her, you gonna regret it."

"She didn't answer the damn phone."

"I know, man, she been in that room crying on and off all day. You
gotta calm yo' ass down–ya gotta do better than this, Troy."

When he turned his back to light a cigarette, he heard the front door
close and lock behind him. The old man shut him out. Troy rubbed his
hand over his face, pressing his forefinger and thumb into his eye sockets.
Francine was making him crazy.

He stared out over the well-manicured lawn to the large trees surrounding the property. He owned twenty acres and most of it was untouched.
Barring the two acres of well-manicured grass and patio out back, the land
was left in its natural state for privacy. Unlike North Carolina, the sun was
shining in Georgia and it was hot as hell. He paced the front of the house
until the sun went down. Butch found him sitting on the stoop, staring into
the darkness.

"Come on in before something bites yo' ass out there."

The air had become thick, and Troy could smell the coming rains. He
had to speak over the loud sounds of the cicada. "So, I have your permission
to come inside my own house."

"Yeah," Butch answered, unmoved. "She doesn't know you're here."

After he entered the house, the old man went home. Troy didn't seek
Francine out, instead he went to the room with the cot, undressed and laid
down. It was after midnight when he woke from images of himself in the
infirmary. He shook his head to clear it, but thoughts of his first year in
prison persisted. It was these thoughts that chased him into Atlanta a week
ago and caused him to collide with Francine. Troy stood, prepared to pace
the house, when he a heard noise from the direction of the kitchen.

* * *

Francine was putting the milk back in the refrigerator; she closed the door
and turned to the counter. Troy stood just inside the kitchen, his anger and
gaze fixed on her. He was dressed in a pair of black boxer briefs–nothing
more. She moved strategically to the island and stood on the opposite side

to give herself room to run. It was almost impossible to hold his stare, but to look away seemed unwise. She pulled his robe tighter around herself. When he spoke, his voice offered threat and follow through.

"You didn't come to the phone."

"I thought you were in Charlotte." Her voice trembled.

"Did you think because I was away, you could break our number one rule?"

Troy crossed his arms and spread his feet controlling the space between them with his presence. His arms and thighs bulged with muscle, but it was the twitching of his bricked stomach that lent to his tension. Francine looked away against her better judgment. She was hypnotized by the beauty of his dark skin.

"My mother and sister already don't believe the marriage is real. If you're going to see other women, please leave me some dignity." She wanted her voice to be stronger—sharper, but her statement was barely audible.

"You didn't answer the question about Jalal Dorsey, and you're not allowed to sleep in any other room but the master."

"I don't want this marriage, Troy, and based on your actions, you don't want this marriage either." Francine finally got up the nerve to bring her eyes back to his. The blank expression on his face gave her pause, but she went on. "You saved my life. I will never speak on what happened."

"You're stuck with me, Francine." His words were matter of fact.

"You have my silence enforced by intimidation… please."

Tears spilled from her eyes and she turned her back on him. She could no longer manage him, his anger, her fear or her inability to face that she was jealous.

"I went to Karyn because I felt I owed her the courtesy of explaining why I could no longer see her. She has been a good friend, and she was hurt by my request to break all contact."

"Troy, we—"

"I want only you, Francine. I won't see her again."

She covered her face and wept, relief flooding her senses. The jealousy strangling her eased. She didn't want him to see other women. This both confused and scared her.

"You never answered my question."

She gasped, dropping her hands from her face. Troy had moved quietly to stand in front of her. He was blocking any escape, and she worried he would punish her. When she tried to look away, he placed both hands around her neck. The pressure was slight, still the control he displayed overwhelmed her.

"No, Troy, I don't want Jalal."

"But you were attracted to him."

Francine swallowed past the weight of his hands about her throat. "Before you—but not now."

"Take off the robe."

He didn't release her neck as she shrugged from the robe, revealing one of his t-shirts. Abruptly, he stepped back dropping his hands before lifting her to sit on the ledge in front of him. He grabbed her ass, yanking her to the edge of the counter. She could feel his erection pressed against her. Francine's breaths were coming in shaky puffs as she placed her hands on his chest. His skin was hot to the touch.

"Troy…"

He leaned down, inundating her senses with the smell of Egyptian Musk oil and him. Troy kissed her shoulder and pressed his mouth to her ear. "Can I have some pussy, Francine? Please."

"No," she breathed.

He chuckled as he continued kissing her shoulder. It was a deep rumbling sound that reverberated through her. "No what, Francine?"

She panted. "No, you may not have some pussy."

"Say it again. I wanna kiss your mouth when you talk dirty."

Still breathless, she repeated. "No pussy, Troy."

He caught her mouth in a stormy kiss and shoved his tongue deep. She moaned when he caught her bottom lip between his teeth and murmured, "Why not, I'm behaving myself. I asked nicely."

When he freed her lip, she leaned back and stared into his eyes. She hadn't expected to find him so relaxed. He didn't appear angry about being refused. It was her husband—Troy. The same man, but he was different.

"Who are you?"

He wrapped his right hand about her throat. "I'm the only man in your life."

"Why didn't you let me go after the auto shop?" she changed the subject.

"I followed you because I wanted you. I honestly thought you recognized me. When it became clear that you didn't know me, I figured it was only a matter of time. I stole you because the situation bonded us together. I won't let go."

"Do you still blame me for having to kill–them?" she stammered.

"I never blamed you for my having to kill them. I fault you for not taking better care of yourself and wandering down a dark street alone. I would have killed them anyway. The blood on my hands binds us."

"Your lawyer, George Ingalls, you killed him." The fact was she knew he murdered the lawyer; her words were a statement, not a question.

"Yes."

She realized that the more she spoke, the more entangled she became with him. Troy must have read her mind. "You will never be free of me, Francine. So, what you know or don't know will not make a difference. It's better if you know the real me."

"I'm afraid of the real you."

"Are you afraid of the real *me* or the real *you*?"

Her husband hit the nail on the head. She feared her attraction to him, and he was aware of these feelings. There was no answer she could give that would hide her thoughts, so she went with silence. Ernest Stephen Bryant was clever as hell, he circled back to the original matter with ease.

"It appears, Francine, that nice guys really do finish last. I was pleasant when I asked for some pussy, but it hasn't helped my cause." He laughed at her shock. "You will at least sleep in the master bedroom with your husband. Everything can't go your way."

Releasing her neck, Troy abruptly stepped back. He scooped her up off the counter, forcing her to wrap her arms about his neck and her legs around his waist. Turning, he strode toward the master suite and Francine, well–she felt safer, now that her kidnapping husband was home.

5

CHARLOTTE, NORTH CAROLINA
MAY 1995

They spent two extra days in Georgia before heading to Charlotte. Francine had slept late on the first morning of Troy's return. She donned a yellow sundress with black flip-flops and was about to leave the bedroom. She opened the door as Butch was about to knock, his expression one of relief. Francine realized then that he was worried about Troy's anger. Before she could think better of it, she reached out and touched his forearm. The old man smiled weakly.

Butch drove them to the airport in Atlanta, and Levi would meet them on the Charlotte side. Troy didn't speak much during their travels, but he was watchful. He caressed her shoulders, the small of her back and held her hand. When she would catch his eye, there was possessiveness in his gaze. Francine studied the man who was now her husband. She noticed the triggers that caused him to become aggressive, and sadly, she was one of them.

After all that happened in the last week and a half, she had become anxious in the company of men she didn't know. While at the airport, if she made eye contact with a man in the crowd, she would avert her gaze and move closer to Troy. Twice, he followed her line of vision and stared the man down until he looked away. By the time they were in the car and her luggage loaded, she was exhausted. Francine was thankful their stay in

North Carolina wouldn't be in a hotel. She was way too overwhelmed to deal with more people.

The condo was furnished nicely, but it didn't feel lived in. She found the place lacked coziness. The colors were natural, earthy and masculine, but no warmth. While the rest of the house seemed disconnected from Troy, the master bedroom was lived in. The master suite had a large round bed with lots of pillows and black satin sheets. One wall bragged of floor to ceiling windows with thick black drapes that moved by remote. The connecting wall was mirrored, while the opposite wall housed a large black armoire. This space even smelled of Egyptian Musk.

It was about 6:30 in the evening and the sun was still shining when she climbed into bed. Francine slept for hours, and her sleep was dreamless until it wasn't. She found herself hanging from a hook in that damn auto shop. The men who stole her off the street were dead, propped up staring at her with sightless eyes. She couldn't look at them, but she couldn't look away. It was the dark stranger that moved to stand before her that commanded her attention. She couldn't get his face to come into focus, his hand was large and when he touched her, she whimpered.

"Please... please help me."

When the man with the blurred features spoke, his voice was sinister and base. "Quiet, Francine, or I will punish you."

"Please...no," she began to sob.

"No one can save you!" he yelled.

She leaned her head back and released a blood curdling scream. The stranger reached out both hands and choked her.

Francine woke to the sound of her own screams. She was disoriented, but when she opened her eyes, the fogginess in her brain continued. Her surroundings were foreign, but everything smelled of him. She sat up in the bed, panting as she gathered herself. The room was dark except for the splash of light from the bathroom and the moon. Troy's voice slammed her into reality. He stood naked in front of the windows–his back to her.

"I'm here, Francine. You're safe."

She saw his silhouetted form against the night sky and experienced familiarity, but not ease. Flopping back against the pillows, she tried to calm her heart. She turned her back because the nightmare was about him, and she didn't want to need him. The bed dipped under his weight and she stiffened when he pulled her into his arms. He nuzzled her neck and the warmth of his body lulled her.

"The nightmare–is it about them or me?"

"You," she answered softly.

When she had gotten ready for bed, he insisted that she sleep in her bra and panties. Though everything about him was sexual, he still had not forced sex. They shared a bed nightly, but he did nothing more than spoon her. At times, his erection was unfailing and while he didn't try to hide his need, he didn't place demands that she couldn't meet. Troy reminded her of a lion playing with a baby deer; but the lion doesn't realize the fawn is stunned.

"I've been behaving myself, don't you think?" he said into the quiet of the night.

"No."

"No?" He feigned shock.

He turned her to face him before pulling her on top of him. All her senses were engulfed by her husband. Francine's face fit in the crook of his neck, so there was no visual. Still, she could smell him, taste him, feel him and hear him.

"You ain't a nice man, Ernest."

He laughed, and the rumble in his chest made her body tingle. "I said I'm behaved–I never said I was nice."

"It's all the same."

"No, baby, it's not. I'm controlling my hostility–that is behaving. I'm sure you think it would be nice if I let you go, but I won't."

Francine was so relaxed that she closed her eyes before murmuring, "Hmmm."

Troy rubbed her back in small circles. "What was your dream about?"

She didn't want to talk about the dream, but she did have curiosities. "Are you going to give in and choke me one day? Why do you always grab me by the neck?"

"Oh, Francine, I want to exert my will over everything that is you and I want you to love it."

"So, you're aggressive with women?"

"No, sweetheart, *you* and *you* alone make me crazy."

"I should feel honored then?"

He shrugged. "I have never felt crazy over a woman before you."

Francine was still draped over him. "I don't think you're aggressive because of me."

Troy hooted, "No, baby, you're not to blame for my hostilities. I spent too much time on lockdown–shit, my aggressions are too numerous to count."

"You never answered my question."

She could hear arousal in his voice. "No, I won't give in and choke you. I will, however, be rough with you and you'll learn to love it."

Francine gasped, and Troy chuckled. She slept in his arms all night, his hard on tucked between them. Still, she snuggled closer.

When she woke the next morning, Francine found herself in bed alone. She showered and dressed quickly before venturing out of the master suite. Male voices drifted from down the hall. She had been hungry until she realized Levi was with Troy. About to turn back to the bedroom, she heard. "Good Morning, Francine, nice to finally meet you. I'm Brenda."

The hall was brightly lit in patches as sunlight spilled from the open doors. A brown skinned woman stood at the end of the corridor, her gray hair braided in two thick cornrows. She wore jeans, a white button down shirt and white gym shoes. Brenda looked to be about sixty. Francine stood frozen for moments before she found her voice.

"Good morning, Brenda. Please, call me Frankie."

The woman smiled. "Come, you must be hungry. I'll fix you something to eat."

"Thank you, Brenda but…"

"Troy said you wouldn't eat, especially when you found out Levi was here." She cackled at her own cleverness.

"No, really, I'm not hungry."

"You want Troy to fire me?"

"Of course not," Francine replied.

"Good, then come have some coffee and a scrambled egg."

There was a standoff before Francine conceded. She followed Brenda around through the living room. A large, brown couch with overstuffed pillows sat to the right of the room facing a huge entertainment unit. The couch was expensive and ugly, yet it looked good in this setting. Off to the left was another hall and she could see Troy seated behind a gigantic desk while Levi paced.

At the back of the living room, the drapes were pulled back revealing a lovely day. Yet, Francine couldn't appreciate the situation because of the anxiety within her. Brenda walked fast, leading her into a black and chrome kitchen. The space was sizable but not as big as in Georgia. The stove and island were in the middle of the kitchen with three stools around the small bar. Even the refrigerator was black.

"How do you take your coffee, Frankie?"

"Just milk."

The lighting in the kitchen was better, and Francine could see that Brenda was a striking woman. She had light brown eyes and keen features. The smile she offered was warm against white teeth. She looked familiar, but Francine couldn't put her finger on why.

While contemplating the woman before her, Francine caught a whiff of Egyptian Musk. "Good morning, Francine."

She met Troy's gaze, noticing that his hair was freshly cut; his mustache and goatee were also perfectly trimmed. Sex emanated from him and she was embarrassed to be affected by him in the company of others.

"Good morning, Troy."

"Troy, Levi come eat with Frankie," Brenda said.

Levi was behind her, but she never acknowledged him. Francine moved closer to Troy and he hugged her. He bent to her ear, "We have an event tonight. You will go out with Brenda to get your hair and nails done."

"No."

Troy backed away and glared down at her. His eyes never left hers. "Levi, I will see you later tonight. Brenda, I'll have breakfast with my wife, then she and I will leave to handle some business."

"Good morning, Francine." Levi said from behind her.

She didn't reciprocate, treating him as if he didn't even exist. When Levi spoke once more, she heard humor. "I'll see you this evening, man. Have a good day, Francine."

"We'll be there early," Troy said.

When her nemesis departed, Francine relaxed, and Brenda took charge. "Come sit, both of you."

Troy led her to a black table in the corner with four matching chairs; he pulled her chair out. When he sat opposite her, she realized nothing about them would ever be normal. In the background, Brenda began cooking and the smell of coffee filled the air. Her husband was annoyed because she declined his request. But, like her, he would have to get over it. She didn't shy away from his upset, rather she faced it head on. He scowled, and she remained deadpan.

Brenda sat two cups on the table and filled them both with steaming coffee. She then placed two plates before them with fluffy eggs, breakfast sausages and buttered toast. Francine broke eye contact to smile at the woman serving them.

"Thank you, Brenda. It looks delicious."

"Yes, thank you." Troy chimed in.

"You two enjoy; I'm going to clean the bedroom."

Francine turned her attention back to the problem brewing across the table. As he sat with the plate in front of him, she tried to remember if she had ever seen him eat. His voice was tight when he spoke.

"So, you think you can tell me no whenever you feel like it?"

"I think I can tell you no when I don't want to do something."

"You are breaking the number one rule, Francine."

"We discussed this, Ernest, but you wanted to marry me."

His words were razor sharp. "I have asked you to do something that is not unreasonable—"

"Everything that has happened to me in the last two weeks has been an unfortunate series of events. Unreasonable doesn't touch what I'm feeling. I don't want to go out with Brenda. Maybe you should punish me, so I can see what you're really about."

She had to fight not to avert her gaze. His speech was void of all emotion. "You trying to provoke me?"

"No, Ernest."

"Everyone calls me Troy." There was salt in his words.

"I'm not everyone. I'm your wife, besides I don't like Troy as a man right now. I prefer Ernest, he tries to behave."

"You like Ernest because you think you can boss his ass around."

She didn't even try to dignify his statement, instead she spoke on what was truly upsetting her. "I don't want to go out with Brenda. She can't help me if someone tries to hurt us."

He stared at her for a time before dropping his gaze and throwing his left arm protectively around his plate. And there he was, the inmate that would forever be part of their marriage. The brown shirt he wore was short sleeved and Francine noted the tension in his bulging forearms. She wanted more softness from him, but he was attempting to disengage. Francine wanted the man that held her all night.

He shoveled a mountain of eggs into his mouth and when he began chewing, she went on. "I don't want to be out and about without you."

When it was clear he wasn't going to respond, she pushed her chair back, scraping the gray stone-like flooring and stood. Troy's head popped up and he looked as though he were about to order her to sit. Francine picked up her food and dumped it onto his plate. She then rounded the table, seating herself in his lap. Dropping his fork with a clink, he leaned back to give her room to settle herself.

He sighed. "You have to go to the event, Francine."

"I know."

"I won't let anyone hurt you."

"You let Levi come here, and he wants to bump me off," she whispered.

He grabbed her chin, forcing eye contact. "Levi doesn't want to bump you off. He would not be welcome if he did. We are serious about your silence–don't misconstrue, but my cousin understands that I want my wife. He's entertained by your distress; he likes to aggravate me."

"Cousin?" she couldn't hide her alarm.

"Our fathers are brothers."

His words added to her stress and now she wanted to disconnect. She stabbed a fork full of eggs and fed him. While he chewed, she fed herself and found that she was starving. When she held the toast up, he bit first, and she did the same. They kept on this way until the food was gone. She was about to get up, and he stayed her with his hand.

"You're a public figure, and I don't want to be bothered with people. How is this supposed to work?"

He grinned down at her and she felt some of his earlier aggravation dissipate. "The public is interested in you, Francine, not me. The press has never shown me this much interest."

"I have never even seen a news truck up close. The public is interested in me because of you."

His face lost all humor. "They can't ever hurt you, again."

Francine knew he spoke of the men with the van. She could do nothing but nod her agreement.

* * *

They didn't go out, instead Troy had three women come to the condo. Faith, a slender dark-skinned woman with wild hair, dark eyes and a sincere smile, permed Francine's hair. Simone, a short plump woman with dark brown eyes and light skin gave her a pedicure and manicure. Neicey, a brown skinned woman with freckles, tiny eyes and huge lips removed all the hair from her lower extremities. When they packed up, they left Francine with a glass of red wine and a promise to see her in two weeks.

It was 4:45 by the digital clock on the nightstand. The event would start at 8:00 p.m. and Troy wanted to be there by 7:00. Francine sat in a straight-backed, blue chair brought in from another room. She faced the windows pondering the dying sunlight and the evening to come. When asked, Troy offered no explanation of the event. His only words were he hoped she enjoyed being out with him.

As the sun faded, Francine began to dress. She started with a black strapless, lace bra and matching lace panties. After rubbing a lotion called Heavenly on her arms and legs, she walked about to let the oil settle on her skin before putting on her dress. She stood in the mirror observing her reflection as if it wasn't her. The woman before her looked well-kept and didn't resemble the waitress she had been for years.

The little black dress she donned was off the shoulders and form fitting. Her hair was parted in the middle with loose spiral curls falling around her face. On her feet were a pair of black strappy sandals that buckled about the ankles; her blood red toenails peeked out ever so slightly. In her hand, she held a small black purse and over her arm hung a black wrap. Troy had given her a gold armlet that wrapped about her bicep in a swirly design. Around her neck hung a gold locket that was fashioned with the same carvings.

It was 5:55 when she finally turned toward the door. She found Troy standing in the living room facing the windows. He turned toward her dressed in his tux, and she drew in a sharp breath. His left hand was in his pocket and in his right a drink. His large eyes were explosive as a slow seductive smile crawled across his face. The meticulous trimming of his mustache and goatee added to the beauty that was him; the small gray patch of hair on his chin added to the sex dripping from him.

"Woman, you are breathtaking." His gaze was intense.

"You look handsome as well," she countered, but in her mind, breathtaking better described him.

"The limo is out front. Are you ready?"

"Yes."

He put his drink on the coffee table and moved toward her. Troy kissed her shoulder before helping her with her wrap. He whisked her from the condo, down the elevator and through the lobby before she could blink, greeting the doorman who held the door for them. An older black man held the door to the limo and Troy helped her in. The evening with the Silent Activist had begun.

They rode Independence Boulevard until the traffic got thick. On the right side of the street and from the passenger window, Francine could see a large brick building. The sign out front read: African-American Cultural Center. The limo slowed, then idled as it waited in line to set them out at the front door. Troy sat across from her, legs spread wide, his attention on their progress. He didn't speak, and she accepted that he was on duty.

When the limo pulled to the curb in front of the building, there was a small delay before the door opened. Troy grinned at her. "You will be at my side all night, except when I have to address the crowd. At that time, you will be placed in Levi's care. He will watch out for your well-being for about forty-five minutes. I will have my eye on you always. You are safe."

Francine nodded, and then the door opened. Troy got out first, blocking her view, before reaching back to help her out of the vehicle. When she stood next to him on the sidewalk, time suspended for seconds as she adjusted to her surroundings. The night air was balmy, offering a gentle breeze. She felt her husband's protective hand at the small of her back. Out in front of them was a path to the entrance, which included about ten staggered stone steps. On either side of the walkway were groups of spectators. Once she acknowledged the hordes of people, she was blinded by the merciless flash of cameras.

As her apprehension transferred to her husband through touch, Troy leaned down and kissed her temple. "You are gorgeous, Francine."

"Flattery will not help you, Ernest."

Troy threw back his head and laughed–more flashes happened. While her nervousness lessened, it didn't go away. Francine took comfort in his nearness as she allowed him to usher her past the onlookers, up the stairs and into the building. It was like Christmas in May as little white lights dangled from the ceiling. The lobby was crowded with well-dressed black couples and several white couples. When the gathering became aware of Troy's presence, they gravitated toward him. He smiled a lot and introduced her to so many people, she couldn't keep the names straight.

As she stood, taking in the atmosphere and the people, Francine made one observation that couldn't be missed. The people at this gathering, while well-dressed, looked hard. This was inclusive of the men and the women. There wasn't a person that approached that didn't look criminal, and she wondered if this was due to her own prejudices. She certainly had prejudgments of her own relatives and friends who moved through the judicial system repeatedly. It was why she naively left New York, believing crime only happened in the ghetto where she came from.

People stood about the lobby, mingling. At the far end of the hall, on the left were two steel doors propped open. On the right of the entrance was a big sign that read: The Black Think Tank. Francine noticed that while Troy socialized, he kept them on a course that led to the open doors. She experienced genuine patience rolling off her husband as he answered the same questions repeatedly.

She peered inside the large open space to find an elegantly appointed dining room. Medium round tables dressed in white cloth sat in clusters of three. The chairs were arranged to make the small podium the center of attention. Standing on either side of the dining area was a waitstaff of about twenty men and women dressed in the customary black and white. They, too, looked rough as hell.

Levi appeared on her left with a salutation. "Good evening, Francine. You look breathtaking."

Francine looked up as he smiled broadly. It was the best she could do, she would not speak to Sean Levi Bryant. She didn't like him. He shocked her when he tipped at the waist and whispered, "Still not my friend?"

She stepped back from him and looked away. Troy was correct, the bastard enjoyed taunting her and she didn't like it. Levi took the hint and addressed her husband. "I will speak first, giving updates and progress. I will also answer questions if necessary."

"I will discuss the new nigger and release our guests to socialize." Troy answered.

Levi nodded and walked away, leaving her alone with Troy. He smiled down at her before holding his hand out to gesture. "This way, my love."

They were about to move into the dining room when a couple approached. Francine saw something dark cross Troy's face and then disappear. The man was the same height as her husband and dressed for the occasion. He looked harder than Troy with a nasty scar on his left cheek that had long since healed. Still, one couldn't help but see the pain he must have endured. The man was light of skin with eyes that were a dark brown; his eyebrows were two angry black slashes that added to his intimidating features. He had curly, black hair that was cut close and no facial hair, making the scar prevalent. His lips were thick and full; he licked them before he spoke. Francine thought him extraordinarily handsome.

"Good evening, Troy."

"Akeel." Troy responded and then paused before continuing. "This is my wife Francine. Love, I'd like you to meet Akeel Marshall and Karyn Battle."

Francine recognized Karyn, she was even more beautiful up close. She wore a spaghetti strapped, black dress that belled out just above her knees. On her feet were black, three-inch heels that made her Troy's height. Karyn had smooth, dark skin, and her hair was pulled up in a French roll with curly tendrils framing her face. In the other woman's eyes, Francine saw pain and love when she looked at Troy. Karyn's beauty made her feel inferior, and Francine's jealousy was smothering. Another reminder that she wanted her husband.

"Good evening," Karyn managed, and her voice trembled. She tried to smile as her eyes bounced around uncomfortably.

"Nice to meet you both," Francine said, when she found her words. Karyn didn't look hard.

Akeel checked her out from head to toe. "You really are as beautiful as I was told."

Francine smiled as she felt Troy's hand go possessively around her waist. His tone had bite. "Have a good evening, Akeel–Karyn."

Akeel smiled down at her and then at Troy before moving Karyn along with his hand on the small of her back. Francine turned to her husband. "You don't like Akeel?"

"Later," Troy responded.

As the crowd flowed into the dining area, Francine allowed Troy to escort her to a table. He pulled out a chair for her in the middle of the room before seating himself next to her. The lighting was soft, yet the place was well lit. Every other table had six chairs, but their table had only three and she was seated in the center. Down front, a large screen hung behind the podium. Around them, the buzz of conversation and laughter filled the air.

Troy sat with his hand on her knee and periodically, he would allow his fingers to slide up her thigh. When she tried to pull away, he leaned in and spoke for her ears only. "No, Francine."

She would have answered him, but the lights flickered, causing the conversational buzz to die. After about five minutes, Levi stepped up to the microphone. "Ladies and Gentlemen, welcome to the Black Think Tank."

The crowd clapped and when Levi raised his hands, the applause died. He stared about the room as if attempting to engage in eye contact with everyone seated in the audience. After complete silence fell, he went on. "I'm honored to be here tonight discussing our accomplishments and our ability to recognize black excellence. We have a few newcomers, and for those people, I will give a brief synopsis of who we are. In late 1993, Troy and I reached out to several men of color who had spent time in jail for crimes they didn't commit. In civil suits carried out against various states, these men were paid for the years they lost. The problem–monetary compensation cannot replenish lost time. The men in this room have decided to help younger black men get a better understanding of the value of time."

The lights dimmed and the screen behind Levi lit up with the words: The Black Think Tank.

He continued. "This group believes working with black youth will help them regain time lost. The men and women in this room are black excellence."

Francine was awed and applauded with the rest of the guests at Levi's last statement. He then offered a roll call. "Our original members, in no order of importance–Akeel Marshall, Tyrell Knox, Hassan Peterson, Troy Bryant and myself. As you can see, we have grown and it's all good."

The people laughed, and when they quieted, Levi continued. "You will be pleased to know that our scholarships have seen seven black men graduate college and four enter law school. As of April, our dollars have sent three black women to medical school. At Bryant and Associates, we have hired a new paralegal and two new lawyers–all black. We have also partnered with Rothstein and Rothstein to offer free legal advice in black and poor communities. Please know that you can't defend your rights and the rights of your loved ones if you don't know your damn rights."

As Francine listened to Levi speak, she saw no trace of the thug she met in Troy's kitchen. Yet, his ability to do violence was still visible. He described the new initiatives and goals for the group. There were charts on where the group's money was being invested. He explained where they were on a new finance scholarship, and then concluded his speech.

"While we are proud of our aforementioned accomplishments, it is the Second Chance Program that brings our hard work together. We, in this room, realize that people make mistakes in their lives. Unfortunately, we live in a society that is unforgiving of the poor and people of color. And often times as black folks, we fall under both categories. We have set up employment opportunities to help people with records rebuild their lives."

Francine thought Levi's last statement thought provoking, she watched as people stood and clapped. Troy leaned in and whispered, "I'll be back, my love."

She nodded as Levi closed out by saying, "Thank you all for your hard work. I have learned much from being in the struggle with you all. Please welcome Troy."

The lighting got brighter as Francine watched Troy approach the podium. The crowd offered a welcoming applause as the men shook hands. Troy leaned in as Levi said something in his ear. When her husband backed away and nodded, she saw tension in his shoulders. Troy moved around Levi and stepped up to the microphone. He waited for the audience to settle, and then spoke; his voice–deep and rich.

"Good evening, everyone."

"Good evening." The crowd responded in unison.

The lights dimmed, and the screen came alive with three words: The New Nigger

"Thank you, Levi, for keeping us informed." Troy paused to look around. "The drug crisis in the black community has produced a new type of nigger and his name is Felon. During my time in lockdown, I observed a rise in young black men doing hard time for nonviolent drug offenses. When released, these men experience legalized discrimination. They are unable to find work, housing or receive public assistance and their right to vote is stripped."

As if he had struck a nerve, individual discussions sprang up around the room, and Troy waited for the crowd to hush before continuing. "This problem is far more reaching than–*we don't hire niggers*, which is an illegal practice in mainstream that still persists. Lack of job opportunity is what forces black men into the arms of law enforcement. And if they survive the encounter, they will come out on the other side a new type of nigger. They will be felons, and it will be legal to employ the practices that were illegal when mainstream shut them out in the first place."

Francine thought back to the summer of 1992, when every guy she knew had been arrested. Several of them were still in prison, all for nonviolent drug charges. She remembered when her cousin Terrence was sentenced to ten years; she thought he had killed someone. It turned out to be a drug charge and his third offense. Troy's movement at the front of the room transported her back to the here and now.

Her husband gazed about, before he began again. "As a black woman, your counterpart is fine to date and fuck when you live with your family.

Even without a brush with the law, mainstream has shut your black man illegally out of the job market. But once he has had a brush with the law, he can't secure housing for you, and he can't find work to support you. And if you tough it out with him, his name can't be on the lease where you and his children live. He is essentially deadweight in his own home. Your man is now a felon, and in many cases, will *never* have another encounter with law enforcement."

Conversation around the room started again in earnest and took longer to quiet. Troy didn't raise his hands to get the attention of the onlookers, instead he waited. When the sidebar discussions ebbed, he went on. "I shouldn't have to make this next statement, but I feel it's necessary. America has a drug problem that plagues all communities and all social classes. Yet, the war on drugs is policed only in the black community. We, in this room, are the new black elite and we must be vigilant in our quest to preserve the black family."

The people stood and clapped, but this time Troy did raise his hands—everyone quieted. "I'm going to close by stating, I unashamedly love my people."

Francine watched as the screen went black and the waitstaff moved about serving food and drink. She found herself seated between Troy and Levi, while the clink of silverware and dishes became the background of the evening. Turning to her husband, she spoke softly.

"I need the ladies' room."

Troy helped her with her chair and held out his arm. Francine placed her hand in the crook of his elbow, allowing him to lead her from the dining room. Once in the lobby, people approached to speak with him, and she saw for the first time this evening, signs of impatience.

"Which way to the restroom?" she whispered. "I'll be right back."

He stared down at her before conceding. "Straight down to the other end of the lobby, make a right. It's the second door on the left. I'll be right here."

Francine nodded and rushed away. She found the facilities with no issue and was washing her hands when she heard the outer door swing open. She stood facing a large mirror, and behind her eight, white swinging doors concealed the commodes. She dried her hands with a thick disposable hand towel, realizing no one had entered the stall area. It felt spooky and tossing her towel in the trash, she headed to find Troy.

Francine stepped into the lounge area of the bathroom and came face to face with her sister, and behind her stood Jalal Dorsey. Shocked, it took her a moment to understand what was happening; Jen and Jalal seemed so out of place together.

They were blocking her way out of the sitting area. Francine sighed. Her heels clicked on the wooden floor as she moved to seat herself on the gold sofa positioned against the far wall. A new kind of weariness settled over her.

"I came to take you home. We're sisters, let me help you, Frankie… please."

Jennifer's words weren't aggressive or rude. In fact, she sounded hurt and afraid. Francine saw that her sister was trying not to cry. Still, when she addressed her lifelong best friend, she was firm. "Jennifer, I'm at an event with my husband. Are you serious, right now? Why in the hell would you bring him?"

Jalal spoke, sounding jealous and indignant. "Come with me, Frankie. I'll keep you safe. If you can keep him off your mind, I'll keep him off your ass."

She knew Troy would be along shortly, and when he saw Jalal, there would be hell to pay. He could tolerate Jennifer, but not Jalal.

"Jalal, me and you had one date. Please go away."

"We were into each other. How you meet this mafucka and marry him in a day?" he growled.

Francine remembered Jalal as polite. Never did he engage in profanity in her presence. The truth was, they had all been through a lot and it was taking a toll. But she still had to get him told. "I'm married, Jalal, and I want Troy. I won't discuss my husband with you."

"Frankie, please." Jennifer pleaded.

Francine cut her off. "How did you get here?"

"Leave with us through the back. We can help you," her sister continued.

"I'm sorry," Jalal said.

She would keep her sister with her and send Jalal on his way. Though she hated to admit it, she needed Troy. Better to go find him than be found like this. When she stood and headed for the door, Jalal grabbed her by the arm. Francine had a new awareness after what happened that fateful day. She couldn't stand Jalal's touch.

"Take your hands off me. Please don't touch me again." Her voice was strained.

He released her, but he blocked her from the door. "You're afraid of him, baby. I can see it. Please, Frankie, come with me."

The door swung open, and several women walked in. Seeing Jalal made their eyes widen, and Francine took that moment to rush for the door. Once in the hall, she headed toward the front lobby, but he grabbed her arm again. This time, his grip was bruising.

"Jalal, please." Francine whispered as she tried to free herself.

"Come with us through the back." Jennifer said, trying to defuse the fact that they were one step from abducting her.

Francine was trying to untangle from Jalal when Troy and Levi appeared at the end of the hall. If nothing else, she considered herself a quick study. The look on her husband's face told her that shit was about to get real basic.

* * *

Troy had reluctantly given his wife directions to the restroom and watched until she was out of sight. He never ate at these affairs because people approached and expected answers while he was chewing. Two new members of the group and their spouses came forward to ask about job opportunities for a young man who was fresh out of prison. Behind them a small line of the usual women formed, and even with a new wife, they were flirting.

He smiled graciously while looking down the hall for Francine.

"Ladies, may I borrow Troy." Levi moved in to save him, and Troy was thankful.

"Only for a few minutes," Keisha Sloan replied.

Troy found her attractive; she was a light skinned woman with green eyes and long, black locks that fell around her shoulders. Her mouth was shaped like a heart and she always had a smile for him. But he steered clear, her husband was an older man and a big contributor. *He ain't want no problems.*

The women walked off in the direction of the restroom and still there was no Francine. He would give her a moment more before seeking her out.

"Are you staying in Charlotte until after the next event?" Levi asked.

"It's two and a half weeks until the next event. I'll have to think about it, Francine may want to see her sister."

Levi turned and looked about. "Where is Francine?"

Troy began moving toward the restrooms. "Walk with me."

The men were trying to coordinate their schedules when they rounded the turn to find Francine struggling with a man by the bathroom door. Troy assessed the scene before him, recognizing Jalal Dorsey and his sister in-law. His wife could be heard pleading with Dorsey to release her. Suddenly, the corridor became chaotic, and when Keisha and the few women she was with spilled from the restroom, Levi sprang into action.

"Ladies, this way."

Most, if not all the men present had done hard time. The women in this circle ran with rough dudes and nothing fazed them; they continued on without a backward glance. As Troy unbuttoned the jacket of his tuxedo, it occurred to him that he hadn't had a fight in a long time. Shit, truth be told, he ain't had no pussy in a while either. He was filled with pent up aggression and a good brawl was just what he needed.

"Dorsey, take your hands off my wife." His voice was calm.

"Fuck you, Troy... activist, my ass. Francine is afraid of you–her family is afraid of you. But I'm not. Something ain't right here. Is she with you against her will? It was you in that black Mercedes, wasn't it? What the fuck did you do?"

Francine was still struggling, and her sister had gotten into the fray. Jennifer was helping Dorsey. She was trying to pull his wife toward the back door. Troy was done talking.

He started toward Jalal, causing him to have to release his grip on Francine. The younger man had no choice but to address the immediate threat. Levi backed the women against the wall as Dorsey threw the first punch. Troy tried to step out of his reach, but the blow connected, and it was solid. He shook his head to clear it, but Dorsey was already delivering another swift combo. The corridor was close confines like a jail cell, and for Troy, it had a ring of familiarity.

When Dorsey threw the next set of punches, Troy blocked them before hitting him in the solar plexus. He was instantly winded, but Troy didn't relent. Stepping into his opponent's personal space, Troy rained blow after blow, leaving the other man stunned. This was no damn brawl, and it alleviated nothing. He grabbed Dorsey by the collar and slammed him hard against the wall.

Jalal was out on his feet when Troy wrapped his right hand about the younger man's throat. He squeezed with intent while looking Dorsey straight in the eyes. "That's it, son, I'm 'bout to lullaby yo' ass."

All sound in the hall lifted, and there was nothing but the feel of Dorsey going limp against him. Troy continued to apply pressure until he felt dude's full body weight. Slowly, he allowed Jalal to sink to the floor in a crumpled heap. As Troy stepped back, the noise around him restarted. Francine was crying, begging for Jalal's life and her silly ass sister was doing the same.

His wife ran forward as if to help the other man; sobs racked her little body. "Did you kill him?"

Troy caught her by the arm, his anger still unchecked. He kicked Dorsey for not being man enough—his tone conveyed his disgust. "His ass ain't dead, but he'll be out for a lil' bit."

Akeel was standing next to Levi as Troy started issuing orders. "Edit the tape down to where he had hold of my wife and struck me first. Send the edited version to his ass; the unedited version goes to Levi. When he wakes, send him on his way in a cab."

"Your car will meet you out back," Akeel said. "We got it from here."

Troy nodded before he turned and dragged his wife out the back door. Francine was stumbling and still crying for the next man. Behind them, Levi had thrown Jennifer over his shoulder. Jesse was indeed out back with the door already open. His wife looked like she was going to refuse to get into the car.

"Get in, Francine."

"Troy..." she hiccupped.

"Get. In. Now."

She turned and did as he ordered; he climbed in after her. Levi tossed Jennifer in before getting in himself. When the door closed, the car immediately started rolling toward the street. The alley was dark, but ahead of them Independence Boulevard was well lit. Jesse made a right, and Levi barked directions.

"My house, Jesse."

Troy listened as the partition rolled up, shutting the driver out of the conversation. His sister in-law was still hysterical. She started yelling at him and Francine.

"He killed Jalal… What are you into, Frankie? Oh God, poor Jalal."

Troy remained quiet, he was pissed beyond words. Across from him, his wife could be heard sniffling.

"Jennifer, close your damn mouth." Levi shut her down. "This was an event meant to help the community. You and Dorsey trespassed on private property and accosted the main speaker's wife. Do you understand what I am saying? Because of you, Jalal Dorsey assaulted a public figure. Who on the staff helped you two get in?"

Levi's last question got Troy's attention, but Jennifer didn't answer. She did, however, shut the hell up. They sat opposite the women, but his wife wouldn't even look at him. She kept her attention trained on the window. It would be an hour to Levi's house in Gastonia. Troy hoped he didn't choke to death on his jealousy before they reached their destination.

He had worked hard to control his temper and his urges. After the incident with Butch, he tried to be softer with Francine. She had accepted comfort from him and had in turn given him comfort. He had backed away from intimidation, but he couldn't lie to himself. Her fear of him sexually excited him. He had not forced sex, allowing her time to get to know him. But Jalal Dorsey had set him back. Troy could taste her concern for the other man, and it turned his stomach sour.

The four of them rode in silence until they pulled through the gates of Levi's home. The house was well lit as Jesse pulled up the driveway. The land was wooded, and in the center sat an imposing brown bricked structure. The garage opened automatically, and Levi opened the door on his side. Francine and Jennifer didn't move.

"Out!" Levi bellowed, and both women scrambled from the limo.

Once alone, Troy got out and began undressing in the driveway. He removed his tie, vest and untucked his shirttails. His suspenders hung about his hips and after he unbuttoned his shirt, he lit a cigarette. He paced the full drive, standing in the darkness to sulk. The door inside the garage opened, and he heard Levi talking to Jesse.

It was cooler than it had been earlier in the evening, and Troy welcomed the breeze. The leaves rustled on the wind and the insects offered a rhythm that helped him relax. He inhaled deeply and when he exhaled, Levi spoke into his space.

"I'll start handling Jennifer."

"You can't beat her with a bag of oranges, man." Troy replied.

Levi chuckled. "They told you what I said that day at the police station."

Troy dropped his cigarette and stepped on it. He didn't answer. Jennifer was the least of his problems. Francine shutting down on him was his biggest fear, but he wouldn't discuss it with his cousin.

"You ain't been up in her, have you?" Levi asked.

"She is my wife, man, back off."

"So, Imma take that as a '*no*'," Levi continued. "Love sick ass."

"Fuck."

Levi laughed out loud. "Francine won't go farther than the kitchen without you. Jennifer is on the floor by her feet. I need you."

Troy took a deep breath and turned heading for the garage. When he stepped into the kitchen, it was as Levi explained. His wife was leaned against the marble island and Jennifer sat at her feet with her knees pulled into her chest. Francine's eyes caught his, and her terror was tangible. He was sorry he hadn't killed Dorsey.

"This shit obviously needs to be cleaned up and since I'm Troy's lawyer that honor goes to me. Jennifer, you're going to help me straighten this mess out since you caused it." Levi said.

Francine was still staring in Troy's eyes; she was shattered, but not crying. She looked as though she wanted to bolt. Jennifer reached for her hand, and his wife reciprocated.

"Troy, you and Francine will go home. Jennifer will stay with me until this is cleaned up. She and I will meet with Dorsey." Levi explained.

Francine looked as though she would pass out at the mention of Jennifer staying with Levi. Her sister whimpered, "Frankie, please don't leave me with him. He wants to kill me."

"Oh, sweetheart, I don't want to kill you, but I do want to spank your bare ass." Levi replied.

Jennifer breathed in sharply but didn't speak. Francine's gaze was pleading on behalf of her sister. Troy wanted to wring Jennifer's neck; the woman was safer with Levi. He was tired, and it would be a long drive back to Charlotte.

"Let's go, Francine."

His wife made no sound, but tears spilled over her brimming eyes. Jennifer stood and hugged her. Francine's shoulders shook with effort to control herself. When his wife backed away, Troy started for the door and she took the silent message. Francine followed. Jennifer could be heard crying, but she stayed in the house while Levi walked them out.

When Jesse saw Francine, he dropped his cigarette and opened the car door. Levi spoke, causing Troy to stop and look at him. His words were for Francine.

"I promise to bring your sister to you in two days. She will be mad, but I won't hurt her."

Francine looked at Levi but offered no response. She got in the car, leaving his cousin staring after her. "Ya wife is mean as hell."

If he weren't so tired, he would have laughed. Instead, he reached out and shook Levi's hand.

"Two days," his cousin reiterated.

Troy sighed as he got in the back seat and allowed Levi to shut the door. The ride home would be about an hour and twenty minutes. He fixated on the floor lights and the back of Francine's head. She planned to ignore him; he was both angry and hurt. As the car pulled away from the house, his wife started sniffling again.

"Francine," his voice was thick.

"I know Jennifer is difficult, but she loves me. I have never shut her out before and she is afraid for me. She knows I wouldn't have married a man I just met without reason. My sister knows me, Troy. Please don't hurt her."

In his mind, he had already weighed Jennifer's actions. This debacle confirmed that his wife hadn't spoken about him to anyone. His sister in-law was annoying as hell, but she was safe. Dorsey was his issue.

"You said you didn't want him, but you cryin' for his ass."

Francine turned to him. The glow of the interior lights outlined her pain, but the detail was lost in the murkiness of the backseat.

"I'm ashamed, Troy."

His body tensed at her words–*ashamed of what?* It must be as he suspected, she still wanted Dorsey and was embarrassed to say. He would keep her–it didn't matter; he wanted Francine. Troy turned his attention to the window. He didn't want to hear her admit to wanting a next man. When he didn't prompt her to continue, he figured they were done conversing.

Her voice broke on a sob. "I wanted you to beat his ass. I couldn't stand his touch. It wasn't until you started choking him…"

Francine was huddled against the door, her words dying mid-sentence. She had his full attention. "Finish."

"My sister thought she was helping me, but she almost assisted Jalal in abducting me. I thought he would break my wrist. He wouldn't let go. Jennifer doesn't know what I been through–I was dying inside. But when you choked him…" She paused, her breaths coming in short puffs to mask her crying. "I thought you killed him. My sister doesn't understand; I can't go back to who I was before all this happened."

Francine moved him; she had explained what he had been unable to articulate. He would never be who he was before prison. His own sister was hurt because he shut her out. But there could be no other way between Monica and himself.

"Come here, Francine."

The lighting on the floorboards provided ambiance, but not the fine points of her beauty. He felt her hesitancy before she moved over, pressing herself against his side. Troy didn't realize it, but he had been holding his breath. He felt her shudder as she tried to settle in next to him. She squeaked when he reached out and pulled her to straddle him.

Troy was instantly assailed by her softness and femininity. Francine snuggled close to him, hiding her face in the crook of his neck. The perfume she wore wrapped about him, shoving him further under her control.

His words were rusty. "Let me see your wrist."

She leaned back and held up her right hand. He felt her sharp intake of air when he gently caressed and kissed her wrist.

"Oh," she gasped.

"Better?"

She leaned her forehead against his, their breaths becoming one. "Yes, Troy."

"Ahhh, so I'm Troy not Ernest." He couldn't help teasing her.

It was his turn to be surprised when she kissed him all over his face. He had never experienced such intimacy. His need to tease her came from his need to protect her. He was trying to lighten the mood and his own temper, which was still raging with her confession; *I thought he would break my wrist.*

"My humiliation comes from knowing what Troy is capable of and encouraging it. I don't want you to be arrested. But, tonight, I needed Troy not Ernest."

"Let me take the burden from you, my love. I became a bad man long before you."

He thought she would make some witty quip to counter his remark. Instead, she leaned in and kissed him, shoving her tongue into his mouth. He groaned as she broke the kiss but not the contact. It was like she couldn't get enough of him and with her lips still against his–she spoke.

"I figured some things out."

"What did you figure out?" he asked.

"I don't like strange men. I worry that the situation will become violent before I can help myself. You, on the other hand, don't like other men– period. I think it's from your time in prison. I'm still trying to figure that part out. I need to be careful not to set you on some poor unsuspecting guy who means me no harm."

Francine nuzzled his neck as he inquired, "So you view what happened this evening as your fault?"

"I have to try to find a way to deal with my sister, and I don't know if I can. Jalal…"

Troy couldn't stand hearing his name on her beautiful lips. He could see the thought was unreasonable, but he couldn't step away from the feeling. His wife was smart, but she only understood some of what made him tick. She had been correct in realizing that other men made him aggressive and her presence in his life greatly increased this problem. But it was the circumstance under which he found her that heightened his need to keep her from harm. It also awakened a sexual need he had been trying to curb. He wanted her complete submission to him in all things.

Achieving this type of power in their relationship had been baffling to him at first. He could bully her, as he had in the beginning, but he wanted something real. Now, it was as plain as the nose on his face. He needed to be patient and control his temper. Troy almost laughed out loud as he came to the understand that he would have to submit to her–to get her to submit to him.

"Don't say his name," he snapped.

She giggled, and the sound was like music to his ears. He didn't know what she had been about to say. She whispered, "I only want you, Ernest."

"I thought it was Troy you liked tonight."

"Is Troy jealous of Ernest?"

"Neither one of them is getting any pussy–so, no, they ain't jealous of one another," he attempted to shock her.

Francine kissed his chin and then along his jawline; she panted in his ear. "Growing up in a house with my mother and grandmother, they always warned me and Jennifer against being loose women. Would you consider me a floozy if I gave Troy and Ernest some pussy?"

Troy breathed in sharply; he could barely speak when he choked out. "No."

He could hear her smile. "I want you to show me how to make love to you–here, in the car."

"I want–"

She cut him off. "I'm choosing here and now to control how rough you'll be with me. At times, I feel like I am drowning in your presence. I need to feel connected to you physically but not overpowered by you."

He was going to say he wanted whatever she wanted. But she stopped him, and her words made clear that she understood he wanted to exert his will over her.

"Talk me through loving you… please, Troy."

"Yes." He did something he had never done with a woman–he submitted.

Francine's breath caught as she offered her tongue to him. She pushed his unbuttoned shirt open, laying her palms flat against his bare chest. When her hands traveled down his stomach to the button of his trousers, he lifted his hips, shoving his slacks and underwear down until his dick sprang free. Troy relaxed, placing his arms across the top of the back seat. His voice was deep.

"Take off your bra and panties."

She pushed her dress down around her waist and unclasped her bra. He watched as she backed away, removing her heels and then her underwear. Troy felt sad that the lighting limited his visibility —but his other senses were sharper. The feel and the smell of his wife was heady.

"I want to smell your panties."

He thought she wouldn't do as he asked, but she placed her lace panties under his nose and he growled, "Closer," before taking a healthy whiff of her sweetness.

"Can I touch you?" he asked.

"No."

She kissed his chin and then his neck; his body quivered like a school-boy when she began placing open mouthed kisses down his chest. Francine bit his nipple and his head fell back in pleasure. He tried to remain focused, but he was losing the battle.

"You ever take a man in your mouth?" His voice was strangled.

"No."

"Will you take me in your mouth, Francine?"

"Yes."

"Lick me twice and then suck me twice–no more than that, baby. You understand?"

"Yes, Troy."

She moved off him and knelt beside him on the seat. He felt her hand at the base of his dick first, and he hissed at the contact. There was no skill in her touch and that observation alone almost made him lose his shit. He was about to tell her that she didn't have to take all of him in her mouth, when she licked him from base to tip.

"Ohhh fuck," he groaned.

He thought she would lick him again, instead her hot mouth closed around him. She only took a little more than the tip, but she was going to be the death of him, all the same. When she released him, she immediately licked him again before pulling him deeper into her mouth.

"No more, baby—too good." He felt like he had been running. His heart was slamming in his chest, and his dick pulsed to the same rhythm.

She leaned up and kissed him. "You taste good, Troy."

He could taste himself on her lips and the feeling was intoxicating. "Can I touch you, now?"

"No."

"Are you wet?"

"Yes." She gasped into his mouth.

"Show me, baby—please, touch yourself and let me taste it."

Francine backed away, and again he was sad about the lighting. When she came back to him, she placed two wet fingers against his lips and he sucked.

"Troy…" she moaned.

"Climb back on top."

He marveled at her willingness to follow his direction. Once she sat astride him, he pleaded, "Take me inside you."

Francine reached down and placed him at her opening. Troy could think of nothing that would have prepared him for the moment she shared her body with him. She had taken him halfway before she gasped and stopped. His wife was tight and hot, it was he that was drowning.

She leaned her forehead against his and breathed, "Troy… you're too much."

"Let me touch you, baby—let me help us get there."

"Yes."

She almost brought him to his knees with that one word. Slowly, he reached out and cupped her face. He kissed her because he loved the mingling of their breath, and he was trying to pace himself. He allowed his hands to trail gently down her back until he was palming her ass. Sweat broke out on his brow as he began to teach her.

"Take a deep breath." When she did as he asked, he offered praise. "That's it, baby, you feel so damn good. Again, breathe."

He plunged deeper into her tightness, and she moaned. They repeated the process until she was seated flush against him, and he could go no farther. The need to throw her onto her back and rock into her until he was spent was so real, he felt faint.

"Troy, I'm full," she breathed.

He didn't move to give her time to adjust to the intrusion. She must have realized, he was waiting for her because she whispered, "I'm ready."

But Troy wasn't ready. Several issues sprang up in a matter of seconds that he could never have foreseen. He never engaged in sex without a condom; bareback with his wife was exquisite torture. It was as if she had never been with a man before this moment–Francine was unbearably tight. He actually turned and stared out the window, lending his attention to the traffic. He had to get ahold of himself or this would be over before it started.

"Troy?"

The anxiety in her voice caused him to turn back to his wife. "Do you still want me?"

"Oh, baby… yes. I'm trying to calm down, so we can enjoy each other."

She adjusted in his lap to look him in the eyes and her already tight sheath constricted around him like a vice. The action caused his hands to shake as he clutched her ass. She squeezed from him indecipherable words and thoughts. "Don't… shit… ohhh, sweetheart. Imma cum–don't move."

Francine snuggled against his chest and stilled. All that could be heard was his own labored breathing as he tried to calm himself. After a time, he asked, "You ready?"

"Yes."

Troy's body was humming when he lifted his wife and dropped her back onto his hard shaft. He groaned, and she moaned–loudly.

"More?"

"Yes please, Troy."

It was all the encouragement he needed. He raised and dropped her repeatedly onto him while thrusting upward to meet the ecstasy her sweet body promised. They found a rhythm, and Francine commenced to throwing her ass while grinding her clit against him. Up inside her began to shudder and with each contraction of her inner walls, she wrung from him strangled cries of satisfaction. His wife desired him, and that knowledge, coupled with the feel of her wrapped about him–pushed him over the edge.

Troy threw his head back and howled his release. "Ahhh, Francine–mine."

He was still spasming when she fell into a violent orgasm. Troy leaned forward and kissed her breasts before latching onto a nipple. As they rode the frenzy to total completion, he continued to switch nipples until she cried out, "Troy… Troy," and fell against him spent.

As he held his wife, Troy found that he was emotionally taxed. But sexually, he could take her again and again. He felt the wetness of her tears on his skin, understanding the weight of their connection. They were still physically joined, and he wanted to stay inside her heat, but the limo had exited the highway; the condo was about twelve minutes away. He kissed her face and cheek before untangling her from him. Troy produced a handkerchief, so she could clean up.

"We're almost home, baby."

She fumbled with her clothing and pushed her feet back into her shoes. He handed her his jacket as the condo came into view. Troy was about to ask her to shower with him when they got upstairs, but the blue lights in front of his building caught his attention.

"Troy, you want me to park or keep going?" Jesse inquired over the loud speaker.

"They've spotted us, Jesse, go ahead and park. Call Levi and watch out for my wife if this doesn't go well."

"Troy, what's happening?" Francine's concern was evident.

"I'm sorry, sweetheart, but police harassment is part of my life. It's now your issue by proxy. Stay quiet, Francine–they will try to use you to provoke me. It'll be all right, baby."

Jesse parked the car in front of the building. Three cops with their guns drawn approached the vehicle. Troy rolled the window down and spoke politely.

"Good evening, gentlemen."

6

REINSTATING PLAN A
MAY 1995

It was the same bullshit with a different twist. Three bruising white cops stood on the sidewalk staring at him through the window of his limo. The situation was lit by several floodlights, placed in the gardens around the front of his building. Although it was after midnight, other tenants were returning home from an evening out to witness his fall from grace. He could see the doorman, not Charlie, watching through the glass of the lobby. Behind him, his wife sat mired in fear.

"Troy Bryant?" Cop number one asked as he holstered his weapon.

"That would be me."

"Please step out of the vehicle, sir, and keep your hands where they can be seen."

Troy placed both hands out the window and the cop pulled the door open. When he stepped from the car onto the pavement, he was immediately cuffed. Cop number one then pulled his flashlight and shined it into the back of the vehicle.

"My wife is in the car." Troy's anger was rising. "Why have I been cuffed?"

The officer didn't answer him. "Ma'am, please step out of the car."

Troy watched as the cop moved back, allowing his wife room to get out of the back seat. Francine had pulled her hair up in a ponytail and little curls escaped around her face. Her eyes grew huge when she saw that he was cuffed. She pulled his tuxedo jacket tightly around her while trying to comprehend what was happening. Her lips were still swollen from his kisses–his wife was beautiful and sexual. When she tried to move closer to him, the cop's voice became sharp.

"Step back, ma'am." He reached out as if to touch her.

"Officer, please–don't touch my damn wife." Troy's words were tight. He couldn't stomach her being handled not after what they shared.

Francine must have sensed his anger and to defuse the situation, she stepped back from him. All three of the cops moved in as cop number one explained.

"We received a complaint that you assaulted a Mr. Jalal Dorsey."

At that moment, in his periphery, a fourth cop appeared on the scene with none other than Jalal himself. Troy was seething. Dorsey hadn't been restrained, and he was sure it was for two reasons. The police didn't appreciate the presence of the Silent Activist in Charlotte, and Dorsey was pretending to be the victim.

"He choked me, and now my friend Jennifer is missing. We came to help, Francine; Bryant is abusing her." Jalal yelled as he and the fourth cop approached.

The press started showing up, and Troy figured the incident must be on the police scanner. He knew the game. They would all be going downtown, and he wouldn't be uncuffed until after the reporters were long gone. When Dorsey saw Francine, he tried to talk to her.

"Frankie, where's your sister? Are you all right?"

Francine frowned as the cop with Dorsey spoke. "Ma'am, I'm Officer Roberts. We got a report that you and your sister are being abused by Troy Bryant. Mr. Dorsey states he was assaulted while trying to help you."

"I'm married, Officer, and Mr. Dorsey won't take no for an answer. I'm not being abused by my husband–I'm being stalked by Mr. Dorsey."

"What the hell, Frankie!" Jalal shouted.

"Mr. Bryant, did you choke Jalal Dorsey?" Officer Roberts asked.

The camera flash started and hadn't stopped. Troy stared from cop to cop, his nostrils flared, the only sign his temper was churning. The press was allowed within earshot to slant the issue. Still, he had choked Dorsey unconscious, and this could be bad for him.

"I want my lawyer," Troy responded.

"You're not under arrest," Roberts answered.

"Then why am I restrained?"

Cop number one yelled in his face. "Hey, we're just trying to sort this shit out!"

"We can all go down to the station if you'd prefer," Roberts threatened.

"He wants a lawyer because he choked me!" Jalal countered.

"Mrs. Bryant, will you come to the station to help sort this out? Officer Williams can take you."

"My wife is not under arrest. She will ride in our car."

"Am I under arrest officer?" Francine asked.

"No, ma'am." Cop number one answered.

"Then, I'll meet you down at the station." Francine moved toward the car. "Jesse will follow."

Troy watched as Jesse helped his wife back into the limo. Dorsey was then escorted to a police car, while he was shoved, non-too gently, into a separate vehicle. The trip downtown smelled of urine and unwashed bodies, a reminder of his old life. He knew he would be caged until Levi showed up, but if Francine was safe, he could manage. Out the rearview window, he could see that Jesse followed the squad car and the press followed Jesse.

The fallout from this would be big, but he would deal with the organization. After issuing a few well-placed threats, he would reinstate plan A. Everything in his life had been derailed since he encountered Francine, but all the chaos had been sweet. He leaned back in the squad car and thought about being deep inside her. His wife pleased him, and he wouldn't allow Dorsey, Jennifer or the organization to separate her from him.

The police station was a large, two-story building. Squad cars were parked to the left of the entrance in several rows. When the vehicle transporting Troy stopped in front of the station, he noted the press was already in place. It appeared they intended to make certain he was discredited in the court of public opinion. He chuckled, causing the lone cop to look in the rearview mirror.

Looking out the window, he saw Jesse escorting Francine up the stairs and through the doors. Next, Dorsey was walked in by the two cops who were at the scene. The cop, who had driven him, yanked him out the back seat and just missed bumping his head against the door frame. Other cops were thrown into the mix, halfheartedly trying to keep the media at bay. Still, they hurled insults in the form of questions while he ignored them.

"Troy, is it true you assaulted your wife's lover?"

"Troy, is your wife cheating on you with Jalal Dorsey?"

"Troy, is it true that your wife has left you for Jalal Dorsey?"

He kept his sights on the entrance, disregarding the reporters and the annoying flashes of light. Troy was at the steps leading to the door of the police station when someone to his right asked, "Troy, is your wife being used to deflect attention from the real issues?"

Normally, he never made eye contact with the press. Unable to help himself, he turned to find an older white man with wild hair, sharp eyes and a grin. The assessment was brief, given the circumstance, but when he turned back toward the steps the man continued.

"You don't give interviews, but does your wife?"

Troy didn't comment as he was ushered up the stairs and into the building. The lobby had white linoleum flooring that led to a large black desk. Seated behind the desk was an older black cop with salt and pepper hair. He was brown skinned with beady eyes, a large nose and an even bigger mustache. There were no chairs, just two steel, brown doors on opposite ends of the lobby. His wife was taken through the door on the right and he was taken through the door on the left.

Once behind the door, he ended up in a long corridor with offices on either side. The hall spilled out into a room that housed two huge cages. On the opposite side of the room were three black, metal desks. Several cops were gathered in a huddle speaking to one another. Inside the cages were five men ranging from age twenty-five to fifty—three Black men, one Hispanic man and one White man who looked to be asleep.

All conversation stopped among the cops and detainees upon his arrival. He was placed in a mesh like cage by himself and uncuffed after the door was slammed shut. The furnishings were scant, three wooden benches and a toilet.

Just as suddenly as the conversation stopped, it restarted with everyone ignoring him. The cops moved down the hall, leaving two on babysitting detail. Of the remaining cops, one had blond hair that was cut to a buzz. He stood over six feet with eyes that never left Troy. Next to him was a female cop with brown hair, brown eyes and a crooked smile. Troy looked away, he didn't need to appear challenging. He picked a bench facing away from the others and waited. He noted it was cold, but he could do nothing about it.

Three hours passed, and the sound of laughter from the other holding cell happened in sudden outburst. A radio on one of the desks played country music. Periodically, a toilet flushed; his stay was uneventful. When his craving for a cigarette got beyond him, someone called his name.

"Bryant." Troy looked up but didn't move. The cop, Roberts was staring at him. "I'll take him, Randy—no bracelets."

Roberts was taller than Troy with a long face. He had brown hair, a sausage nose and a wide mouth. His eyes were fixed on Troy, and he looked irritated. It meant Levi was here and he was handling the matter but not to their liking. The cop held the cage open.

"Please follow me."

Troy didn't speak, but he followed. He was taken to a conference room occupied by Levi and Jennifer. Williams, the cop who cuffed him, was also in attendance, but Francine was nowhere in sight. Though he wanted to know his wife's whereabouts, he remained quiet.

"They're asking if you want to press charges against Dorsey and Jennifer," Levi explained.

Troy glared at his sister in-law who greatly resembled Francine. She had on Levi's jacket. "No, but I want Dorsey to stay away from my wife."

His cousin looked pissed, but Jennifer looked contrite and afraid.

"Where's my wife?"

"She is in the conference room next door. Francine is refusing to see Jennifer," Levi replied.

"Obviously this is a family matter that has gotten blown out of proportion," Williams said. "If you press charges, Dorsey will face trespassing and assault charges. Ms. Adams could face trespassing charges."

Troy looked at the cop who had yelled in his face. He was a brown-haired man with unfriendly eyes. Williams was slightly shorter and fat; he stood against the wall on the opposite side of the wooden table staring at Troy. Turning to his cousin, Troy asked, "Am I free to go?"

"Yes," Levi answered. "But Francine is a different matter. Jalal is also facing assault charges for his encounter with your wife. She has opted not to press charges, but the state will probably pick up the charges against him. He can be seen on the video entering the woman's restroom and trying to restrain her against her will–manhandling her, really."

Jennifer sniffled, but stayed quiet. She had incited this bullshit, and he was left with the clean-up. Troy couldn't even stomach to look at her again, and he didn't give a damn what happened to Dorsey.

"Is Jennifer free to go?" Troy asked.

"Yes." There was bite in Levi's tone.

"Francine?"

"Gentlemen is there anything else?" Levi addressed the cops.

"You'll be hearing from the District Attorney's office. They may have questions," Roberts said.

"I want to go on record. All contact with Mr. and Mrs. Bryant will be made through my office and me." Levi stood with his arms folded over his chest.

Roberts nodded before turning to lead them into the open squad room. Williams moved to open the door to the right of the conference room. He waved his hand to an unseen person before Francine's small frame appeared in the doorway. Troy watched as his wife scanned the room until her attention fell on him. The stress of the situation was apparent in her face, and he hurt with the realization. She rushed forward, her concern for him evident.

Francine wrapped her arms about him and squeezed tight; Troy reciprocated. Over her head, he glared around the squad room as both uniformed and plainclothes cops looked on. He was not into public displays of affection, but it had been a trying evening. When his glare settled on Jennifer, she looked to the ground. Abruptly, he stepped back before bending to whisper in his wife's ear.

"You all right, baby?"

"I'm sorry all this is happening," she answered.

"I'm good, sweetheart," he hesitated. "The press is outside."

"I want to go home with you."

He searched her face, taken aback by the level of emotion he felt for her. Francine's desire to go home with him said much. Troy wasn't sure if he was falling in love or already in love with his wife. He was about to straighten his stance and cue Levi when she cupped his face and kissed him. It was a pressing of their lips in chaste contact, but the action floored him. In the background, he heard his cousin advising Jennifer that it was time to leave. Troy sighed before he stepped back and took his wife by the hand.

They gained the lobby from the opposite door he was originally ushered through. The same older black cop was still on duty. It was almost dawn when they met Jesse in front of the station, but there were no reporters.

"The press was told you wouldn't be released and that your wife left through the back entrance." Levi said, understanding his confusion.

Troy nodded, and Levi went on. "They were dismissed to make certain the story of your arrest goes undisputed."

Jesse held the car door and Jennifer climbed in first, then Francine. Levi waved him in next and got in last. They pulled out of the parking lot onto the main drag, and Troy said, "This can no longer be avoided."

"I stand at your back always," Levi said.

"Set the meeting up."

"Done," Levi answered.

Francine snuggled against him, never acknowledging her sister. Troy turned his attention to the window to cut the tension he was feeling. Jennifer broke the quiet of the backseat.

"I miss you, Frankie, and I'm worried about you. Sorry for all the trouble I caused… please talk to me." Her voice was small–hurt.

His wife closed her eyes, feigning sleep. Levi took charge. "Jennifer will be staying with me. I'll work on shit today and come to you tomorrow with the details."

"Aiight." Troy responded.

The limo pulled in front of the building and Troy helped Francine from the car. His wife didn't look back at her sister who c ould be heard crying softly. Levi nodded as the car door swung closed. They made their way through the lobby and onto the elevator. Troy unlocked the condo allowing Francine in first. Once in the foyer he spoke.

"You must be exhausted, go shower and rest. I'll be along shortly."

His wife stared at him. "You all right, Troy?"

"Yes, sweetheart."

He kissed her forehead and smiled down at her. Francine looked as though she wanted to say more, instead she turned and headed down the hall. Troy headed to his office where he removed his shirt and shoes. He needed to be alone with his temper and insecurities. The shit rolling around in his head made him unfit for female company. He lit a cigarette and inhaled deeply.

Carefully, he began to work through the issues on his plate in order of importance. He would start with his wife's safety. Troy would make Francine the addendum to plan A. Tyrell and Hassan would be difficult, but he would give them no choice. If they refused to see reason, he would suspend plan A long enough to do violence. He was prepared to follow through.

Everything revolved around the plan, and he would see it through, but he wouldn't give her up. He understood his personal life and the arrest drew unwanted media attention, leaving the organization open to suspicion. Standing before the windows in the corner of his office, he watched the sun ascend to the sky. His mind settled on Jalal Dorsey. Witnessing another man's hunger for Francine set him to murder.

He would stay in his office until he calmed down. She did not want rough, but he did.

"Troy?"

Turning away from the windows, he found Francine standing in the doorway of his office. She was dressed in a pale rose nightie that clung to her curves and stopped mid-thigh. Her eyes were wide with concern as she stepped over the threshold. She had loosened her hair from the ponytail leaving a riot of curls. His wife was sensual and sweet. Troy wanted Francine to go away; she wasn't ready, and neither was he.

* * *

Francine stared at her husband. Troy stood before her wearing only the black trousers to his tux. His arms were crossed over his powerful chest as he regarded her. He was trying to hide his anger, but it consumed everything in the space between them. And though she felt his rage, she also felt his fear.

"I don't want him."

"I know it in my head…" He sighed and turned away from her. "Did more happen between you and him? Is this what has him challenging me as your husband? Is there shit you don't want to tell me?"

She giggled. "No."

He turned back and glared at her. "This is funny to you?"

"It is a little comical."

She felt a sharpness in his words that hadn't been present in the limo. He was trying to dismiss her, so he could be alone with his temper, but Francine realized it wouldn't help him or her to let him stew. He would only be more intimidating, nastier.

"Why is this situation funny?"

"Because you know I don't want him, and you know I haven't lied to you."

"You're with me because I forced you…"

"You going to let me go?" She felt nervous for his answer.

"No," he replied swiftly. "Your sister and Dorsey think you don't want me. They see your fear."

"Maybe in the beginning they thought that, but no one thinks that now—not even you. You're tired Troy, come shower and rest."

"You go relax. I'll be in later."

He turned his back ending the conversation, but Francine went on. "Are you afraid I'll be rough with you? If I promise to be gentle, will you come to bed?"

Troy didn't turn back to her, but he hung his head as his shoulders shook with mirth. The muscles in his back bunched and released with the effort. She moved to stand behind him and kissed his back. He tensed when she wrapped her arms around him; he leaned his palm flat against the window. She moved around him, squeezing between him and the glass.

He took her mouth in a rough kiss and whispered, "Francine."

She splayed her hands over his chest, feeling his muscles. His skin was kissed by the sun as he stood before her and the floor to ceiling windows. He smiled weakly and beseechingly as he breathed, "Francine."

"Yes."

He stared at her for a moment, allowing the word to hang in the air. She felt shy in the light of day but held his gaze. There could be no doubt or he would back away. She was nervous, still she wanted more of him.

Troy didn't inquire again, instead he reached down, grabbed the hem of her nightie and pulled it over her head. Lifting her, he carried her to his desk and settled her in the middle.

"Open your legs," he demanded.

Francine spread her legs wide, and Troy dropped to his knees, shouldering her limbs further apart. She cried out when his tongue lashed at her clit. Her head fell back, and her eyes rolled up in her head. She was panting and quivering. Francine was about to explode when he stopped suddenly.

"Please, Troy... don't stop."

He didn't respond verbally, but he did lean forward and thrust his tongue inside her. She let her eyes drift close as he began spanking her clit—again. The noises that came from her were disjointed babblings, all meant to encourage. When ecstasy snatched all thought from her mind, she was hoarse from moaning and straining. Troy pulled away—stood and shoved himself inside her, causing orgasm to hit her in waves.

"Ahhh shit, baby." He groaned.

Francine felt full as her body spasmed around him. In the distance, she heard him speaking; she had to try to focus. "Look at me, baby, don't close your eyes."

She did as he instructed. Troy was a sight to behold as the sun shone down on him and sweat beaded his body. His masculinity flexed as he rode her body hard; he was stunning. She looked down between them, watching as he retreated and slammed home over and over. Francine had never experienced the like and though she tried to stay with him, her head fell back in absolute pleasure. Troy pinned her legs wider and banged into her roughly until she felt his manhood pulse. He leaned over and pulled on her nipples before taking her mouth in a bruising kiss.

"Ohhh fuck, Francine. I love you," he cried out as he stiffened and collapsed on top of her.

She wept his name as she locked her legs and arms about him. When the room stopped spinning, he didn't speak. He stood, and she felt him slip from her body. Troy carried her down the hall to their bedroom. She thought he would take her to the shower, so they could clean up. Instead, he climbed in bed with her and snuggled close. Francine felt the essence of him dripping from her. She was about to suggest they shower when he spoke.

"I don't want you to wash me away."

She fell asleep in his arms.

* * *

It was early evening when Francine woke, alone. She was disoriented until the last two days came rushing back. Groggy, she climbed from the bed, showered and dressed in a forest green nightie before going in search of her husband.

She found Troy in the kitchen, garbed only in a pair of white boxers. He stood at the island with all the makings for a sandwich spread out in front of him.

"Come eat," he said.

Francine moved into the kitchen, seating herself across from him at the island. There were several types of lunch meats and cheeses, along with lettuce and tomato, and white or wheat bread. She made a turkey and swiss cheese on white. Troy was cutting his own sandwich in half when he spoke.

"The state may pick up the charge of assault on Dorsey for the shit with you."

"I know, Levi told me. I want all this to go away."

"This could cause me a problem as well."

She paused from the bite she was about to take and put her sandwich down. "What kind of problem?"

He took a bite of his food, as if to stall, but she held his gaze. "We could both be charged with assault. I choked him unconscious, it will be considered excessive."

"It's not on the video."

"The validity of the video can come into question if he has a good lawyer. If it were me, Levi would question if the video was altered."

"Levi invited them to come see the setup of the equipment. Apparently, the camera is on a timer, alternating around the cultural center. It cut to the lobby before you choked him. I don't think they had to do any editing," Francine explained.

He stopped chewing and tilted his head to one side, really looking at her. "How do you know whether we altered the evidence?"

"I love photography. I edit and splice film as well."

"Interesting… I have a meeting with Levi in the morning. He'll have the video for me to view."

Francine didn't want to think about the beginning of the video. She would let Levi work that out with him. Troy wasn't going to be pleased. She looked away, but not before he saw her concern.

"What is it?" he asked.

"Two of the wait staff can be seen opening the back door for Jalal. When they went back to their duties, he let Jennifer in."

Troy's nostrils flared as he stared at her. He placed his food on his plate and reached for two wine glasses. Francine continued to eat while he poured chilled, white wine into both glasses. He also added potato chips to their spread, and she knew he was trying to keep busy. Since he was already aggravated, she decided to ask the questions that were most pressing in her mind.

"What did you mean when you said, 'this can no longer be avoided'?"

Troy put his glass down. "When we formed the organization, it was to help young people and make a difference in our community. We–meaning the original members–also have an agenda that is not public. Tyrell, Hassan, Akeel and I have all done time. Levi, who has never been incarcerated, represents us and the organization."

She frowned, "Levi has never been to jail?"

Troy laughed. "No, Levi has never done time."

Francine shook her head. "You mean he has never been caught."

"No," he responded, "Levi has never been caught."

"Why doesn't the organization like me?" She thought to be blunt because he had not answered the question.

"There is an unwritten rule that we would not step away from the agenda for personal reasons until the mission was complete. The press and our marriage has brought unwelcomed attention to the group.

"So, the women in the circle are part of the organization, and I am the outsider who has sidetracked you?"

He sighed. "It's a little more complicated than that, but yes."

"What is the agenda?"

"Do you trust me to keep you safe?" he asked.

"Yes, I trust you to keep me safe…" she paused, then exhaled before she went on. "I don't know what to think about you or us."

"You're mine. The organization, Dorsey or your sister won't separate us. Do you understand me?"

"Yes, Troy."

"I have friends I want you to meet. We'll be having dinner with them soon. Don't worry about this anymore."

Francine understood that he was fighting with his irritation. She backed off to allow him to level out. After several moments of stifling silence, she got up and began putting the food away. Troy helped and when they were done, he led her back to their bedroom. She laid in his arms and told him funny stories about when she and Jennifer were children. He laughed, and she felt some of the stress leave his body. She fell asleep listening to the sound of his heartbeat.

It was morning when she emerged from the bedroom to the sound of Levi's voice. Francine could see Troy standing behind the desk in his office, glaring at his cousin. When he spied her, he reached out his hand and she went to him. Troy kissed the top of her head and dismissed Levi.

"Did you sleep well?"

"I did," she answered.

"I put Jennifer on a plane to Atlanta. Jewel will pick her up from the airport and see her home. Your mother is angry with her. Ms. Dot asked that you call her today," Levi said.

Francine didn't want conversation with him, but anxiety for her sister won out. "Thank you for taking care of Jennifer. She isn't in any trouble, right?"

"No, she's not in trouble, and the DA has decided not to press charges against Jalal. In return, he has agreed to stay away from you. So, are we friends now?" Levi asked.

"No, we're not, but thank you."

She left the office to give the men privacy and to escape the strain of dealing with Troy and Levi. The day pressed on with her eating breakfast alone. She explored the condo and finding the laundry room, she began cleaning. The phone rang as she was placing their bedding in the wash. Troy appeared, handing her the receiver. He looked apologetic.

"Hello."

"Didn't Levi tell you to call me?"

"Oh… Hi, Ma."

"You all right? Jennifer told me what happened. I ain't never sure what that girl be thinking."

"I'm fine. Troy and Levi got it sorted. I don't know what she was thinking either."

"We're both worried about you, but your sister goes too far. She told me Troy was arrested, and Levi had to get him out of jail."

"How are you, Ma? When you coming back?" Francine changed the subject.

"I don't know. We'll see."

"I'll pay for your ticket. I think Jewel and Butch miss you."

"I'll bet they do, neither one of them can boil water."

Francine laughed, realizing she missed her mother. She also felt unease about Jennifer being alone in Atlanta. "I miss you, Ma, but I want you to know–I'm fine."

"Okay, my little Frankie. Imma get off here before my bill be too high. I love you."

"I love you too, Ma."

"I understand you upset with Jennifer, but she's heartbroken that you ain't speakin' to her. She doesn't know what to make of all your changes. We both don't know what to make of Troy."

Francine's voice softened. "I want my husband."

Her mother laughed. "Troy is too intense for an old lady like me. In my younger days, I would have fainted if a man like him set eyes on me."

"Bye, Ma… stop it." Francine giggled.

"I love you." Dot said before hanging up.

Francine went back to setting their bedroom to rights. She also cleaned the bathroom and the kitchen before finishing the laundry. The afternoon creeped in, and she looked up to find Troy standing in the doorway of the master suite. His face was serious.

"We have dinner plans this evening."

"Oh," she didn't want to deal with people.

He smiled, but it didn't reach his eyes. "We'll have dinner with friends tonight. It's causal, I'm wearing what I have on."

Troy was dressed in blue jeans, black work boots and a plain black t-shirt. She smiled weakly and nodded. Francine didn't want to dine with people who didn't like her. It was one more thing on the list of shit she couldn't control. She also didn't want to see Karyn, who was clearly part of the circle. Francine didn't want to deal with Troy's other woman.

"I'll start getting ready."

"Good," and before turning to walk away, he added, "Jesse will be out front in two hours."

"All right," she answered, her voice tight.

"What's wrong?"

"Nothing."

"Francine?"

"Is Karyn going to be there?"

"Whether Karyn is there or not, doesn't change your status in my life."

"She's in love with you."

"I know."

"I don't want to see it."

Troy folded his arms over his chest and crossed his feet at the ankles. He leaned against the door frame as he regarded her. "I'm in love with you, Francine."

"I know."

"Do you think you could ever love me?" he asked.

"I'm confused about you, Troy."

He looked away, but she didn't miss his hurt. "I understand."

"Do you—really? Because I don't. I'm mad at Jennifer for trying to save me from the man who abducted me. I only want to be with this man and I only want his touch. I'm falling for him, and I forget he's a bad man."

They stood staring at each other for a time before he stretched away from the door frame. Francine didn't look away and she saw relief in his eyes. He offered no remorse when he said, "I'm not sorry for stealing you and I would do it again."

"I know."

"I'll leave you to get dressed." He disappeared from the doorway. She was no different than her mother, Troy made her feel faint.

Rush hour traffic was thick at 5pm, and the heavy rains added to the congestion. Troy sat in the center of the back seat with his right hand possessively on her knee. Francine stared out the tinted window, trying to control the unease she felt at having to dine with people who didn't want her company. Jealousy sat opposite her; she couldn't stay away from thoughts of Karyn.

Troy was agitated, and it couldn't be missed. If she didn't know better, she would think he didn't want to dine with these people either. It was the same as the airport, he didn't speak, but he continued to caress and stroke her. Outside the limo, rain came down in buckets with the occasional thunder and lightning. The morning had been sunny and bright, but the day had taken a turn. Like his mood, it was now stormy and unstable.

They rode in silence for almost two hours until Jesse finally maneuvered them off the expressway and to the gates of Levi's home. Even in the rain and gloom of night, floodlights brought the imposing structure to life. The first time she was here, she hadn't been able to concentrate on her surroundings.

Jesse opened the door and handed Troy an umbrella; her husband, in turn, helped her from the vehicle. He walked her between four other cars, sheltering her from the downpour. All three of the garage doors were open and Butch stood inside the middle entrance. He was dressed in a pair of blue carpenter pants, a white t-shirt and brown work boots. His hair was rough, but his face was clean shaven. He didn't smile, but he caught her eye and nodded. The old man spoke to Troy.

"Everyone's inside." He paused for a moment and then went on. "Jesse, how you been?"

"I'm good, Butch, I can't complain."

Once she was in the garage, Troy shook the umbrella free of excess water. After placing it against the wall, he turned and asked, "Ready?"

"Yes."

Troy smiled as he reached for her hand and gave it a reassuring squeeze. "Come."

He led her to a door inside the garage that opened in the kitchen. Butch was behind them and Jesse remained between the cars as if keeping watch. Francine hoped Troy wouldn't walk off and leave her with the women. She wasn't good at small talk.

The three moved into a large dining room. Francine hadn't been this far in Levi's home the first time she was here. In the center of the dining room sat a large wooden table with seven mismatched chairs. Around the table stood four men and they all looked agitated. She recognized Levi and Akeel, but the other two men she didn't know. This was no dinner with friends.

Francine looked Akeel in the eyes, there was nothing warm about him. He was dressed in a pair of black jeans with black combat boots–a black t-shirt stretched across his bulging muscles. Levi was dressed the same, except his jeans were blue, his work boots black and his t-shirt navy-blue. Next to her, Troy cleared his throat.

"Hassan."

The man Hassan was dark of skin with slanted brown eyes and thick lips. The bridge of his nose was wide, his nostrils–fat. His black hair was almost shaved making the frown lines on his forehead obvious. Like the other men, he was dressed casual in blue jeans, black boots and a black t-shirt. Hassan was shorter than Levi but taller than Troy. He was all muscle and exuded danger.

"Troy," he replied.

The man next to Akeel was of a brown skin tone with light brown eyes. His features were hard, adding to a coldness that emitted from him. He had a sharp nose with angled cheekbones and dark brown lips–with a hint of pink. His black hair was cut close, and he had no facial hair. He wore black jeans and boots with a white t-shirt. This man didn't wait for Troy to acknowledge him.

"Troy," he sneered.

"Tyrell." Troy replied.

As Francine assessed Tyrell, she realized she was wrong. Levi was not the biggest man she had ever seen. This man was a hair taller than Levi and broader. While it wasn't by much, he was still larger, and his presence gave her pause. She moved in closer to her husband who addressed the room in a commanding voice.

"I have come to reinstate plan A, effective immediately."

"If you have decided to discuss plan A, why is your wife here?" Tyrell's demeanor chilled her to the bone.

Calmly, Troy explained, "Francine is the addendum to the plan."

"Addendum? Where the fuck she come from, man? Why the fuck are you always in the news, bringing attention to our shit?" Hassan growled.

All eyes were on her, and she looked to the ground to keep from collapsing. She wanted to fade away, but Troy squeezed her hand lightly. "This group operates as if we're equals, but we're all clear that I'm the man in charge—correct?"

"So, you pullin' rank?" Akeel asked.

"I am." Troy's speech conveyed boredom.

"I think Hassan asked a valid question. Why are you always in the news for bullshit?" Tyrell continued.

"The organization won't control my personal life. You will offer your loyalty to me and all extensions of me. My wife will have allegiance from the group I formed. You are either with me or against me—there are no other choices."

"So, you are threatening us?" Tyrell stepped back from the table.

"Let me get this straight, you fucked up and now you're issuing threats. Yet, your wife and her damn family have caused us nothing but grief," Hassan said.

Levi spoke up, "Jennifer belongs to me now, and you will offer her the same loyalty."

Francine was so overwhelmed with everything that was happening, she couldn't process Levi's words. But she was aware that something bad was happening where Jennifer was concerned.

"I have not asked for what I'm not willing to give; you all have my loyalty. If we can't reach an agreement…" Troy let his threat trail off.

"You is one cocksure mafucka," Hassan's tone dripped with menace. "I guess it ain't no sense in putting this to a vote. Akeel, you and Levi is family. It's me and Tyrell being put on notice here."

Troy never let her hand go, but she felt him shrug in response to Hassan's words. The room fell silent, and Francine couldn't breathe. Tyrell spoke first, his words were tight.

"How do you propose to reinstate the plan with all this media attention?"

"The media attention is the diversion we need to move forward. We'll play our positions and after each phase, we will suspend the plan until we're ready to begin again. What's important is for everyone to recognize that Francine is nonnegotiable." Troy answered.

There was more smothering silence before Hassan addressed her. "Little one, are you aware of the power you hold?"

Francine couldn't answer, her mind was rubbed clean of all thought. She looked to Troy for help and found him glaring at Hassan. It was Levi who stepped in. "Let's take the vote for shits and giggles. All those in favor of the addendum, raise your hand."

The old man stepped from behind her and raised his hand, Akeel instantly did the same. Levi followed suit as he eyed the other two. After several heartbeats, Hassan reluctantly pushed his hand in the air. All the attention in the room shifted to Tyrell as his gaze fell on her. She couldn't help herself, she started trembling. Dread engulfed her, and it was literally suffocating her. She knew he wasn't going to raise his hand. Instead, he spoke directly to her–his voice coarse.

"Francine, you have my loyalty."

BOOK 2

Made in America

1

CHARLOTTE, NORTH CAROLINA
JUNE 1995

It was after midnight, and Troy paced the house with painful thoughts of the life he lost. He had been twenty-four with big dreams and aspirations–a kid, really, who had never been in trouble. The old him wore highwater pants, thick glasses and a pocket protector. He humorlessly chuckled because the old him didn't have a violent bone in his body. Ernest Stephen Bryant trusted law enforcement.

Troy stood naked at the windows of his office. He was trying to clear his mind from the nightmare still haunting him. His breathing was labored as he reminded himself that he was no longer incarcerated. He could still see himself handcuffed while being patted down by two white officers. Akeel had demanded to know why they were being stopped; he was dragged from the car and beaten. They were told they fit the description, and shit was never the same.

At times, the hurt was so great his eyes watered. But he had not been able to shed tears for himself, and he had become who they claimed to have arrested. There was however, one bright spot in his existence–Francine. She saw his ugly and still she shared herself with him. He was thankful for his wife, no matter how he acquired her.

Images he couldn't shake weighed his brain down. He leaned his forehead against the coolness of the glass and closed his eyes. It all came rushing back, and he was powerless to stop it. He could still hear the judge's voice.

"Ladies and gentlemen of the jury, have you reached a verdict?"

An older white woman, with grim features, stood and moved forward. Her salt and pepper hair was pulled back in a severe bun. She wore a white button down shirt with blue slacks. He noted the serious expressions of the seated jurors. But she wouldn't look at him as she answered the judge.

"We have, Your Honor."

"Bailiff." The judge said, and a portly Black man with a small afro and blank gaze stepped forward. He wore a brown and beige uniform, and the sound of his shoes hitting the stone floor echoed in the courtroom as he retrieved the slip of paper from the head juror's hand.

"Will the defendant please rise?" the judge asked.

Behind him, Troy could hear his mama praying, "Lord, please—take care of my baby."

His legs could hardly carry him to an upright position. He clutched the back of his chair for support and looked to the jury. The judge spoke as Troy tried to gauge the people who would decide his fate. The seven white men and five white women did not look like his peers.

"For the charge of murder in the first degree—the People vs. Ernest Stephen Bryant, what say you?"

The judge, who seemed above the law, sat in a black robe with his hands folded in front of him. He had red hair, and from the defendant's chair, his eyes appeared blue. The white gentleman on the bench looked to be about forty and his face was void of all emotion.

"For the charge of murder in the first degree—the People vs. Ernest Stephen Bryant, we find the defendant—Guilty." The head juror replied, her words flat—lifeless.

"For the second count of murder in the first degree—the People vs. Ernest Stephen Bryant, what say you?" the judge continued.

A humming noise started in Troy's head, his lawyer grasped his shoulder to steady him. Behind him, he heard his sister scream and then a dull thud. The courtroom became chaotic as he realized his mama had collapsed.

"Order! Order in the court!" The judge yelled as he banged his gavel adding to the disorder.

Instinctively, he tried to go to his mother, only to be tackled and shoved face down onto the table; he was cuffed immediately. His sister was hollering and crying, "Get a doctor! Please, get a doctor!"

"Mama!" he yelled as he was dragged from the courtroom.

They left him in a holding cell while he waited for news of his mother. After thirty minutes, his sister was allowed in to see him. Monica was twenty-two and hysterical when she told him their mother died.

"Troy?" Francine's voice brought him back from the past but not from the pain.

He couldn't respond, and when she touched him—he cringed. She never questioned why he paced the condo or what made him leave their bed. Francine kissed his back and hugged him.

"I can't sleep without you."

Stepping back from the window, Troy lifted his wife into his arms and carried her back to the master suite. She wrapped her arms and legs about him, holding him tight. Once in bed, she reached for him, stroking his erection. His body tensed as he gently pushed her hand away.

"No, baby."

"I'm sorry, Troy," she whispered, and he heard the sting of rejection.

His wife thought he was refusing her, but nothing could be further from the truth. He was having trouble regulating his mood, and Francine's innocence was a real thing now that he had been inside her. Yet, after such horrific memories, he needed total control over everything in his path. He wanted to orgasm while exploring his urges. Troy sought to dominate her, but she wasn't ready for what he needed. In fact, it was seeing her strung up and exposed that brought what he was trying to bury to the surface. He was too fucked up to safely engage her right now.

She turned her back to him, and impulsively, he yanked her to face him once again. His voice was raw. "Don't turn away from me, Francine."

His wife gasped, but she didn't speak. The drone of the air conditioner, the dull light from the bathroom and the moonlight spilling into the bedroom set the stage for what he wanted. Even the coolness of the satin sheets against his skin heightened his need to exert his power over her. But knowing what she had been through, and his firsthand knowledge of bad memories, he couldn't take from her. He couldn't become her nightmare any more than he already had.

He slid down in the bed, so he could be eye to eye with his wife. The perimeter of the room glowed and shimmered, leaving her features shadowed. He was still submitting to her, but it was a process that did not come easy. In the past, he never felt it necessary to explain himself to anyone. As for the women he fucked, he always left before clarification of his feelings became a factor.

"I have too many thoughts in my head—a lot of mental noise. I'm afraid it will blot out my ability to measure the pain and pleasure I want to inflict."

"Inflict?" she questioned, softly.

The apprehension in that one word made him even harder. Francine was young, but she respected the danger that lay between them. And he was appreciative because he *had* abducted her and threatened bodily harm if he didn't get his way. He was still that man even while loving her, and she knew it. The fact that she didn't take for granted that this was still a perilous joining made his affection for her deepen. He would compromise and submit, but his masculine flexibility could snap if too much pressure was applied.

As he leaned forward and kissed her lips, he took inventory of who he was at that moment. He was a man who was learning to accept that he wanted to spank and fuck his wife. He was a man who was always comparing who he was before jail and after jail. He was a man who was engaging in barebacked sex for the first time with a pussy so tight it owned him—testing his precious control. He was a man who had never explored his sexually dominant self and he feared hurting her through ignorance.

"I want to give you pleasure and pain." He kissed her again and then warned. "Go to sleep, it's safest for both of us right now."

Francine was quiet for a time. "Will you always be a bad man?"

"Yes."

She snuggled close and fell asleep in his arms, but he and his erection remained awake. At dawn, he climbed from the bed and closed the drapes casting the room in darkness. Troy dressed in another bedroom, so as not to wake his wife. He found that her sleep was broken by his nightly pacing.

As he entered the kitchen, the strong smell of coffee drifted through the air, clinging to his senses. Brenda sat at the table making a list. She looked up at the sound of his voice. "Good morning."

"Morning, Troy, Frankie still sleep?"

"Yes, Francine is still resting. I'll be home late." He ignored the name Frankie.

Twenty minutes later, he was climbing into the limo headed toward his first meeting of the day. He pushed all thought of Francine from his mind, so he could be productive. When he arrived at Levi's house, he dismissed Jesse. He would take possession of one of Levi's cars and drive himself around.

There was one car in the drive that didn't belong, it meant his first appointment had arrived. He lit a cigarette as he stood in the shelter of the garage. The middle door was open, and the smell of motor oil and dampness beset him. Though the sun shone brightly, the smell of the previous day's rain still lingered. The trees were in full bloom, leaving the woods thick and private around the house. He could no longer see the limo or the gate. Throwing his cigarette to the ground, he snuffed it out before looking up to find a deer watching him. Two babies followed, and Troy figured the larger one must be female. He removed his left hand from his pocket, and she darted off, babies and all. The bushes rustled as they made their getaway. He wished Francine were here to see. Troy sighed. The rule–he wasn't allowed to think of her until he was done with work. It was already a long day, and it was still early morning.

He stepped into the kitchen to find Levi and Georgia's Fulton County D.A., Larry Wright pouring over paperwork. They stood at the island with a stack of manila folders piled neatly. Larry looked up at his entrance.

"Troy, how goes it?"

"I'm good, Larry, how about you?"

"Good... good," Larry said.

Levi nodded, and Troy jumped into the business at hand. "What's all this? I thought we would only take two cases at a time."

"I have only given one case. The rest is information I thought you all may need. A bad pattern has emerged," Larry said.

"Pattern?" Troy replied.

Larry was a dark-skinned man with a bald head and astute brown eyes.

His beard was neatly trimmed, but it brought attention to the wideness of his nose. Troy gauged him to be—not quite fifty, but over forty-five. Larry stood about five feet, nine inches and he was soft in the middle from too much good food. He backed away from the island.

"Yeah, man, I came to speak with you. Levi told me that you reinstated the plan. I realize I'm not part of the group, but I'm desperate."

"This wouldn't have kept until I returned to Atlanta?" Troy asked.

"Levi called in a favor. The D.A. in Charlotte dropped the charges against Jalal Dorsey at my request. You know how these things go. I owed Levi, and the District Attorney of Mecklenburg County owed me. Besides, they have serious shit to handle and not enough hours in the day."

Troy was following the gist of the conversation. He realized that not only should Dorsey have been charged with assault, but he should have been charged as well. The Fulton County D.A. was letting him know without saying that he now owed a favor.

"I'm listening," Troy said.

"We have a kid in custody; his name is Darrell Jenkins. He is awaiting trial for the shooting death of an elderly white man. The victim's family has money, and they have been quietly applying pressure to get a conviction," Larry explained.

"The victim's name is John Unger—seventy years old," Levi added. "When the neighborhood experienced white flight, the old man stayed. The people in the community say he was kind to everyone."

"The detective on the case is Chris Logan," Larry said.

The men fell quiet and Troy knew they were waiting for his reaction, but he had nothing to give. In his mind's eye, he could see Detective Logan on the witness stand lying his ass off—during his trial. It had been a toss-up between killing his attorney, George Ingalls or Chris Logan, the detective who ripped his family apart. It seemed there would be no reprieve from his nightmares as they had followed him into the light of day. His body stiffened, but he finally found his voice and addressed Levi.

"You obviously don't think the kid killed this old man."

"No, we don't," Levi answered.

"Who do you think did the old man?" Troy asked.

"If plan A is back in effect, I'll leave it to you and Levi to find out.

You should know that Darrell Jenkins' family has involved the media. They have brought attention to the case by protesting and shutting Old National Highway down. College Park has become a political hot bed, and the people are calling for an investigation of Detective Logan."

Larry then stepped away from the island to retrieve his belongings from a chair by the table. He shrugged into his suit jacket. "*When* you take this case–you will file the proper requests as if you never saw these records. I'm in North Carolina because my wife's mother is having surgery. I felt it was better to see you and Levi here. How long before you're back in Georgia?"

"I should be leaving Charlotte in four days. I have another speaking engagement, after which, I'll be heading home." Troy answered.

"Congrats on the nuptials." Larry chuckled. "I won't ask how you ended up with the missing woman from New York."

"Oh, Larry, you could ask." Troy didn't smile, and the shorter man took his leave.

Later, Troy met with Akeel and Hassan to discuss the case left by Larry. Tyrell did not show up. It was clear he was still pissed about being strong armed. Interestingly, Troy had chosen well with these men. Tyrell was angry, but he could be trusted. Whenever he missed a meeting, he met with Troy privately and while his attitude was apparent, he worked through what needed to be done.

The day pressed on with the men addressing items on the agenda in order of importance. First, they would vet the staff for the next speaking engagement and make certain all was secure. Troy took a personal interest in this because Francine felt unsafe. Next, they would head back to Atlanta and investigate the case of Darrell Jenkins. The men were discussing how to proceed when the phone in Levi's kitchen rang.

Levi pushed back from the table and headed for the phone. Akeel yelled after him. "Yo, why you don't have furniture?"

Levi yelled back. "Fuck y'all," and they all laughed.

Troy had been about to ask Akeel his thoughts on Logan when Levi called his name. "It's for you, man."

He stood, heading for the kitchen and Levi handed him the phone. "Troy speaking."

"It's me, Jesse. There's no problem, but Brenda wants to take Francine to dinner. Your wife has agreed, but I didn't want to take her anywhere without your knowledge. I'm running errands with Tyrell, but I can take them and wait. If that's all right with you."

"Which restaurant and what time?" Troy asked.

"The Soul Food Joint at 7 p.m. I think Brenda begged until your wife finally gave in. I don't think Francine wanted to go, but she likes Brenda."

"I'll meet you there. Thanks, Jesse."

"Sho' thing, Troy."

He hung up the phone and stared at his watch. They had been at it all day, handling one issue or another. Troy was ready to see his wife and call it a night. Levi spoke before he could ask. "Take whichever car you want."

Troy nodded and headed for the garage, Akeel stood to follow. Troy took the keys for the Benz from the hook by the door. Once outside, he stopped at the sound of Akeel's voice. It wasn't what he said that made him take notice, it was the strain in his speech.

"I'm gonna head back to Atlanta early."

"No," Troy answered. "You can't compromise yourself."

"Listen, man—"

Troy cut him off. "She didn't marry him."

Akeel sighed and then nodded. "Yeah, I know."

The two men stared at each other for a time before Akeel turned and went back inside. Troy had never referenced their past or anything they lost that night. Still, he saw the defeat in Akeel's eyes when he alluded to Monica. It was unfair, but it was enough to get his friend grounded. They had not discussed it, but Troy was filled with guilt about many things, and Akeel was at the top of his list.

As he drove back to downtown Charlotte, Monday night traffic was lighter than usual. He didn't turn on the music because the extra noise wouldn't have helped his mood. Larry's mention of Detective Logan had pushed him back in time. His mind flashed to the moment when everything had gone wrong. 11 p.m. on a Saturday and the Camry he had driven for a year stopped on the edge of Buckhead. He walked several blocks to find a pay phone.

He called his sister's boyfriend to pick him up; he would decide what to do with his car the next day. Akeel showed up twenty minutes later, exhausted. Monica, his sister had gifted Akeel with a son, two months prior. Troy remembered his best friend being over the moon, Akeel had wanted to marry Monica.

"We need to stop for pampers," Akeel said.

"That boy is a pooping machine."

"I know right—all my funds is going to keeping him dry," Akeel snickered.

"Is Monica mad at me for getting you outta bed?"

"Naw, her and little man were asleep."

"Everybody is tired of my damn car," Troy chuckled.

"Yo' car is a piece of shit."

Akeel's conversation faltered when he noticed an unmarked car following them. "The cops is on us."

"How you know?"

"Don't turn around—let me get us the fuck outta Buckhead."

When they came to a red light, a patrol car cut them off. Two plainclothes cops and two uniformed cops drew their weapons.

"Get out the car with your hands up!" The uniformed cops were yelling.

"Officer, what's going on? Why are we being stopped?" Akeel asked.

"Where you boys coming from?" a plainclothes cop asked.

Troy had gotten out of the vehicle and was being patted down. Akeel kept his hands on the steering wheel but demanded, "Why are we being stopped?"

In his side view, Troy witnessed Akeel being dragged from his vehicle and beaten. One of the cops patting him down joined the plainclothes cops in what would later be described as securing a suspect. He thought Akeel was already dead when the ambulance arrived. It was explained later that an elderly, white couple had been murdered in their home, along with their Pomeranian. The EMTs and cops actually discussed letting Akeel die.

"We could save the taxpayers money if we let his ass go now." The shorter ambulance worker said.

"Don't I know it." One of the plainclothes cops answered.

Troy had been distraught; the police and EMT workers were all white. And so, the conversation continued in the same vein.

"What they do?" the taller EMT worker asked.

"Got us a double homicide—fuckers even killed the dog."

"I hate these kinda stops. Me and Rick call it workin' for the bad guys." The taller EMT worker said.

"We need to save his ass, so the family can see justice." The plainclothes cop replied.

The beeping of a car horn brought him back from his reverie. He took in a deep breath as he maneuvered off the expressway. His old car dying that fateful night had set off a chain of events from which he nor his family would ever recover. The worst, his mother dying of a heart attack in the courtroom. And if that weren't enough, his sister and Akeel were torn apart; their son forced to grow up without a father. Troy didn't know his nephew, and he no longer knew his sister. He couldn't face all that Monica lost in the tragedy that was his life.

When he parked his car behind the Soul Food Joint, he had to take a moment to collect himself. The reinstatement of the plan had bombarded his senses. Taking another steadying breath, he climbed from the vehicle and made his way around to the front of the restaurant. It was 6:30 in the evening and the sun was still shining. The temperature on the digital clock tower across the street read eighty-three degrees. Troy didn't venture inside because he wanted to wait for his wife.

While watching the people mill about, he lit a cigarette. There were several benches placed strategically around the establishment for the comfort of waiting patrons. A blue awning stretched to the curb, offering shelter from the elements. Large bushes added to the character of the restaurant. At the left of the entrance, three white men in business suits stood in a circle conversing. A black Land Rover pulled up, and four chocolate beauties exited onto the sidewalk. The Soul Food Joint was bustling for a Monday night. The windows were enormous, and customers could be seen eating, drinking and making merry.

At 6:55, Troy saw his limo pull to the curb. He moved forward to assist his wife and Brenda from the backseat. But the door popped open, stopping him in his tracks. Tyrell stepped onto the sidewalk and turned back, helping Brenda from the car first. The older woman wore her gray hair in two thick cornrows with the braids trailing down her back. She sported a brown Indian print skirt with an orange spaghetti strapped top, draped over her arm was a cream-colored sweater. On her feet were a pair of brown, leather slide-on sandals. Brenda smiled, thanking Tyrell for his assistance.

Tyrell then turned back to the car and propped his hand on the roof, before bowing down to look inside. Troy could see that he was speaking, but nothing was happening. After about five minutes of what looked like debating, Brenda stepped back to the car and looked inside as well. Tyrell shook his head and looked around. When he spotted Troy, his face became impassive. Still, he turned back to the car, bowed once more and started speaking. He pointed in Troy's direction before moving back to make room as Francine stepped onto the sidewalk.

His wife was dressed in a black pair of silk shorts that flowed to just above her knees. She wore a pink shirt that had only one sleeve, leaving her right shoulder completely bare. On her feet were a pair of black wedges that showed off her pink toenails. Francine's hair was parted in the middle and lightly curled; her hair framed her beautiful face. She looked composed, if you didn't know her, but her eyes gave away her fear. Even at this distance, Troy could see the tremor at the base of her throat. And he was suddenly jealous of Tyrell for riding in the limo with her and of the damn business-men for stopping their conversation to appreciate her.

Brenda walked over to him. "Hello, Troy. I think I pushed Francine too much today, but I do find it interesting that she only feels safe with you."

"Good evening, Brenda, and why is that interesting? I'm her husband."

Tyrell placed his hand at the small of Francine's back as he walked her over to him. She instantly moved away from Tyrell and pressed herself against him. Troy placed his arm possessively around her while mean-mug-ging Tyrell, who grinned.

He turned his focus on his wife. "You look gorgeous, Francine. Are you ready to go inside?"

"Yes, I'm ready. I missed you today, Troy–hope your day went well." Her voice was throaty and thick.

He stared down into his wife's face, her sincerity didn't lessen his jeal-ousy. Troy still wanted to punch Tyrell, but he wanted to kiss her more. He leaned down and planted a chaste kiss on her forehead. "I missed you more."

Brenda placed her hand on Tyrell's arm, and they walked into the restaurant, leaving him to speak with his wife. "I'm sorry, Troy. I tried today, but I almost couldn't get out of the car."

"We'll go out more, so you can get used to people again. It doesn't help that you're trying to work through shit, and the press is always on our heels."

Francine looked distressed, but she nodded. Her eyes became glassy and wide as she tried to contain herself. "I think I worked Tyrell's patience."

"He ain't the man in your life, I am. It don't matter what his ass thinks."

She smiled, and he asked. "You find me funny?"

"I do."

"Why?"

"Because you're mad that he rode in the limo with me and Brenda."

"I'm pissed he rode in the limo with you. I couldn't care less if he rides with my aunt."

"Your aunt?" her shock obvious.

"Yes, Brenda is Levi's mother."

"You don't tell me anything," Francine said, annoyed.

"I just did." He countered before adding, "Don't be upset, I didn't think of it. I'll do better."

"I see I'm going to have to get a list of interview questions for you."

"I don't give interviews."

"You don't speak with the press, this is different. I'll let you interview me." She cajoled.

This piqued his interest. "When will we start?"

"Tonight, when we're alone."

Troy decided to leave the conversation right where it was, so he could get through dinner. "Let's go inside."

In response, she tangled her fingers with his and whispered, "All right."

They stepped into the restaurant and up to the hostess's podium. Charlene immediately smiled at him. She had smooth, mahogany skin with large brown eyes. Her hair was dyed black and blonde adding a bad girl feel to her persona. Charlene was plump in all the right places and sexy. Troy had forgotten about her or he would have changed restaurants. The upside, he didn't fuck her, but if Francine hadn't come along when she did, he would have.

"Good evening, Troy."

"Charlie, this is my wife Francine."

"Good evening, Charlie." His wife said, and he heard the humor in her greeting.

"My aunt and Tyrell are already seated."

"Yes, follow me." Charlie retrieved menus and tableware.

Troy noticed Charlie didn't respond to Francine's greeting, but his wife didn't seem to care. He also knew his willingness to call Charlene–Charlie would spark a debate. Francine didn't mind laughing at him, and at first, he hated it. But now, he loved to pretend annoyance when posing the question–*You find me funny?*

They followed Charlie through a maze of big and small tables with different colored cloths draped over them. Along the walls were huge booths where one had to step up to be seated. They were crescent shaped and burnt yellow in color. The dining area smelled heavenly and Troy realized he was starving.

Tyrell and Brenda were seated in a booth at the back of the eatery. Troy allowed Francine to scoot in first and he sat opposite Tyrell. When the women settled, his wife still managed to be pressed against him. Troy loved it. The lights in the dining area were dim and a lone lamp hung above their table.

Brenda jumped right into conversation with Francine about clothes, and Troy threatened Tyrell. "How are we out to dinner and you missed the meeting?"

Tyrell's eyebrow popped, but he knew better than to push. "Can I meet with you in the morning? I'll come to the condo. Jesse was going to drive me to Levi's house later, but the women wanted to go out and here we are."

"Be at my house at 10 a.m. Don't miss another meeting," Troy said.

Tyrell grinned. "Aiight."

The waiter, a thin man, dressed in all black appeared with a pad in hand. "How are we this evening?"

Brenda spoke up. "We are wonderful. I know what I want."

"Shoot," The waiter said, his pen poised.

"I'll have the collard greens, baked mac and cheese with beef brisket. Oh, and cornbread, please."

Francine ordered chicken and waffles. Tyrell ordered fried chicken and collard greens. Troy ordered barbequed chicken, collard greens and potato salad. They all ordered a beer. The conversation continued to flow, but Francine spoke only to Brenda. It was apparent that she was trying to avoid Tyrell. Periodically, she would adjust and snuggle closer to him as she laughed at something Brenda said. He and Tyrell listened to the women, nodding when necessary.

Tyrell decided to push the envelope. "So, Francine, you're from New York—Queens, right?"

"Yes."

"What part?" Tyrell inquired.

"Sutphin Boulevard, near Hillside Avenue."

"Ah, I'm from Laurelton." Tyrell responded.

"Really," she said, flatly.

Troy could feel her shaking, but she needed to be engaged, and he needed to be all right with other men conversing with her. The waiter interrupted to serve them, and Francine turned her attention away from Tyrell. He shrugged and grinned when he looked at Troy. The dinner continued this way with his wife trying to ignore Tyrell and the other man refusing to be disregarded.

Francine shared her chicken and waffles with him and Troy let her eat from his plate. She picked between his food and her own while chatting with Brenda. He and Tyrell didn't talk about much, their business was confidential. When dinner ended, his wife and Brenda went to the ladies' room, and Troy discovered he was more than overprotective. He went to pay the bill, but Tyrell held up his hand.

"I got it. I'll order something for Jesse too."

Troy stood, headed for the ladies' room.

"She won't get any better if you're in the hall when she comes out." Tyrell added his two cents.

Troy stopped in his tracks. "I waited too long last time."

"Levi explained some of the shit to me. She gotta be stronger for how we live."

Troy nodded before sitting back down. Tyrell continued, "She wouldn't get out the car until I promised you were out there. Your wife is a sweet thing, I think I'm jealous of you."

"Are you trying to help or piss me off?" Troy asked.

"Both."

The women came back without incident, and the men stood, leading them from the dining area. Once on the sidewalk, Brenda hugged Francine. "I'll see you day after tomorrow."

"Okay," Francine answered as she twined her fingers in his.

"Tomorrow, man." Tyrell said, helping Brenda into the limo.

The clock tower showed the temperature had dropped from eighty-three to seventy-five degrees. A balmy breeze blew as patrons chatted around the entrance while waiting for their vehicles. Horns blew, and people laughed; complete darkness fell, alleviated only by signs and streetlights. Troy tugged her along to the parking lot at the back of the building. Before opening the door, he pushed her against the car and kissed her deeply; she reciprocated. Francine climbed into the passenger's seat and dozed off as he drove them home.

When they were getting ready for bed, she asked what he would consider to be an interview question. "Everything in our house is always so quiet. Why don't we have a TV in the bedroom?"

He liked her use of the word "*our*". "I don't watch TV, it doesn't interest me. Do you want a television in our bedroom?"

"Will you watch it with me?"

"I guess," he answered.

Her amusement made him smile. "Again, you find me funny."

"You sound pained at the thought of watching television."

"We'll only be here a few more days. I'll have a TV installed in our bedroom in Georgia."

She nodded. They showered separately, and he wore nothing but a towel. Francine had pulled on a blue nightie with matching panties. It was his turn to ask a question. "Why have you dressed for bed?"

"Why haven't you dressed for bed?" she shot back.

"Sooo, you can't answer a question with a question." He said, establishing the rules.

She sighed. "Sleeping with a man is all new to me. Do you want me to sleep naked?"

"Sometimes… Tonight I do."

She removed her nightie and underwear before climbing into bed. Troy dropped his towel and got in next to her. She lay facing him, and he settled on his side, giving her his full consideration. Enjoying the intimacy, he decided not to turn his lamp off.

"Are you still sexually pent up from being in jail?"

Troy fell flat on his back and barked out a laugh. Francine was unexpected and so damn sweet. She leaned up on an elbow, so she could look down into his face. Her eyes were big with curiosity and he offered the truth. "Yes."

"Is that why you want to inflict…" she paused for a heartbeat. "Pain?"

"I have a need to be in control–so, yes."

Swallowing hard, she asked, "You want to hurt me?"

"I want to help you teeter between pleasure and pain. I don't want to just hurt you–no."

"You scare me, Troy."

"You scare me, Francine."

She frowned at his words as she gazed down at him. Still, she didn't back away. "Why are you afraid of me?"

"Because you make me feel too good."

She giggled. "What are you talking about, crazy man?"

"I can't explain it any better than that."

"You are overpowering, but you make my world bigger." Troy hadn't bothered to inquire about her fear of him, but she offered enlightenment just the same. "You make me think about things I never considered. I'm not enough for you, Troy."

He reached up and cupped her face, pulling her into a turbulent kiss. Francine was already too much for him; he was done being interviewed. Rolling her onto her back, he shoved himself inside her tight body. When his hips were firmly planted against hers, he sucked in a ragged breath. She called his name, and he couldn't tell whether from pleasure or pain.

"Francine," he grunted, "too rough?"

Gasping, she answered, "No…"

His mind quieted, and there was nothing but the feel of her body wrapped about him. He pulled out and slammed home, causing sparks of pleasure to ricochet between them. She was going to kill him with delight, but he would die happy. Leaning up on his palms, he set a relentless pace of pound and retreat. Sensation pooled in his lower belly as his wife began chanting his name. Her soft sighs and pleadings pushed him toward conclusion. Abruptly, he pulled out of her and reared back on his haunches. He wasn't ready.

"Troy?" she begged.

"Shhh…"

Reaching out, he hauled her up to straddle him, while still on his knees. He cupped her bottom to defy gravity as he scrambled to the left of the bed. He got to his feet and flipped on the overhead light. The room was clinically bright–the mirrored wall captivating. He placed Francine on her feet, but her legs were weak, and he had to keep her upright. Turning back to the bed, he pulled the comforter and pillows onto the floor. Troy navigated them closer to the mirror and when he spoke, his voice was laced with aggression, arousal, and authority.

"Get down on all fours–facing away from me."

Francine didn't hesitate; she dropped to her hands and knees. "Move closer to the wall in front of you–hold out your hands as if to brace yourself at the baseboard."

She adjusted like he asked. "Head down–spread your legs and get that ass higher in the air."

When she did as he commanded, his breath caught. Silently, he backed up until he felt the edge of the bed. He was experiencing his wife in all her naked glory and the sight had him shaken to his core. He was so quiet, her head popped up as she tried to locate him.

"Troy?" she whispered.

He heard uncertainty when she called his name. Moving away from the bed, he knelt beside her. "I'm here, Francine… you're so lovely like this."

His hard on had not subsided. In fact, it worsened with the sight of her submitting to his demands. Kissing her shoulder and hip, Troy groaned. Francine's arched back pushed her bottom further into the air, and moving behind her, he found moisture on her inner thighs. He separated the chocolate globes of her ass, then licked and kissed her rear entrance. Her breasts dangled, and he pinched her erect nipples, making her sob incoherently.

Francine's body trembled, but she didn't attempt to change her position.

His tongue danced lower, sliding through her wet folds. He pushed a finger inside her and her muscles clinched. She almost fell over and he had to right her. His wife was close. Unable to help himself, he slapped her ass twice in rapid succession. His palm stung, and his control snapped.

Frantically, he pushed himself inside her wetness, while thumbing her rear muscle. He gripped her right hip to steady her as he slammed home and bottomed out. His stride was rough–hard, but he couldn't stop.

"Fuck me, baby...please." He begged.

Shifting, he grabbed both hips to keep her in place as he drove into her. Their connection was electric, but they did not have rhythm. What they had was frenzy. Troy was blissed-out and barreling toward completion when he realized his wife was meeting him thrust for thrust. He dropped his head to watch as his dick slid in and out of her wet heat. Her body began spasming and he had to lean his hand against the wall above her head to steady himself. His ejaculation hit in three powerful bursts. The first spurt made the edge of his vision go black. The second eruption cleared his mind and the third jet, dismantled him.

As they fell in a tangle of legs and arms, his wife lay with her head on his chest. Troy stared up at the light fixture in the middle of the ceiling; he was too weak to move them back to the bed. They would sleep on the floor. When their breathing calmed, he reached for the light switch, flipping it to the off position. The lamp on his side of the bed was still lit and too far away for him to care.

Silence persisted until Troy muttered. "Shit."

Francine leaned up on her elbow and looked down into his face once again. Her eyebrows were furrowed, her concern apparent. "Something wrong, Troy?"

He was frustrated and snapped. "Yeah, Francine, something is wrong."

"What is it?" She caressed his cheek.

"I think I'm pussy-whipped."

Laughter bubbled up from within her as she hunkered down next to him. He failed to see the humor, and Troy was still scowling when Francine dozed off.

2

INSIGHT
JUNE 1995

Francine found Troy looking over paperwork in his office. His head snapped up at the sound of her heels striking the floor. He had been up all-night pacing, and his eyes were red from lack of sleep. She wished he would speak more about what troubled him. He did, however, answer her inquiries–no matter what she asked; she made it a point to ask him one question per day.

He stood and moved around to the front of his desk. Leaning back against the edge, he spread his legs and held his hand out to her. Her husband was dressed in black dress slacks, a black pair of oxfords, and a crisp white shirt. He wore no cufflinks and his sleeves were rolled up, revealing his powerful arms. His shirt was open at the throat, adding to his maleness.

Francine didn't come forward, instead she dawdled in the doorway taking inventory of him. His hair and goatee were freshly cut and trimmed. The patch of gray hair on his chin marked him as stunning while making him appear sinister. His eyebrows were creased in the center, showing his contemplation of her. She was nervous. They would be leaving for his speaking engagement and then heading to Georgia right after. The timbre in his voice was all gravel when he spoke.

"Our luggage is in the living room. You glad to be going home?"

"No."

Troy had moments when he spoke about any and everything with her. He also had times when he wasn't verbal at all. Her husband was an open book and a mystery all at once. What made him complicated was how simple it was to live with him. And beneath the surface of Mr. and Mrs. Ernest Stephen Bryant, peril was present. He was still the man who had murdered three people and still the man who stole her from her life. Francine had not told him so, but he was also the man she loved.

"I'll speak, and then we'll mingle for a bit. Afterwards, we'll meet Butch and he'll take us home. I know you don't want to fly."

She nodded. "I'll get my wrap."

"Come here, Francine."

She stopped in her tracks. They stared at each other for seconds before she moved to stand between his legs. Reaching out, he curled the fingers of his right hand about her throat, applying pressure.

"I failed to keep you from harm at the last event. I'll do better."

"Troy…"

In the background, she heard the front door open and deep voices carry down the corridor. Francine didn't have to turn around to know it was them. Troy released her neck, his expression becoming impassive. He looked over her head to the door and nodded.

"Troy, Butch will drive you and Francine to Georgia. Jesse will take the rest of us." Levi's words floated over her shoulder.

"What about the event?" Troy asked.

"We'll ride with you to start out," Levi answered.

"Troy," Akeel greeted.

"Akeel."

Hassan and Tyrell spoke next, and Troy nodded his acknowledgment. As was his way, Tyrell spoke to her, forcing her to turn and face him.

"Good evening, Francine."

"Hello, Tyrell… Gentlemen."

"Hey, Francine," the men said in unison.

As she studied the men standing in the doorway, Francine couldn't help thinking of the fact that they all wanted her dead at some point. She was leaned against Troy who whispered into her ear. "Go get your wrap."

They would all be riding together–her stress knew no bounds. She couldn't show fear in passing them in the hall. Revealing her discomfort made Tyrell converse with her more than Levi. She hated it, and he didn't care. Once in the bedroom, she retrieved her wrap and purse. The men were at the front door and ready to go when she returned.

"Do you have everything?" Troy asked. "We won't be coming back."

They all turned to look at her.

"I do," she responded.

The men carried the luggage, and when they exited the elevator, it all made sense. Hassan and Tyrell took the lead. Akeel and Levi brought up the rear. Francine was swept along, holding Troy's free hand. They strode through the lobby with purpose, bidding Charlie good evening. At the curb, the men loaded the baggage while her husband helped her into the back seat. She sat between Levi and Troy. Akeel, Hassan and Tyrell sat opposite them. The night was underway whether she was ready or not.

There was no conversation on the ride to the venue, and after thirty minutes, Jesse pulled the limo in front of a three-story building. Troy told her that this event would be smaller than the last, but after a quick assessment, it was clear he was wrong. The structure was older, gauging by the type of windows that could be opened and closed manually. Everything was lit up like a Christmas tree, and the crowd was thick.

"Are we ready?" Levi asked, not waiting for a response. He popped open the door and stepped out. Across from him, Hassan got out next. At the opposite door, Tyrell and Akeel stepped onto the street. Hassan reached back into the car to help her out, and Troy exited behind her. She couldn't breathe, it was all too much. Had all these people come to hear Troy speak?

There were police barricades with several uniformed officers directing the crowd beyond the wooden horses. The press was in place, and the moment Troy stepped from the car, bursts of light started as the cameras began to go off. Her husband, unfazed, leaned down and whispered in her ear.

"I got locked up after the last event, and I have a sweet young wife. People wanna see you close up."

"So, you're tryna tell me all these people are here for me?"

"Yes." He grinned when she frowned at him.

They moved toward the stone stairs, and Troy tangled her fingers with his own. A red carpet led from the curb across the sidewalk, up the stairs and through the main entrance. Francine found that she was sheltered from prying eyes because the men surrounded her as they made their way. On the sidelines, the press was merciless with their rude questions.

"Francine, will you continue to see Jalal Dorsey?"

"Troy, are you still a person of interest in the George Ingalls' disappearance?"

"Francine, where were you for four days? How did you end up with the Silent Activist?"

"Troy, what kind of charity is this and where does the money go?"

"Troy, what do you say to the people who don't think you're innocent in the murders of Mr. and Mrs. Dotson?"

"Akeel, do you think the judicial system worked for the Dotson family?"

Francine kept her eyes on the steps and the entrance, but she was listening. She would ask Troy later about the rantings of the media. Mixed in with the press were people that stood about peacefully with signs that read:

I AM A MAN

MY HUMANITY SHOULD NOT BE UP FOR DEBATE

THE WAR ON DRUGS IS A WAR ON BLACKNESS

I'M A FELON–SO FUCK IT

They were almost to the stairs when a woman started screaming, "Mr. Bryant! Mr. Bryant! Please help me. My son was arrested, and he is innocent. I need help! Please!"

The police tried to push the crowd back, but Troy responded. "Please let her through!"

Hassan broke from the group to assist the woman who sobbed, "Thank ya. Thank ya so much."

As they gained the stairs, Troy never released her hand. Once in the lobby, the men spread out with Hassan, Akeel and Tyrell herding the approaching guests toward two large open doors. Everything was happening so fast, Francine couldn't think. Following Troy's lead, she allowed herself to be whisked onto an elevator with Levi and the crying woman. Francine was in the corner with her husband standing in front of her.

When the doors opened on the second floor, Levi waved the woman out first and then followed. Troy protectively stepped out next and then reached back for her. The doors closed smoothly behind them and with all the commotion gone, Francine could finally concentrate. The woman was brown skinned with eyes that were red and brimming with tears. She looked to be in her mid-forties with a poorly done weave that was brushed into a ponytail. The bridge of her nose was straight with nostrils that ballooned into what looked like a pear. She wore jeans and a gray t-shirt, and on her feet were black gym shoes–a hole in the left toe.

"This way," Levi said.

Against one wall were several glass offices and then an art gallery. In the center of the room were several partitions that sported large pictures representing black life. Each photo was something she had lived. In one black and white picture, two girls sat on a porch–one girl braiding the other's hair. There was yet another photo of a black family praying at the dinner table. Another picture showed black children in the summer running through water spraying from the fire hydrant–their goal to cool off. The lighting had an orange hue and the floors were hardwood. The place was beautiful.

Levi picked the first office, ushering them all inside. He handed the box of tissue on the sleek chrome desk to the woman and waited. When she calmed, he spoke.

"I'm Sean Bryant, I'm an attorney. What's your name?"

"Ursula Howard," she whispered.

"You live here in North Carolina?" Levi asked.

"Naw, I live in Austell, Georgia. My boyfriend drove me here. We was hopin' to ask for help from the Silent Activist." She eyed Troy.

"What's your son's name?"

"My son is Julius Howard, and he's a good boy. He ain't never been in no trouble. Julius been charged with trying to kill someone and having a gun. They ain't told me who he tried to kill or why."

"Who is his lawyer?" Levi continued.

"They give him a public lawyer, but he don't answer the phone. I ain't been able to see Julius. The lawyer is named Theodore Hanna."

"How old is your son?"

"Julius just turned eighteen." Ursula answered before she started crying again. "I been an addict and even sold myself on the street. The boy the only good shit I ever done. My mama raised him, mostly, until she died. This is killing me."

"I can't make any promises, but I'll look over the case." Levi pushed a notepad at her. "Write all your contact information down and take my card. I'll be back in Georgia by tomorrow. My office will call you the day after."

Ursula flopped over, pressing her forehead to her knees. She sobbed uncontrollably. Francine felt her pain so acutely that she stepped forward and rubbed her back.

"Where is the ladies' room?" she asked, both Troy and Levi looked relieved that she was intervening.

Levi pointed. "By the elevators."

"Come, Ursula." Francine said, gently.

The white and yellow restroom smelled of lavender with a hint of vanilla. Ursula rushed straight into one of the four stalls; she could be heard hiccupping. When she collected herself, she came out and washed her face. She gathered two plush paper towels and patted her face dry. Ursula turned to Francine and fanned herself before speaking.

"I ain't think they would help me, but I had to try." More tears fell as they stared at each other. Francine smiled as the other woman took a steadying breath. "I'm ready."

"I'm not." Francine laughed, before pulling the silver handle and allowing Ursula out first.

Troy was waiting for her in the hall, his face pensive. Francine felt his tension as she moved forward and pressed against his side. Levi took charge.

"Ursula, is your boyfriend outside?"

"Yes, Earl is out front."

"The two of you will be my guests for the evening. Let's go find Earl. I hope he doesn't mind sharing his date for tonight."

Ursula's smile wobbled as she said, "Thank ya."

Turning to Troy, Levi said, "We're late."

Troy nodded as the elevator dinged and the mirrored doors slid open. They all got on, and after moments, the door opened again to a busy lobby. Akeel, Hassan and Tyrell were standing to the left of the entrance with a short dark-skinned man. The man pointed to Ursula, and they all began moving toward them. When they were close enough, Levi greeted the man.

"Earl, I'm Levi, and this is Troy."

"Hey, man," he said, shaking both Troy and Levi's hand.

Francine watched as Levi moved everyone toward the evening at hand. "This way."

Tables dotted the left side of the ballroom and on the right, the wood flooring was polished to perfection. A large screen and podium was set up in front of the tables, and dim lighting offered ambience. Well-dressed people laughed and huddled in clusters, and unlike the last event, there were white people in attendance. On the walls were more pictures with individual lights dancing over the huge frames.

One picture caught her eye, and Francine moved in closer to get a better view. It was of a black man walking along a white paved path toward an open gate. On either side of the path was a barbed wire fence. The sky was vibrantly blue, and behind the man loomed the Hoover State Penitentiary. The photographer caught the essence of *change*. Francine breathed in sharply as she recognized the man to be Troy; the photo was evocative.

She couldn't stop staring at him, it was as if she thought the Troy in the picture would speak. Francine wanted to touch the image to gain insight into the man he was now. Behind her, she felt his presence and turned to him. He did not acknowledge the photo, his eyes remained on her.

"We're about to start." He said, his voice low.

Placing his hand on the small of her back, he led her to a table down front. Already seated were Ursula, Earl and the other men—minus Levi. Francine found herself sitting between Tyrell and Troy. The crowd hushed as everyone settled in. Levi walked slowly to the podium, and the screen behind him lit up with the words: Welcome to the Black Think Tank

Levi smiled when he addressed the group. "Good evening, beautiful people, I'm happy you all came out."

The crowd clapped, and he adjusted the mic, giving them a moment to quiet. Levi's voice boomed as he opened the night. "We have seen much progress in our endeavors and tonight, we will bask in our accomplishments. So, let us dive in."

There was more applause as the message on the screen behind him changed. A bullet point agenda appeared, and Levi continued. "We have collected one-hundred and fifty thousand dollars toward our new finance scholarship to push black youth toward financial health. As you all know, my aunt – Troy's mother, Minnie J. Bryant died shortly after his incarceration. And tonight, I am pleased to announce the Minnie J. Bryant Scholarship is in full effect."

Francine stared at Troy's profile. He stiffened at the mention of his mother; still, his attention stayed on his cousin. The handclapping started and faded swiftly. Levi beamed. "We have partnered with several black owned businesses to offer jobs to men and women newly released from jail. Our goal is to help folks get back on their feet. The Second Chance Program works because of places like Carmichael's Import/Export, Ebony's Hair and Makeup, Lucy's Diner and Tammy's Temp Service. Last, but not least, we are also thankful to Chuck's Janitorial Services and Jones Automotive. These establishments employ more than three hundred men and women who are making change. We add stipends to some of the jobs, allowing people to make money that will provide a real life."

Levi paused and looked about. "In conjunction with the Second Chance Program, the organization encourages all participants toward other assistance programs. We help folks prepare for the G.E.D. and beyond. We will help at any level. If someone can't read, we will teach them. The organization has the resources, and we will share. All of you here tonight make change possible, and you all deserve a pat on the back."

Conversation broke out around the room from Levi's last statement, and he raised his hands to gain control. "Before I turn the evening over to Troy, there is one more group I want to thank. Our volunteers are a special breed of dedicated men and women who give selflessly to the literacy program. We appreciate them every hour of every day."

The crowd stood and clapped, thunderously. "Please welcome Troy."

Francine felt his hand brush over her bare thigh and squeeze lightly before he stood heading for the podium. She stared straight ahead, praying Tyrell didn't see the exchange. As Troy approached, Levi reached out and shook his hand before leaning in to whisper something in his ear. Her husband nodded as he moved around his cousin to the microphone.

The room grew quiet as Troy looked about. He cut quite the figure of sex, menace and ripe masculinity. His back was straight, his attire elegant but not flashy. He exuded power, and Francine could feel the audience collectively holding their breath. Ironically, her husband was an arresting man, and everyone present was prisoner to his brooding charm. When he finally spoke, his voice was the equivalent of an iron fist–dressed in a velvet glove.

"Good evening, everyone."

"Good evening," The crowd returned.

"You're all probably wondering what Levi said to me." Troy's words were slow, his face serious. "He has informed me that I can't light a cigarette and absolutely no profanity."

The crowd laughed and while what Troy said was funny, Francine noted that he was annoyed. It was in the lines around his eyes and the stiffness of his body. Next to her, Levi chuckled then shook his head. Tyrell leaned over her, addressing Levi.

"You know he hates speakin'. Why you gotta piss him off?"

"My bad," Levi answered.

Troy pulled a pack of cigarettes from his pocket, tapped the bottom twice and then lit one. A young man from the waitstaff ran forward with an ashtray. Troy inhaled slowly and exhaled audibly. Francine looked around at the hypnotized crowd. He took another pull before laying the cigarette down. His eyes bounced around the room.

"Shall we get shit started?"

There was more laughter, and someone yelled out. "You got married, Troy, and didn't introduce your wife to us."

"I guess I have been remiss."

An older black gentleman seated at a table next to theirs shouted. "My wife has been inconsolable, son. She was hoping to leave me for you."

The older woman next to him simpered. Troy chuckled. "My wife may decide to give me away, so all hope is not lost, Ms. Priscilla."

The woman shook her head and giggled. Francine did not laugh because she knew what was coming. Troy gave a curt nod of his head, and Levi pushed back from the table. He moved behind her chair and she allowed him to help her stand. Placing his hand at the small of her back, he marched her over to Troy. Francine was shaken to the center of her person.

Stepping away from the microphone, Troy reached out and hugged her. In her ear, he murmured, "You're safe, I promise."

"I know," she whispered in return.

"I didn't introduce you the last time because I knew you would hate it. I can't get away with it this time."

Francine realized he was speaking to her while the crowd waited. When she looked up into his eyes, he was smiling. He kissed her, and behind them was a shared *awwww*. Troy turned her to face the crowd, his fingers twined with her own.

"Ladies and gentlemen, this is my sweet wife, Francine Marie Bryant."

The crowd applauded, and a female voice asked, "Where did you all meet?"

Troy was a bold man, and Francine knew what he was going to say before he opened his mouth. "I stole her right off the streets of Atlanta."

"You're awful," Francine said.

Levi came out onto the floor and ushered her back to her seat. Once she was settled, the screen lit up with the words: Black on Black Crime

And just like that, Troy successfully steered the evening back to the matter at hand. The gathering grew quiet as his rusty voice reverberated around the room.

"I often receive correspondence from businesses explaining why our Second Chance Program wouldn't be a good fit for them. Often, we are encouraged to check back in the future and at times, we have gone on to make great partnerships. Our organization understands that working with a program like this one is not for the faint at heart. Still, the goal is to offer people who have made nonviolent mistakes an opportunity to move forward."

Discussion exploded around the room, and Troy waited. When everyone simmered down, he continued, "I get plenty of hate mail, but one letter caught and held my attention. The letter writer cites black on black crime and drug use as the reason for the woes in our community. I contemplated the concept and wondered if as contributors you all felt the same–at one time or another."

"Can I get a show of honest hands, please?" Troy paused, though his eyes kept moving.

Francine looked around, and almost every person in the room had their hand up. At the front of the room, Troy spoke again. "Ah, so you all have hope, or you wouldn't be here."

He had changed the dynamic and energy of the event. His words caressed the spectators creating intimacy. "I won't debate black on black crime, but I do have a story to tell. Many of you may not be aware that I am originally from Brooklyn, New York. My father died young, leaving my mother to raise me and my younger sister alone. When I turned ten and my sister eight, my family came to Georgia. My mother wanted to move us out of Brooklyn to a slower paced life. She wanted out of the ghetto. As a man, I now realize her concern was for me, her son, a young black male."

He stopped speaking as if to give everyone time to catch up. "Naturally, we went back to visit friends and family, regularly. As time passed, each visit found more and more of my male friends and cousins locked up. The charges ranged from muggings to drug possession and even murder. My mama felt like she had dodged a bullet by getting us out. But when I was old enough to start moving around Atlanta as a teen, I was shocked to find there was a ghetto there too—filled with black people. I thought the ghetto was in New York, so I wasn't sure why we moved."

Troy sighed before going on. "My sister and I complained about missing friends and family, so my mother bought us a fish tank to give us something to focus on. The project was elaborate in that my mama purchased the fish based on an ecosystem. She wanted the tank to be self-cleaning according to the fish we picked. Some of the fish were scavengers, others ate the algae off the sides, and still, others kept the top of the tank clean. It was beautiful. Monica and I spent a lot of time choosing the fish; we even did our homework in front of the aquarium. The fish lived in a silent harmony, and it was perfection to watch. There were about twenty fish in the tank, if I remember correctly."

Francine hated learning about him this way, but she was fascinated, nonetheless. Troy smiled at the memory before he began again. "Summertime rolled in, and we were headed to Brooklyn to be with family. Mama paid Mrs. Phillips from across the way to come by once every other day to feed the fish. She was a sweet old lady, and she was happy to help. Our aquarium was safe with her. We were gone from the first week of July until the first week in August."

Troy stepped back from the podium and shoved his hands in his pockets. His voice became deeper. "When we made it back to Georgia, my mama went to Mrs. Phillips first to get our key. Sadly, we found out that Mrs. Phillips had a stroke a few days after we left, and she had been in the hospital the entire time we were gone. When Mama opened the front door of our house, Monica and I raced straight for the tank. Inside the aquarium was one fish, and it was dead."

Individual conversation broke out and then quieted. Troy rocked back on his heels as he waited for the audience to follow. "My mama didn't want to say that the fish ate each other in order to survive. But the reality of this story is when the basic needs of life for the fish stopped being met–anarchy ensued. When opportunity in the form of food ceased, so too did the utopia we created. Why would people be any different?"

"This country has set the right conditions for ghetto life." He looked around. "The media is then sent in to record the results, reporting only half truths. I shouldn't have to say this, but I would be negligent if I didn't. All races commit crimes against their own. People perpetrate corruption where they are most comfortable. Statistically, black on black crime is no higher than any other race. It's prejudice that keeps a slanted black experience in the forefront of the nightly news. This tactic is meant to douse hope, but again, you are all here. You have seen past your fear and that's a start."

Troy moved from behind the podium, leisurely walking back and forth. He was pulling the crowd further under his spell. "Unfortunately, after all my mother did to save me, I still ended up in prison for a crime I didn't commit, and she died never knowing that I had regained my physical freedom."

The crowd took to their feet applauding as the waiters began bringing out the food. People immediately flocked to Troy to speak with him about one thing or another. While he wasn't as large a man as Levi, he was still a big man. He towered above most of the folks gathered around him and over their heads, he locked eyes with her. His facial expression offered the smallest amount of sadness, and she was sure it was because of the memories of his family.

Levi and Akeel left their seats and made their way over to Troy. They smiled, chatted and surgically removed him from the crowd. Troy came back to the table, seating himself next to her. There was no conversation between them. Suddenly, a waiter appeared, placing two plates on the table. The meal consisted of steak, asparagus and baked potato. Troy didn't eat, instead he answered questions from guests who wanted more from him.

Francine wasn't serious about her own food either, and instead, listened to the sidebar discussions happening. Several chats ended with more donations to the Second Chance Program and the different scholarships. When the music started, it seemed Troy could take no more. He stood, then helped her from her chair.

"Let's make our escape. We have a long ride home."

She noted the strained lines around his mouth and his tired eyes. He maneuvered them toward the doors where Akeel, Tyrell and Hassan were standing. Troy spoke briefly with the men, and they all walked her to the restroom in the small alcove behind the elevators. Francine rushed inside, worried the men could hear as she relieved herself. Everything echoed in the hollow sounding restroom. She splashed water on her face before heading back out to the hall.

When she stepped from the bathroom, Troy was exiting the restroom as well. She was beyond embarrassed that she needed this many escorts. Her husband was trying to make certain she felt safe, but she was going to have to make change. Still, while having them all in the hall was uncomfortable, it was better than thoughts of being abducted. She had to regain her mental freedom, and she had no clue how to go about it. A therapist was out of the question—what could she say? Two men tried to kill me, but Ernest killed them, then forced me to marry him.

Levi joined them as they moved toward the entrance. There were more people out front than when they first entered the building. Some of the folks called Troy's name and he waved, but the men kept them moving to where Butch waited with the limo. Francine was pleased when the car door closed behind them and the vehicle pulled slowly away from the event.

Inside the limo was her favorite pair of black leather flip-flops, a red t-shirt and a blue pair of shorts. She folded her blue cocktail dress and placed her black heels in the corner. Troy unbuttoned his shirt, pulling the tails from his trousers. He stared out the window, and she knew he was trying to disconnect from her and the entire evening; the notion made her sad. Francine didn't delay; she dived into conversation.

"Is your story about the fish tank true?"

"You plannin' on interviewing me?" he snapped.

"Correct me if I'm wrong, but didn't you establish the rule: You can't answer a question with a question?"

She sat opposite him in the darkness of the back seat, chilled from the air conditioner and pulled a small blanket around her shoulders. Outside, the street lights played with the angles of his face. He turned from the window, allowing her access. She didn't look away, but she left the burden of dialogue on him.

"Yes, the fish tank story is true."

"What happened to Mrs. Phillips?"

He sighed. "She died shortly after we made it back from New York."

"When I was seven, my mom and dad took us to a fair in upstate New York. I wasn't all that happy about it. They sat me on a camel, and it slobbered on my new jacket. It stank too, now that I think about it. Then, Jennifer pushed me, and I almost fell in a large pile of shit. The whole thing is just one bad memory."

Troy was quiet, but the outline of his body showed he was interested. His frame was less stiff as she continued with her story. "My dad won me some goldfish—four to be exact. Jennifer was jealous, but that's a story for a different day."

He chuckled. "Ah, insight into what makes you tick."

She giggled. "My mom put them in a bowl, and I couldn't take my eyes off them—the first day."

"And the second day?"

"The second day, I turned the bowl up to my mouth and drank all the water—poop and all. My dad spanked me and then flushed the fish down the toilet. I still feel some kinda way."

"What happened to your dad?"

"He left, and my grandmother moved in to help my mother. She died when I was eighteen. It was like being brokenhearted twice—once for my mom and once for us. My nana was wonderful."

"Why didn't you tell me before I kissed you that you drank fish shit?" he asked, straight-faced.

"I told you not to marry me." She said, unapologetically. "But you like it dirty, so I really didn't think it would have mattered."

He was quiet, as if contemplative. "I see your point."

"It's not like you didn't have choices. Ms. Priscilla is inconsolable after all."

The highway was well lit, but they remained cast in obscurity. His laugh was easy. "You jealous?"

Troy's voice rubbed against her skin, seductively; the smell of Egyptian Musk oil caressed her senses. Women wanted him, and she knew it. Francine looked out the tinted window and sighed. She was edgy about Karyn, but she hadn't seen her this evening.

"No. I'm pointing out your options."

"I appreciate your thoughtfulness." The timbre of his chuckle was low—erotic.

"You hate the speaking engagements. Why do you do them?"

He was quiet for several heartbeats. Francine thought he wasn't going to respond, but then he did, and she was sorry she asked. "I do the events to stay alive."

He wasn't overexaggerating and Francine was sure she didn't want to know anything more. Still, she asked. "How do the speaking engagements keep you alive?"

"The events keep me before the public eye. I don't like the press, but they make it hard for my enemies. The media also keeps my enemies safe from me for now... I had decided against doing anymore events, but then you came into my life. I want you, so I am not as preoccupied with my own death."

"I don't understand." Desperation laced her voice. "Please, Troy, show me who you are."

She was trying to figure out her feelings for him. But he was letting her know that he welcomed his own demise.

She sat at the edge of the seat opposite him. Outside, the countryside rushed by in shadowed figures. The muscles in her body contracted and released with the effort of balancing herself as the limo glided down the highway. Troy leaned forward, placing his elbows on his knees. His posture was intimate, but not sexual. She needed to see more of him—the parts light couldn't reach.

"You know me, Francine, better than most."

"Better than most is not good enough, Troy. We're stuck in this together, but it's not unreasonable for me to want to know my husband."

"Are you trying to understand me, or are you trying to comprehend why you want a man who *would…*" he stopped speaking as if to suspend the word *"would"* between them, "kill your mother and sister if you tried to leave him?"

The connection between them felt fragile, yet unbreakable. He was attempting to intimidate and antagonize, so he could regulate the direction of the conversation. She closed her eyes to give herself a moment. Reaching out, she touched his lips with the tips of her fingers, and then stroked his cheek. She brushed her palms gently against his goatee, enjoying the prickly sensation before pulling him close to press the tip of her nose to his. The act was beyond intimate as she inhaled drowning in his nearness.

"I'm trying, Troy—you're not." She whispered, before kissing his nose.

Abruptly, he sat back out of her reach, his body ramrod straight. He was stepping away from the softness, attempting to cut off all roads to gentleness. She felt the loss but moved back to settle in the corner by the door.

"I think we need to set another rule between us."

"You don't make the rules," He snapped.

"The new rule: You're not allowed to try to intimidate me to get out of speaking the truth to me." Francine said, her attitude blossoming. "I see what you're doing. You're starting a fight on purpose."

"Am I?" he asked, condescendingly.

"Hell wit' you, Troy—The. Hell. Wit'. You."

"Watch your mouth," he countered.

She turned her back on him and stretched out on the seat. Pulling her blanket around her, she dozed off, effectively ignoring his rude ass. They still had about four hours of travel, but she wouldn't spend it dealing with his spitefulness. His mood swings were unsettling and meant to keep her off kilter. Francine refused to play the game. She would disconnect and feign indifference. Those were her last thoughts before sleep claimed her.

3

BACK TO BUSINESS

They had been riding for two hours with Troy staring at Francine's back for an hour and fifteen minutes. His wife was correct in her assessment of him. He had started a fight to shut down communication between them. Troy didn't want to discuss his family, and he didn't want to talk about himself. He did, however, need to make her aware of how things would be going forward.

Butch stopped at a designated gas station, but he didn't come to open the door. Three pumps over, Jesse pulled the other limo up and parked. Reaching out, Troy rubbed her back as he spoke her name.

She stirred, and then woke. "Are we home already?"

"No, we're at a rest stop. Come."

Troy watched as she pushed her feet into her flip flops. He opened the door–got out, then turned back to help her out. Her smaller hand was cold and shaky in his as they moved across the parking lot to the entrance of the store. Stubbs was a major gas station chain with a diner attached. Truckers frequented establishments like this for food and showers. It was a smart stop as a black man.

In his side view, he saw Hassan and Tyrell making for the entrance as well. It was quarter past midnight, but the rest stop was moderately busy and well-lit with a count of fifteen pumps. The weather was hot and sticky, yet inside the store was freezing. He moved them through the maze of cookies, potato chips and candy to an aisle with t-shirts and umbrellas. In a little alcove, a neon sign read: Bathrooms.

Tyrell and Hassan didn't speak, but Hassan stayed in the corridor between the men's room and the ladies' room. Tyrell continued on to the stalls while Troy followed Francine into the ladies' room.

"You can't be in here," she hissed at him.

There were at least ten stalls lined up against the far wall with ten sinks. The bathroom was beige and not well lit like the rest of the store. He bent down to see if anyone was in the stalls, but there were no feet in front of the toilets.

"Go," he said, before stepping into the stall next to the one she entered. Troy could hear her tinkling and pulling off toilet paper. The sound of him relieving himself drowned out the sound of her finishing up. He gave himself a shake, fixed his trousers and stepped out to find his wife at one of the sinks. She washed her hands and splashed water on her face. Troy washed and dried his hands, then waited by the door.

When she finished, he pulled the door open, allowing Francine out first. Once back in the center of the store, he asked, "Is there something you want before we head out?"

"A chocolate bar."

Tyrell and Hassan left the store when Akeel and Levi entered. Troy stared down at Francine who was still ignoring him. Her hair was curly and a bit wild; she pulled it back in a ponytail as they waited in line to pay for her candy choice. In front of them were two black men closer to his wife's age. Both men were tall and thin. One man was light of skin–the other man was brown skinned. They noted his woman. Francine kept her head down, but Troy kept his eyes on them.

The brown skin dude stood sideways speaking with his friend who was facing forward. His eyes bounced to Francine several times, then finally up to meet Troy's glare. The youngster wore jeans with a tank top and expensive red sneakers. His homey was dressed the same, except his sneakers were black. When a second register opened, the line moved quicker. The men moved over to the other cashier, leaving he and Francine to a short, plump white woman with gray hair and thick glasses — her voice was cheerful.

"You two find everything ya need?"

Troy smiled, but Francine answered. "Yes, thank you."

"Is this gonna be it for you, hon?"

"A pack of Newport." Troy laid a twenty-dollar bill on the counter.

The cashier reached behind her, pulling the pack of cigarettes from the bottom shelf. Once she handed him the change and the cigarettes, he placed his hand on Francine's back, guiding her out to the muggy parking lot. As he moved them toward the limo, he noticed the two young men from the store standing in their path. The brown skin fellow stepped forward.

"You Troy Bryant, right?"

"I am."

"My brother was in prison with you. Terrence Carter, you prolly know him as Gun."

Troy stared at the younger man for a moment, the resemblance was clear. "Yes, I know Gun."

"Terrence says you still take care of him even though you back in the world. I see you on the news and all the good you doin'. I send him books when I can and newspaper clippings on how you livin'. Shit makes his day." He glanced at Francine. "Pardon me."

Levi stepped up behind him, and the tension Troy was feeling lessened. His cousin took Francine by the elbow and led her back to the car. Akeel, Tyrell and Hassan moved within earshot.

"What's your name?" Troy asked.

"Patrick Carter," he extended his hand to shake.

Troy smiled, it *was* Gun's youngest brother. Terrence Carter, also known as Gun, was doing life for a crime he *did* commit. The whole thing was some sad shit. His old cellmate–shot his baby mama in the head. Gun caught her with his best friend; he offed the friend too, then dropped the son he shared with the woman to his grandmother's house. It was a year before they caught him. He pled guilty and got life instead of the death penalty.

Troy sent him one care package a month. He wouldn't have survived without Gun and Butch. He offered little to the exchange, but he was glad to meet Patrick. Gun was proud of his little brother. The light skin dude he was with hovered in the background as if to give them privacy. Patrick leaned in and spoke softly.

"Gun say it was you who paid our mama's house off."

Troy smiled. Gun's mother ended up with his son. Ms. Pam came to him and thanked him. He also put lil Terrence in private school. The kid was smart based on his grades. Troy never met the boy or the rest of the family. He thought it best that way.

He didn't respond to Patrick's statement about the house, but he did give him his card. "Call me if ever you need me."

Troy clapped the younger man on the shoulder, then stepped around him headed for the limo and Francine. Butch and Jesse were the last to use the restroom before they hit the road. Thirty minutes passed with no words from his wife, only the rustling of the candy wrapper as she popped small pieces of chocolate in her mouth. When he could take no more, he moved to the middle of his seat and plucked her onto his lap. She squeaked and then settled sideways against his chest, her face pressed into the crook of his neck.

Francine's skin smelled of strawberries and her breath of chocolate. Troy loved the feel of her weight against him. But before his thoughts could turn sexual, his wife hit him with a question.

"Why did you decide to stop doing the events?"

Francine must have felt his body go rigid; she said, "I can go sit back by the door if you want to be left alone."

He tightened his grip on her. "I want you to sit with me."

Her head popped up, bumping him on the underside of his chin. "Do you want a real marriage with me, Troy?"

Francine was telling him in no uncertain terms, if he wanted a real marriage, he better answer her damn questions. Her breath was warm and sweet as the scent of chocolate lingered between them. He felt her lips brush his cheek as she spoke. Angling his head, he kissed her, but she pulled away. He knew he was being an ass, but he didn't want to upset and worry her. Telling her anything beyond what he'd already told her would trouble her, and he didn't want more anxiety for her.

"I backed away from the organization even though I was still funding it. There were issues I wanted to address faster than the group could afford. But my own frustrations…" he sighed. "I thought to leave the other men blameless is what I'm trying to say."

"The situation with me—sidetracked you from your goal." Francine stated rather than asked.

"When I ended up with you, I decided to bide my time." Troy explained, before adding. "I had cancelled several engagements, and Levi made excuses. After you, I resumed my schedule to keep the peace. The men were angry with me before you."

"You were separating from the organization—to do what? What did my falling into your life stop?"

"Enough for now, Francine. I don't want to answer any more questions."

It was his wife's turn to sigh. He thought he was off the hook until she said, "In the store, you thought those guys were interested in me, but it was you they recognized."

He didn't want to talk anymore, but Francine wasn't done. "The guy said you still take care of his brother even though you're not in prison."

"I send him a care package once a month."

"When is this Terrence getting out?"

"He's not."

"Oh… Is that why you take care of him?"

He chuckled, but there was no humor. "No, I take care of Terrence because at the lowest point of my life, he took care of me. Gun and Butch took me under their wing. I got the shit beat out of me regularly for the first year, and I almost starved to death from getting my food taken by the other inmates."

It was more than he intended to divulge, but his wife seemed undaunted. "Do you think one day, I'll be strong like you, Troy? I gotta start doing things by myself—like using the damn public bathroom. The men are right, I'm too weak for you."

Her question made his chest tight. "You're not weak, and no other man's opinion matters but mine."

Francine snuggled close, dozing off in his arms. He wasn't strong, his anger had been the only thing holding him together—until her. His wife was young, this had to be why she couldn't see his frailties. He held her until they pulled onto his property. It was four in the morning and still dark when he woke his wife.

Butch opened the door, and Troy stepped from the car still holding

Francine. She wrapped her arms around his neck while nuzzling into him. "I can walk, ya know," she whispered.

"You want me to put you down?"

"No."

The Georgia weather was oppressively hot, even at this hour of the morning. It was pitch dark and the lighting around the house did nothing to break the spell. As he moved up the path carrying his wife, he saw Jewel standing on the small stone porch. She looked anxious, and Troy figured it was because she missed Butch. When he reached the stairs, Jewel was jumpy.

"Good morning, Troy–Francine, we have unexpected company."

Jewel moved back, opening the front door before he could ask what she was talking about. He stepped into the house to find that they did indeed have guests. Francine wriggled in his arms, causing him to let her down as he stood facing the woman and boy standing in the middle of the water colored area rug. The woman looked unsure and tired, the boy looked nervous yet protective of her. She was thin with black skin, an untamed head of hair and stiff posture. Her eyes watered upon seeing him.

The boy was bright skinned with dark brown eyes and eyebrows that were pressed together as if deep in thought. His hair was cut close and his face was round. He didn't smile nor did he fidget. He looked to be about ten, but he was big for his age. Troy hadn't seen him since he was a newborn, but he would know him in a crowd. The child was dressed in an orange t-shirt with black jeans. Neither he nor the woman wore shoes.

They all must have been waiting for him to speak, but he couldn't find the words. Francine whispered, "Troy."

He cleared his throat. "Francine, this is my sister Monica and my nephew Akeel. Family, this is my wife Francine."

"Hello, Francine, nice to meet you. I was hurt to find out that Ernest got married and didn't invite me." His sister gestured at him with her hands.

"It's nice to meet you, Monica. My own mother and sister were upset about the same thing. Please forgive us. I'm glad you're here."

His sister's voice was tremulous, and Troy wished the floor would swallow him whole. "Akeel, this is your Uncle Ernest."

"Hey, Uncle Ernest." The boy said in a low uncomfortable tone.

Troy stepped forward and shook his little hand. He was so manlike for a kid, and he looked just like his father. "Hey, little man. It's nice to meet you."

"Yes, sir."

"This is your Aunt Francine."

"Hello, Auntie."

"Hey, Akeel. How old are you?" Francine asked, and Troy was thankful for the distraction she offered.

"I'm nine," he answered, minus any elaboration.

Troy felt it, the boy was worried about his mother. Francine must have sensed it too, she was cheerful when she asked. "Akeel, I was going to make myself a peanut butter and jelly sandwich. Would you like to help me?"

The boy wouldn't look at Francine, he kept his eyes on his mother. Monica turned to the child and pulled him into her embrace. "We talked about this, remember? Uncle Ernest looks mean, but he would never ever hurt me. He's my brother."

Akeel turned his gaze on him. The boy was skeptical, leaving Troy no choice. "No, I wouldn't hurt your mother."

Francine placed her arm around Akeel's shoulders, propelling him toward the hall, and Jewel followed. When they were alone, Monica faced him, and her words caused him physical pain.

"You and Akeel turned your backs on us while in prison. Since you both regained your freedom, neither of you deal with me or my son. You refused my visits and he..."

Troy stared at his sister, her misery visible. He took a deep breath. How could he explain that they disassociated from her to keep her safe? He nor Akeel wanted her to experience loss again on their behalf. They certainly thought their absence would be better for the boy. Akeel tried to give Monica most of the money he received from the state, but she refused. Troy had tried the same, but his sister penned him a note saying she missed her brother.

Monica had been living with an older man whom she planned to marry. After Akeel was released from prison, she called off the wedding and moved out. Troy knew it was because she still loved her son's father. His friend had been devastated by the thought of her in another man's arms, but he stayed away. They were no longer the same men.

"Do you want me and my son to leave?"

He was up in his head and wasn't participating in the conversation. Still, he was honest. "No, I don't want you to leave. But you gotta know Akeel will come for you when he finds out you and the boy are here."

Monica didn't respond about Akeel, but she did speak to the ache growing within him. "I don't blame you for anything. I always knew you were innocent. This wasn't your fault. Our mama would want us to stick together. I love you, Ernest, we're family."

"Shit, Monnie, I can't have this talk. Stay as long as you want, but no fuckin' talking."

His sister flinched at his words, and to his dismay, he felt no remorse. He wanted to stop her from pushing before he snapped. The man he had been would never have cursed in the company of his mother or sister. But the man he was now would steal a woman at the most vulnerable point in her life and threaten to kill her if he didn't get his way. He embraced the motherfucker he had become because while he was emotionally weak, he was no one's physical victim.

His sister wanted to discuss their mother, their past—his murder convictions, and he could not. The notion panicked him. He was overstimulated from the speaking engagement and warding off Francine's questions. Now, Monica was picking at all the same scabs, and she had more knowledge than his wife. Suddenly, he needed Francine. He was about to explode.

Monica stood in the center of the living room, blocking his way into the rest of the house. He almost backtracked out the front door and around to the garage. They were at a quiet standoff and it occurred to him that Monica may not be who he remembered. The truth is her story had merit as well, after all she had been through as a new mother, freshly in love and looking to the future. In the blink of an eye, their mother died, her brother was locked up for crimes he didn't commit and Akeel, her lover was snatched from her in much the same way. Troy shocked them both when he started yelling.

"Francine! Francine! Francine!"

Monica jumped but didn't speak. Francine came rushing back into the living room, followed by Jewel and the boy. His nephew immediately searched for Monica, relief flooding his feature when he found her unharmed. They all stood staring at him as if he'd lost his mind. In the hallway behind Jewel, Butch waited for instruction. But it was Francine he addressed.

"Please help my sister and nephew get settled."

Troy didn't give Francine a chance to comment, instead he stepped past everyone and headed for the master suite. Once inside, he shucked his clothes, tossing everything onto the huge four poster bed. He began pacing, yet the action alleviated nothing because of his restriction to the bedroom. As he circled the space, even adding the bathroom for distance, Troy realized why the room seemed smaller. At his request, Butch had moved a fifty-inch television in to surprise Francine. He wanted to open the door and shove the damn thing into the corridor. The irrational gripped him, and he couldn't think his way out of it. He lit a cigarette and inhaled deeply–Monica had him cornered.

It was after dawn when his wife stepped into their room. Francine went about undressing and dressing for bed without looking at him. It annoyed him that she planned to sleep in a t-shirt and panties. He waited for her to acknowledge his presence, but she continued to ignore him. She went into the bathroom, and after a time, he heard the toilet flush, the water begin running and what sounded like her brushing her teeth. When she reappeared, she moved to the bed, pulling back the thick burgundy covers. She was about to climb in when he called an end to being disregarded.

"Why the hell are you mad at me? Surely after your sister's shit, you understand where I'm coming from."

"Jennifer came to an event uninvited with a man I don't want to be bothered with. I worried you would kill her–cutting her out of my life was partly to keep her safe."

"You telling me you fucked me in the limo to save Jennifer." There was no inflection in his voice. He couldn't hide his pain.

Francine dropped the blanket and instantly moved to stand before him. He folded his arms over his chest to keep from touching her. The light of day was gradually brightening, leaving his wife bare to his scrutiny. She didn't look away when she spoke.

"My sister caused you to be arrested. I was upset with her for hurting you, but I feared your reaction to her actions. *Partly* is the word to concentrate on—I cut her out of my life only *partly* to keep her safe."

"What is the other part—the other reason?" His question cracked like a whip.

Unlike his sister, Francine didn't shrink away from him. "I'm in love with you, Troy, and it's complicated. I don't want you interacting with my mother and sister because I don't want to deal with the guilt of loving you. I cut Jennifer out because I'm not who she knew me to be and because I'm in love with the man who stole me from my life. I shared my body with you because I needed you—then and now. Jennifer's ignorance can only add grief to this situation. I already submitted to you, Troy, I can't go back."

"So, you still don't trust me around your mother and sister?"

"No, and it comes with responsibly loving you and them."

"Why are you mad at me, Francine?"

"I'm upset with you because your sister came with a child who is nervous for his mother. I get it. Monica gets it, but Akeel doesn't understand. Stop being an ass, Troy."

When Francine made to walk away, desperation overtook him. He reached for her, needing to stop her dismissal. "Please, baby, I'm sorry."

She looked up at him and whispered, "You need sleep."

He released her arm and climbed into bed after her. Francine tried to turn away, but he pushed her flat on her back and propped himself up on an elbow. "Can I have some pussy, please?"

"Yes."

Troy felt clingy in light of her confirmation of love. What fascinated him was his need for softness from her, yet he didn't know how to articulate such a longing. Francine lay on her back, staring up at him and he wondered if his true anguish were evident. Did his wife see his emotional fatigue—brought on by the speaking engagement, the long drive home, the unwanted memories and the coincidence of his sister and nephew's arrival? He hoped she could grasp his full misery, it would weaken him further to have to explain.

Francine sat up, pulling her shirt over her head, then wriggled out of her panties. When she settled on her side, she reached out and caressed his cheek. He closed his eyes reveling in her touch. Every prison recollection made him belligerent and sexually aggressive, but this morning he was too weary to entertain his baser self. He could feel the spent time that, unlike money, couldn't be earned back. Troy could acutely feel the disconnect where all the important relationships in his life were abruptly severed, only to be replaced by violence, incarceration and lies.

He realized that his wanting to be physically connected to her was not about sex. The reason was elementary. Troy was sad, and he wanted Francine to hold him. He wanted his wife to make shit better. This trait in a woman—in his wife—made his masculinity potent, but this same trait in a man—in him made him bitch-like. While he wrestled with this thought, Francine got on her knees next to him. The air conditioner chilled the room, leaving goosebumps on her skin. Her puckered nipples, flat belly and pleasing thighs made him swallow hard. She was alluring and when she spoke, to his surprise, his eyes smarted.

"I love you, Troy."

She understood what he needed, but he feared closing his eyes. He worried if the tears started, he wouldn't be able to stop them. His first year in prison, he had cried in the wee hours unable to believe his circumstance. The second year, he had dried up, accepting that only the fittest of the fit survived. But in this moment, with his wife, he was nothing but the kid who had been wrongfully convicted. He didn't respond—it was safest for his manhood.

Francine, it appeared, wasn't looking for a verbal exchange. She leaned over him and began placing hot, open mouthed kisses on his belly and chest. He turned his head toward the window and the sunlight slanting though the portal. His brain had gone foggy; he needed a moment, but she whispered, "No, Troy."

She scooted up the bed and cupped his face. Apparently, there would be no disengaging from himself or what she was offering. She brushed the tip of her nose against his before kissing his entire face. The act was so affectionate that without warning, a sob broke from his chest.

"Fran-cine…"

"Shhhh."

He sat up abruptly, pushing her against the pillows. She opened her legs, and he stared down at her in awe. It was the glint of the morning sun, her chocolate skin, and his need to be comforted that kept him emotionally and physically befuddled. Earlier, in the limo he had tried to hide from intimacy, but Monica's presence forced his hand. When his vision began to blur, he leaned forward pressing his face between her neck and shoulder. She wrapped her legs and arms around him, but he didn't enter her. He was unmanned from the contact. Troy didn't sob audibly, but he did cry hard to the point of depletion.

Francine made a small noise that punctured the haze of his shame. He pulled back and grunted, then flipped them onto their sides to remove the brunt of his weight from her. But she curled right into him, not giving him a chance to withdraw. She used her thumbs to wipe the tears from his face, and he closed his eyes. It was all too much. He moaned when she pushed her tongue into his mouth. She was being strong for him, and he was thankful.

She gently flipped him onto his back and straddled him; his erection nuzzled up against her wet folds. He was suspended between his grief and his need. Troy felt exposed, and he resented being forced into sharing this part of himself. But he was also mesmerized when Francine reached down between them and angled his hard on, so she could ease onto him. She had to work her way down his thick shaft, and he gritted his teeth while trying to maintain. Melancholy, rage and ecstasy danced through his veins; the combination almost caused him to spill his seed like an untried adolescent.

It was the contraction of her knees and thighs along his hips as she sat bestride him. Undeniably, it was also the feel of her ass seated flush against his groin and the feel of his dick buried within her to the hilt that caused him to shake. A light sheen of perspiration covered his body as his wife placed her palms flat against his chest and began rolling her hips.

"Not gonna last, baby—easy... shit." He groaned.

"Ohhh."

Troy couldn't get enough of his beautiful wife. He watched as her lips parted, eyes fluttered shut and her tits bounced in concert with the rolling of her hips. And still, more tears fell from him; he could no longer control the pain that shook loose and resonated in his soul. Francine leaned forward, rubbing her clit against the roughness of his lower belly, changing the angle of sensation. But his undoing came when she opened her eyes, revealing enlarged pupils; Francine was dazed.

She pressed her chin to her chest as pleasure overtook her, and it was fantastic to witness. This was a frail moment in his existence made extraordinary by their connection. When she gasped and orgasmed, she dragged him along. He felt her insides clamp down and seize before her head fell back in utter surrender. A moan ripped from deep within her–his wife's words scraped his ears.

"Troy... Troy, I'm so in love with you–so in love–so in love."

His climax was wrenched from him, and it was deliciously painful. Completion for him was a series of bright colors and the urgent colliding of their hips. But he wasn't the one in control, and for Francine, the orgasm was painstaking slow. She rocked on him unhurriedly, grinding her pussy down on him–clinching and releasing one stroke at a time. His wife milked him deliberately, lovingly–perfectly, until he was empty.

He groaned when she finally crumpled against him still whispering, "So in love with you, Troy."

Damn, he thought, before he burst out crying again.

4

EXECUTIVE DECISIONS
JULY 1995

I t was eleven p.m. when Troy climbed out of the silver Yukon parked at Sparks gas station off Old National Highway. Levi stepped from the driver's side along with Tyrell, who emerged from the front as well. Troy took in the scene before him as he headed for the entrance. Loud music thumped from a white Suburban with the hatch up and all the windows rolled down. On the side of the vehicle leaned a man with thick locks tied back from his jet-black face. He glared at Troy, and the air between them smelled of weed.

The parking lot was full of expensive cars and young black men standing about. The area was well lit and to the right of the entrance, seven men huddled together shooting craps. Some squatted and others stood as they watched the dice dance. There were sudden outbursts of cursing and bragging as money exchanged hands. At the left of the parking lot, several more dudes were paired off with young women, chatting. The Georgia weather was stagnant–hot.

Troy pulled the door open, and a bell chimed as he entered the establishment. Coolers lined the interior with the glass door farthest from the front of the store labeled "Beer." He surveyed the joint looking over the racks of cookies, potato chips, and candy. Next to the snack foods were dusty shelves of overpriced motor oil and canned soups. The pinball machine in the far-left corner was unplugged. The scent of incense and weed smelled like a felony in the making.

The lottery machine sat flush against the cash register with scratch tickets in a wide range of colors draped over both contraptions. On the back wall was an assortment of cigarette brands. Behind the bulletproof glass at the counter, a woman who looked to be about twenty stared at him. She was plump with chestnut brown skin and glassy round eyes; her dark hair was pulled back in a ponytail. The woman before him wore a black tank top-no bra and what he thought were denim shorts, given the counter obstructed his view. As Troy approached, she moved in as if anticipating his words.

Troy looked back to the parking lot to find Akeel and Hassan standing in front of the Benz, watching him. Tyrell was outside the door with only his back visible. At the back of the store, another door squealed on its hinges, and Troy turned his attention toward the advancing footsteps. Into his line of vision stepped a man of average height and thin build–his skin dark and his eyes red. Dude wore a blue t-shirt and faded jean shorts, on his feet were an expensive pair of sneakers. When he reached the end of the snack aisle, he grinned.

"Troy."

"Justice."

The man came forward, his hand outstretched to shake Troy's hand. "Been a minute."

"It has," Troy agreed.

Justice's dark skin was pockmarked; he was high, yet alert. While in lockup, they weren't friends, but neither were they enemies. In prison, Troy knew him to be ruthless, and it appeared nothing had changed, on his right hip a nine millimeter and on his left, a pager. The man oozed *careful,* and Troy paid heed. Interestingly, he felt more at ease with Justice than he did at an event.

"Where you wanna talk?" Justice asked.

Troy nodded toward the Yukon, and without words, Justice followed. When they stepped into the stillness of the Georgia heat, all eyes were on them. Turning to Justice, Troy asked, "Which one is she?"

Justice didn't respond; instead, he walked over to a group of people standing off to the side of the store. Troy saw him gesture their way as a cocoa skinned young woman stepped forward. She looked at him and Tyrell before she followed Justice over to where they stood.

"Troy, this is Jasmin Walker." Justice said.

"Jasmin."

"Hello, Mr. Bryant."

She looked at Tyrell first and then to the ground. Jasmin wore a yellow sundress that was wrinkled based on the bright lighting at the entrance of Sparks. She was afraid, and he couldn't miss her fear of Justice—it was clear she thought him dangerous. Troy gave her points for seeing Justice for what he was—cutthroat.

"Please, call me Troy," he said, while gauging the goings on around them. "Come to my truck."

He and Justice led the way with Tyrell bringing up the rear. When he glanced back at Tyrell, he observed Jasmin walking between them with her head down. At the Yukon, he opened the door allowing her to climb into the back seat. Her right sandal clamored to the ground as she got into the truck. Justice retrieved the leather shoe, handing it to her. She tossed it to the floor before her, while trying to smooth her dress over her thighs. It was as if she were trying to wipe away her own clumsiness and ward off the awkwardness happening.

The men didn't get into the truck with her, instead they formed a small circle at the door. Troy began the questioning, and Jasmin was receptive.

"How old are you?"

"I'm nineteen, Mr. Bryant."

"How long have you known Darrell Jenkins?"

"Me and Darrell been knowing each other since first grade. Darrell wouldn't kill nobody."

Levi chimed in. "What is your relationship to Darrell?"

She turned to look at Levi. "We been dating for about three years."

Troy found Jasmin to be sincere, not in her responses, but in her deportment. It was also clear this wasn't her scene. He would question her more in depth once they were away from Justice and Sparks nightlife.

"I take it you don't live far from here." Troy asked.

"No, sir. I live off Godby Road."

"Call me Troy, behind me is Levi, Tyrell, Akeel and Hassan." Jasmin nodded, and to Justice, he said, "We'll take her home."

Troy felt the inner conflict radiating from Justice. He didn't want to let her out of his sight, but he relented as if coming to an unspoken decision. He addressed the girl. "Don't come back. Troy will take it from here, and if I'm needed, he'll get wit' me."

"Thank you, Justice," Jasmin whispered.

Troy noted they both looked relieved to be done with the other. He suspected Jasmin wanted no contact with Justice because of her fear. Justice, on the other hand, appeared to want no contact, because he *desired* his cousin's woman. Reaching into his pocket, Justice pulled out two wads of cash—both were neatly wrapped with a rubber band. He compared the two and handed the thicker roll of cash to Jasmin.

"Justice... I live wit' my mama. I don't need..."

"Until Darrell is outta this shit, take the money. Troy will let me know the cost going forward."

Jasmin was going to refuse again when Justice bit out. "Jasmin, do what the fuck I say."

She looked to Troy for help, but he remained expressionless. Her hand shook as she held it out to Justice. He dropped the cash into her palm, careful not to touch her. When he turned to walk away, he stopped and spoke for Troy's ears only.

"I'll be here if she needs me. If you page me twice and I don't call you back, I'm dead."

The men dispersed with Akeel and Hassan driving off in the Benz. Troy got in the back seat with Jasmin, and Levi and Tyrell got in the front. As Levi pulled the truck away from Sparks, Troy watched Justice head back into the store. Assessing the scene once more, he concluded that there was no concern for the interference of law enforcement, which meant Justice had police permission to carry on as he did. He wondered which officers patrolled this area and turned a blind eye.

He and the men had been down several rabbit holes that led nowhere, but today was a breakthrough.

"Troy, I live down by the post office," Jasmin said.

"We're going to ride around for a little bit, so we can talk."

"Okay."

"Can you tell me the events leading up to Darrell's arrest?"

"My mama works at night. Darrell usually waits for her to leave and then he spends the night with me. He leaves my house around five in the morning for work. I called his mama's house later that evening when I didn't hear from him, but no one else heard from him either. The following morning, I got a call from Darrell. He said they were holding him for murder."

"When did you find out about Mr. Unger?"

"I saw the police in the neighborhood all day. Johnny lives about three blocks over from my mama's house. I knew something bad happened, but I thought he died. He old ya know."

"Johnny?"

"Mr. Unger—everyone called him Johnny." Her voice caught with emotion.

"So, you and Darrell knew the victim." Troy stated.

"Everyone knew Johnny, and honestly I can't think of anyone who would want to hurt him. Darrell surely wouldn't harm Johnny."

Troy noted the sorrow in her voice for the old man as well as her boyfriend. She was believable, still it didn't mean Darrell was innocent. He was about to ask her another question when she continued her thought.

"Johnny didn't have many visitors, but lately some of his family started coming around."

"Family?" Troy repeated, his eyebrows furrowed.

"This a black neighborhood—we notice when white folks come. His visitors were white—just assumed they were his family."

"Darrell's mama is distraught, but she's strong. She say we gotta keep this in front of the news, but..."

"But what?" Troy asked.

"I'm afraid that going to the news and making a ruckus might get Darrell killed in jail. Ms. Jenkins asked Justice to stay away. She says she don't want people to know he's related. Ms. Jenkins feels his presence will hurt Darrell's credibility."

Troy couldn't see Jasmin's face in the shadow of the backseat, but he knew she wanted his opinion. He didn't give advice in situations that might cause riffs and hurt the person incarcerated. He hadn't approached Darrell's mother, not while he was still trying to piece the puzzle together. In remembrance of his own mama, he didn't want to give false hope. But he would have to speak with Ms. Jenkins now that he made contact with Jasmin.

"You said Johnny had guests, how often?"

"I can't say how often—but I grew up in this neighborhood. Old man Johnny was alone, far as I knew, until a white man who drives a blue BMW started coming around. He had a woman and two little girls with him. Once he came with another white man who looked rough. This was last month—I only remember because they argued. I was walking to Darrell's house around seven o'clock one Saturday evening. A few people saw the exchange. The scruffy one walked away, cussing to himself. I told all this to Detective Logan."

At the mention of Logan, Troy asked, "Which house is yours?"

They parked in front of a small brick house with a lonely street light that did nothing to relieve the darkness. The insects were loud and behind them the Yukon idled at the curb. The front yard inclined slightly as they reached the porch. Jasmin maneuvered her way by familiarity, and he followed. She unlocked the front door and flipped on the foyer light, but Troy promptly reached in flipping the light off. He heard voices, even at this late hour, and gauged it to be about three porches away.

"That's old Ms. Joan and her sister, Ms. Vivian. They always sit on the porch in the early morning. Ms. Joan don't sleep well."

Still, the light remained off as he spoke. "We will reach out to Darrell's mother. Levi will keep you posted."

"I'm normally in school, but I haven't been attending since this happened. I can't function." She sniffled. "Please don't tell Darrell's mama that I reached out to Justice. She would be upset with me."

"Why did you reach out to him?"

"I thought since Justice did time, he might visit Darrell. I figured his presence would make Darrell's time easier if some of the inmates knew of the relationship. I didn't think he knew you—I didn't see this coming."

Troy was alarmed. He feared Jasmin stepping away from the reality of the situation. "Sweetheart... I..."

"I know, Mr. Bryant, but I still have to be in awe that you're here. I love

Darrell with all my heart and standing here with you makes me feel like I'm helping him."

Troy nodded, he had nothing to add. "We'll be in touch."

He didn't give her time to answer before he walked away. Levi pulled away from the curb and Tyrell said,

"The time is now, Troy."

All he could manage was, "Have Jesse watch that gas station." Tyrell was right.

* * *

It was three in the morning when Troy reached home. His sister and nephew were living with him now, and the situation was filled with tension. They both adored Francine, it was *him* they could do without. His wife had a way about her that made people want to be in her presence. She was even managing her own sister, and the three women got along famously. The added strain for him was his sister in-law, Jennifer stayed about three nights a week to be near Francine. She still didn't like him, but she behaved, and she did like Monica and little Akeel. It was strange, but now that Plan A was in effect, he felt better having them near to make certain they all were safe.

Akeel came every other day, and little Akeel was warming up to his father, but he avoided his uncle. Monica was polite to Akeel to help their son, but she avoided him on a personal level. Troy couldn't understand what Levi and Jennifer had going on, but there was a lot of comings and goings from his house. He stayed focused on Francine and the plan, everything else was background noise.

Troy parked crooked in front of his house and entered through the front door. There were no lights on in the living room, but as he reached the hall, he saw a light coming from the kitchen. The sound of a spoon hitting the inside of a cup came from the same direction. He followed the clinking sound and found Monica seated at the head of the table with a cup of hot tea. The rest of the high-backed chairs sat at attention like soldiers on either side of the table. She didn't look up when he filled the doorway. The night light from the hood over the stove made her appear even smaller in frame.

"The air conditioner in this house gets to be a bit much." She said and then added, "Francine just went to bed."

She was dressed in a white shirt with blue shorts and on her feet were fuzzy red socks. He stared at her, but Monica had not made eye contact since he cursed at her during their first exchange. She appeared more hurt by the interaction than afraid. He was about to turn and go to his room when she spoke again.

"I came here so Junior could get to know his father and uncle. It's been slow going between my son and his dad, but there is progress." Monica left unsaid that there had been no growth between him and his nephew. "Junior doesn't mind seeing his father without me. He can travel to his dad for the holidays and summers. I'll be leaving for New Jersey in a few days."

"Francine tells me you gave up your apartment."

"I did, and I now realize it was a mistake. I could have worked with my son and his father while still in Jersey."

"You are not allowed to go back to New Jersey, it's safer here. There are only two choices–stay in this house or with Akeel."

After such a statement, he expected her to look up at him, but Monica's gaze remained in her cup. When they were children, a conversation like this would have caused her to complain to their mama, and she would con-firm what he already knew–he wasn't her father. He almost smiled at the memory, but he couldn't trust her. If he let his guard down, she would want to speak about their mama and he wasn't ready. He would never be ready.

"I'm not afraid of you, Troy. I'll do what I want." Her penetrating eyes finally locked on him. "Save the intimidation for your wife and her sister. I'm not interested."

Troy's eyebrows shot up to his hairline, a reaction he meant to conceal. But he was calm when he said, "Akeel has backed off because you're in this house. If you try to disappear, it won't be me you have to contend with. My bullying is stretched thin between my wife and her sister. But I can say for certain you won't leave, or whatever progress your son and his father have made will evaporate. Especially, when the boy sees how aggressive his father can be over you."

When her eyes widened, he said, "Ah, so you see the change in Akeel, and he *does* scare you. You pushed for this, Monnie, and there's no going back."

"Fuck you, Troy and Akeel too," she whispered as her eyes fell back into her cup.

He chuckled. She was calling him Troy, acknowledging his changes; saying without saying that she didn't care for who he had become, but he was shocked at her use of profanity. "Watch your mouth, Monnie."

She kept her head down, and he felt the hurt too. He tried compromise. "I'll try harder…"

"You'll try harder at what, Ernest? You'll try to be meaner or will you try harder at ignoring me?"

"I don't wanna talk about Mama. Unless you go to Akeel, I don't want you and the boy to leave."

"How did you meet Francine?"

"Monnie…" He sighed.

"So—no talking about our mama *or* your wonderful wife."

"No."

He turned, headed for his room, when he heard her say, "I miss my Akeel. The man who comes to get our son is not him."

Troy hovered in the corridor on the edge of the entrance beyond the soft lighting. The clock on the wall to the left of him ticked loudly, denoting the vicious passage of time. He could offer no comfort, so he turned and walked away. Behind him, the clinking of the spoon in the cup resumed.

When he stepped into the privacy of their room, he began undressing. Francine was propped up on several pillows fast asleep. Once naked, he climbed in bed next to her, and she murmured his name. The day had been a long one, it felt good to hold his wife. He rested but sleep never happened.

It was 10:00 a.m. and though the curtains were drawn, the sun was still present in slivers that marked the edge of the room. He could hear voices and small feet running down the hall toward the living room. Troy also heard Francine gently admonishing his nephew.

"Akeel, no running. You're going to wake your uncle."

"Sorry, Auntie."

"It's almost time to go. You want to watch TV while you wait?"

"Yes. You gonna watch cartoons with me?" Akeel asked.

"Absolutely," Francine countered as they walked away.

Troy showered and shaved with purpose. He wanted to see his wife before his day started. Once dressed, he went in search of Francine. He found her in the kitchen laughing at his nephew. Akeel was dressed in blue denim shorts, a red tank top and blue sneakers. It seemed he was trying not to make a sour face but failing. His wife, on the other hand, couldn't stop giggling.

"I won, again," Francine said.

Akeel started laughing too. "The candy is too sour, Auntie. You ain't playing fair."

"I'll let you pick the candy next time."

Akeel was about to answer when he spied Troy. The boy became serious, his facial expression going blank. Francine turned to see what caused the change. Unlike his nephew, she smiled at the sight of him.

"Troy, did you sleep well?"

"I slept all right." He didn't, but he gave the polite answer. He turned to his nephew. "Good morning, Akeel."

"Good morning, Uncle Troy."

It was uncanny how much the boy looked like his friend. If anything, Akeel Jr. seemed to assess him more than fear him. Francine, trying to help them along, said, "We're going to tour Atlanta–waiting on his dad. Monnie, Jennifer and I are all going to tag along."

Before Troy could answer, Monica spoke from behind him. "Come, Junior, and brush your hair again."

The child looked up at him. "See ya, Uncle Troy."

"Have a good day, Akeel."

When his nephew followed his sister out of the kitchen, Troy focused on Francine. He could feel her anxiety. "You don't have to go."

She smiled weakly. "I have to go out, Troy. I can't continue to live in fear. I've been out with Monica and Jennifer, it wasn't so bad. Junior is always a wonderful distraction. Besides, Akeel and Jesse are there, so, I'm safe."

Francine was dressed in yellow shorts that flowed to above her knees. She wore a matching shirt with black sneakers; her hair was pulled back in a ponytail. She made his chest tight.

"I think I want to volunteer with the literacy program. It'll give me something meaningful to do."

He stared at her, the statement unexpected. She wanted to work. It made sense but...

"Some of the people—the men in the program are rough." Troy grimaced. "No, find something else to do."

Francine placed her hands on her hips. "Akeel told me you have two facilities. One for young people and one that is part of the Second Chance Program. I'll work at the one for the young people. I'm told most of the participants are young pregnant women who are trying to make change."

"I'll think about it," he snapped.

Softly, she asked, "Is this how it's going to be? Am I a prisoner, Troy?"

"No, you're not a prisoner, but you are restricted to my demands."

Francine continued to stare at him, until he sighed. "I'll take you tomorrow and see how I feel about it."

She smiled at him, and again his chest constricted. "I haven't agreed to anything, yet."

His wife stepped forward and hugged him as Jennifer's voice floated down the hall. "Frankie, come on."

Francine cupped his face and kissed him urgently. She whispered, "Thank you for helping me. I'll see you later."

"Frankie!" It was Monica who yelled after her this time.

"I'm coming!" Francine shouted back, and then she was gone.

Troy braced his hands against the island as he stared out the kitchen window. Akeel spoke into his quiet space.

"Imma take my son out for the day, and the women will be with me. I'll meet you this evening."

Troy turned to look at him. The man looked pained. "You have the boy and Monica here. Why so glum?"

"Monica is afraid of me. I don't like it, but I can't be different." He had dark smudges under his eyes, still, he smiled. "My son is beautiful."

Troy nodded. "Give Monnie some time."

"I think she wants to leave." Akeel's words were hard and desperate. "I can't let her go. She can either stay here or move in with me. The real truth— I'm tired of them staying here, but it's better than nothing."

His friend was strung tight. Troy decided against telling him that Monica did indeed want to leave. No good would come from revealing what he and his sister spoke about. He took the safe route. "I'm meeting

Levi, Hassan and Tyrell, we're headed to speak with Darrell Jenkins' mother and girlfriend. We'll also canvass the neighborhood; shit will get hot today."

"Butch and Jesse will be here with the women later. Where do you want to meet?"

"Your house tonight, around 10:00." Troy replied.

"Aiight."

As Akeel walked away, Troy weighed him. The gun strapped to his right hip signified his friend's willingness to follow through. Monica would be safer with who Akeel had become. The man he used to be couldn't keep his own self safe. Troy shook his head to clear his thoughts before exiting the house by way of the garage. It was time to start his day.

5

WHAT'S DONE IN THE DARK

I t was noon when Levi slowly pulled onto Hanover Street in College Park. The day had shaped up to be cloudy, even as the heat kept its powerful hold on Georgia. The men noted the squad car that sat in front of the third house on the right. It was the home of the murder victim, John Unger. The yard and front door were roped off with crime scene tape. According to the case folder, the old man had been dead seven weeks. Yet, the police presence at the scene, and in the neighborhood, was continual.

Levi would offer to take the case, and they all would investigate—collect the facts. They would speak with Darrell last, thereby strong arming him into letting Levi represent him. Troy set the pace for the day, and he would control the outcome. When night fell, all of Atlanta would know he was in charge. As for Detective Chris Logan, he would know what it felt like to be publicly hunted.

At the end of Hanover Street, about half a mile down, Levi parked in front of Shirley Jenkins' home. It was a small brick house with a carport big enough for two cars. The driveway could park four more vehicles. The lawn was patchy, but the place sang—poor but proud. A thin white, stone walkway led to a tiny porch and brown front door. Before they got out of the truck, Troy went through the checklist.

"The media has been called, correct?"

"In about twenty minutes, the media will appear. They understand there will be no statement if they're here before 12:30," Tyrell answered.

"Jasmin is already here," Hassan said.

"Ms. Jenkins' is rough–she ain't no easy win." Levi chuckled.

Troy opened the back door and stepped onto the pavement, the other men followed. A woman about five feet, six inches in her late forties appeared on the small porch. She wore black slacks and a floral print shirt with big pink flowers. Her hair was natural and the kink prevalent; bobby pins pushed the afro away from her face. She had dark skin with a tiny nose that made her cheekbones stand out and coffee black eyes hooded by long lashes. Her lips were dark like the rest of her skin. Levi was right, Darrell's mother appeared tough as nails. She was also a beautiful woman.

Behind Shirley Jenkins stood two young men who looked like her. Troy gauged the man on her right to be about twenty-two and the other looked to be about seventeen. Each had a small amount of facial hair and both were dark skinned–standing right at six feet. Between them stood Jasmin, dressed in blue slacks and a white shirt. Given the atmosphere at Sparks, Troy couldn't assess her during their first encounter. She was gorgeous with mahogany skin and huge brown eyes. Her hair was pinned up in a French roll with a small curl that draped over her forehead.

Now, as he stared at Jasmin, he felt sorry for Darrell. A thought bloomed in his mind unbidden; the media would spin shit badly if given the opportunity, and Troy didn't want a replay of his wife shutting him out. He would leave Jasmin to Levi whenever possible–Francine had him shook.

They reached the bottom of the stone stairs and Troy spoke first. "Good afternoon, Ms. Jenkins. I'm Troy Bryant."

"I know who you are, Mr. Bryant. Have you come here thinkin' to use my son and me for political gain? Me and my family won't be pimped out, so you can be mayor or some shit."

The young men behind her remained expressionless. Jasmin gasped and looked faint. Levi snickered, while Tyrell and Hassan made not a sound. Troy was impressed, and he immediately saw the difference between his mother and this woman. This woman owned the situation; she trusted no one. His mother had been desperate, trusting anyone who said they could help. She had been victimized trying to obtain his freedom.

"I can assure you, Ms. Jenkins, I'm not seeking a political career."

"Why are you here, Mr. Bryant? What do you have to gain? I have not asked for your help." Shirley Jenkins questioned.

Troy made a point of not looking at Jasmin. "Justice sent me. He thought I could help. We were in prison together, but the truth is–I would come to you anyway. Detective Logan is the reason I've come."

"Revenge then..." she narrowed her eyes.

"Revenge has its place, but it's a little more complicated than retaliation." She continued to stare at him, and Troy knew he would have to be rough. "Look, Ms. Jenkins, I came here because you have already placed your family in the public eye. We could have gone to Darrell with promises, and he would have accepted. He *is* the one in prison. But I thought to come to you and not undermine your efforts. I came to you because I wanted to work with you. The media needs to see a united front. If I go to your son, I won't come back. And I won't need to because he'll be calling the shots."

The woman before him was pissed, silence hung between them. Troy looked at his watch. "The news outlets will be here any minute. It's up to you, Ms. Jenkins. I can't promise to get Darrell out of jail, but I can promise to honestly help your son and you."

"They're here." Levi nodded in the direction of the news vans and squad cars moving slowly toward them.

Troy turned back to Darrell's mother and smiled. "We're out of time."

Shirley nodded curtly as if it pained her to be bested by him. Troy chuckled. "Later, Ms. Jenkins, you can be mean to me later. As for right now, I'm not going to answer any questions. But I am going to make a statement. Please trust me."

She sighed, a sign she was softening toward him. Troy reached his hand out to her and she placed her hand in his. "I'm Shirley, and these are my two sons–Jerrell and Michael. This is Jasmin, Darrell's girlfriend."

Troy nodded, "Justice tried to introduce me to Jasmin, but she wouldn't speak to me or him without you."

She turned, looked at Jasmin and smiled. Troy didn't want to set Ms. Jenkins on Jasmin. It was best this way; he helped her down the steps and they moved to the top of the driveway. The press spilled from their vehicles to the front of the house, and the family moved in behind Troy and Darrell's mother while Levi, Tyrell and Hassan pushed the reporters back to a safe distance. Three squad cars were parked to the right of the house—on the opposite side of the street. Three black and two white police officers stood in a huddle watching the events unfold.

Troy felt his body hum with anticipation. He had been waiting a long time for this moment. The residents of Hanover Street came out of their homes, standing in the street and on the lawns of the nearby properties to see Ms. Jenkins and the Silent Activist address APD. Troy looked at the crowd gathering before him and thought of his wife. One of two things would happen: he would be killed, or he would be incarcerated for life. In the case of the latter, he would take his own life. Either way, Francine would eventually be free, still he would enjoy her until his last breath.

The snick, snick, snick of cameras and microphones being shoved past the men in his direction was a means to an end. He had to remind himself of this fact as the questions started.

"Troy, are you still married?"

"Is your wife aware that you're a person of interest in the disappearance of George Ingalls?"

"Troy, rumor has it your wife is seeing her old lover? Are you and Francine still together?"

He stepped forward and held up his hands; the questions stopped, but the cameras did not. Troy's tone was warm, friendly even, when he threatened. "The rude questions will stop, or we will not make a statement."

A thin blonde woman with sea blue eyes and perfectly shaped eyebrows stepped into his line of vision. She wore a navy blue skirt suit with a white shirt, and the shoes she wore matched her suit, adding about three inches to her height. She was attractive and looked to be in her mid-thirties. Troy had seen her on the news a time or two.

Boldly, she spoke. "I'm Lacey Bowers, Channel 55 Action News. Are you attempting to control the media, Mr. Bryant?"

Troy chuckled, "No, Ms. Bowers, I'm being clear about what I'll tolerate."

They stared at each other for moments. He could see her weighing whether she wanted to continue verbally sparring with him. She relented, and Troy suspected it was because she didn't want to be the reason shit got shut down before it got started. When he was sure he won the exchange, he dismissed her and addressed the crowd—voice heavy and laced with excitement.

"The people of College Park have questions for APD. As taxpayers, to inquire about the local government is a right. Why are dirty cops moved from all white areas and placed in the black community rather than fired?"

Chatter started again amongst the reporters. They were all speaking at once, and Troy held up his hands again. "The people of College Park demand to know when APD will take responsibility for the actions of Detective Chris Logan. Why has Detective Logan gone through so many partners?"

A breeze blew, alleviating the heat of the day. When Troy paused this time, the reporters remained quiet, only the click of cameras continued. He took in the bevy of media outlets and then spoke calmly. "We have an unfortunate situation which has resulted in two victims, Mr. John Unger and Darrell Jenkins. The people of College Park want the murder of their beloved neighbor solved, and they want Detective Logan removed from the case. We, as citizens of Georgia, want Detective Logan removed from the force—we want him to face the consequences of his behavior. We want every case he worked reevaluated."

The reporters started firing questions at him, but the nature of the inquiries changed.

"Troy, are you accusing APD of negligence?"

"Troy, are saying Darrell Jenkins was wrongfully accused?"

"Are your actions a direct result of your own experience with Detective Logan? The murders in your case have never been solved, correct?"

"Troy, are your statements retaliation against Detective Logan?"

He didn't attempt to answer the barrage of questions, instead he went in for the kill. "If you have had a violent encounter with Detective Logan that has gone unaddressed by APD, please contact Bryant and Associates. There will be someone on hand to hear you and help you address the ignored brutality running rampant in our community—perpetrated by the very institution sworn to protect us."

When the questions started again, Troy turned toward the family of Darrell Jenkins and walked away. He took Ms. Jenkins by the elbow and helped her up the stairs and into the house. Jasmin entered next; the men and Darrell's brothers brought up the rear. Levi closed the door on the media as they stood packed together like sardines on the driveway.

Shirley turned to Troy. "What next?"

"Levi will stop by the jail and speak with Darrell. He will become the defense attorney on the case."

"We can't afford—"

Troy cut her off. "This is pro bono."

She looked as though she were going to argue, but her eldest son stepped in. "Mama, Darrell needs this. Let them help us."

Shirley Jenkins nodded. "Thank you, Mr. Bryant."

"I'm Troy–this is Levi, he'll be the one taking your son's case. Behind him is Tyrell and Hassan. They will help me investigate the case while also helping keep your family safe."

"Safe?"

"Yes, ma'am. I have called into question the integrity of the Atlanta Police Department. I am attempting to shed doubt around Detective Logan while bringing his caseload into question."

Troy knew all that he was saying was a lot to take in, but it needed saying. She finally asked, "What about Jasmin and her mama?"

"We have property that we would like to move you all into; we can provide better protection when familiarity is a factor," Troy replied.

"So we are prisoners as well?" she asked.

"You will all go about your day–but we will be in the background."

"When do we have to move?" the older son Jerrell asked.

"We will move you all today after the press leaves," Tyrell said. "But the police will be watching; you will pack like you're staying with friends for a while."

"I need to go and speak with my mama." Jasmin said.

"I'll go with you, child." Shirley said.

"I'll go with them." Tyrell said.

Troy nodded. "Butch will be here in about thirty minutes to help you all move. We'll get them settled and meet at Akeel's at 10:00."

The men dispersed to handle the tasks given to them while the police and media lingered on Hanover Street.

* * *

Levi went to meet Darrell at the Fulton County Jail, and Troy tagged along to assess the situation. When he stepped through the metal detector, shit got real. His soul shook as the bars closed behind them in the gray and white corridor. There was a black line in the middle of the floor and force of habit made him walk to the left of the divide. A light sweat broke out on his body, but he maintained an outer appearance of calm.

"You good?" Levi asked.

"Yeah."

They followed a tall, brown skinned correction officer down the hall to a small conference room. The man sported a box haircut and clumsy gait. "It'll be a few minutes," the guard said, directing them to a chrome legged table with an orange surface and matching chairs. He shut the door behind him.

The room was windowless, the walls gray. Levi sat, but Troy was too high strung. He stood with his back to the wall as they waited for Inmate 211357 to be brought out. Forty-five minutes passed before the door opened and Darrell Jenkins appeared cuffed and shackled. At Levi's request, he was unchained. Troy couldn't breathe.

Darrell was just under six feet and thin of frame. His skin was the darkest, and still it was obvious that his right eye was swollen. His attire–an orange jumpsuit with white socks and rubber sandals. He had an afro that was unkempt and a patchy beard. The kid had been here six and a half weeks. Troy knew the shock in his eyes wouldn't fade for a year. He was being shoved back down memory lane.

"I'm Sean Levi Bryant with Bryant and Associates. We would like to take your case pro bono."

"Pro–what?" Darrell asked, staring at Troy.

"Pro bono, it means free legal service." Levi explained.

"What my mama say?" Darrell asked.

"Do you want to keep the lawyer you already have?" Troy asked.

"No. I saw him for about fifteen minutes in court six weeks ago. My mama left messages on my behalf, and my girl called for me a few times. He ain't been to see me. Jason Toliver is his name."

"Do you want my help?" Levi badgered Darrell on purpose.

"Can you get me outta here? I ain't killed nobody, and if I was thinking about offing someone, it wouldn't have been old man Johnny."

"First of all—never speak of offing anyone while in here. Refrain from conversation about your case with the other inmates or while on the phone speaking with loved ones." Levi instructed.

The kid's eyes watered, but no tears fell. He stared at Levi for minutes and then nodded. Darrell's voice was thick. "This fuckin' place makes you wanna kill a mafucka. I ain't never been in trouble in my life. I was too scared of my moms, but here I am."

Troy laughed. "We met Ms. Shirley Jenkins."

Darrell's eyes softened. "How she holdin' up?"

"Better than you. She's fueled by indignation." Troy answered.

"You that activist dude?"

"I'm Troy Bryant, we want to help you. Sign the paperwork, so Levi can represent you. Your mama knew we were coming."

Levi extended the hand with the topless black pen. Darrell took it, scribbling his name with harsh fast strokes. Unceremoniously, he dropped the pen on the table and leaned back against the wall opposite Troy.

"Tell us everything that happened from the last time you saw Mr. Unger until you were arrested." Levi instructed. "Don't decide what's important, tell us every little thing."

"We lived on the same street. I saw the old man pretty regularly. When I got off work and drove home, Johnny was out on his porch. If the weather was good, that's where you could find him. He waved—I waved. Same shit every day—no variation."

"Had to be a variation, the old man is dead." Troy said.

"I got off work early; it was 2:00 o'clock. I made it to my neighborhood around 3:00, Johnny was on his porch. At 5:30—quarter to six, my brother drove me to Jasmin's house because he wanted to borrow my car. He met some girl and wanted to hang out with her. Jerrell promised he would meet me at 5:00 in the morning at Jas'."

"Did he meet you?" Levi pressed.

Troy noted Darrell was hesitant to answer the question. Levi, being trained in the art of reading people said, "So he didn't meet you at 5:00 a.m. as agreed."

"No, he didn't."

"Continue," Troy said to make Darrell uneasy.

"I tried to call Jerrell at our house, but he didn't answer. I gave up and walked home. My brother can be inconsiderate at times."

"Did you tell the police the same story?" Levi asked.

"I left off the part about my brother—not that they would have heard me. I cut through Mr. Mitchell's yard and then Mrs. Montgomery's, which backs up to Johnny's yard. I walked right into the police. When I climbed the fence, I felt something wet and sticky—turns out it was blood."

"What do you do for a living?" Troy asked.

"I work at Brooks Memorial Hospital. I'm a janitor."

"Do you normally get off early?" Levi countered.

"Me and Jas had a fight—no, I don't normally leave work."

Darrell was frustrated, but they kept hammering him. "What did you and Jasmin fight about?"

"I was considering the Marines. She thought I didn't want her anymore…"

"All this sounds like deviations from the norm. Did you kill Mr. Unger?" Levi asked.

Darrell stared between the two of them, understanding dawning. The kid looked hurt by the question. Still, he answered. "No, I didn't kill Johnny."

"Let's hear the story again." Levi barked. "And Darrell, it's important that you know—the story only matters to us. The rest of the world believes they know what happened."

Troy felt Darrell's defeat when the younger man nodded and began retelling the story. This time, he took care to note even the smallest change in his day. Levi began badgering him anew regarding the arrest.

"Were you questioned on the scene or at the station?"

"I was questioned in Johnny's yard. I figured since I didn't kill anybody, what harm could it do. But Detective Logan started putting words in my mouth, and I stopped talking. Next thing I know, I'm being told that I have the right to remain silent. They cuffed me—brought me to the police station and started questioning me again. When I asked for a lawyer, Logan's partner, Detective Rayner slammed my head into the table."

"Did you understand your rights?" Levi asked.

"I understood once they started repeatin' that shit I see on cop shows, I wasn't goin' home." Darrell said.

"Aiight man, they started questioning you–then mirandized you. Rayner slammed your face into the table. Did you tell your lawyer?"

"I did, but Toliver said it would be hard to prove." Darrell answered.

"Okay, Darrell, we talked around it, but Johnny *was* murdered. The old man was shot in the back of the head."

Troy watched as Levi kept working Darrell's reactions. It was important for them to see how he would present in a courtroom. He looked hurt and confused; Darrell didn't speak.

"Tell me in your words how this makes you feel," Levi asked.

"You will be disappointed." Darrell countered.

"Why?" Levi leaned back in the chair. He twirled the black pen between his fingers while offering Darrell intense scrutiny.

"My last memory of Johnny was of him sitting on his porch waving at me. I know he's dead because I've been told, but me being locked up feels like a bad nightmare that has nothing to do with Johnny at all. I am so fucked up in the head about being here that I forget it's because my neighbor was murdered. I don't understand why I'm here."

Levi stared at him and Troy understood the message. He had explained feeling disconnected from the murders when he had been in Darrell's shoes. The crime for him was being incarcerated for an act he didn't commit. When he got out of prison, empathy for the victims hit him like knives slicing through flesh; he saw himself as a victim of the same crime. In his head, someone had brutally killed this unsuspecting elderly couple and stolen his life in the process.

Levi stood. "We'll be in touch."

They both shook Darrell's hand, and then he was taken away. The men reached the truck and started pulling away from the jail as Levi laid out his thoughts. "Here's what we know. Darrell last saw the victim Johnny Unger alive at 3:00 p.m. on June 6th. According to the police report, 911 received calls around 4:20 a.m. on the 7th of June about gunshots. Shortly after 5:00

a.m., our client cut through the yard of the murder victim. Darrell was caught at the scene with the blood on his clothes."

"The report sights robbery as a possible motive," Troy added.

"Naw—they always say that shit when they don't know what happened." Levi explained. "Here is what we don't know. Why was Darrell reluctant to tell us his brother borrowed his car? How often did he lend his vehicle to his brother? Why couldn't Jerrell meet Darrell? Where was he at 5 a.m. and what was he doing?"

Troy nodded as he stopped at a red light. "We need to see the clothes Darrell was wearing the night of his arrest. Tyrell and I will question the neighbors. Can you request all video of Darrell at the station? I want to see from the moment he was brought in."

"I'll get all the proper motions and notices filed." Levi promised.

By the time they left the jail, the day had pressed on to rush hour. On the ride to Levi's office, pockets of silence enveloped them with each man in his own thoughts. Troy was drowning in anger and revenge and finding it hard to stay focused after reliving prison life with Darrell.

He parked in front of an orange, bricked high rise on Paces Ferry. Bryant and Associates took up the top three floors. Troy had an office there but rarely used it. About to get out, Levi asked. "You comin' up?"

"No, I'm going to meet Tyrell and walk the path Darrell took through Unger's yard."

"Aiight. See you tonight at Akeel's."

Easing back into traffic, Troy headed for the safe house to meet Tyrell. It was an hour before he pulled into the Woodland Subdivision off Fulton Industrial. At the end of Harriett Street on the left was a large, red brick-faced house with a two-car garage. The siding was beige with black shutters. He parked in front of the house instead of on the long, steep driveway.

Troy stepped into the foyer, thankful for the coolness of the air conditioner. Greeted by an image of himself on the evening news, Lacey Bowers was reporting on his shitty attitude and his attempt to manhandle the media. The large television in the corner of the living room held everyone's attention. Ms. Bowers wore a cream colored short sleeved shirt and in her hands were cue cards. Seated opposite Lacey was her black co-host Thom Flint, an older man with silver hair and leathery brown skin. His eyes crinkled around the edges as he blinked. He wore a blue sports jacket and kept adjusting his cue cards as she spoke.

This ten-minute segment of the news featured Lacey and Thom debating matters affecting Atlanta and the surrounding areas. Troy had seen them battle on issues of race, politics and policy. He hated to admit it, but Thom Flint was a bit of a house nigga and Lacey tended to lean toward the people. She was fair, still she was the media.

The foyer was hardwood, the ceiling vaulted with a decorative chandelier suspended overhead. On the left, a beige carpeted staircase led to the second floor. The same beige carpet picked up again in the living room. In front of the television, on an angle, was a tan leather couch and across the room was a matching love seat and ottoman.

Michael and Jerrell sat at opposite ends of the couch, and Ms. Shirley sat in between them with her legs crossed. On the love seat sat Jasmin and an older woman who looked to be about fifty. She wore jeans and a blue t-shirt that read, "I heart New York."

Troy's attention was drawn back to the television screen. The camera had zoomed in on Lacey Bowers as she reported on the death of Johnny. "Channel 55 Action News broke the story of John Unger. For those of you who are unfamiliar with the events—Mr. Unger, a long-time resident of College Park, was murdered inside his home—early June. Darrell Jenkins was taken into custody shortly after 911 was called by neighbors to report gunshots."

The camera focused on Thom Flint long enough for him to say, "Such a sad state of affairs for the Unger family."

"Yes, it is, Thom. We were out on Hanover Street where the victim and the accused lived mere yards from each other. Shirley Jenkins, mother of the accused has been vocal with the media about her son's innocence."

The camera cut away to a rally with Shirley standing in the middle of Old National Highway backed by hundreds of protesters. She was speaking bluntly about the lack of investigation into John Unger's murder and the crime happening against her family. "Free Darrell Jenkins," the crowd chanted.

Gaining control of the gathering, Shirley Jenkins stared right into the camera. "If the Atlanta Police Department thinks I'm going to go quietly into the night while my child is railroaded, they have another thing coming. My child will not be a scapegoat because the victim is white."

The camera cut away, and again Lacey filled the screen. "While Channel 55 was on Hanover Street today, we witnessed the Silent Activist, Troy Bryant joining forces with Ms. Jenkins in the cause to free her son, Darrell."

Thom Flint filled the screen. "The question here: Is Ms. Jenkins making a mistake by throwing her lot in with Troy Bryant?"

The camera angle widened, so that both Lacey and Thom could be seen. Lacey responded, "Why would Troy Bryant's presence make the situation worse?"

Flint shuffled the cue cards in his hands. "I get it, he was exonerated for the murders of Mr. and Mrs. Dotson, but he has also been implicated in the death of his own lawyer, George Ingalls. This could hurt Darrell. I think his mother is desperate. It was a bad choice to join forces with Troy Bryant."

Again, the camera cut away to the clip of his press conference in front of the Jenkins' house. And to his shock, they played the video in its entirety. When the clip ended, Lacey and Thom filled the screen.

"Well, Thom, it's no surprise that we would disagree. In my research of Troy Bryant, he has used the money from his own exoneration to help those less fortunate. His organization offers a literacy program, several scholarships and jobs. Mr. Bryant stepping in to help the Jenkins family seems in line with the work he's already doing. If this doesn't work out for Darrell Jenkins, it won't be because of Troy Bryant. His presence, I think, can only help. He has called for a proper investigation into the murder of John Unger while holding APD accountable for the behavior of their own."

"Lacey, this smells of revenge against Detective Chris Logan," Thom countered.

The music started, signaling the end the segment. Lacey replied, her tone mocking. "Does it really seem like revenge? I mean black men get such a fair shake in our judicial system. You can't be that far removed from the plight of the less fortunate, Thom."

A commercial started playing and the older woman seated next to Jasmin looked up at him. It caused everyone to turn his way. Shirley stood upon seeing him.

"Good evening, Troy."

"Shirley."

"This is Patricia Walker, Jasmin's mama." She pointed at the other woman. "Patricia, this here is Troy Bryant."

"Patricia." Troy said, by way of greeting. She smiled and nodded, but she wasn't verbal. Like Jasmin, her mother seemed reserved–shy. Patricia had the same skin tone as her daughter. Her black hair was pulled back in a ponytail. She had tiny dark eyes and a plump face–from her ears dangled gold earrings that resembled Nefertiti.

"We really raised the four of them together. I met Patricia and Jasmin when Darrell was in the first grade. Jas ended up in his class. Poor Darrell came home complaining about the little girl in his class that hit him when he refused to marry her."

Troy stared at Jasmin, and she bashfully looked away. He shook his head and chuckled. Behind him, Tyrell and Hassan stepped into the living room; he turned to them. "I just came from seeing Darrell."

"Is he all right?" Jasmin's face held concern.

"Yes, Troy, how is my baby?" Shirley added.

"Darrell is fine. He signed the paperwork, and Levi went back to the office to begin working on his case."

"What now?" Jasmin asked.

"Hassan will stay here and monitor the house." Troy's eyes locked on Jerrell. "Tyrell and I will walk the path Darrell took from Jasmin's house the morning he was arrested."

Troy felt Jerrell's anxiety as he continued to stare. "Jerrell, you will join us."

The younger man nodded. He knew what was coming, Troy could see it on his face. "Ladies, we'll be back later."

Tyrell turned for the door first and Troy waited, allowing Jerrell to exit the house before him. When they got to the vehicle, Troy tossed Tyrell the keys. As the truck pulled into the light traffic of the side street, Troy turned to Jerrell.

"Why didn't you meet your brother the morning of June 7th?"

"I was with a friend and lost track of the time." Jerrell replied.

Troy turned in the front passenger seat to eye him. Jerrell wore his nervousness like a bad suit. Everything about him seemed out of place and awkward. "Your brother said you borrowed his car to meet up with a woman. What's her name? Where did you two meet up?"

"I missed meeting my brother—what does this have to do with anything?" Jerrell's frustration was evident.

Troy offered his most intimidating glare while remaining quiet. He placed the burden of easing the tension in the truck on Jerrell. Tyrell added pressure by pulling the vehicle to the side of Camp Creek Parkway; he too glowered at Jerrell through the rearview mirror.

"Did you kill Johnny?" Troy asked.

"I'm a fuckin' murderer now because I didn't meet my brother on time?"

Tyrell's tone was soft. "You betta get control of yo' tongue or we'll beat yo' ass— and you'll still tell us what we wanna know."

"Fuck you." Jerrell sneered at Tyrell, who was about to pop the door and get out.

Troy grabbed Tyrell's arm to stop him. Jerrell turned and stared out the window, ignoring them. Troy threatened. "We could have this discussion in front of your mother. Both you and your brother are lying, but he's covering for you. You ain't covering for him. I won't be lied to while offering my help."

"When a person doesn't show up on time, it makes them *late*–not a killer."

"Your brother is facing years in prison. Georgia is a death penalty state–Dude, you do the math. Is what you're hiding more important than Darrell's life? It was you who pushed your mother to accept our help. Now you can't be truthful, even to save your brother." Troy countered.

Jerrell was back to staring out the window, his jiggling leg revealed his disquiet. He never looked at Troy. "I've been dating someone for two years. I haven't introduced them to my family. Darrell met them by accident..."

"Name?" Troy pushed.

Jerrell sighed. "Brian West, he lives off Six Flags Road."

Troy was reticent as he turned over what Jerrell was saying in his head. The silence caused the younger man to turn and look at him. When he was sure he had Jerrell's attention he asked, "You would rather live under a cloud of suspicion than admit you're gay?"

"I'm not gay. I'm bisexual, Brian is my first long term relationship. I like women, too."

Troy passed Jerrell a card. "Have Brian call Levi. We won't discuss your business with anyone else unless it affects Darrell."

Jerrell nodded, and Troy continued. "Do you know the path your brother would have taken between houses?"

"Yeah."

They arrived in College Park about 7:30 in the evening. They had an hour and a half of daylight left, and Troy wanted the people of Hanover Street to become familiar with him and his men. Tyrell parked in front of Jasmin's house and they all got out. Godby Road was the cross street, and with the sun still up, he realized the house was several yards to the right of the corner. Foliage separated the cross street from the small brick structure that faced Prince Street.

The grass was freshly cut, and this concerned Troy. Jerrell moved to stand next to him on the lawn while Tyrell retrieved supplies from the back of the truck. Turning in a complete circle, Troy inspected the neighborhood with its little red brick houses and built on carports. Three doors down, two elderly women sat together on their porch watching him. Troy smiled and then waved. They reciprocated by nodding their heads.

Directly across the street, a curtain danced in the window, but no one was visible. Troy made a mental note to speak with the people on Prince Street as well. Tyrell appeared shoving his hands into a pair of latex gloves. He carried a backpack on one shoulder, and around his neck hung a thirty-five-millimeter camera. Before searching Jasmin's front yard for clues, he handed out gloves.

They spread out and walked down the small slope. This upset the gnats and other bugs, causing Troy to wave his hand in front of his face. He didn't know what they were looking for, but they would know it—when and if they found it. Troy, followed by Tyrell and Jerrell, rounded to the back of the house, but nothing stuck out.

The men stood facing away from the house. At the edge of the backyard, there was no fence separating the unkempt underbrush. "This way," Jerrell said. "It's not as bad as it looks. Beyond the bushes is Mr. Mitchell's yard."

Troy stepped into the thick brush behind Jerrell; he was sorry he hadn't worn a long sleeve shirt. When he looked back at Tyrell, it was clear he thought the same. They found themselves in another backyard and still nothing seemed amiss. As they moved around to the driveway, an elderly man was making his way down the steps.

Jerrell moved forward and spoke. "Mr. Mitchell, good to see you. Troy–Tyrell, this is Mr. Mitchell. He has known me, Darrell and Michael our whole lives."

The older man was dark skin with bleach white patches around his mouth and ears. He stood about six feet, and when he reached out to shake Troy's hand, there was patched white skin about his knuckles. Mr. Mitchell had hair so gray it was white. His bushy eyebrows covered perceptive eyes. He wore brown slacks and a white tank top. The man before him was not feeble.

"Good to meet you," Troy offered.

"The pleasure is mine, son," the older man said. "Jerrell–here is correct when he says I been knowing his family a long time. They cut through my yard and piss me off, but they run errands for me and check on me. Darrell didn't kill Johnny."

"Sorry, sir," Jerrell said.

"You ain't sorry yet. I want my grass cut on Saturday." Mr. Mitchell demanded.

"Yes, sir." Jerrell grinned.

Tyrell stepped up and shook Mr. Mitchell's hand. "Tyrell, I work with Troy."

The older man nodded, and then turned to Troy. "I was out in front of the Jenkins' house when you held the news conference. The police picked the boy up and ain't asked no questions. They not even working this case, they got Darrell–so case closed. It's a damn shame."

"Is there anything you can tell us?" Troy asked.

"Naw, I can't think of shit. The boy ain't been through my yard in a while–since he got himself a car. I got up early for coffee–around 5:15 that morning. The back of my house lit up when Darrell got close. I have motion detectors–saw Darrell through the kitchen window. He was alone."

"Did you hear the gunshots?" Tyrell asked.

"Naw, I didn't hear a damn thing." Mr. Mitchell confirmed. "Gunshots kinda common around here. I prolly wouldn't have called nobody if I did."

"What street is this?" Troy asked looking for a sign.

"This is Rose Street." Jerrell and Mr. Mitchell said in unison.

"Do you get up early for coffee regularly?" Tyrell asked.

"My wife died about five years ago. I don't sleep well since she left. Coffee in the morning gives me something to do."

"Did anyone else come through your yard before or after Darrell?" Tyrell countered.

"No, and I only recognized Darrell because he looked up when the floodlights came on. He didn't wave, I don't think he saw me."

"Is it all right if we come back to talk with you?" Troy asked, trying not to sound overly eager. The truth of the matter was the old guy knew more than he thought, and he was corroborating Darrell's statement.

"Absolutely," Mr. Mitchell answered.

"In the meantime, if you think of anything else, please give me a call." Troy handed the man a card.

"Will do."

They were about to head toward Mrs. Montgomery's house when Mr. Mitchell cautioned. "You can't walk through Johnny's yard. The police have it closed off."

"I figured as much," Troy said with a smile. He was aware of police presence in the neighborhood, but he would get as close as possible. "Which house belongs to Mrs. Montgomery?"

"It's the second one across the street." Jerrell pointed to the house with the white door.

Turning to Mr. Mitchell, Troy said graciously, "Again, it was nice meeting you, sir."

He didn't wait for a response, instead he headed toward the house. The old man's voice followed them. "Cordelia ain't home. Her daughter came and carried her to Alabama. They came for her about two days after all this happened."

Behind him, Troy heard Tyrell say, "Thank you, sir, we'll be in touch."

The sun was in the last stages of daylight as they crossed the street. Troy noticed that the lawn had been freshly cut at the Montgomery house and winced. The driveway was a gradual hill and the home sat at the top to the right. The curtains were drawn, making the place appear dead. When they reached the side of the house the smell of cut grass and pine assailed them. A wooden decorative fence was bolted into the red brick, encompassing the whole yard.

At the back of the yard where the brush was thick, the fence and the foliage was cut away. What separated the land now was police tape. When he got closer, Troy could see right into Johnny's yard.

Turning to Tyrell, Troy said, "Get a picture of this."

Peering beyond the crime scene tape, Troy saw that the grass in Johnny's yard had not been cut. They were trespassing in the Montgomery yard, so they couldn't add to the bullshit by breaking the seal. Levi would kill him. Tyrell took pictures while he and Jerrell stood to the side. He wanted to walk through the property.

When they backtracked to the front of the Montgomery house, a crowd had gathered. Troy removed his gloves as he walked down the driveway. There were about ten people standing about trying to see what was going on. Troy addressed them as a group.

"We are here trying to get justice for Johnny and Darrell. If you know something, don't be afraid to come forward."

The people spoke amongst themselves but not to him. Troy understood this dynamic in the black community. They did not trust authority. He and Tyrell moved forward, handing out business cards.

"Please give us a call if you know something. We can meet in private if necessary."

The buzz grew louder in the gathering, still nothing was directed to them. When the people dispersed, the three men walked the long way back to Jasmin's house. Tyrell loaded the supplies in the back of the truck. Troy got in the driver's seat, and Jerrell climbed in the back. They did not speak on the way back to the safe house. It was dark when they pulled into the driveway.

Tyrell got out, "I'll relieve Hassan."

"Will you let me continue to help?" Jerrell asked.

"Don't you work?" Troy inquired.

"I work at a bottling company from 7 a.m. to 4 p.m. It's warehouse work."

"It'll be better if you're there when we go back to Hanover. You're one of them." Troy confirmed.

Jerrell stared at him in the rearview and then nodded. Opening the door, he climbed out of the backseat and disappeared into the house. Seconds later, Hassan appeared getting into the front passenger side.

"S'up?"

"We headed to Akeel's. I need to talk shit out with Levi." Troy replied.

It was after 9 p.m. when they headed for Dallas, Georgia. Hassan was quiet by nature, and Troy needed the peace to collect his thoughts. They turned onto Seaboard Drive and then Toulouse Street at 9:45. Levi's Benz was parked in the driveway of Akeel's modest home. The lights were on at the bottom of the house.

"It's dark as shit out here," Hassan said.

Troy laughed as he parked behind Levi's car and got out. The front door was pulled open by Akeel, and Hassan stepped into the house first. Unlike Levi, Akeel had a couch and a television in the living room, and in the dining area, he had a new oak table with six matching chairs. Levi was seated at the head and there was paperwork all over the surface. He looked up when they entered.

"How did it go?" Levi asked.

"The grass had been cut at the Mitchell and Montgomery house, but Johnny's backyard hadn't been cut." Troy answered.

"Darrell's brother?"

"The brother spent the night with his boyfriend, Brian West. Ms. Shirley doesn't know, but Darrell does. The boyfriend will give you a call to confirm their whereabouts."

Levi nodded. "I filed a Notice of Appearance and spoke with previous counsel. I also subpoenaed Detective Chris Logan's personnel file and requested discovery."

"Will that get us a walkthrough of Johnny's house?" Troy asked.

"Police presence on a crime scene that's seven weeks old isn't common. They know something we don't. I'll see what I can do." Levi answered.

Hassan sat and leaned back in a chair situated to the left of Levi. Troy stood at the opposite end of the table and when his eyes fell on Hassan, he saw tension. Levi's gaze bounced between them.

"We can't kill Detective Logan. He would die a slain hero rather than a dirty cop. People like Darrell would suffer, and Logan's cases would never be scrutinized."

"The longer Logan goes unchecked, the bigger the clean-up." Hassan said to no one in particular.

"I feel the same," Akeel said.

Levi stood. "Let me make one thing clear. I took Darrell Jenkins' case, so ethically I'm obligated to do what's best for him. I'll get my hands dirty, but I won't compromise the kid. I have my fuckin' limits–I won't let what happened to you all happen to Darrell."

Abruptly, Hassan stood and glared at Levi. Troy thought he was going to have to break up a fight. Akeel moved to the end of the table between Hassan and Levi. His words were calming.

"We all want what you want, Levi–ain't that right, Hassan?"

"Yeah." Hassan broke eye contact with Levi and looked at Akeel.

Troy noted the muscles in Hassan's neck and shoulders were still tense. The pain was visible in Hassan's black face. He sighed as he moved his hand over his tight jaw. Hassan turned to Levi and apologized.

"I been with Darrell's mother and girlfriend all day. It's hard to watch their pain. I'm sorry, man."

Levi nodded. "We'll fix this, man. I promise."

And just like that, the strain in the room lessened. It had been a long day, it was time to call it quits for the night. "Akeel and Levi will come home with me. Y'all can help with the safety of Francine, Monica and Jennifer."

"Aiight," Akeel said.

"Hassan, you and Tyrell will stay at the safe house. Butch and Jesse will help in both places." Troy continued.

"Yeah." Hassan agreed. "What are we doing tomorrow?"

"I gotta take Francine down to the literacy program in Marietta. She wants to volunteer." Troy glared at Akeel.

"I was trying to help. She wanted to work somewhere that we couldn't control. Monica and Jennifer were encouraging her." Akeel explained.

Troy shook his head. "I'll be dealing with my wife the early part of the day. I'll come to the safe house when I finish."

Hassan drove Levi's car back to Fulton Industrial and the Jenkins family. Troy, Akeel and Levi took the truck and headed for Calhoun, Georgia. As he sat in the backseat, Troy thought of Francine. He wanted to hold his wife; he needed her.

6

SHIT STAY HAPPENING

Francine had gone sightseeing with Monica, Jennifer and Junior—escorted by Akeel. The day had been exhausting. Twice, she had to go into the restroom to get herself together. The saving grace was Akeel's patience. When they got back to the house, it was 8:30 in the evening. She had feigned sleep as they sat in the living room until Monica pushed her toward bed.

Once in the bedroom, Francine dug into the wicker basket at the foot of the bed. She donned the t-shirt her husband wore the previous day. He wasn't home, and she missed him. Francine turned on the television, so she could have the comfort of chatter in the background. But the image of Troy on the evening news, discussing the wrongful arrest of a young black man, filled the screen. She was transfixed as he laid out his list of demands. Francine was sure she was witnessing Plan A.

When the newscast was over, she turned to other channels trying to get their take on her husband. She found that the consensus surrounding Troy was that he was an angry black man with an agenda. Francine was indignant on his behalf. It also made clear that her husband had real issues to tend. Babysitting her shouldn't be a burden he had to carry.

Francine had been asleep for about two hours when she felt Troy's hot mouth between her thighs. She was dimly aware that her bikini underwear had been ripped. Groggy, she welcomed the tip of his tongue as it lashed at her clit. Her husband brought her to the brink of climax, then backed away. Troy was a windstorm of urgent need, moving over her; she couldn't breathe.

"T-shirt... take it off," he whispered.

Frantically, his hands groped at the shirt to help her pull it over her head. But before she could push the garment away, he latched onto one of her nipples and crammed himself inside her. He slammed his mouth down on hers and grunted. His breaths were labored, and the sound of his need caused spikes of ecstasy to gather low in her belly. He bowed his back, shoving his face between her neck and shoulder. Troy rode her hard and fast.

Their bedroom was illuminated by the television that sat in the corner with the volume turned down. In the mirrored ceiling, she saw his body rocking roughly into her. The lighting lay over his black skin, accentuating the tightening and releasing of his muscled form. The sight was stunning, but when he pulled back to look in her face—it was erotic. His features were shadowed on one side making him appear barbaric.

"I need it, baby." He ground out, his words confirmed the image. "Oh, Sweetheart, I'm gonna explode."

Sparks started in the place they were joined and radiated outward, plunging her into spasms so wrenching she feared she would pass out. Mindlessly, she began chanting his name as if her mind had broken. His every thrust was magic, pushing her uncertainties to the outskirts of pleasure. Feeling his desperation for her sent her crashing into sensations so intense, sobs tore from her soul. Yet, she couldn't look away.

Troy's eyes closed, and his lips parted. In a hoarse voice, he cried out. "Shit, baby, I'm gonna..."

Endlessly, orgasm rode him as she felt him pulsing within her. He grunted, groaned and panted as he rode out his own end. It was the way his body strained against hers, the hardness of his thighs as they pressed her legs further apart. The weight of him anchoring her in safety that allowed her rhapsody to drag on.

When the rapture ebbed, he pulled them onto their side. And the lovers fell into a deep slumber, still tangled into each other.

Francine was still adapting to sharing intimate living space with a man—with Troy. She showered first and while it was evident that he wanted to join her, he didn't. Instead, he gave her a small amount of personal space within his lair. She was thankful.

She brushed and combed her hair, trying to get the thick strands into a neat bun. The large mirror in front of the double sink allowed her to watch as Troy stepped into the shower. She left the bathroom to offer him privacy and give herself a chance to breathe. Troy was overwhelmingly dangerous and coarse while at the same time gentle and compliant. He was acquiescent when he was not trying to frighten her.

Troy bought her a black, leather fold up chair that she sat in after bathing or showering. She liked to watch television while applying scented lotion to her limbs and belly. But today, her mind was on the literacy program. Francine wondered if she bit off more than she could chew. Troy was taking her to meet the staff. This was a biddable act on his part; he didn't want her to work and his compromise was real.

It was 10:00 in the morning, and the local news was on. Francine grabbed the remote from the nightstand on her left and turned up the volume.

"When Channel 55 Action News returns, two families want to send a heartfelt plea for help to the Silent Activist."

Francine was staring down at her feet trying to decide if her toes needed painting when she heard the coming attraction. The program had already cut to a commercial when her head popped up. The shower was still running as she focused on the television, waiting for the news to continue. She didn't think to get Troy because she was sure he was already aware, but this was another opportunity for her to learn the man she married.

The theme music started playing as the camera rolled around the news station offering an intimate view of the news anchors. An older black man sat opposite a young white woman. Both held cards in their hands as they stared into the camera. The gentleman wore a black suit jacket with a white shirt and black tie; his gray hair was neatly trimmed.

"Welcome back. I'm Lacey Bowers and this is my co-host, Thom Flint."

"Welcome back." Flint said with a smile.

"Our top story—two Southwest Atlanta families are asking for your help in the search for their loved ones." Lacey Bowers' face was filled with empathy.

She wore a blue dress with a cream-colored sweater. Her thick blonde hair was curled loosely around her shoulders. Francine went back to her toilette when the lady reporter began weaving a tale.

"Mrs. Sylvia Dawson and Mrs. Mattie Fields are asking for information in the whereabouts of their sons."

The screen changed to two elderly women seated on a blue couch staring into the camera. It appeared the younger of the two was doing the talking. Around them stood several young men, women and children—family, it seemed.

"My son, Harold Louis Dawson been missing since April. We ain't heard from him. It ain't like Harold not to come see 'bout me." The gray-haired woman in a brown dress stated. "Mattie here ain't heard from her Samuel in the same amount of time—they's friends."

"I sho ain't heard from my baby. His name Samuel Hubert Fields. I cain't sleep—we done been to the police, but they ain't had no luck." The older of the two women added, her black wig in conflict with her elderly face. The green dress she wore looked more like a robe.

The camera cut away once more showing the front of a rundown brick house with children playing in the yard. A young black woman, who looked to be in her mid-thirties, appeared on screen. She had oily skin and missing front teeth. Her hair was cornrowed to the back, adding to her roughened camera presence. It looked to Francine like the woman had done a nickel for assault.

"My name is Pumpkin Fields. Sammy Fields is my uncle. We askin' the Silent Activist for his help. Neither family is getting nowhere with the police." The woman explained before smiling.

Francine stood as photos of the men who tried to rape and kill her filled the screen. She ran for the bathroom door on shaky legs screaming.

"Troy! Troy!"

Shutting the water off, he stepped from the shower. He moved swiftly toward her in the doorway. "What is it, baby?"

"Hurry, Troy... hurry!"

Troy rushed past her into the bedroom, looking as if he were ready to fight an intruder. When his gaze fell on the television, he stopped short. He appeared unworried at the sight of Sammy and Harold on the screen. Francine waited for the gravity of the situation to sink in; she *waited* for her husband to show signs of stress. But Troy showed no reaction as he stood naked with his feet spread apart, arms folded over his chest and water dripping from his magnificent body.

"If you have any information leading to the whereabouts of Harold Louis Dawson or Samuel Hubert Fields... The Dawson family and the Fields family are sending a heartfelt plea to the community and the Silent Activist. I'm Lacey Bowers, Channel 55 Action News."

Troy turned to her, his expression void of all emotion. "I think shit just got basic."

Francine couldn't breathe, the edges of her vision grew dark–until there was nothing.

BOOK 3

Smoke and Mirrors

1

MARIETTA, GEORGIA
JULY 1995

Amanda Gaither stood to the left of the scarred wooden table in Chris Logan's kitchen. On the counter between the white toaster and the red bread box sat a portable color television. She kept her eyes glued to the set as she watched the Silent Activist join forces with the mother of Darrell Jenkins. It had been three days since the original airing of the newscast, yet each station played the clip as if it was being shown for the first time. There was no relief–Homicide Detective, Christopher Daniel Logan was now synonymous with corruption.

He reached out turning the TV off before placing his blue coffee mug in the sink. When she got up the nerve, Amanda gave him her attention. Chris stepped back from the counter folding his massive arms over his broad chest. She viewed him in profile while he kept his eyes on the now black screen. Amanda needed to unplug from the power struggle that throbbed between them.

"Listen, I'm sorry about how things turned out. I gotta go–I won't be back," she whispered. It was time to leave and distance herself from him.

"You dumpin' me?" Chris's tone was cold.

"We both know you pursued me because of the investigation."

Chris was just over six feet with brown hair that was fashionably shaved on the sides and spiked on top. He had a wide forehead with bushy eyebrows and a penetrating gaze. His ears stuck out from his head, which somehow brought attention to his square jaw. His white skin was sun-kissed perfection. The man before her was so handsome–he was pretty. He was model quality with a large muscular frame. Logan wreaked of maleness and sexual promise. Amanda felt shame in his presence because she was thankful for his interest in her. She didn't care that he had come to notice her because she was assigned to investigate him.

"Are you going to pretend you don't want my attention?" he countered, unfazed by her words.

"No."

When he turned to face her, his unwavering inspection caused her stomach to lurch. Chris was dressed in a plain gray t-shirt and blue jeans–his feet bare. He uncrossed his arms before rubbing a hand against the two-day stubble on his jaw. She couldn't breathe, and he knew it. The waiting game was killing her, so she looked away to regain control.

"You'll sleep here tonight."

"I can't help you, Chris," she said softly, bringing her eyes back to his.

"What time will you be back?"

He spoke as if she hadn't said she was done with this thing between them. She took a steadying breath and used her cop voice. "Logan, I won't be back."

Chris had blue eyes that changed with the color of the shirts he wore. Today, his glare was silver because of the gray t-shirt, and it was unnerving. He smiled though his eyes remained mean. She hoped to convey that she wasn't challenging him, but rather making decisions for herself. The truth was simple–she was trying not to be entangled by him. Amanda went back to concentrating on her surroundings.

The back door was glass in the middle with a white frame. A custom venetian blind draped the door allowing sunlight to spill onto the floor. Next to the door, one window was partially covered by a white refrigerator. The stove, also white, had several unused pots piled on top. The black coffeemaker sat on the opposite counter along with a green and white dish rag. Chris kept a tidy house, still it was lived in.

She turned her back to him, about to walk away when he said, "You had yourself removed from the investigation the day after we slept together. I have been forced out even though they found nothing to implicate me."

Amanda looked at the weeks' worth of unopened mail on his black dining room table, cringing at his words. The gold colored curtains were closed. She guessed they were from the previous owner because they didn't fit him.

"Tonight." He pushed.

She started toward the front door and her maroon Camry parked in his driveway. In the living room, she retrieved her overnight bag from the floor by the forest green couch. Amanda was almost free when he grabbed her by the arm. He placed his other hand on the door above her head but didn't turn her to face him. When she stilled, he caged her in, and she dropped the bag. His body heat was at her back as he leaned in, bulldozing her senses. She closed her eyes.

"Mandy, are you wantin' me to beg?"

"No," she panted softly. "I think…"

"Please," he growled against her ear.

Amanda didn't move, instead she basked in his scent, his warmth and her own need. When she could finally contain herself, her voice betrayed her pain. "I won't be back, Logan. Please… back off."

Chris bent and gently kissed her cheek, then abruptly retreated. She placed her hand on the knob and fought with herself before pulling the door open. Amanda didn't look back as she rushed to her car and tossed her bag in before driving off. When she got to the corner of Whitlock and Powder Springs Road, she burst out crying. Amanda loved him, and she was certain about one thing–Chris Logan didn't love her.

* * *

Chris Logan had been smart in his willingness to do dirt while on the force; but there was one rule he never broke. He worked alone, and if it became necessary to break the law in the company of another–he did so with civilians. Chris didn't engage in crime with other cops, it was the fastest way to get caught. His reasoning was simple; cops had more credibility than citizens. The people he dealt with had records and this lent to his integrity when he had to lie. What galled him was being investigated for two years while knowing Troy Bryant killed his attorney and was getting away with it.

George Ingalls's whole caseload had come into question, so Bryant was a suspect by formality, along with his other clients. Chris couldn't shine light on the situation and risk his own freedom. What grated—the Silent Activist was unaffected by his knowledge of George's demise. Troy Bryant was actively hunting him while the public unwittingly looked on. He would be lying if he said he wasn't bothered by the thought. He had handled everything correctly and that included fucking Amanda Gaither from internal affairs; still, he had been removed from the force with all haste.

He stepped to the foyer window and watched as Amanda backed recklessly out of his driveway. She loved him, he was certain of it. The problem—he had fallen for her as well. Chris had experienced his fair share of beautiful women, and he enjoyed all the perks of being an attractive white male. When it came to his attention that Amanda was assigned to investigate him, he had been smug in his pursuit. She was plain—unattractive, really, if he were being truthful.

Amanda had brown hair that she kept cut short with unremarkable brown eyes. She did have beautiful plump lips and when she smiled, it was disarming. Lucky for him, Amanda didn't smile much. She was chubby, by his standards, and the pants suits she wore for work were less than flattering. Chris had mistaken her for easy prey. He had also thought to control the investigation of his activities through her, but Amanda had shown herself to be stronger than she appeared.

The first time he'd fucked her, he had been unprepared for what transpired between them. Amanda's ordinary brown eyes had lit up when she dropped to her knees and took him into her hot mouth. It was the way she held eye contact while sucking him, each lick thanked him for noticing her. Chris had not been ready to be humbled in bed.

Undressing in front of him made Amanda shy, but she didn't hide from him. She allowed him to see her not so flat belly and thick thighs. Her white skin was pale from lack of sun and from the nerves of being exposed to him. When Chris eased into her tight body, it confirmed what he'd already guessed; it had been a long time for her. He had been on the edge from the moment he entered her, and it didn't help when she began moaning...

"Oh, Chris—thank you… thank you… thank you. It feels so good."

He sighed as he stepped away from reminiscing about the best orgasm of his life. But backing away from thoughts of Amanda only pushed him towards thoughts of Troy Bryant. Chris had been bested on all fronts; he only had one move. It was time to silence the Silent Activist, and he would do so by not losing his shit. There were no other options, he needed to come out on top.

The first step in slowing Troy Bryant down would be to have him picked up for questioning in the murder of George Ingalls. He would call in a few favors that would publicly discredit Bryant. His actions would of course be recognized for what they were—petty, but it was all he had for now. Still, requesting that Bryant be questioned would make several guys on the force nervous. Chris would push the issue to get what he wanted, and more than anything, he wanted Troy Bryant laid low.

* * *

Francine had not left the room in three days, and she refused to see anyone but her husband. As she lay in bed, she listened to life beyond their bedroom door. Francine could hear Troy doing damage control as he spoke with her sister.

"Jennifer," her husband sighed, "Francine is not feeling herself, she doesn't want to see anyone."

"What did you do to her, Troy?" Jennifer accused.

"I know you love your sister. You also know that I love your sister. I don't wanna fight with you, Jennifer."

"You scare me, Troy. I don't know what to think about you and Frankie— ya just scare the shit out of me." Her sister's voice wobbled.

Troy chuckled. "This is you fearing me?"

Hours after Jennifer had accosted her husband, there came another knock at their bedroom door. Francine heard Monica's soft voice, and she felt guilty about Junior. She faced the window and the evening sun, while Troy attempted to make his own sister stand down.

"Ernest, I want to speak with Francine. We are all worried."

"Monnie, please."

"Junior is worried about his auntie."

"Please gives us some time." Troy pleaded. "I can't look after my wife and deal with you and Jennifer."

"Ernest, how did you meet Francine?" Monica pushed.

"No, Monica."

It was all her husband said before she heard the door close behind her. Troy's footsteps retreated into the bathroom, and she was sure he needed space. Francine turned, facing the fireplace and bathroom entrance. The toilet flushed, and the water ran before he reappeared. Their eyes locked, his were filled with concern.

"What are you going to say to the media? These two families are asking for your help."

"I'm not going to answer the media—that's not how I work. You don't need to worry, Sweetheart."

"What if they find something that links you to this crime?" Francine whispered, her pain evident.

"You haven't killed anyone. Levi knows what to do."

Troy was dressed in black jeans and a white button down shirt. His sleeves were rolled up and a gold watch with a large face flashed from his wrist. He moved into the bedroom and stood next to the swept-out fireplace. His mustache and goatee were neatly trimmed. Her husband's dark skin was hypnotizing as he tried for nonchalance.

"What did you do with them?"

Troy's eyebrows shot up; his words were emphatic. "I will not discuss that with you."

"Why?"

"This is my worry, Francine—not yours."

"Troy…"

"I have let you stew in this room, concerned about shit you can't change. Your sister and my sister are about to kill me. You will get yourself ready for the literacy program. We will continue in normalcy."

"I'm worried they will arrest you for saving me." She said in a soft voice.

He sighed. "Three women have reached out to Levi's office to ask for a meeting with me."

"Why?" she croaked.

Troy stared at her as if gauging her response. Francine whispered, "Please."

"I believe these women are victims of the men who tried to harm you, and they are wanting to ask me not to assist in the search."

"Oh, Troy," she sobbed. "I hadn't thought there might be other victims."

"I had, Francine. I'm sad only three women came forward–makes me think other women didn't fare so well."

"Can I help you meet with the women?" She held her breath waiting for his answer.

"Will you be able to handle this? Will you be able to pull yourself together?"

"I want to help, Troy."

"You're going to have to leave this room and deal with the people in this house if you want me to believe that, Francine."

She nodded.

Troy left their bedroom soon after issuing the challenge, and once alone, Francine attempted to manage her emotions. He was giving her time to gather herself. Turning back to face the window, she continued in fear and misery until darkness engulfed the room. Beyond the door, she heard the voices of her new family and thought back to her first time with Troy. It was a far cry from how she felt at this moment. Francine pulled herself out of the bed, washed her face, brushed her teeth, then headed to find her husband.

She stepped into the hall, listening to her surroundings. In the direction of the kitchen, she heard Monica and Jennifer as they prepared dinner. Opposite the kitchen, she heard male voices and followed them to the threshold of Troy's office. Inside stood Levi, Akeel, Tyrell and Hassan. Troy was seated behind the desk, and he smiled upon seeing her. He stood and moved toward her in the doorway; Francine was thankful.

Allowing herself to be drawn into the office, she heard the door click behind her. She stood next to Troy as the men formed a closed circle. Levi started speaking in an informative tone.

"My office has received a call from three women." He looked through a file in his left hand. "These women have requested a meeting with you, Troy. They wish to discuss Harold Dawson and Samuel Fields."

Francine found her voice. "Will we meet with these women separately?"

Levi didn't miss a beat. "Yes, and I think your presence will make it easier. If a statement needs to be made to the media, the meetings will give us a better gauge on how to proceed."

"We know what these women are going to say–this is a formality," Tyrell said.

"My concern is why would this pop in the news after Troy joined forces with the Jenkins family?" Akeel asked.

"Same here." Hassan added. "I'm tryna figure out if this is a coincidence or is someone saying they know what really happened."

Francine noted Troy's cool exterior and to her own shock, she said, "Hassan is right. We need to determine if this is a threat or a fluke."

Levi smirked. "If we dig and find out it's a threat–then what?"

Francine held Levi's amused eyes and whispered, "Kill them."

The smirk fell from Levi's face and the office went silent. Francine's gaze bounced from man to man, and it was clear that everyone in attendance felt the same.

* * *

It was 12:30 in the afternoon, and it had been a hard morning for the former detective Logan. Chris had been on the move since the night before. Now, he was calling in a favor from Frank Simms, who was working the George Ingalls case. Frank was an older, white detective who had been on the force for seventeen years. He didn't like the pressure being applied where Troy Bryant was concerned; but Frank owed, and it gave Chris leverage.

The men met for lunch at a hole in the wall, deep in Douglasville. Chris had gotten there first to observe Frank and make certain he was alone. Frank was dressed in a wrinkled gray suit with stains on his blue tie. His trousers dragged the ground, almost hiding the cheap black dress shoes he wore. Detective Simms looked as though he had been drinking all night. He was forty-two with bleary, runny eyes that were a faded brown. At his temples the hair was white and matched the coloring of his unkempt mustache. The blood had drained from Frank's face, and Chris guessed it was the stress of meeting with him that caused it.

"Frank, thanks for seeing me." Chris offered his hand to shake.

"Logan."

Frank ignored his outstretched hand, but Chris wasn't the least bit put off. He followed Frank inside and adjusted his eyes to the dim lighting. Jack's was a pool hall that saw little action around lunchtime. There were five patrons, two sat at the bar and three sat at separate tables around the room. He and Frank took a table at the back of the establishment. Country music played in a static filled haze, allowing for a small amount of privacy. Frank didn't beat around the bush.

"You want me to hassle Troy Bryant. I dislike the way he speaks against cops and hate the way you been treated…" He fidgeted, looking about before he continued. "But Bryant is a powder keg and fuckin' with him can end the career of any cop who handles him wrong."

"Bring him in for questioning, Frank, and make certain the media is present."

"Logan, are you even listening to me? The damn world is watching."

Frank had become entangled with a prostitute about three years ago. She went missing after filing a complaint. Chris had become aware and though he didn't lord it over the other man—they both understood how it worked. Leaning back, he looked Frank in the eyes, his words matter of fact.

"Make it happen, Frank." Chris stood as a man in his twenties with spiked hair started toward them. He was obviously the waiter. "And clean yourself up, the cameras can be harsh to alcoholics."

When Chris was back on the street, he took a steadying breath and walked to his black pickup. He would not linger on Frank's fear of Troy Bryant's celebrity. There were other matters that needed his attention. He climbed in the driver's seat, turned the key in the ignition and pulled out of the diagonal parking space. The radio came to life, but it seemed the song playing was coming to an end.

The noon sun shone brightly on Bankhead Highway, causing Chris to pull the vinyl visor down to protect his eyes. He was crossing over Highway 92 when he began to focus on the radio announcer. It was the news segment, and while brief, it was troubling.

"Welcome to 104.4 The Boom—I'm Nancy Gold. Some have called College Park a political hotbed. Residents in the area say they have been subjected to profiling as well as stop and frisk. The racial unrest came to a head with the arrest of Darrell Jenkins by former detective Christopher Logan. Logan is also known for the wrongful arrest of Troy Bryant, the Silent Activist. In dealing with the cry for justice, the Atlanta Police Department has dealt swiftly by removing Logan from the force. Mayor Trina Clemmons issued the following statement–*We are here to serve the people and we will work hard to achieve better communication*–As for the residents of College Park, they say it's too little too late. Again, I'm Nancy Gold for 104.4."

Lost in the news segment, honking horns caused Chris to look up. The light was green, but he had not proceeded through the intersection. As his foot found the gas pedal, he was seething from the constant media onslaught. Meeting with Frank today had definitely been the right choice. Chris couldn't deal with emotion; he had to be as calculating as Troy Bryant.

Turning the radio off, Chris rode in quiet to the one place he never ventured unless under the cover of night. Forty minutes later, he arrived in Acworth, Georgia, at the home of Richard Unger–nephew of murder victim John Unger. Richard lived in a sprawling estate off Mars Hill Road with his wife and two daughters. A large black wrought iron gate loomed and to the right was an intercom. Chris pressed the button and waited for moments until a man's voice broke the silence.

"Yeah."

"It's me, Logan."

"Shit." Chris heard before the gate slowly opened to him.

He drove half a mile down a dirt road until a large house came into view. The garage door began to slowly lift, and Chris continued inside. He parked and cut the engine before stepping out of his truck as the garage door descended in a loud rumbling noise. A side door leading into the house swung wide with Richard appearing red-faced and agitated. Like his earlier encounter with Frank, Richard wasn't pleased to see him, but in this instance, it pissed him off.

Chris stared at the smug Richard Unger while collecting his thoughts. He had given up much, and Richard had remained in the shadows taking care to protect himself. They needed to speak, and Chris would no longer be relegated to the cover of night. His inquiry was met with sarcasm.

"Are your wife and children home?"

"It's a little late for that question—don't you think?" Richard sneered.

Chris assessed the tall thin man dressed in black slacks and a white shirt. His sleeves were rolled up with the top button open at the throat. Richard had a slim face with brown scheming eyes and a big nose with tight lips that conveyed his annoyance. He was clean-shaven with close cropped brown hair that was finger combed. Chris gauged him to be under six feet tall, and in his own pettiness, he was glad the other man was shorter.

"We didn't kill John Unger, Richard. My being here will cost you nothing."

"My wife and children have gone to visit relatives. What do you want, Logan?"

"I'm here to find out if you located your uncle's will."

"No."

"Come with the long answer, Richard. When will I get my money?"

"My uncle's estate has been moved to probate court. You will get your money, Logan—when I get mine. That *was* the agreement, remember?"

"When I got involved in this clusterfuck, you didn't tell me that your uncle had a will that didn't include you."

Richard stepped down into the three-car garage and began pacing. There was an open space where a car was obviously missing; in the next space sat a blue BMW. Across the back wall was a work bench and from what Chris could tell, it was there for show; all the tools appeared to be brand new. The faint smell of gas, motor oil and grass permeating the air made Richard look out of place.

"I didn't know the old bastard changed his will." Richard's voice was laced with bitterness.

"I'm empathetic to your problems." Chris stated without empathy. "But I lost everything on this venture, and I expect payment regardless."

Richard stopped pacing to fix his glare on him. "Or what, Logan? You can't get blood from a rock and as you stated—*we* didn't kill him."

"It was me who locked up the Jenkins kid for murdering a man we were going to kill had we gotten there first. How long do you think it will take for them to figure out that Darrell Jenkins didn't kill your uncle? Where the fuck will that leave me? You will pay, Richard, or you will pay."

"My lawyers are handling things, we have to be patient."

"I'm outta patience, Richie. Find the will and pay me–those are your fuckin' choices."

Richard Unger didn't respond, instead he pushed the button on the wall to open the garage door. They stared at each other for moments, then Chris climbed into his vehicle, started the engine and backed out. His threat was clear, he would kill Unger if shit didn't go right. As he traveled the dirt path back to the gate and Mars Hill Road, Chris moved to the next item on his list–Amanda.

The afternoon morphed into evening, and Chris had driven about trying to avoid himself. He hadn't many friends, only the women he chased to break the monotony. Even in his dealings with women, he did not engage in pillow talk; it was the difference between prison and freedom. No pussy made him talk. He was in love with Amanda and still orgasmic chatter didn't happen.

Chris stopped at a diner and had a burger with fries to kill time. It was eight o'clock when he drove to Amanda's apartment complex in Vinings. He spotted her maroon Camry in front of Building Seven and breathed a sigh of relief. The two front windows of her third-floor apartment were lit up. She lived at the back of the complex not too far from the dumpsters; across from the entrance of her building was thick with trees.

The heat and the smell of the community garbage hit him when he got out of his truck. The lighting in the parking lot was sparse as only two streetlights fought back the darkness. Chris made his way to the outside staircase and climbed until he stood at her door. He didn't knock right away, he gathered himself bracing for rejection. If she turned him away, he would come back tomorrow.

He knocked on her door much harder than he intended. The peephole was lit in a peach hue of light and then suddenly went dark. Amanda was staring at him. When she moved away from the hole, the peach light was back, but the door didn't open.

"Baby, I know you're home… please." His voice was thick; he tried to clear his throat. "Open up."

Minutes ticked by with no sound. He leaned his forehead against the door, and then came the sudden clicking of two locks. Chris had a hand on either side of the doorframe to hold himself up. Amanda stood before him dressed in yellow gym shorts with a small slit up each side and a white t-shirt. She wore no bra. Her white skin was pale, and her eyes were red. She wiped at the wetness on her blotchy cheeks, and he felt like crying too. He couldn't have picked a worse time to fall in love.

"You said you wouldn't come back, so I came to you. Can I come in?"

Amanda stepped aside to allow him entry. The house smelled of chocolate chips; a sheet of cookies lay cooling on the counter. When he focused his attention on her, she began to tremble.

"You shouldn't be here, Logan."

He didn't respond right away, as he tried to think of what to say. Amanda's apartment wasn't big, behind her and to the right was a small living room. Against the far wall, before the tiny terrace door was a gray and black couch. At the left of the television was a gray recliner. There was a blue blanket on the chair and on the black coffee table was a pint of butter pecan ice cream, a spoon in the container.

"It backfired on me, chasing you." Amanda grew even paler. She knew he chased her because of the investigation. But he hadn't admitted why he stayed after she could no longer benefit him. "I can't let go."

Amanda backed away, but he followed. When her body bumped the wall, Chris stepped forward; she whimpered. He grabbed her by her short brown hair, angled her head and kissed her. She didn't try to fight him when he stepped back and picked her up.

"Bedroom—which way?"

"Down the hall, straight ahead." She whispered.

Once in the dark room, he stood her on her feet and helped her removed her t-shirt and shorts before shucking his own clothing. When they were both naked, they fell into bed. She was still crying and emotional, and truth be told, so was he.

There was no foreplay. Chris pushed inside her to the hilt and stilled. The room was dark, offering no visual. He was forced to rely on his senses. Amanda smelled of vanilla, her body was hot and tight, even with the condom he frantically rolled on. He was on the edge, and it was the same each time he touched her.

"Fuck, Mandy." He retreated and then slammed home.

"Chris." She panted.

He banged into her none too gently. The feel of her body cleared his mind, eased his hurt and pushed him toward conclusion. His testicles drew up and sensation gathered behind them. Chris didn't try to stop himself–he allowed release to take him. He was thankful when her body clamped down on his erection, pulling the orgasm from him.

"I love you," he groaned as his whole being gave in to what she offered.

Slowly, he moved off her, then disposed of the condom in the waste-paper basket beside the bed. He pulled her against him, his breathing still haggard as he spooned her. She melted into his touch. When their breathing evened out, she whispered into the quiet.

"Nothing good can come of this, Chris."

He wasn't going to let go, he had made that clear when he entered her apartment. There was no sense in repeating himself. His only answer was to hold her tighter. Still, she asked another question.

"Will you stop this with Troy Bryant?"

"No."

2

THE PUZZLE
AUGUST 1995

Troy stood in the reception area of Bryant and Associates with Francine by his side. In the conference room at the end of the hall, a woman named Cynthia Duke awaited an audience with him. Levi had chosen a Saturday afternoon for this meeting to protect her identity. His staff had been put on notice that there would be no weekend work. Akeel was posted up in front of the building. Tyrell was in the corridor leading to the office. Hassan remained at the safe house with the Jenkins family.

Francine was quiet as she stood next to him. Troy twined his fingers with hers to offer support and still, she trembled. When he asked if she were ready, Francine gave a curt nod. He turned and began moving them toward their meeting. Along the hall were beautiful paintings, rich in color. On either side of the corridor were office doors; straight ahead was the *Fish Bowl,* the all glass conference room.

When they reached the doorway, Troy's eyes landed on a woman who looked to be between thirty-five and forty. Fear stiffened her posture upon seeing him but gave slightly at the sight of his wife. The woman before them was black in skin tone to put it mildly. She had a scar over her top lip and the bottom lip, unlike her top, was two-toned with pink on the inside. The bridge of her nose appeared crooked, it was disarming to think her nose had been broken. She had large black, untrusting eyes that conveyed the courage it took to meet with them. Her eyebrows were done to perfection and her hair was shaved close with enough wave to be stylish.

"Mr. Bryant, thank you for seeing me."

"Please call me Troy, and this is my wife Francine."

"Hello, Francine, both of you please call me Cynthia."

"Hello, Cynthia," Troy said, and Francine echoed.

Cynthia wore an orange, v-neck blouse that was short sleeved. She remained seated as Troy pulled out a brown leather chair from the long, cherry wood conference table. The natural light from the floor to ceiling windows added to his ability to gauge her as they spoke. Francine sat first, and Troy took the seat next to his wife.

The room smelled of leather and freshly brewed coffee. A stiff silence blanketed the situation, causing Troy to gesture toward the coffeemaker and small refrigerator.

"Can I offer you something to drink?"

"Coffee with cream—no sugar," Cynthia replied.

Troy nodded, then stood, thankful for something to do. He worried for his wife and how this meeting would affect her. But he didn't place demands to keep her out—he couldn't for he was part of Francine's nightmare. He wasn't delusional about his role in all this and killing her abductors didn't excuse him. His hands shook as he poured coffee for Cynthia and tea for Francine. Placing the paper cups before each woman, he retrieved his own beverage and sat. Cynthia stared down into her coffee as she spoke to the room at large.

"Sam Fields, Harold Dawson and I grew up in the same neighborhood. They were older than me by a year or two, so we didn't travel in the same circles. My mother wouldn't have allowed me to keep company with anyone from those two families. She called the whole lot of them—*trouble*."

Cynthia paused and sipped the brew as if trying to gain strength before continuing with her story. "The Dawson family consisted of four girls and three boys. The Fields family had four boys. The two families banded together and basically terrorized everyone in the neighborhood. I saw the newscast of their mothers asking for help. Those two old bitches were as rough as their children. They often instigated the shit their kids got into."

"I've met people like that in my life," Troy said.

"I came home from school one afternoon and checked the mail. I was preoccupied; my grandmother had promised to send me something for my sixteenth birthday." Cynthia held her head high, "They forced their way in on me when I opened my door. Samuel Fields and Harold Dawson took turns raping me while the other held me down."

"Did you report it?" Troy asked.

"I was sixteen. I even hid it from my mother, who would have been more broken than me. So, no, Mr. Bryant, I didn't report it."

He stared at Cynthia as his wife fidgeted in the chair beside him. She had called him Mr. Bryant, so he was sure he offended her. Francine stepped in and saved him. "Troy's not judging you, Cynthia. He's trying to get the facts. Especially, since you're here to ask my husband not to help these women find their sons. That *is* why you're here, right?"

Francine sat taller in her chair as she waited for Cynthia's answer. He noted that his wife's voice was strong. Cynthia sighed, before directing her words to him. "I've heard you speak several times. I admire the work you do in the community. Helping in the search for men like Sam Fields and Harold Dawson will take away from all you do. I can't be their only victim."

Cynthia stood, reached for her purse and started for the door. She was shorter than Troy expected. When he got to his feet, Francine did the same. He spoke at the other woman's back.

"I will not be helping the Dawson or Fields' family. Thank you for trusting us enough to tell your story. We won't betray you."

Cynthia stopped moving and dropped her head. Troy heard what sounded like a sniffle. Finally, she replied, "I know it sounds petty, but your wife is correct. I don't want you to help them."

"I'm feeling petty too." Francine said, causing Cynthia to turn and look at her. "Can I walk you out?"

Cynthia nodded, and Francine offered him a reassuring smile. As he watched them exit the conference room, Troy found a new respect for his sweet young wife. He stared through the glass enclosure at their retreating backs and noticed Levi standing at the receptionist desk. His cousin was speaking on the phone and the tension in his person was visible. It caused Troy to follow the women.

Staring over the women's heads, Troy watched as Levi hung the phone up and stood to his full height; his words strained.

"We have two situations. I'll start with the shit we can't put off."

In front of him, Francine stopped, turned sideways in the hall and gazed between him and Levi. Cynthia's steps faltered, then stopped before she dropped her eyes to the wood floor.

"What happened?" Troy asked, while conveying that Levi should take care around Francine.

"That was Akeel calling from the lobby. There are two squad cars out front and several news vans. Akeel says he thought he saw Chris Logan at the gas station across the street."

"Troy?" Francine whispered.

He didn't answer or look at his wife. Instead, he addressed Levi. "This is not about Darrell, is it?"

"No. Detective Frank Simms is outside."

"Cynthia shared her story with me. I would like to maintain her privacy. Please have Tyrell escort Francine and Cynthia home."

Levi nodded, then went in search of Tyrell. When he was gone, Troy addressed the women.

"Cynthia, for the purpose of discretion, Tyrell will escort you away from here." And to his wife he said, "I will meet you at home."

"That's fine," Cynthia replied. "I came by cab."

Troy could see that Francine wanted to protest, but she remained quiet. He removed his wallet from his back pocket—took out his license, one credit card and handed the wallet to his wife. Francine stared up at him. Levi reappeared with Tyrell, and the women were ushered back to the conference room. When the elevator doors opened, Troy let Levi enter first. The elevator dinged, signifying that they were moving.

"What's the other issue?" Troy asked.

"I received a call from the lab we commissioned to test the evidence in Darrell's case."

"And?"

"They're saying the evidence hasn't been turned over. The head of the lab we're using believes the samples were lost on purpose."

"Shit."

Levi sighed. "Let's get through this first. You will not answer any questions. We knew this was coming to vilify you. Logan is trying to show that you should be locked up."

"I'm good at silence."

"They're following you; how else would they know to come here?" Levi said more to himself.

"Logan's been following me since they fired him. He sometimes makes himself visible to make certain I understand he's out there."

"You ain't said shit." Levi was agitated.

Troy shrugged. "Can you get the case against Darrell dismissed?"

"The evidence hasn't been declared missing yet, just undelivered."

The dinging sound echoed and the elevator settled before the doors slid open. Akeel stood to the left of the elevators at the security desk. Mildred, the guard was nowhere in sight. Troy guessed she was making her rounds. His attention fell to the large windows and the parking lot. Indeed, there were two squad cars and a throng of reporters. Levi's voice came from behind him.

"They have nothing, but they want you in the police car to embarrass you."

"Let them cuff me and take me to the station. Don't fight them here or prolong shit with my wife upstairs."

"If they take you, me and Akeel will follow."

Troy wanted to send Akeel back to his house with the women. He wanted his wife and family protected. All he wanted Akeel to do was deal with his son—not this old hurt. But when he met his friend's eyes, he knew there would be no sending him away.

"I'll drive." Akeel said, heading for the back of the building to get Levi's car.

"Let's go." Levi said.

The front of the building had a small round drive for drop off and an overhang for bad weather. The squad cars and media lay just beyond the shrubs, adding to the illusion of privacy. Still, this didn't stop the slowing of traffic and the rubberneckers. As Troy moved away from the front doors, he schooled his expression. Detective Frank Simms approached, his demeanor cool and business like.

"Mr. Bryant, we are investigating the disappearance of George Ingalls. We would like to chat with you down at the station."

"You could have called and asked for time with my client. This was tactical—meant to slander." Levi stared in the direction of the gas station. "Do you have evidence against my client?"

"We are trying to fill in the gaps in a murder case. Mr. Bryant is a person of interest. We figured he would want the opportunity to clear his name." Detective Simms replied.

"Are you looking this hard into the disappearance of Tiffani Burkes. She's been missing for three years. I'm sure you're concerned about the young woman who complained that you took advantage of her." Levi countered.

Troy watched as Detective Simms blanched. The older man looked as though he were going to pass out at the mention of this Tiffani woman. Simms cleared his throat, but still stumbled with his next words.

"I'm here to do my damn job."

"Well, Frank," Levi countered, his contempt obvious. "I'm doing my job too. If you don't back the fuck off, our next news conference will be about yo' ass."

Simms took a step back as if slapped, then turned and walked away. Troy watched as the detective made a circling motion with his right pointer finger. The signal to wrap things up was met with enthusiasm. Moments later, the squad cars were gone, leaving the media with an anticlimactic finish. Akeel pulled up in the Benz and Levi got in the front; Troy slid into the back seat. The reporters started for the car, yelling questions. But Akeel rolled slowly toward the street.

"Francine?" Troy asked.

"Tyrell already left with the women. We are giving them time by creating a diversion." Levi answered.

"I thought we agreed to let them take me."

"I'm your lawyer, Troy. If you're being followed, I should have been made aware." Levi snapped.

Troy sat quietly in the backseat, dismissed. They were mad, but he was too tired mentally to explain his stance. He closed his eyes, willing himself to relax. His thoughts drowned out the strained tone of Levi's voice and

Akeel's clipped responses. Unable to stop his brain, his mind wandered back to the night in question.

It was a January evening in 1994, and strangely, it was unseasonably warm even with the hazard of an ice storm approaching. Atlanta had buckled down in anticipation of bad weather. But what the south thought was inclement weather was nothing compared to what Troy had experienced in New York. He meant to exploit this occasion of ice, rain and freezing temperatures. He'd been out of prison four months; he couldn't wait a second longer to kill George Ingalls.

He remembered watching as Levi pieced his case together. His cousin had been trying to save him and Akeel. Troy recalled the moment he realized Ingalls was negligent in the handling of his case, his life and his mama. A pattern had surely emerged of extortion, abuse of power and coercion. Ingalls had made it a point to insinuate himself in the lives of the people arrested by Logan, and then navigate their cases poorly. It wasn't every collar because the goal was to go undetected. The clients he shook down were poor and offered some unseen reward for Logan.

He had followed Ingalls for weeks, learning how he spent his free time. Troy gleaned where his woman lived, where he ate most frequently and who he met with in private and in public. How often Ingalls secretly met with Detective Chris Logan had shocked and enraged him; this caused him to grapple with who to kill first, but in the end, he decided to stay the course.

The storm was scheduled to hit Atlanta and the surrounding areas around 2:00 a.m., and Troy was giddy with how easy it was to predict George's evening activity. The night in question, Troy didn't follow the man who had bled his mama financially and emotionally dry; instead, he lay in wait for his prey. Ingalls, it seemed, had planned to get stranded with his girlfriend while the city froze over–then thawed.

Powder Springs was submerged in darkness by 5:15 that evening. Dressed in a black hoodie, black jeans and black boots, Troy had parked the blue Honda on the corner of Horse Shoe Bend. His gloved hands gripped the steering wheel and he didn't move. It was 8:45 when headlights turned unhurriedly onto the street and cruised past where he was parked. Troy watched as the BMW pulled onto the driveway of Teresa Greenberg.

When the tall form of George Ingalls stepped from the sports utility vehicle and moved to the back door, Troy slipped from his car. Silently, he moved in behind his target, placing the barrel of his nine millimeter flush against the back of George's head. Instantly, Troy began to sweat as his body flooded with two dueling sensations: to flee and to do violence.

"Hands behind yo' fuckin' back."

"Ernest, you tryna end up back in population. My man—you don't wanna take dis no further." George warned and pleaded.

Ingalls stood about six feet, two inches with an athletic frame. A plain looking white man with brown hair and eyes, George wore black rim horned glasses, and Troy suspected it was to appear intelligent rather than for sight. The lawyer was an unremarkable figure who wrapped himself in fine suits and a lavish lifestyle. He had a straight nose with a mole at the edge of his right nostril, which made his spectacles sit slightly askew on his face and added to the dishonesty of his eyes.

Troy disliked this man immensely, but what he hated most about George Ingalls was his attempts to sound black. Shoving the lawyer hard against the side of the vehicle, he gritted.

"Get. Yo. Hands. Behind. Yo. Damn. Back."

He felt himself coming unglued. Troy had to fight the urge to shoot Ingalls right there in the driveway. Suddenly, he felt the cold steel of a gun barrel pressed hard against the back of his own head. Seconds later came the icy voice of Detective Logan.

"Bryant, you shoulda quit while you were ahead. Place your gun on the roof of the truck and put your damn hands in the air."

"Shoot this mafucka." Ingalls growled with renewed vigor now that he had back up.

Troy didn't move, but his body stiffened. He was pissed that he hadn't seen this coming, but he had anticipated that he might bitch up. The possibility that he might not be able to follow through with killing Ingalls was real. He had emerged from prison a changed man, but how much he had changed was still unclear. As he contemplated who he was and this predicament, he heard a swift thud before Logan fell into him and slid to the ground.

Butch came forward, cuffing Ingalls for him and hitting him twice in the head with the butt of his gun. The old man was in place to make certain he settled shit with the lawyer and to make sure shit was cleaned up. They carried a dazed Ingalls to the blue Honda and crammed him in the back seat. As for Logan, Butch hit him again, then dragged him to the back of the house and left him there.

"It's not time to kill the cop." The old man said, before he turned and walked to the black Civic parked in the distance.

It was 11:30 p.m. when they arrived at Troy's home in Calhoun. Ingalls had been taken to the partial basement, where he begged for his life. Troy's hand shook when he shot him in the temple.

"Don't sell this house until ya too old to care if the basement is dug up," Butch said.

"Logan knows I killed Ingalls." Troy countered.

"The cop 'bout himself. He ain't gonna draw attention to his own shit."

The ice storm hit on schedule, but the freeze didn't last as long as predicted. They buried George Ingalls in the cellar floor—then recemented the foundation of the house. Now, the below stairs portion of his home holds some of the best wines and the lawyer who used people for personal gain.

The sound of car doors slamming brought Troy back to the here and now. He looked about to find that Levi and Akeel had exited the vehicle. Following suit, he made his way across the parking lot of Chuck's Bar and Grill. The afternoon sun was bright with the heat adding to his discomfort. It was the first time in years that Troy felt like he needed a nap, though his exhaustion was far from physical.

Inside the cool restaurant, the men followed the short plump hostess to the back of the dim eatery. A round table with four chairs sat in the far corner, and each man took a seat. As the men got comfortable, the older black woman handed out menus.

"What can I get you gentlemen to drink?"

"I'll have a Heineken," Troy said.

Both Levi and Akeel nodded in agreement; the hostess smiled. "Carmen, your waitress, will bring your drinks and take your orders."

"Thank you." All the men murmured in unison.

When they were finally alone, Troy looked about trying to ignore his companions. The dining area was half full of laughing—conversing patrons. Several televisions played the latest sports highlights in the background.

Large windows with the blinds pulled at an angle allowed the smallest amount of sunlight. The place was tranquil.

Troy sighed as he turned his attention back to the table. Both men were glaring at him, but Akeel looked indignant. The waitress appeared with three Heinekens. She dropped a napkin in front of each man, then placed the beer on top.

"I'm Carmen," A tall, thin, young lady with dark skin and thick glasses announced. "I'll give you all some time to look over the menu."

Akeel never took his angry eyes from him. Troy knew what was coming; it was the words he could do without.

"This issue…" Akeel stopped to look around the dining room at the collage of faces, "doesn't belong to you–man. What happened all those years ago–happened to both of us. The time lost with Monica and my son is not your fault. I'm unclear about the fuckin' plan; this ain't plan A."

"It's like there's a whole other agenda that you haven't told us about." Levi's vexation was palpable.

Troy fixed his eyes on the green bottle before allowing his gaze to bounce between Akeel and Levi. He leaned back in his chair to make certain his lack of response put him back in the driver's seat. They weren't in control–he was quarterbacking. This was his show–he was walking this dog. Troy was prepared not to answer when Levi abruptly stood and threw two twenties on the table.

"Where we headed?" Akeel asked.

Levi kept his attention on Troy. "We headed to Troy's house."

"You calling a meeting?" Akeel inquired.

"Naw." Levi countered while staring Troy in the eyes. "We going to Troy's house, so I can beat the fuck outta his smug ass."

Akeel scooped the two twenties off the table and pressed the cash back into Levi's hand. "The beer is on me then."

Levi and Akeel led the way out of the restaurant. Troy followed, realizing Levi was dead-ass.

3

Mutual Understanding

Francine sat quietly as Troy maneuvered his truck into a parking spot facing the two-story structure on the corner of Roswell Road and Fairground Street. She didn't look at her husband because Troy would let her off the hook, and she needed this interaction with the unfamiliar. It was time to start living outside of him. Monica and Jennifer wanted to come with her, but Francine had refused. Both women were understanding of her anxiety. Still, they manhandled Troy in hopes of getting to the bottom of what they believed was his fault.

The lobby door opened, and out stepped Levi dressed in black slacks with a white button down shirt. Francine had not asked, and Troy had not offered. Her husband had a black eye with a gash on the bridge of his nose. Levi sported a deep cut over his left brow, a bruised cheek and split lip. Francine was sure they had a fight. She worried it was because of the addendum, but Levi treated her no different.

"I have an office on the first floor, the classrooms are on the second floor." Troy informed her.

"Do you come here to work often?"

"No," he replied.

Troy was agitated, and Francine decided not to try to manage his mood today. The goal was to bring her own emotions to heel. She blew out a loud breath, then opened the passenger door; her husband followed suit. When she rounded to the front of the vehicle, Troy took her hand. They moved toward Levi who looked a step above annoyed. This threw Francine for a loop because Levi wasn't serious about anything in her presence.

"Troy-Francine."

"Levi." Troy greeted in return.

She didn't speak, and as always, the tension between the men seemed both hostile and brotherly. Francine disengaged from them, trying to avoid overstimulation. It was the only way to survive without breaking down. Levi opened the door and both men allowed her to enter first. She stepped into a small lobby with a narrow corridor and rickety elevator. At the end of the hall was a conference room with a desk to the right of the door. The walls were white with several bulletin boards dressed in colorful flyers. Under her feet, the beige, industrial carpet crunched a bit as they moved along.

The building was old, and the smell of fresh paint clung to the atmosphere. Francine could see people standing about in the conference room. On the wall next to the door hung a makeshift sign that read: Staff Meeting. When Troy entered the room, all conversation stopped. Francine stood next to her husband, but she didn't press herself against him. Two women and a man stared at her before the man stepped forward.

"Troy—Levi, what's up?

"Eric." Troy responded. "This is my wife Francine."

"Nice to meet you, Francine."

She had to clear her throat before speaking. "Same here."

Behind her Levi said, "Eric, good to see you. How's Club Confidence holding up?"

Eric focused over her head. "The program is good, not having steady instructors is killing us. But beggars can't be choosy."

"Yeah, Troy and I realize the shit you deal with on the regular. We appreciate you."

While Levi spoke to Eric, Francine stared at the unfamiliar man. Eric was shorter than Troy, yet way taller than her. He was dressed like Levi in black slacks and a white button down shirt. His collar was opened at the throat, and his sleeves were rolled up. Eric looked to be no older than twenty-five with light brown skin, black curly hair and green eyes. When he smiled, dimples appeared. He had light stubble on his square jaw with a mustache and goatee that outlined his masculinity. He was also well muscled.

Eric's attention fell back to her. "Francine, this is Rachel and Courtney. Today is their first day as well."

She looked to the women standing in front of the coffeemaker. They smiled. "I'm Courtney," a dark-skinned woman with thick glasses and a huge afro, who looked to be Francine's age introduced herself. Like Levi and Eric, she too was dressed in black slacks and a white dress shirt.

"Hi, Courtney." Francine replied.

"I'm Rachel." The woman standing to the right of Eric said.

Dressed in a blue pants suit, Rachel looked to be thirty something with light skin. She had wavy brown hair that was pulled back in a ponytail. "Nice to meet you." Francine replied.

Eric took control of the situation. "Francine, we were going over how things work around here. Please, join us."

Next to her, Francine felt her husband's tension. But Levi's words floated out from behind her. "Troy and I will work out of his office today. We'll see you all later."

Francine turned to find her husband even more upset than when they arrived. She glanced around the room, and everyone was staring at them—witnessing their strain. But she didn't shy away from his concern for her; instead she stepped closer, causing him to bend and whisper in her ear.

"I'll be down the hall."

"I know," she whispered back.

"All right, people," Levi said, "Troy and I will leave y'all to it."

Reluctantly, Troy stepped back, eyeing Eric before turning to leave. As she stood frozen and alone at the door, Courtney broke the silence. "Your husband is a pretty intense dude."

Francine blinked, and Rachel added. "Both of them are freakin' scary. My father would say they look like brawlers."

"All right, ladies, let's cut Francine some slack." Eric's hilarity was unmistakable.

Francine smiled weakly as she moved to seat herself at the scarred wooden table. A whiteboard hung to the left of the room; the word *dignity* was written in neat block letters. Courtney and Rachel sat, while Eric remained standing.

"Let me start by thanking you all for your time. I won't lie–programs like this are hard for two reasons. Either, we encounter volunteers that are not serious, or we deal with attendees that aren't willing to put in the work. The goal here is to give people a level playing field while offering opportunity where there is none."

Eric paced for several moments as if he expected them to get up and walk out. When that didn't happen, he continued, "We are selling dignity, confidence and pride. When *down on their luck* people step through these doors, we want them to know we care."

"How many volunteers do you have?" Rachel asked.

"We have experienced a bit of a revolving door. At this moment, we have two volunteers, plus me." Eric replied.

"How many people apply to this program?" Courtney asked.

"Countless—we turn lots of people away. We also keep strange hours because we're dealing with people's free time."

"How long are the classes?" Francine asked.

"We do four hour classes, which amounts to half a day." Eric explained. "Why don't I give you ladies a tour? The building is old but clean."

In the hall, Francine got a closer look at the flyers on the bulletin boards. There was information on WIC, rooms for rent, as well as free STD and pregnancy screenings. They took the tiny elevator to the second floor where they found a class in session. Francine was shocked to find Akeel standing at the chalkboard. He winked at her, but he didn't stop teaching. There were two other rooms that were set up like classrooms with the chair and desk combo. The last room was a library of sorts with large bookshelves against every wall. The lighting was great, and there were comfortable chairs all around the open space.

Back on the first floor, Eric began asking questions about scheduling. They all agreed to start on the next business day. He dismissed Rachel and Courtney, which left Francine alone with him. She stood behind her chair studying a chip in the table. Eric's voice was deep and patient.

"You all right, Francine?"

She brought her eyes up to meet his green ones. "Yes."

"Akeel and Levi mentioned that you get nervous around men you don't know. I'm glad you're here, we need the help. Please know I would never do anything to hurt you or any woman."

Francine blew out a shaky breath, then nodded. She couldn't find the words—not without crying. Eric smiled, "Soooo—I have a favor to ask."

She stared at him—still no words, and he continued. "Will you tell me to back off if I make you uncomfortable? I won't be offended. I promise."

Francine gave him a feeble smile, then answered. "Yeah."

* * *

The first week at Club Confidence, Francine experienced three anxiety attacks. When she looked back over the week, she was thankful for the small things; the anxiety seemed to take its toll at night, and though she was crippled with fear, she dealt with it in private. She threw up twice in the wee hours of the morning from an unsettled stomach. It was the apprehension of leaving for work in a few short hours to do it all over again.

She hadn't done any teaching, and it was clear that Eric was giving her time to become acclimated with the set up. Courtney had shadowed Akeel and then Eric in the classroom, by day two she was handling a session on her own. On day three, Rachel had decided this wasn't for her and quit. Eric had taken the news in stride and didn't appear the least bit shocked.

Akeel came and went throughout the week. Courtney did the afternoon sessions, while Eric did the morning sessions. Francine, by default, became the person handling the front office. She tackled the never-ending trays of unopened mail. Next, she helped sign up several young, expecting mothers for the program. And though she was nervous, she slowly became at ease with Courtney and Eric.

Troy had been asked by both her and Levi to give her some room. As a result, she saw little of her husband. Butch or Akeel drove her to the office and picked her up in the evenings. And there were at least three mornings where Troy was climbing into bed as she was getting out. Francine had been too self-absorbed to question the strangeness of his schedule.

It was Friday and the last day of week one when matters took a turn for the worse. Eric had taken an early lunch to run some personal errands. Courtney was teaching a class of eight. Francine had been dropped off by Butch, and she had not seen Akeel all morning. The first floor of the building was set up weird to her way of thinking. There was the entrance, the conference room and the two offices, both at the far end of the hall. She stayed at the receptionist desk, so she could see who was coming and going and to answer the phone which rang constantly.

The lobby door was shoved open, giving a scraping sound. Francine peered up to find a young girl who looked as though she were about to give birth. She wore a pink maternity top with little teddy bears all over it. If Francine had to guess, she would have gauged the girl to be about seventeen. The door gave another scraping sound and the mailman walked in. He was a big burly, white man with dark blue eyes.

"You new?" The mailman asked while handing her a large stack of mail. Francine almost fainted.

She didn't reach for the mail nor did she respond. A humming started in her ears as the lobby door gave another scraping signal.

"Victor, I told you to stop bringing us bills." It was Eric's laughing voice.

"You all right, Miss?" The mailman asked.

Francine didn't answer, instead she rushed for the bathroom. Once inside, she picked the smaller of the two stalls and immediately lost her breakfast. The oatmeal tasted as lumpy coming up as it had going down. She finally stopped heaving and became aware of someone else.

"Miss, you okay?" It wasn't Courtney.

"I'm fine." Francine answered with a shaky breath. She felt sweaty and unstable on her feet as she leaned heavily against the wall.

"Come out and let me see you or the guy with the green eyes will come in."

Francine slowly twisted the lock and stepped from the stall to face the brown-skinned girl with two cornrows in her hair. She was so pregnant, and Francine experienced a moment of guilt for making her worry. At the sink, she washed her hands and splashed water on her face. When she looked in the mirror, the girl smiled.

"You pregnant? Yo' belly seems sensitive like mine was in the beginning. The man with the green eyes–that yo' baby daddy?"

Francine was confused. It took a moment to register, but when it did, she gripped the sink. "I'm married and not to Eric."

"I'm Shelia." The girl beamed. "So green eyes ain't yo' man?"

"No." Francine replied. She was about to ask the girl to give her a moment, but the door opened again.

"Francine?" the voice belonged to Levi. She was annoyed with herself. This was a lot of drama because the damn mailman tried to do his job. Levi looked to Shelia. "Give us a moment."

The girl nodded, then disappeared. "You good?" he asked.

"Yes." Francine whispered.

They stood in silence for what seemed an eternity; she lifted her head to find him staring at her. "You need me to call Troy?"

"No."

Levi continued to stare at her a few beats more. "Troy is handling some business. He's not here—"

"Give me a minute."

Levi nodded and backed out of the women's restroom. Turning, Francine gazed at her reflection, assessing all her frailties. She was plain old embarrassed to face everyone. Taking a deep breath, she pulled the door open and stepped into the corridor. The girl, Shelia, was gone. Eric was gone. The mailman was gone–only Levi remained, leaned against the edge of her desk, feet crossed at the ankle, arms folded over his chest.

"Tomorrow is Saturday," he said.

"I know."

"We have another lady coming to meet with us about the Harold and Sam case. If you show weakness, Troy will shut you out."

"I know."

"Would you rather not be part of the next interview?"

"I want to be part of the next interview." Francine replied, and more staring happened between them until Levi finally stood and walked away.

The rest of the day was uneventful, and it was Levi who drove her home at the end of business. As they rode along in absolute quiet, it occurred to Francine that she was well into her last pack of birth control pills. She wasn't pregnant, but she would be if she didn't see a doctor. There could be no going to Troy; she didn't want to have to ask for permission on this issue. She needed to speak with Monica because going to her own sister was out of the question. Jennifer was a loose cannon where Troy was concerned. And she still wasn't sure what her sister had with Levi.

* * *

Although Troy had his own office at Bryant and Associates, he preferred the conference room. The receptionist, Denise, a plump woman in her late thirties with deep chocolate skin and brown eyes kept him plied with coffee. She dressed colorfully with beautiful wraps about her locks. Denise was blackness set on fire, and she had become his personal assistant.

When he finally turned his mind away from worrying about his wife, Troy had thrown in shoulder to shoulder with the other men to get to bottom of the Darrell Jenkins' case. Levi and Akeel dealt with Jennifer and Monica. They also went back and forth to the jail to work with Darrell. Troy wouldn't visit the prison again. The experience left him too rattled. He worked with Hassan and Tyrell to investigate the facts.

The conference room had folders, photos and paperwork sorted across the entire table. They had begun sifting through all that was given to them by the Fulton County D.A. Larry Wright. It had taken Troy some time to recognize the significance of the information supplied and now that he had latched on, he was like a dog after a bone. But it wasn't just the paperwork, it was the residents of Hanover Street that got his brain going.

While the neighbors of the Jenkins family refused to speak with him publicly, they had begun calling the law office and setting up private appointments. He, Tyrell and Jerrell Jenkins had gone out several times to interview folks. The welcome they received was anything but warm. Troy thought this was because of him until the interviewees requested that Jerrell not be included or informed of their willingness to come forward.

There were a total of four interviews from the people of Hanover Street. Yet Troy, as well as Tyrell, experienced great disappointment. A girl named Bridgette West was their first interview. She looked to be about nineteen with light skin and long black hair. The worst part–she was attractive, but everything about her screamed gaudy. The makeup she wore was thick. It made her appear as though she were headed to the club rather than a meeting at a law firm on an early Tuesday morning, and the black dress that barely covered her ass didn't help matters.

Since Troy had the conference room sewn up, he took interviews in his unused office. There was a large mahogany desk with a black leather chair.

In front of the desk in one of two smaller chairs, sat the woman, Bridgette. She had a nasal twang that rubbed Troy the wrong way.

"Shirley Jenkins ain't shit." Bridgette informed them. "When I started dating Jerrell, she stepped in because my father is white. She told him she ain't want him running wit' no half black girl."

Troy blinked, while Tyrell asked. "What does Ms. Jenkins not wanting you to date her son have to do with Darrell's case?"

"She a bitch. I just told you what." The girl replied.

Strangely, the next two interviews happened in the same vein. The sit down was with a girl about twenty named Raven Coleman. The tag fit her well because her skin was jet black, and she had dark beady eyes. She wore her hair shaved close with pink framed glasses. The woman before them was unattractive. She was dressed in blue slacks and a yellow shirt; her voice, oddly seductive.

"Shirley Jenkins thinks her and her sons are above everyone else; fuck her."

This time it was Troy, who asked, "What does this have to do with the case against Darrell?"

"It has to do with Shirley thinking she better, now the son she ain't want me to date is in jail."

"Do you have anything to say about Darrell?" Tyrell asked.

"Yup… fuck him, too."

In the interest of time, meeting number three was over the phone and screened by Tyrell. A woman named Michelle Scott wanted to know why her interview had been cancelled. Tyrell informed her that there was a scheduling conflict.

"That bitch Shirley prolly told y'all not to meet with me." She complained.

Troy stood by quietly. Tyrell sighed, "Ms. Scott, Shirley Jenkins doesn't know we're meeting with you."

"At first, I didn't want her to know that I was talkin' to y'all, but I decided I don't give a shit if ya tell her."

"Do you have anything that would be helpful to the Darrell Jenkins case?" Tyrell asked, attempting to get control of the conversation.

"Yeah. I got something to add. I bet Ms. Shirley ain't so smug now."

Troy did the phone screening for meeting number four–Tyrell refused. They were prepared for the interview to yield no fruit when what sounded like an older woman began speaking.

"Glad you called, Mr. Bryant."

"Thank you for working with me, Ms. Moore. Scheduling conflicts have set us back three days."

"Please, call me Judy."

"Well, Ms. Judy," Troy said, "do you have anything that might help us with the Darrell Jenkins case?"

The woman sighed. "You know, Mr. Bryant—"

"Troy."

"Troy," She supplied before continuing. "I can tell you that Shirley has three good boys. She, on the other hand, is a dishonest bitch. But she did good wit' them boys."

The last thing Troy wanted was another conversation that crossed into gossip about Shirley Jenkins. He had been about to cut the discussion short, when Judy said something that brought his thoughts to a grinding halt.

"I have the will."

"What will?" Troy asked.

"John Unger's will."

And so it began, a paper chase that sent Troy's mind reeling. There was so much he hadn't considered. He needed to speak with Levi and the other men. Their list of suspects had grown due to the number of people who hated Shirley. They would have to check into the background of each woman who came forward. It was possible Darrell got shafted, so someone could get even with his mother.

* * *

Francine stared across the table in utter shock at the woman meeting privately with her husband. The day was overcast and muggy, which seemed fitting to the task at hand. When she glanced at her husband, Francine had to admit, he was better at hiding his surprise. Pumpkin Fields, the niece of Sam Fields, sat opposite them. She appeared nervous, still she looked Troy in the eyes.

"My family don't know I'm here."

"I gather you're here to ask for my assistance in person." Troy countered.

Pumpkin cleared her throat. "Yes, Mr. Bryant, I'm here to ask for help. I don't want you to look for my uncle or his friend. Both families is better off without 'em. My grandma don't see shit so right."

Francine gasped. "You *don't* want my husband to look for your uncle? But you were on the news asking for his help."

Pumpkin turned her attention to Francine. She was as rough in person as she appeared on the television. Dark, oily skin with sharp eyes and freshly braided hair. She wore a blue dress layered with a white sweater. Yet, there was nothing feminine about the niece of Sam Fields. When she spoke, her tongue fell in and out of the space where her front teeth were missing.

"I have been raped by my uncle repeatedly. I hope he's dead."

Francine held her gaze. She could find no words for such a statement. Troy asked, "Why ask for my help publicly?"

"My family… it's what is expected of me." She said in a shaky voice.

Francine had missed the intelligence in the other woman's eyes when she first saw her on the television, but there was no mistaking it now. Pumpkin broke her train of thought.

"I have a daughter. Tiara is a great kid. The children in my family don't need him back."

Francine was still speechless, and apparently, so was Troy. But Pumpkin wasn't. "I thought because he is Tiara's father, I wouldn't love her–but I do."

Troy finally recovered. "Ms. Fields, I have no intention of looking for your uncle or his friend. I think this situation is best left for the police."

She nodded, then stood. "Thank you for your time, Mr. Bryant."

Before she walked out, Troy asked, "Who decided it was a good idea for your family to ask for my help?"

"You were recommended by Shirley Jenkins. The lady you was on the news with about her son."

"What did you say?" Troy's voice dropped to the tone of menace.

* * *

As the day pressed on, Francine was aware of a shift in her husband's demeanor. Pumpkin Fields had long since gone, but her words changed everything. Troy and Tyrell had an intense conversation in the conference room, then Troy packed his briefcase. They rode home in complete silence while Tyrell drove. When they reached the house, the men headed for Troy's office. Hassan wasn't present.

Francine was concerned because she didn't understand what she was seeing. She also couldn't push aside the pain she witnessed in Pumpkin Fields; the mention of a child had stunned. Francine felt shame because she had offered no support. In fact, when she initially saw who they were meeting with, she became angry—only to find that Pumpkin had been victimized too.

The hour grew late, and Francine woke to find that Troy had not come to bed. She felt disconnected from him, but she wasn't angry. He had been asked to back off, and he had done as requested. She didn't feel neglected since he had put all kinds of safety nets in place. There was always someone looking after her. If she were being honest, she liked that he was distracted. She couldn't deal with her fear and his intensity. Francine had another major issue; *she did not want to become pregnant.*

The state of her life didn't bode well for a baby, her brain was too scrambled. She loved her husband, but Levi's words still haunted her: *Since you ain't gonna kill her, marry her, fuck her and knock her up.* This was also part of the reason she didn't want children. Troy had enforced Levi's demands… yeah, both men were part of the problem. Strangely, Butch wasn't part of her nightmare, but the old man was frightening as hell.

She climbed from her bed and headed for the closet where she found Troy's robe. The air conditioner was humming, making the chill in the house almost unbearable. When she stepped into the hall, she heard the clinking of a spoon hitting the inside of a cup. Francine followed the noise, but before she did, she glanced to the left. Troy's office was dark.

Stepping into the kitchen, she found Monica seated to the table sipping tea. The light over the sink cast a soft glow, and the clock on the wall to her left read 1:45 a.m. Monica had an orange blanket wrapped about her waist with hot pink wool socks on her feet; her hair a huge untamed afro. Francine smiled, and Monica spoke.

"The men left a little before midnight. Junior and Jennifer are in their rooms. Butch and Jewel went home. What are you doing up?"

Francine moved to the dish rack and retrieved a red mug, before adding hot water and a teabag. She sat opposite Monica. "I couldn't sleep."

The quiet enveloped them until Monica said, "It's August, and I haven't attempted to get Junior registered for school. I wanna go back to Jersey, Akeel scares me."

Francine didn't know what she had expected Monica to say, but it was her turn to offer a small amount of honesty. "I need you to take me to get birth control. I don't want Troy to know."

"Ernest will kill us both." Monica shrugged. "What the hell? Akeel is going to kill me anyway."

"I can't talk to Jennifer. She might get angry and tell Troy."

"Or my cousin Levi outta spite."

"How could we go to a clinic, we're always being watched?" Francine said.

"You have a place in mind?"

"Yeah, the bulletin board had information about free screenings and birth control."

Monica nodded. "I'll borrow Jewel's car and pick you up for lunch on Tuesday."

Francine couldn't help it, her eyes watered. Still, she managed, "Thank you."

Monica studied her for a few intense moments. "How did you meet my brother?"

"Please… don't." Francine shook her head. "What's important is that I love him, but I'm not ready for a child."

"Why can't you tell Ernest how you feel?"

"Why can't you tell Akeel how you feel?"

The last two questions hung in the air between the women until Francine stood and placed her mug in the sink. She squeezed Monica's shoulder and turned to exit the kitchen.

4

CAT AND MOUSE

Troy stood in the living room of the safe house facing Shirley Jenkins. The woman was smug and unapologetic as she glared at him. Speaking with her was against his better judgement, but Levi wanted to see her reactions to the questions. The anger rolling off her was palpable and what it meant was not yet clear. Behind him stood Levi, Tyrell, Akeel and Hassan. The hour was late, and everyone else in the residence was asleep.

"We are working as a team to free Darrell. Why would you volunteer my services and take away from your son?" Troy asked.

"He is *my* son, Mr. Bryant. I was doing fine without you–you inserted yourself where you weren't welcome."

Troy couldn't say that her nephew Justice and the D.A. himself had asked for his help. He also needed to be careful in the amount of interest he showed in the Sam Fields and Harold Dawson case. What he did not need was for her to piece together his concerns. Why had she picked a case where he was the perpetrator?

"How did you set this up? Did you contact these families offering false hope?" Troy asked.

"I do my homework, Mr. Bryant. There are several cases where black victims are overlooked and more where black men have been arrested for crimes they didn't commit. I planned on using the data at my next protest– then you came along. I thought to get you out of my way or give you some other family to focus on."

Troy was incredulous on so many levels. Levi took over the conversation. "Darrell needs us—we will deal no further with you."

"I did this when I was angry—when we first met." Shirley protested.

"You will keep your mouth shut in public." Levi countered.

She nodded, contrite. "Don't shut me out."

"What else have you done that we don't know about?" Tyrell asked.

Shirley sighed. "I volunteered you all for five other missing person cases. The families of the two men were the only ones that asked for your help."

Darrell's mother stood before them dressed in jeans and a wrinkled blue shirt. It was obvious she had clothed herself quickly to meet with them. Troy's head was ringing, and he still didn't know what to think. One thing was for certain—they couldn't trust Shirley Jenkins. She was a controlling bitch.

Before they left, Levi added another log to the fire. "Tyrell and Hassan will move everyone out of this house in the morning."

"I am willing to work with you all… please." Shirley said.

"This set up was to keep the press and the police at bay." Levi replied. "Since you're contacting the media and making more work for us, this is a waste of manpower. We'll let you tell your sons and Jasmin what happened."

As soon as Akeel pulled away from the house, Levi asked, "What do you make of Darrell's mother?"

"Fuck if I know." Troy answered. "But my mind keeps coming back to someone killed John Unger and left Darrell to take the heat to get even with his mother."

"We gotta think logically." Akeel added.

"Logically?" Troy repeated.

"All the cases she picked are from the Atlanta area. The shit with Francine happened in Atlanta—I think this is a coincidence. What I think is Shirley got something to hide."

"Like what?" Levi snapped.

"I don't know what she's hiding, but it's something." Akeel answered.

"Shit." Troy muttered.

"What next?" Levi asked.

"Next, we meet with Judy Moore." Troy said. "She has agreed to let us see John Unger's will."

"I'll leave it to you and Levi." Akeel said.

"Did she say why she hadn't submitted the document to the probate court?" Levi asked.

"No," Troy said, "but I got the feeling she wasn't going to tell me about it–then changed her mind. She lives in Austell now and advised that we shouldn't come until after 10:00 pm tomorrow night."

"You mean tonight–it's almost 2:00 a.m." Akeel corrected.

"Yeah." Troy countered.

The house in Calhoun, Georgia, was dark when Akeel parked the car. The men entered through the front door and separated heading for their beds. Troy began moving toward the clinking sound coming from the kitchen. He figured he would find Monica; instead, he walked in on the tail end of a conversation between his sister and his wife.

"Thank you." Francine said, sounding emotional.

"How did you meet my brother?"

"Please… don't." His wife answered. "What's important is that I love him. I'm not ready for a child."

"Why can't you tell Ernest how you feel?"

"Why can't you tell Akeel how you feel?"

The conversation stopped, so he stepped into the kitchen. His wife looked nervous at his sudden appearance. Monica, however, had no reaction to seeing him.

"Good morning, Ernest."

"Monica." He responded, but he never took his eyes from his wife.

"Good morning, Troy." Francine managed.

"You're up early." He replied, dismissing his sister.

Francine couldn't hold eye contact; *what the fuck*–he thought. His sister left the kitchen, but his wife stood by the island dressed in his blue robe. She looked like a deer in headlights.

"How are things going at the program?" he asked.

"I'm tired, Troy. It's been a rough week, but I made it."

He slanted his head and stared at her the way a dog might when confused. Still, he didn't push the issue. "Come, let's go to bed."

Francine nodded, then stepped past him. Once in their room, she removed the robe and climbed into their bed without looking his way again. Troy undressed, took a piss, then brushed his teeth. She lay facing the window, basically trying to ignore him. He lay flat on his back, trying to control his anger. She was shutting him out again and with all that was going on, he couldn't take it.

Troy tossed over in his mind the words between his wife and sister. Francine had said she didn't want a child. Was his wife pregnant and refusing to tell him? What had she thanked his sister for? He had backed off to give her room, now she was avoiding him. Francine was fuckin' hurting him. There was too much shit in his head. As for Monica... he would make certain Akeel dealt with her.

He never did find sleep, so when the morning sun rose, it found him staring at his reflection in the mirrored ceiling. Next to him, his wife pretended to still be resting and he allowed it. It was Sunday, there was much to do; he shaved, showered and dressed. Troy would bide his time.

He stepped into the hallway at the same time Monica and Junior came into view. They were coming from his nephew's room and heading for the kitchen.

"Good morning, Uncle Troy."

"Morning, Little Man." Troy managed a smile.

"Is Aunt Francine up yet?" Junior asked.

Troy shook his head. "Your partner in crime is still sleeping."

"Come eat." Monica said to her son–then to her brother she offered. "Morning, Ernest."

Troy nodded his head curtly in her direction before walking away. Once in his office, he closed the door quietly and turned his mind to the mistakes he made while researching this case. He was an amateur at placing the facts, but today he had a strategy. Shirley Jenkins was correct about one thing–she didn't ask for his help. He had assumed she would be like his own mother looking for anyone to save her son.

Levi stepped into his office followed by Akeel. Troy was still unpacking his briefcase and trying not to appear wrung out. He offered his ideas, throwing himself and them into work. It was better than discussing Monica and Francine.

"We need to look into the background of John Unger. Chris Logan has been our focus, yet nothing points to him other than being the arresting officer. Shirley is correct about my need to get revenge clouding my judgment."

"What I find interesting is all the complaints are about Shirley and not Logan." Levi said.

"I agree." Akeel chimed in. "But most of the gripes seem to be chick shit. Darrell's mother being a bitch doesn't make or break this case. Let's not forget that Logan is good at what he does."

"What we got is cops witnessing Darrell with blood on his clothes. I'm meeting with Larry Wright on Monday. The physical evidence–meaning the clothing Darrell was wearing when he was picked up has not been made available to our experts. My office has been notified that there is no video of Darrell entering the precinct, so the brutality issue is my client's word against theirs." Levi said.

They worked through the facts, trying to gauge the correct avenue. They all agreed to back into the problem and start with Unger. As the day progressed, Levi and Akeel wandered in and out of his office. Troy didn't venture out and his wife didn't seek his company. It was 7:45 p.m. when he finally left his office.

He found his wife watching a movie with his nephew in the living room. Francine smiled up at him, but she never came to greet him. When she spoke, her voice was strained.

"Hey, Troy, Junior and I are trying to guess the outcome of this movie."

He leaned against the wall for moments, gazing at her before he nodded. "Well, you two have fun. I gotta step out this evening. I'll be back late."

"All right." She whispered.

Troy didn't respond to the relief he saw on her face at the news of his departure. He turned on his heels and exited the house through the side door. Levi and Akeel were already at the truck, and they pulled away from the house ten minutes later.

Sunday traffic from Calhoun was light and the men arrived in Cobb County with forty minutes to spare. Akeel parked at the Friendly's Supermarket next to Tyrell on Floyd Road. The day started off bright but had turned overcast, causing the sun to go down early. Troy smoked a cigarette as they stood between the vehicles talking.

"Jasmin was hurt when we moved them out of the safe house. She worried we're not going to help Darrell." Hassan said.

"Shirley admitted what she did—but tried to justify it with the fact that she didn't ask for our help." Tyrell said.

"Let Shirley's ass stew." Levi countered.

"I got a list of all the cases she tried to refer to us." Tyrell continued. "Jasmin was distraught in a big way. She will come to the office in the morning. I think she wants to hear from Troy that we'll still be helping Darrell."

"Yeah." Troy agreed, then he and Levi headed to Judy Moore's home off Hicks Road, and Akeel left with Tyrell and Hassan.

Ten minutes after ten, Troy and Levi pulled up to the gray house at the end of Merriweather Trail. Once on the porch, Levi rang the bell. A dark-skinned woman, who appeared to be in her late sixties—early seventies, answered the door. Her white hair was pulled back in a bun that was streaked with black strands. She wore jeans and a red button down shirt, and on her feet were a white pair of gym shoes.

"Come in," she breathed, stepping aside.

Troy entered the house first. She closed the door and locked it after Levi. The house smelled of peaches, and one lamp was lit beside a burgundy leather couch. The television was on in the far corner of the living room but muted. A dining table sat before a set of sliding glass doors and to the left was a light coming from what Troy guessed was the kitchen. Judy walked toward a large table that was covered with paperwork.

"Ms. Judy, this is my cousin Levi. He is also the attorney representing Darrell Jenkins."

She turned to look at Levi, and her eyes softened at the mention of Darrell. "I have seen you all on the television. Both of you are bigger than I would have thought."

Troy smiled, hoping they didn't make her nervous. Levi stepped up. "Nice to meet you, Ms. Judy."

"Can I offer you gentlemen something to drink?"

He and Levi declined, so they could get down to business. Levi asked, "Why didn't you come forward with the will?"

Her expression was rueful. Judy waived them toward the table and allowed them to settle before sitting opposite them with her hands folded over a stack of papers.

"When I first met Shirley, she was a young single mother with three small boys. I took her under my wing because I couldn't have children and the boys were so sweet. They still are–Jasmin too. John was forty and I was thirty-eight, we had been seeing each other for about two years."

She stopped as if in thought. Levi coaxed her onward. "Please… continue."

"Shirley was young and pretty. John left me for her. I was devastated, so I moved away. He found me, and we managed to save our friendship. Shirley didn't know that we remained friends. When John started getting older, she dropped him. But he remained loyal to Shirley. How much her boys understood about their relationship–I ain't sure."

Judy stopped talking and pushed the paperwork at them. Troy pulled the documents forward, so they were visible to both he and Levi. There was silence while they read through the papers. It was Levi who whistled. John Unger had left his entire estate to Jerrell Lamar Jenkins, Darrell Nathan Jenkins and Michael Collin Jenkins. The will stated that Unger's holdings were vast– between the properties and money, the total was twenty-three million.

When he and Levi looked up at Ms. Judy, she said, "Darrell doesn't know about the will–none of the boys do. I didn't come forward because I thought it might be worse for Darrell. My brother, Charles and I witnessed and signed the will. Me nor my brother have gained nothing from the will. John gave freely to me while he was alive. Shirley was never part of the will."

"Shit." Troy said.

"Damn." Levi countered.

"Come." Judy said.

She stepped into the small living area and picked up the remote. Troy watched as a white man in his seventies with gray hair and clever blue eyes stared back at him. It was John Unger himself, reciting the will that he and Levi had read over. The older man was making changes to the document and speaking about them in the video.

"If you're watching this video–I'm dead." Unger smiled.

It was unnerving, seeing the victim of their case animated. The video was short and to the point as Unger held up a newspaper to confirm the date of the changes, which was three months prior to his demise. His last statement floored them all.

"I, John Unger, wouldn't have made this video if my nephew, Richard John Unger wasn't trying to control my estate. I refuse to sell my properties in College Park, Georgia, to Aero Loop Tech. The Jenkins boys are my sole heirs."

"Shit." Levi said.

"Damn." Troy countered.

Levi turned to Judy and asked, "Does Shirley know about the will?"

"Shirley was aware that John had money, but I don't think he discussed with her the extent of his fortune. If she knows about the will, he didn't tell her about me; she would have come here by now. John might have been weak when it came to Shirley, but he was a businessman."

* * *

Francine had been so worried about what Troy might have overheard that she couldn't decide if she were nervous about her husband or her new job. He hadn't pressed her, but where Troy once seemed preoccupied–his attention was now definitely on her. Her husband still offered space while being present inside the margins of her life. He continued to be busy, but when they came into contact, his eyes held questions that he didn't ask. She was relieved when he and the men left to handle business. His scrutiny was more than she could bear.

It was well after midnight when Francine heard Troy speaking with Butch in the hall leading to their bedroom. Technically, it was early Monday morning; she would be leaving for work at 7 a.m.

"I would appreciate if you drove my wife to work today. Akeel and I have business."

"I would be happy to drive Francine." Butch replied.

"Levi will bring her home."

"All right." Butch answered.

Francine lay on her side facing the window, and when the room door opened, she closed her eyes. Troy moved around in the dark and then the bathroom light flickered on. The toilet flushed, and water ran before everything went dark again. Behind her, there was no sound for moments, the cat and mouse game growing between them. Suddenly the bed dipped, and Troy pressed his steel like erection against her ass. He didn't speak, but she breathed in sharply.

She was dressed in a black t-shirt and panties. He wore boxers and the fabric brushed the backs of her thighs. Francine didn't want intimacy with him, though not because she didn't crave him. She feared she would confess her plan for more birth control. Francine feared telling her husband that she did not want his children. And if she were honest with herself, she didn't know if that would ever change. Troy was the worst and best thing that ever happened to her.

Troy adjusted himself, before pulling her even tighter to him. Egyptian Musk Oil and maleness saturated her world, reducing all awareness to the man at her back. He kissed her shoulder and still, he offered no dialogue. She allowed herself to drift in and out of sleep, cocooned in all that was Troy. Her alarm sounded, signaling the beginning of week two at the literacy program, and Francine almost cried.

Reaching out, she stopped the alarm clock. When she would have climbed from the bed, Troy pulled her against him once more, his erection still tucked between them. His voice was drenched in arousal, concern and challenge.

"Do you need to talk to me, Francine?"

"No."

She thought he would push for more, but he released his hold on her. The fire between them made her want to jump from the bed and run away. In contrast to her desperation, Francine slowly threw her legs over the side of the mattress and got to her feet. She turned on the lamp at her side of the bed, then moved to the closet selecting a pair of black slacks, a pink button down shirt and undergarments. Francine lay everything at the foot of the bed in preparation for the long day. She didn't acknowledge Troy as she moved about readying herself.

As the warm water flowed down her body, she heard the shower door open and a brief flash of cool air touch her skin. Her gaze was glued to his–avoiding the hard-on that poked at her belly. Troy reached for the peppermint soap and her. When his thumbs slid over her nipples, she squeezed her eyes shut. At the touch of his fingers along her folds, Francine moaned.

He was somewhat rough when his large hand closed around her neck. Troy was demonstrating his physical dominance over her, while displaying his lack of emotional control.

The peppermint soap made her skin vibrate and his touch made her ache. He had turned her, so the water sprayed at his back. His hand still about her neck, he directed her until her back was flush against the glass enclosure. She thought he would kiss her, but he didn't; he ran his nose along her jaw. Francine could barely breathe. She was drunk from his presence.

When she finally got up the nerve, Francine looked up into her husband's eyes. Beads of water dripped from his hair down onto his deep chocolate skin. Troy's eyes were wide with pain and uncertainty. She wanted to reassure him, but she was wrung out. Francine dropped her gaze. Troy backed away, leaving the path clear for her to exit the shower.

Once in the bedroom, she dried herself quickly and donned her underclothes. She heard the water shut off and her husband enter the bedroom. Francine was already seated in her favorite chair, rubbing lotion on her limbs and watching the news. Her husband moved about while dressing. There was no further interaction until they were both fully clothed.

Francine reached for the remote, turning off the television. She then did a full three hundred sixty degree turn to make certain she had her purse and the book she would read while on lunch. She was stalling, hoping that Troy would leave her alone. She needed a moment before seeing Monica and Jennifer. Who was she kidding? She needed a moment before facing anyone.

Turning toward the door, she found Troy waiting patiently with his right hand on the knob. There was no getting away from the embers burning hot between them. Her husband was dressed in navy blue slacks and a white button down shirt. His sleeves were rolled up, revealing powerful forearms and a big faced, gold watch. She almost broke down and confessed her pain, *I don't want children with you.*

Breathing in sharply and exhaling shakily, Francine moved toward him. But Troy made no motion to open the door. When she was close enough, he removed his hand from the knob and placed it about her neck. She tried to stare at the floor, but his free hand forced her chin up; like in the shower, he forced her back to the door. The pressure of his hand at her throat caused her to swallow.

Troy leaned in abruptly, crushing his lips to her own. Shocked by the intensity of his touch, Francine gasped. He bit her bottom lip and shoved his tongue into her mouth; she whimpered. The kiss was bruising–tantalizing, then unexpectedly he jerked away, creating distance. He moved his tongue around as if carefully considering a fine wine. His voice was rough.

"I can taste the lie on your beautiful lips." He crossed his arms over his chest, studying her. "You hiding shit from me, Francine?"

She felt faint, but before she could speak, there was a knock at the door. "Francine, Butch has pulled the car around. You're going to be late for work."

They stood for many seconds staring at each other. Troy conveyed his pain at her dishonesty, and Francine offered a blank expression. Finally, Monica called his name.

"Ernest, Butch is waiting for Francine."

Troy didn't answer his sister, but to Francine he said, "After you."

She turned, pulling the door open. Monica looked relieved. "Sorry to interrupt, Butch is worried about traffic."

It was early morning, so the corridor was dim. Francine headed in the direction of the living room. The house was quiet, save for the hum of the air conditioner. She crossed the pastel colored carpet and looked to the window. The day was going to be sunny, and it did nothing for her mood. She felt him at her heels but didn't look back. Francine pulled the front door open and almost sprinted to the car.

Butch was standing beside the vehicle. He opened the door, allowing her to climb in. Francine finally looked back in the direction of the house, thankful to find that Troy hadn't followed her. They were moving slowly down the long-wooded drive, before she realized two things: Troy was upset with his sister and she hadn't greeted Monica.

An hour and twenty minutes later, the old man escorted her inside. Francine found Eric and Courtney chatting in the conference room; upon seeing her, they both smiled.

"It's going to be a busy day." Eric said.

"Oh," Francine's dread was obvious.

"Yup. We got three interviews and four classes." Eric clasped his hands together. "You gonna be all right?"

"She'll be fine." Courtney said.

"Yeah." Francine reiterated.

The day happened in a blur, and they were so busy, Francine didn't have time to fall apart. The first candidate for the position of instructor, Sebastian Wilder, had done time for assault. He was open about the charge. He had beaten the nephew of his elderly neighbor for abusing her, and the tall white man with ruddy cheeks and black hair was unapologetic.

After lunch, Akeel appeared; he seemed different–tense maybe. But they were all thrown back into the day before Francine could decide. Courtney and Akeel each taught an afternoon class, while Francine and Eric continued with the interviews. The first woman, Sheri Rockford was a substitute teacher and the next applicant was a bored housewife in need of something meaningful to do.

It was almost five o'clock when she realized she had worked with Eric all afternoon and felt no fear. Francine didn't even think about Troy and his calling her a liar–which was a true assessment. At quarter after five, Levi appeared at the conference room entrance.

"Eric." He greeted.

"What up?" Eric countered.

Levi nodded, then turned his attention to her. "You ready?"

"Give me a moment." Francine replied.

She moved past Levi in the doorway and retrieved her purse from the bottom drawer of her desk. Turning, she headed for the restroom to gather herself to ride home with that prick–*Sean Levi Bryant.* Francine splashed water on her face and applied bubblegum lip gloss before meeting him in the lobby. He was chatting with Akeel.

"Good evening, Francine." Akeel said.

"Good night, Akeel," she replied.

The men ended their conversation, and Levi held the door for her as she stepped into the Georgia heat. Along Fairground Street, traffic was at a standstill from a red light at the crossroad. The day was bright and once in the car Francine tried to adjust the visor overhead to protect her eyes. But she was short, so it didn't help. She flopped backward and sighed. There was however, one bright spot to the commute home, Levi didn't engage her.

Levi pulled in front of the house and Francine exited the car without looking his way. She headed straight for their bedroom and changed clothes. Later, she found Monica and Jennifer in the kitchen. Her sister was standing at the sink readying a salad as Monica carried a hot pan of baked ziti to the island. Junior sat at the table drawing, his head popped up at the sound of her voice.

"What can I do to help?"

"Get the plates," Monica said.

"Auntie, I hate that you work. I never see you anymore." Junior said.

Francine smiled. "Awww, I miss you too."

Junior's little face turned red, and he went back to drawing. She made eye contact with Monica and asked the silent question; *Did Troy say anything?* Her sister in-law offered a reassuring smile.

"Today has been uneventful." Monica said.

Francine reached for the plates. "How many for dinner?"

"Let's see there's Jewel, Butch, Levi and us four." Jennifer answered.

She finished setting the table as Levi and the others stepped into the kitchen. Butch brought an extra chair since there were technically only six places. This was going to be awkward, Francine thought. Monica put the large pan of food in the middle of the table so everyone could help themselves.

"Francine, how is work going?" Jewel asked.

"Ahhh, it's going. I haven't taught a class." She answered.

"Butch taught me to read." Jewel said.

Francine's head snapped up, and she eyed the old man who remained focused on his food. "Why don't you volunteer?"

Butch's head popped up; he smiled. "I don't like people."

Francine couldn't help but giggle. Shit, she didn't like people either and was quickly coming to understand that about herself. Junior chimed in. "You don't like me, Uncle Butch?"

"Oh, I like you and the ladies just fine, boy. Levi not so much." Butch replied.

Junior snickered, and Levi rolled his eyes. "Get in line behind Francine."

Jewel chortled and so did Jennifer. Monica shook her head, and the funny conversation carried them to the end of dinner. As she sat with this strange group of misfits, Francine noticed something else. Her sister wanted Levi, but it wasn't clear what he wanted. The poker-faced attorney gave nothing away.

They all moved into the living room, and Jennifer sat next to Levi on the black sectional. Jewel and Butch took the other end. Monica and Francine sat with Junior between them. It was cozy as they watched several sitcoms until the hour grew late. There had been no time to speak with Monica privately, besides Francine wasn't sure if Levi was there to spy.

As Francine stepped into her room and readied herself for bed, she realized that sleep had to be her goal. Lack of rest was adding fuel to the fire that was her anxiety. Willing her mind to relax, she began to drift. It was after 11 p.m. when she felt the bed shake and Troy climb in behind her. She held her breath waiting for him to crowd her, but his touch never came. Francine missed her husband, but not enough to place refilling her birth control in his hands.

She slipped in and out of sleep until her alarm went off. Falling flat on her back in bed, Francine found herself alone. She showered and dressed for work in a blue skirt and red blouse. On her feet were blue strappy sandals that added to her ensemble. Striding into the hall, Francine headed for the kitchen, the smell of strong coffee pulling her along. She found Monica in green pajama pants and a yellow t-shirt.

"I'll be there at 11:30." Monica said.

Francine looked over her shoulder. "All right."

Monica sensed her apprehension. "The men are in Troy's office with the door closed. Butch is out front."

Nodding at Monica, she turned and left the house. They would speak freely when they were away from the house. Francine wasn't willing to chance Troy's ear hustling ass. She would deal with him after the birth control issue was handled. Her stomach was unsettled, she decided against coffee. Instead, she headed for the car and Butch.

The ride into work was uneventful. Butch walked her into the lobby, and they found Eric seated at her desk. He was opening mail and looked up at them with a smile. His demeanor was warm—genuine.

"Morning, Butch." The old man nodded, and to Francine, Eric said, "I opened a few pieces of mail, but not enough to make a difference."

"Every little bit helps." Francine countered.

Butch strode away; Francine knew he wasn't feeling the small talk. Without a backward glance, he said, "5:30."

She watched him retreat, and when she was sure Butch was gone, she said, "I have an errand to run at lunch."

Francine held her breath, waiting for Eric to try to stop her. He nodded before asking, "Okay. What time are you going? Courtney is teaching an early class, but we should be fine while you're gone."

"My sister in-law is picking me up around 11:30."

"Aiight."

The conversation lulled, and they began going through the mail in earnest. The day was slower paced than the previous. About an hour had gone by when Eric asked, "What did you think of the applicants?"

Francine was about to answer when the lobby door offered a scraping sound. She looked up to find Monica walking toward her desk. Confused, she glanced at her watch, 9:45. Her sister-in-law must have read her mind.

"I thought to come early, in case it's crowded." Monica answered a question Francine hadn't yet asked.

Francine nodded and turned to Eric, "Will you be all right if I leave earlier?"

Eric smiled. "It'll be a hardship, but..."

She laughed. "Monica, this is Eric."

"Nice to meet you."

"Same here." Eric smiled.

There was an awkward silence, until Francine said, "Okay... well, I'll be back."

Grabbing her purse, she followed Monica out to the parking lot where Jewel's black Volvo station wagon sat at the ready. They did not speak until they were safely in the car.

"What the hell? He's gorgeous." Monica said.

"Eric is attractive, and he's a nice guy."

Monica became serious quickly and Francine suspected that her facial expression was the reason. She had to remind herself that deciding to continue her birth control wasn't a crime. With everything else out of her reach, this was something she needed to govern. The incident with Sam Fields and Harold Dawson, interviewing other victims and witnessing their hurt, even getting married and falling in love with Troy—all of it felt like a storm that never died down. Her life was turned upside down.

"Which way?" Monica asked. Francine must have gotten lost in her head.

"Left out of the parking lot."

"You all right?"

"Troy knows something, but he's not exactly sure of what."

"He knows you're on the pill, right?"

"He does, but I think he was waiting for my supply to run out."

"Ah."

"We haven't discussed children, but…" Francine's explanation faded. "Make a right, here on South Cobb Drive."

The blinking of the signal was the only sound in the car for seconds before Monica asked, "Do you want to be with my brother? Are you sorry you married him? How did you meet Ernest?"

Francine didn't think it was possible, but she giggled. Her eyes were brimming with tears at the love she heard in Monica's voice for her brother. She sighed.

"I can't leave him, it would hurt me to live without him. No, I'm not sorry I married Troy. I love him beyond words, but he's too much for me at times. No, I won't tell you how I met him. Please don't ask me that again."

Monica stopped the car at a red light and looked over at her. "I won't ask again how you two met. But Jennifer isn't going to back away from the question–I'm just saying."

"I know." Francine changed the subject. "The health station is on the right before the next light."

Francine was thankful for Monica's willingness to accept that she wasn't going to speak about the beginning of her marriage. The women made it to their destination; both sat staring at the entrance. "Let's get this over with," Monica said.

Francine smiled as they exited the car headed for the front of the building. The health station was busy as several pregnant women with small children in tow moved about the parking lot. In her side view, Francine noticed vehicles arriving and others departing. There was much going on, and she was again grateful for her sister in-law. By the same token, Francine was sad that she couldn't talk to her own sister; she and Jennifer were forever changed.

The color scheme in the lobby was a pea green and white. On either side of the small corridor were two glass doors while straight ahead was an elevator; the sliding door was also green. A directory next to the bulletin board stated women and children services on the first floor–STD screenings on the second floor. Monica moved away while Francine was reading.

"Looks like we need to go in here." Her sister-in-law informed.

Francine glanced over her shoulder as Monica pointed to the left. Turning, she hurried through the door Monica held open. The office was decked out in the same color pattern as the lobby. Plastic green and white chairs furnished the space along with small tables stacked with books and magazines. Against the far wall sat another table that held pamphlets. All the chairs faced the receptionist area that was behind a glass enclosure.

A black woman with a stylishly cut hairdo peered at them from behind the desk. Francine approached, and the woman smiled. "How can I help you?"

"I'm here to see the doctor and get my birth control prescription refilled."

"Sign in here and fill this out." The woman handed Francine a clip-board with lots of paperwork and a pen. Her hot pink nails gleaming in contrast to the blue pen.

Turning back to the waiting room, she found Monica seated by the door with an empty chair next to her. Francine sat and began filling out the paperwork; it came to her that she didn't know the address where she lived. It was the last straw in the bullshit that had become her life. Francine broke down and cried.

"Oh, Frankie, what's wrong?" Monica placed her arm around Francine's shoulders.

She couldn't speak enough to articulate the problem. But the issue was clear, Levi had been correct about her. She wasn't strong enough. It was as if she was losing her mind and unable to stop it. Francine sat slumped over the forgotten clipboard and wept in silence. She couldn't look for the bathroom in this state. Monica handed her a tissue.

Eight other women sat in the waiting area; a far cry from the crowd the health station in Queens serviced hourly. From the chatter in the waiting room, it appeared no one was paying her any attention. Monica continued to rub her back, trying to help her calm down. Abruptly, all conversation stopped, and she heard Monica breathe in sharply.

Francine looked up as Troy and Akeel stepped into the waiting room. Both men were upset, and it was palpable. Next to her, Monica muttered.

"Shit."

"Come, Monica." Akeel demanded.

Francine had never seen this side of Akeel. Monica didn't try refusing; she stood. "I'll see you at home, Frankie."

"We'll be in the car." Akeel said.

"Yeah." Troy countered.

Francine watched them go while trying to avoid eye contact with her husband. She waited until the last possible moment before looking up into Troy's beautiful face. The smell of Egyptian Musk oil enveloped her senses. Unlike Akeel, who appeared angry, Troy seemed hurt. The words were thick when they fell from his lips.

"Why are you crying?"

"I don't know our address." She whispered.

His gaze softened as he sat beside her and reached for the clipboard. He filled in the address, then handed it back to her. She stared into his eyes trying to read him.

"Are you pregnant and trying to hide it from me?"

"No. I'm trying to get my prescription for the pill reinstated. I'm on my last pack."

"You don't want children with me?" Troy asked.

"When we first met... that day in the kitchen. Levi's words..."

Troy sighed, then nodded. Francine could tell he knew to which day she referred. She waited, holding her breath, but her husband sat back in the chair and relaxed. Unable to think of what to do next, she sat up straight and went back to filling out the paperwork. When she was finished, Troy handed the papers to the receptionist for her. The woman couldn't take her eyes off him.

Troy seated himself once again, and together, they waited patiently for her turn, kept company by pain instead of conversation.

* * *

Logan couldn't believe his luck when the wife and sister of Troy Bryant stepped from the building he had been canvassing and climbed into a black station wagon. Chris followed Troy openly and at other times discreetly. Simms had failed to bring Bryant in for questioning, and this brought his whole plan up lame. When he attempted to strongarm other cops that he knew had a gripe with Bryant, Logan was promptly turned away. It seemed Troy Bryant had APD in a chokehold.

As the station wagon pulled to the red light, Chris experienced glee at the sight of Akeel Marshall's woman. He had shown up late to watch the building that housed the literacy program. While he missed their arrival, his day couldn't get any better. Pulling slowly into traffic, he covertly followed the women. Tailing them wasn't hard, so engrossed were they in conversation.

The Volvo wagon traveled down South Cobb Drive until the health department came into view on the right. Logan watched as the vehicle in front of him took a sharp turn into the parking lot of the Human Resource building. It was 10:30 in the morning, the sun was bright, and the Georgia heat–unyielding. Several cars pulled out of the parking lot, while more pulled in. The place was transient, a fact that helped Logan in his quest to remain unnoticed. He didn't think Bryant's wife knew his face, but he was sure his sister did.

He parked in the back row of the lot and watched as the women spoke for a few minutes. Bryant's wife was visibly upset. In the next row of vehicles, an older black woman climbed from her car, before helping three small children from the back seat. At the front of the building, two pregnant women emerged from the lobby. After a time, the wife and sister of Troy Bryant got out of the car and hurried toward the entry way. When the women disappeared through the doors, Logan contemplated how long he should wait before venturing inside.

As he sat staring at the front of the building, Chris had to be honest with himself. There were too many moving parts that were beyond his control. It was only a matter of time before it was found out that the Jenkins kid was innocent. His previous arrests had not yet been shoved under a microscope to save the department money and face. Chris needed the will to be located–he needed to be paid so he could bounce. Until then, he would keep an eye on Bryant. But he couldn't be everywhere, and this was why Bryant no longer saw him as a threat.

Being a cop gave him authority on the streets and back at the station. Now, his masculinity and respect had taken a powerful blow. Where he could command informants and associates to do his bidding—now, it wasn't safe to be him. His enemies were sizing him up. Troy sought to isolate him and had succeeded. Time was running out.

There was nothing he could do with the Bryant women in broad daylight. Chris wasn't naïve enough to believe Troy unprepared for even this situation; his woman was always protected. It was a tactical mind game that caused him to get out of the car and stride toward the doors. This action would cause Troy and his men to look over their shoulders even when he wasn't there.

Chris was about twenty feet from the building when a black Benz came to a screeching halt in front of him. The old man was driving and narrowly missed hitting him. Three doors swung open and out stepped Troy Bryant, Levi Bryant and Akeel Marshall.

"Detective Logan… pardon me—I mean, Chris." Levi greeted him.

"Levi."

Troy and Akeel never acknowledged him, both men walked toward the building with purpose. Chris watched as they entered the lobby. The car pulled slowly away leaving nothing but space and opportunity between himself and Levi. Chris waited for the other man to threaten some legal action, but those words never came. They stood glaring at each other.

"You and me gonna settle up real soon." Levi said.

Chris chuckled, then turned and strolled back to his car, but he didn't get in. When he reached the driver's side, he leaned against the door and openly watched the parking lot. After about ten minutes, Akeel reappeared with Monica and they both looked tense. Marshall's eyes bounced to him and held, even as he helped his woman into the station wagon.

And so, it was that Levi paced in front of the building. Akeel sat in the car with Monica. The old man parked and waited. After two hours, Bryant and his wife stepped from the lobby. Chris openly observed the goings on. When Bryant helped his wife into the Benz, Chris turned to get in his own car. As he cranked the engine, a silver Yukon pulled in front of his vehicle–essentially blocking him. He stared at the retaining wall in the rearview mirror and cursed. The tinted window of the Yukon slid down and Tyrell Knox scowled at him.

Chris saw the passenger door on the Yukon open. Hassan Peterson rounded the front of their truck, switchblade in hand and slit his tire. As Chris watched the Yukon exit the parking lot, he began to recalculate his next move.

* * *

Butch was driving, and Levi rode front passenger. Francine sat next to him in the back seat, but Troy couldn't look at her. He allowed his mind to step away from his wife and the fact that she didn't want his children. Troy turned his mind to Logan and the disaster that was averted. Surprisingly, he felt no anger. Still, it was time to reexamine his path.

As the countryside rolled by, Troy began to look more closely at the coincidences. It was a humbling moment to have to admit he was slow in appreciating this endeavor. The facts were not easily identified and his ability to push the puzzle pieces together was less than amateur. But he had arrived at a place where comprehension of the truth lay in his skill to set aside his own hurts. He needed to look deeply at all the players. Troy needed to separate the good, the bad and the ugly.

When they reached the house, Butch and Levi got out of the car as if to give him a moment with Francine. But Troy didn't take it, instead he got out, then turned to help his wife from the back seat. Once inside, they found Junior and Jewel watching cartoons. His nephew was happy to see Francine.

"Hey, Auntie, come watch television with me."

"I'm sorry, sweetheart, Auntie is not feeling well. Later, I promise."

Junior nodded, and Troy noted his concern. "Hey, Uncle Troy."

"Junior."

"Can I get you some tea?" Jewel asked.

"No, thank you." Francine answered. "I'm going to rest."

Troy followed his wife to the hall, but he made a left, while she made a right. He went to his office allowing Francine to roam freely about the house. There was much to be sorted, and strangely he felt up for the task.

He would catalogue his thoughts and chase them in order of importance. The debacle had loosened up as the sight of a real target came into focus. All this was separate from the trouble with Francine, but he could handle both.

He turned to the window of his office and stared out. It was 4:30 in the afternoon, but the day had grown dark with angry storm clouds. The trees on his property were bending in the wind, another sign of the approaching rough weather. Troy had organized and re-organized the paperwork, facts and random acts all afternoon. He made several charts, placing the acts that appeared to be chance in a column by themselves. As the first fat drops of rain fell against the window, he stepped away from Darrell Jenkins to ponder his wife.

When they left the health station, they had come straight home. Eric had done well in his role to watch over Francine and report back. He and Akeel had simply followed Monica. Jewel had informed him of his sister's request to borrow her car. Troy thought his wife and sister were headed to an abortion clinic. The notion that he would be left out enraged him. Tailing them to the Human Resource building had lessened his propensity to violence.

The sight of Chris Logan had set Akeel off, but Troy could think of nothing but Francine. He was thankful to find that she wasn't getting rid of their child without telling him. There could be no recovery for such a betrayal; he loved his wife so much, he ached. She had been trying to refill her birth control, even though she knew he was waiting for her supply to run out. His wife didn't want to carry his child; the thought was sobering. She'd even given him the exact time and moment that caused her to keep that part of herself from him. Shit, he heard Levi's words too: *"Since you ain't gonna kill her, marry her, fuck her and knock her up. I will leave for New York in the morning to follow her mother. Butch will follow her sister. It's your job to make clear the art of blackmail."*

There was a knock on his office door, and Akeel popped his head in. He stared at Troy. "Jewel and Butch took my son to their place. We're ready."

"Francine?" Troy asked.

"She hasn't come out of the bedroom since we got home."

So great was the weight on his shoulders, Troy sighed. Levi stepped up behind Akeel, "You ready?"

The sight of his cousin made Troy pinch the bridge of nose. He loved Levi, and he couldn't part with the friendship—therein lay the dilemma. He would speak with his cousin after he spoke with Francine. Troy needed Levi to help make this right. He felt weak, and he knew they saw it.

"Where is Monica and Jennifer?"

"They're in the kitchen." Akeel said. "Let's get this over with before Junior comes back."

Troy nodded, then followed the men to Monica and Jennifer. His sister in-law immediately noted the expression on their faces and jumped right in. "Is something wrong with my sister?"

Monica had the grace to look at her feet. His sister couldn't meet his gaze, and the action made Troy feel numb. He tried to lessen the aggression in his stance by leaning back against the island. Crossing his arms over his chest and his feet at the ankles, he glanced from woman to woman.

"Francine and I have some things to work through." Troy glared at Monica and then continued. "The next two days will be private time for me and my wife. If either of you interfere, you will be removed from my house."

As expected, Jennifer started in. "What is wrong with my sister? What did you do to her, Troy?"

Levi stepped in, shutting her down. "Jennifer, stop it. Your sister is married, you have to start minding your own damn business."

Relentless, Jennifer asked, "Why won't anyone tell me the truth? How did you meet my sister, Troy? What the hell is going on?"

Troy shook his head and smiled weakly. Turning to Levi, he said, "I want her out of my house. Don't bring her back until she understands that she ain't the fuckin' boss here."

"Let's go, Jennifer." Levi commanded. Troy thought she would argue, but she didn't. Jennifer started crying, but he could give less than a shit.

When his sister in-law was gone, Troy returned his glare to Monica. He had only one question. "Would you have driven my wife for an abortion without telling me?"

"No," she whispered.

Troy continued to mean-mug his sister until the sight of her made him want to throttle her. He pushed away from where he was leaning and left the kitchen. Behind him, he heard Akeel. "Pack your shit, you're coming home with me. I have three private schools in mind for Junior. You will pick one and get my son ready to start the academic year."

Once at the door of his bedroom, Troy hesitated. He stood with his hand on the knob while mentally envisioning his other hand turning the dial of his anger and pain down to a manageable level. Levi's words hit him again: *marry her, fuck her and knock her up.* He almost backed away from the door, the need to hide in his office—real.

Troy turned the knob and entered his bedroom. It had started thundering outside; he could see leaves drifting past the window. The bathroom light was on, and Francine was nowhere in sight. It was obvious she had just finished showering; steam clung to the air along with the faint scent of strawberries. He pulled the t-shirt he wore over his head, then toed off his boots. Dropping his jeans where he stood, Troy reached down and yanked off his socks.

He wiggled his toes trying to relieve the tension in his person. Troy kept his underwear on, he didn't want Francine to be uncomfortable. He moved to stand in front of the window; it had become dark enough that only his image was visible. The white boxer briefs glared back at him, and he contemplated shorts. But before he could move, he saw Francine's reflection step from the bathroom. Next, came her startled intake of air.

She was dressed in a pink t-shirt; her black hair was combed out and left wild. His wife was damn beautiful in this state. He expected to be the one to start this conversation, but she surprised him.

"This is not Monica's fault. I think she agreed to drive me because I was distraught. Your sister asked me to talk to you—but I couldn't. Please don't be angry with her."

Francine stood next to the fireplace and he at the foot of the bed next to the television. Yet, the distance between them was great. Behind him, the storm raged on as he stared at the love of his life. He knew she would defend Monica, and Troy understood that she was right. But it didn't stop the hurt he felt. His anger was directed at Monica but not limited to his sister. No—he was pissed at both women, they had conspired to leave him out.

He had allowed himself to become delusional, but he was back on track. The marriage was forced; this was all his fault. While he understood that Monica didn't know how they met, he was still wounded by the action. Troy couldn't help it; the question fell from his heart.

"Were you gonna tell me that you renewed your prescription?"

"Yes."

"Then why go through all this?"

"Because you would have tried to stop me." Francine wrapped her arms about her middle. "If you would have placed that type of demand…"

Troy didn't ask her to complete the sentence; he knew what she would say. The truth is he wouldn't have let her refill the prescription. He wanted all of her at his mercy.

"Do you know how much I love you?" Shit, his voice cracked.

"Yes," she countered. "Do you know how much I love you?"

"No," he answered, the insecurity he felt oozing from his pores.

"I love you more than words can say. I'm also drowning while trying to be strong enough. I want my old self back. A lot has gone on in the last few months—I'm your *wife*, Troy, not your hostage."

Francine dropped her head to hide that she was crying. His own throat began to burn, and his eyes were stinging. He tried to clear his throat, but it didn't work the first time. When he could gather himself, he asked another question, afraid of her answer.

"Do you want an abortion?"

"They always test me before issuing new pills. I had a day where I had to double up on the dosage, but I didn't expect to be pregnant." Her voice quivered.

"You didn't answer the question, Baby."

"Would you hate me if I said yes?"

"I want you both—so much," his voice wobbled.

"You didn't answer the question, Troy."

He could hear the tears that stained her soul and still there was no room for dishonesty. Yet, his truth with her would be bruising on a simple day. Everything that was him was a contradiction when applied to her life. He had saved her from peril—then abducted her. She was his hostage and his wife. He was the maker of the rules and she was his to command. She was his dream and he was her nightmare.

Who he was without her scared the shit out of him, Troy shook his head trying to clear it. He was Ernest the victim *and* Troy the perpetrator. Was he a good man who did bad things or was he a bad man who did good things? He had been about to raze Georgia to the ground, until Francine. She offered him peace where there was none.

"I could never hate you." His tone was gruff.

She stumbled back against the wall as if he had struck her. His wife looked in danger of passing out, causing him to rush forward. He held his hands up in surrender even as he stood close enough to touch her. Troy didn't want to intimidate, yet his wife looked as though she wanted to back away from him. Hands still palm up, he stepped back a bit trying not to loom over her.

"Troy..." she wept, "I don't know if I can go through with this."

"I know."

"You won't love me after..." she sniffed.

"Can I hug you?"

"No." Francine's answer was swift.

He dropped his hands because he understood what she was feeling. She didn't want to be suffocated by him. Yet, he didn't want to be pushed out of this process—no matter the outcome. He was frantic and needed the intimacy. If she planned to end the pregnancy, he didn't want to spend his time on the outside looking in. He had to fight the urge to not press his will. There were so many things he wanted to say, but his tongue was heavy with dread. Shit, at this moment, Francine *intimidated* him. While his mind shifted from thought to thought, his wife spoke.

"I want to visit my mother..."

Troy felt the blow of reality, and the words tore from him on a sob. "Baby, please—no."

Troy was unsteady when he stepped forward and dropped to his knees in front of his wife. Francine wouldn't let him hug her, so he did the next best thing. He leaned over and pressed his lips to the top of her foot. She smelled of strawberries and her toenails were painted blood red. His wife gasped at the contact, and it broke him too. He was powerless to stop the flow of tears that fell from him against her warm brown skin. His shoulders shuddered with heartbreak; he hadn't felt like this since his mother died— since the night he fit the description.

"Troy," she murmured. "Don't–please, get up."

As the light spilled from the bathroom, illuminating his complete sub-mission–Troy moved to kiss her other foot. He couldn't stand up to face her. His breaths came in ragged puffs and still, he couldn't back away. Francine tried to snatch her foot out of his reach, but she was against the wall and there was nowhere for either of them to hide.

"I want to overpower you. I'm trying…"

"I know," she replied, softly.

"You can decide whether or not you want to carry my child, but you will do it from this house."

Francine wasn't aware of the danger that involved being his everything. He hadn't even made her or Monica cognizant of Chris Logan's presence today. Troy couldn't chase her to New York, Darrell Jenkins needed their help. He wouldn't explain all that to his wife because it was trivial compared to his real reason; he couldn't let her go and still he remained bowed before her.

She attempted to give her thoughts. "I don't want—"

"I'm compromising, Francine, please see that. If I bend any further, all hell will break loose."

"I know," she answered.

"Can I hold you, baby, please?"

His wife didn't answer right away, causing him to keep his head low-ered. When she did speak, he almost missed her response.

"Yes."

Troy didn't stand, but he did look up into his wife's face. He saw defeat and uncertainty in her eyes. Slowly, he reached out a hand, thankful when she accepted. Gently, he pulled her down to straddle his lap.

"I won't push you. I'll wait for you to tell me how it's going to be."

He wrapped his arms about her, holding tight to his woman and child. As Francine snuggled into him, it became clear what his next step had to be. Troy would take another hostage.

5

PLAY–PLAY KILL BIRD
SEPTEMBER 1995

The fact that Troy Bryant seemed undisturbed by his appearance at the health station caused Chris Logan to change tactics, and he found himself, well after midnight, pacing the parking lot of a tiny strip mall off Highway 41. The shopping center consisted of a defensive driving school, a barber shop and a tax joint. Using this place for a meet-up was for the best. There were no signs of life for miles in either direction.

It was past time he started the steady lean on Richard Unger. Chris needed to make certain the man understood that he was in the background–impatient and waiting. The night was coal black, and the perimeter of the parking lot was thick with trees. A lone streetlight blinked repeatedly, casting the front of the driving school, along with the other establishments, into murkiness.

Sweat trickled down his back, making the shirt he wore stick to his skin. The Georgia heat was punishing, even in the wee hours. Chris had parked in the shadows to be invisible to the passersby; although given the time and location, it was unlikely he would see anyone other than Unger. The insects were loud, and it was weird hearing the sounds of nature while standing in a parking lot.

Forty-five minutes passed before the high beams of an old pickup swung into the lot. The vehicle pulled alongside his truck, then suddenly the lights and the engine were cut. Chris watched as the driver sat in the darkness of the cab for a time before opening the door to step out. He witnessed a nervous Richard Unger move from between the trucks and allowed his hand to rest on his gun. Chris left the entrance of the driving school and walked into the blinking streetlight.

He crossed the pavement in sure strides, coming face to face with Unger. Before Chris could utter a word, the other man spoke, his voice laced with irritation.

"Logan, I don't have the will. If I did, you would be the first to know."

"I'm giving you a week to come up with my share of the money. Shit is getting thick for me–not you."

"I don't have six million dollars laying around. Are you fucking kidding me?"

"We're not friends, Richie, I wouldn't kid you. From the beginning of this thing, the risks have been all mine. My situation is becoming a tight one. I need to move on."

"The agreement we had was: You get paid when I get paid. This shit with you and Bryant doesn't have anything to do with me." Richard was almost yelling.

"Hey–you don't know what I got going on, and it's none of your damn business. What is your business is my money, and I want it by next Sunday or I'll be paying you a visit. Look for the will on your own time."

Unger was dressed in gym pants and a hoodie. The lack of light left the color vague to Logan, but it was too hot for that type clothing. And when Richard shoved his hands in the pouch, Chris offered a warning.

"Hands where I can see them."

The other man brought his hands up in surrender. "So you think I'm going to shoot you?"

"Sunday, Richie. I'll let you know where we can meet."

"Logan, you can't change the rules to suit you. I don't have that kind of cash. Why don't you help me locate the documents instead of chasing Troy Bryant around?"

"I just did–I changed the rules."

The mention of Bryant turned his blood cold. He saw the tactics Unger was employing, and it was working. Chris turned, rounded his truck–then drove away. His windows were rolled down, and he heard Unger hollering his name. He didn't acknowledge the other man; he had made his demands known, they would go from there.

Like it or not, he had become Troy Bryant's bitch. Chris felt as though he were in a relationship where the aggressor had cut him off from his support system and became abusive. The comparisons were in his head, unbidden. He could see himself running strong with the herd, then finding himself cut from the pack, stalked and killed. It was clear from the moment Bryant publicly called him out that his life had gotten beyond his control. He couldn't make noise with the department because it was only a matter of time, and Chris needed to avoid a prison sentence.

The worst of it was Amanda. When he had answered truthfully that he couldn't stop the cat and mouse game with Bryant, she had cut him off. They made love over and over that night, but she had not opened the door to him again. After four days of being shut out, he banged on her apartment door early one evening, but the neighbor, an older white gentleman with bulging eyes, stepped into the breezeway and said what Chris didn't want to hear.

"The lady cop moved out yesterday. Gimme a break, wouldya."

It had been weeks since he last saw her. Chris had refrained from seeking her out in the workplace. The notion could be dangerous for them both, but he was getting desperate. Chris had one brother who was much older and lived in Colorado. As for his mother, she died the year before; but he hadn't been a good son. Chris remained disconnected from anything that wasn't his own agenda—until Amanda. He'd never been in love.

Despair, defeat and impulsiveness rode him as he pulled into the driveway of Frank Simms's home. Chris had been to this house at least twice for poker and dinner back when Simms had a woman. He swung out of the truck, bound up the steep driveway and banged on the door. A light somewhere deep in the house came on, but the door didn't open. He had been about to bang again when the door was yanked open to reveal a burned-out Frank Simms.

"Why the fuck are you here? I got me enough problems."

"You owe me, Frank."

"Do all your conversations start like this, Logan? I did the best I could,

Levi was goin' to make hell for us if we took Bryant in for questioning. Why the hell were you there? They saw you, Logan… It's too early in the morning for this shit."

"I need you to locate Amanda Gaither for me." Chris stepped over Frank's rant about the Bryant incident.

"The internal affairs chick?"

"Yeah."

"Why?" Simms narrowed his eyes. "You tryna make trouble?"

Frank hadn't invited him in, so they stood in the darkened doorway eyeing each other. The air conditioner felt good even as the heat danced at his back. The only light in the house came from the top of the stairs. Simms was dressed in boxers and a stained white wife beater. The old bastard was strapped, his gun at his upper left side; the smell of stale liquor rolled off him in waves.

"Be discreet—don't approach her. Just find out her schedule, so I can track her."

"Why?" Simms asked.

Chris ignored his inquiries. "I need to know before the end of business today. I'll meet you at Jack's pool hall at noon."

Before Simms could ask another prying question, Logan backed away. Once in his truck, he sat for a time before finally driving off. Chris rolled out of Paulding County, making for Marietta and sighed. He tried to avoid his own house as much as possible, but this morning he was emotionally and physically worn out. After twenty-six-minutes of travel, he pulled into his garage and cut the engine.

He stepped into the hall from the side door and leaned heavily against the wall. "The more I try to avoid prison, the more powerful Bryant becomes."

And yet, if he could, he would continue to sidestep jail time. Bryant, on the other hand, was now a murdering thug; but it seemed nothing could be done about it. Chris was playing defense all the time, and he was doing a piss poor job keeping the bullshit at bay. Everything about him was stagnant and losing Amanda had only added to these feelings.

Chris wanted to kill Troy Bryant and be done with it, but he also knew he would be the first person questioned. If he were honest, this was the same reason Bryant hadn't already smoked his ass. Troy also had something he didn't have–true loyalty. It was how he kept Chris caged in, and like a boa constrictor, each time Chris breathed, shit got tighter.

The former detective plopped down on his couch, leaned back and closed his eyes. His last thought before he dozed–How could he kill Troy Bryant and get away with it?

* * *

Troy stood facing the window, mentally going over the tasks that needed addressing. His base of operation was now his home office so that he could be near his wife. It had been days since the incident at the health clinic and everyone in his life was on edge. Extra chairs were brought into his office, and Troy turned his attention to the men.

"Tyrell, I want you to find all you can on John Unger. Dig deep; we need a full picture–family background and the women in his life. I also want you to investigate Richard Unger–the nephew. I have a feeling these two trains collide."

"Aiight," Tyrell answered.

"Hassan, I need you to look into Shirley. Bring even the issues that sound like petty chick shit, so we can examine it."

"You got it," Hassan countered.

"Levi, I need you to look into Aero Loop Tech. We need to find the association to our victim." Troy paused, and Levi gazed up at him. "How well do you know the D.A., Larry Wright?"

"Larry is good people. I haven't had reason to distrust him but trying to get a meeting with him is like pulling teeth. I think he's avoiding me." Levi said.

"I'm not saying you have a reason to distrust him. But the D.A. and Justice having interest in the same case concerns me. We're missing something."

"I'm on it." Levi replied.

"Butch and Jesse, I want you two to keep a close eye on Chris Logan. Bring in a third person if needed–one the ex-cop doesn't know."

"Yeah," Both men said in unison.

"This meeting is over. We'll meet back here in three days same time–10 a.m. If you need me before then, come to the house unless I specify otherwise."

All the men stood and began filing out, except Akeel. It was obvious he was looking for a fight, but Troy spoke up before he could go into meltdown mode.

"Levi, I need to speak with you and Akeel on a separate matter."

When his cousin seated himself, Akeel stood. Troy knew what was coming.

"You skipped over me, man." Akeel's voice was low–hostile.

"Francine is pregnant," Troy said.

Both men smiled, but it was Levi who said, "Oh damn–congrats, man."

Troy grabbed the back of his neck, then took in a cleansing breath. Before he could muster the energy to say more, Akeel dropped back into his seat. "Francine doesn't want the baby, does she?"

"No."

"For real?" Levi leaned in to stare in his eyes. "She loves you, so what is it you're not saying?"

"It was how we met, obviously." Troy answered. "The things said that she can't get out of her head."

"Like what…" Levi's words faded on the question.

Troy could see when his cousin understood what troubled Francine. Levi dropped his head and looked to the ground. His voice was thick. "How can I help? Do you need me to stay away?"

The last question hurt Troy too, but he pressed on. "No, I don't need you to stay away. But we do need to speak freely with Jennifer. I'm going to need help with her."

"Damn," Akeel said, softly.

Troy felt befuddled. "I've been trying to be available for my wife, but it looks like I'm going to have to go out." Troy paused, then went on. "Denise, called from the firm several times. She says someone keeps calling and asking for me. The person identified herself as Margaret Hyde. I'll meet with Ms. Hyde tomorrow morning, and I'll see Jasmin after. Today, however, I would like both of you to accompany me to speak with Jennifer."

They all stood heading for the door, and Levi asked, "Do you want me to bring Jennifer to you?"

Troy chuckled, humorlessly. "No, Jennifer deserves the position of power. I'll go to her."

"We'll meet you out front," Akeel said.

"In fifteen," Troy replied.

Troy headed for the kitchen where he could hear his wife and Monica talking. The smell of coffee and cinnamon wafted toward him. He didn't linger unseen, instead he stepped into the kitchen as Monica pulled a batch of rolls from the oven. Francine, who was leaned against the island, moved in to look over his sister's shoulder.

"Those look good–better than the first batch." His wife teased.

"I told you don't bring up those rolls." Monica giggled.

His sister noticed him first. "Good morning, Ernest."

Francine turned to look over her shoulder at him. "Oh, Troy, I didn't see you."

"Good morning, ladies."

His wife offered him a smile, but she didn't venture closer. Troy shoved his hands in his pockets to keep from hauling her up against him. Francine was trying not to drown in the relationship, so he backed off. At night, when they were alone, she did allow him to hold her; it was better than nothing. She set the tone–there was no sex, and he didn't complain.

As for the literacy program, Troy stopped her from going. Francine protested, but he didn't back down. He was still the maker of the rules; she bargained for part-time, and they had reached an agreement. But she wouldn't rush back, instead, she would give herself time.

"I have to step out."

"All right," she replied.

"I'll be back in enough time to watch television with you."

Francine's eyes widened, and Troy grinned. She asked, "You'll be home for dinner then?"

"Yeah."

He turned, walking back the way he came–exiting the house from the front. Levi was driving the Yukon, and Akeel rode in the front. The men traveled in silence until they reached Oak Tree Apartments, Building Ten.

"You sure this is necessary?" Levi asked.

Troy wasn't sure of anything these days, but he believed his wife needed the friendship she once shared with her sister. He was going to try to get it back for her. Still, speaking with Jennifer could make matters worse. Levi was staring at him through the rearview mirror waiting for an answer.

"It's gotta be done."

"I'm sorry, man—for everything." Levi replied.

"I abducted her before your words. Don't stress about it."

"I'm going to stay away from—" Levi tried to verbalize.

"You can't stay away, but you can stop teasing Francine." Akeel snapped.

"Yeah," Levi countered.

Silence fell between them once again as each man tended his own thoughts. Troy hated to add more fuel to an already raging fire; still, he needed them to be aware of all his thoughts, especially with Francine's condition.

"I reevaluated every coincidence, and the more I look at the Sam Fields and Harold Dawson situation, I believe Shirley Jenkins knows I killed them, which means she got this information from someone else. I wanted you both to be aware because of Francine."

"Look man—" Akeel started.

"Later," Troy cut him off, "we'll get to that later."

* * *

Logan stepped into Jack's Pool Hall at ten minutes after the hour. He had waited until he was certain Simms was alone. As always, the place was dimly lit, but unlike his last visit, it was kind of crowded. He spied Frank at a table near the bathrooms and made his way between the cluster of patrons. There was no need to pretend, Chris didn't bother sitting.

"Do you have something for me?"

Simms pushed a slip of paper across the table at him. There was an address, nothing more. Chris dropped two twenties on the table, turned and walked out. At the front of the bar, he had to climb over a few people to get out. Once on the street, he headed for his truck. A couple leaned against his passengers' side kissing; they were in their own world. Fuck—he missed Amanda.

They moved with the quickness when he open the driver's side door. He was several traffic lights from Jack's before he acknowledged that his hands were shaking. Amanda was going to be difficult, but he would get her to see reason. He needed her.

The day was a combination of overcast and sunny. The temperatures had cooled, and a soothing breeze took hold of Georgia. Chris drove through traffic, unable to calm his racing thoughts. The travel time was great as Jack's was in Douglasville, and Amanda was hiding in Dunwoody. When he exited I-285 at the Perimeter, it was congested. Chris stopped at a gas station to get directions.

Plantation Ridge Apartments was tucked behind a shopping center not visible from the street. The community was gated, and he scraped the side of his truck as he forced his way in behind another vehicle. He found her apartment, but the wine-colored Camry was nowhere to be found.

Chris parked in the back of the lot, almost in front of the connecting building and reclined his seat, anticipating a lengthy stake out. But after an hour, he spied Amanda's car moving down the small hill toward him. There were several cars between them, but he could see the driver as he pulled into a spot in front of her breezeway. A white male in his mid-thirties parked her car and got out. Red hot shards of jealousy stabbed Chris in the chest, spurring him out of his own vehicle.

Chris was crossing the parking lot when the brown-haired, slightly taller man looked in his direction. The man angled his body as if preparing himself; his deportment was challenging.

"Can I help you with something, Buddy?"

Chris felt provoked and growled in response. "Where the fuck is Amanda and why do you have her damn car?"

The other man was dressed in blue jogging pants with two white stripes that flowed from the hips to the ankles. He wore a gray t-shirt that read "Navy" in bold blue letters. On his feet were gym shoes that matched his jogging pants–blue with four white stripes on either side of each shoe. The man was clean shaven with brown eyes that appeared to have a better understanding of the situation than Chris. He didn't bother to answer, but he did laugh. Chris was about to get in his space, when he saw Amanda rushing from the building toward them.

"Logan, what are you doing here?" Amanda's tone was no nonsense.

"You moved and didn't tell me. Who the fuck is he?" Chris rasped, using his thumb to point at the other man in a sharp jab.

Amanda looked damn good as she stood before him angry. She wore a pink button down shirt with charcoal gray trousers and black loafers. Her hair had grown some since he'd seen her last. The unremarkable brown eyes that Chris identified with Amanda were whiskey colored today, made extraordinary by the myriad of emotions crossing her face.

"Mandy, go back inside." The other man demanded.

Chris turned his attention back to the man standing next to her. She stepped between them, attempting to block what was sure to ensue.

"Joe, please go inside." Amanda never took her eyes from Chris.

"Mandy—"

"Go inside, Joe." Chris cut the other man off.

The Joe character grabbed Amanda by the arm, causing Chris to reach over her head and shove him. She was quick at defusing the ruckus.

"Joe is my brother, Logan. Stop it!"

"Go!" she said to Joe, who eyed him, and then walked away.

Her brother reluctantly walked away, and Amanda whirled on him. The tone emitting from her was snide. "I don't want this, Logan. Don't make me file a restraining order, so when I shoot you there'll be a record of you harassing me."

Chris blinked at her words before snatching her by the arm. He dragged her to his vehicle and hoisted her into his passengers' seat. Climbing into the driver's seat, he started the engine without preamble. They drove in silence until they reached a sandwich shop about fifteen minutes from her complex. He parked the truck, got out and approached to help her out. Amanda opened the door but didn't accept his assistance.

He didn't back away when she got out; Chris pinned her between himself and his truck and forced her chin up with two fingers. His voice was raw.

"Don't run from me again–no other men."

"Chris…" She panted his name.

She had called him by his first name rather than his last. The sound of his name had been breathy. Still, he warned her again. "No other men, Amanda."

He stared down into her warm brown eyes, brimming with tears.

Fuck–had he been stupid enough to think her unattractive? She tried to pull her chin out of his grasp, but he tightened his grip. Tears slid down her cheeks.

"I hurt my career by sleeping with you. They want to use me to trap you."

"Trap me doing what?"

"They haven't told me, Chris. I can tell you they were investigating George Ingalls and two judges."

He dropped his hands, but he didn't back away. "Is Joe your brother or part of the trap?"

"I don't have a brother," she whispered.

At her confession, Chris leaned in and kissed her. He crushed his lips to hers; the contact was so bruising it made her whimper. "Are you choosing me, Amanda?"

"Are you dirty, Chris?"

Neither of them answered the question posed by the other. He stated rather than asked. "You're obviously not wearing a wire."

"My apartment is bugged," she countered.

"The black car…"

"Tailing me–you, when you're with me," she explained.

"Who are the judges?" He asked, but Amanda shook her head, letting him know without words that she wouldn't tell him. "What do they think they got on me?"

"They believe you killed Bryant's lawyer, George Ingalls." She answered.

If the situation wasn't so pitiful, Chris would have laughed. Of all the shit he'd done, it galled to be accused of a murder Troy Bryant committed. "Who is involved with this investigation?"

Amanda shook her head. "Chris…"

"Who, Baby?" He whispered against her ear.

"Frank Simms… he says you've pushed to get Bryant questioned. The higher-ups think you're trying to cover your tracks in the disappearance of Ingalls. They think you're trying to get the public away from all thoughts of Darrell Jenkins."

Chris leaned in and kissed her once more; the exchange was

soft–agonizingly slow. When he pulled away, Amanda asked, "Did you kill George Ingalls?"

"No."

"But you know who did, right?"

He stepped back and offered his hand to her. She looked as though she was going to refuse, but Chris shook his head. "They're watching."

The delicatessen was in a shopping center with a supermarket, a dry-cleaner and an electronics store. Small trees lined the strip mall to make it more picturesque and beyond the parking lot was I-285. Dark clouds hung heavy in the distance, but no rain fell. Chris strode past the unmarked black car as if oblivious to the white man who watched them. Amanda sighed, but she allowed him to lead her to Stein's Sandwich Shop. As they stepped into the establishment, the sign by the cash register–read: SEAT YOURSELF

The air conditioner was set to freezing, and even though the weather was cooler, the eatery was uncomfortably cold. Booths lined the back wall, while wooden tables and chairs were clustered at the front of the dining area. Chris led her to a booth for privacy. An older white man with dull black hair came to check on them, when he spoke, his teeth chattered.

"Sorry–the wife is going through menopause."

"Oh," Amanda said, before adding empathetically. "Poor thing."

"No poor her–poor me. We don't got no customers because of how cold she keeps the place. I'll bring you all coffee on the house." The man whined.

"Coffee is good." Chris added, giving the older guy the signal to back off.

The man nodded, then walked away. Chris remained quiet until the coffee was served. When the owner was out of earshot, he gave Amanda his undivided attention. Her heart shaped face was pale, and her eyes bright with unshed tears. His tone was rusty.

"I don't do pillow talk."

"I know."

"So, your apartment is bugged." He continued, stating a fact. "Do you care if they hear us fucking?"

"No."

"Good… because they will hear us, Amanda."

$* * *$

Jennifer wasn't home when Troy knocked on her door flanked by Levi and Akeel. The men didn't discuss a plan, but they did go back to the truck to wait. Troy stood leaned against the back of the Yukon smoking a cigarette. It was early afternoon and there was the threat of a storm, but no rain had fallen. He took in the steep peaks and valleys that made up the Oak Tree Apartment grounds. His sister in-law lived in the center of the complex at the top of the highest hill.

The smell of rain and the warm breeze that rolled around him was a nice change from the sweltering heat of the last few months. Young trees were planted throughout the complex, and the way they bowed in the wind was a gauge of the severe weather to come. The buildings themselves were white and beige; the dreary day and their coloring made the violent clouds even more ominous. Troy mentally went through his *to do list* as they waited for Jennifer.

He had several meetings ahead of him, and he wasn't pleased. Troy didn't want to meet with another victim of Sam Fields and Harold Dawson. He also didn't want to have more conversation about Shirley Jenkins. Margaret Hyde, the woman clamoring to meet with him, more than likely fell into one of the two categories. Troy hadn't spoken with Jasmin in a while, so he couldn't cancel on her. He understood that it was his job to collect the facts and provide the men working with him a clear path. Today, however, he would add taking Jennifer hostage to his growing list.

A green car with a dented grill parked haphazardly in front of the build-ing. Troy watched as his sister in-law got out on the passengers' side. She was dressed in blue slacks with a cream-colored shirt. Over her arm was a blue jacket, along with a black purse that dangled from a short strap. Her hair was swept back into a ponytail. Jennifer was smiling when she called out to the driver.

"Thanks for the lift, Stephanie."

"No problem." The unseen driver yelled back before pulling away.

Jennifer was about to turn toward the building when she spied them. Levi got out of the truck and approached first. Troy couldn't hear what his cousin said, but he did hear her ask, "Is Francine all right?"

Akeel got out of the truck, blocking Troy's view of Jennifer. He sighed as he moved in next to Akeel. Levi had already taken her by the hand and was leading her from the parking lot. His sister-in-law peered over her shoulder at him; she was afraid.

Troy was the last one to step into the apartment. Jennifer was seated on a blue denim couch that sat flush against the far wall. A brown coffee table occupied the space in the center of the room. The carpet was landlord beige and slightly worn.

Levi leaned against the bar that separated the kitchen from the living room. Akeel had turned one of the chairs away from the table to face Jennifer. He sat hunched over with his elbows to his knees. Troy stood with his back to the closed front door, but he wasn't leaning. Jennifer spoke first, and her anxiety pulsed between them.

"Did something happen to Francine?"

"No." Troy replied.

"Your sister is fine." Akeel added, before glaring at him.

Troy ignored Akeel. "Jennifer, I came to speak with you about how your sister and I met."

She nodded, but she didn't speak. His sister in-law was trembling. He looked to Levi for help, but his cousin kept his eyes to the floor. Clearing his throat, Troy continued. "I first saw Francine exiting a restaurant in Atlanta. She was trying to get away from Dorsey and a woman who had crashed their date."

"Jalal told the same story. I didn't believe him at the time." Jennifer whispered.

"In trying to get away from them, Francine rushed down a side street. I was parked in front of the restaurant and followed her for several blocks. At the next major intersection, a white van screeched to a halt; a man got out and dragged Francine from the curb into the vehicle. It sped off before I could think of what to do."

Jennifer gasped, but he went on. "I followed them to an abandoned auto shop..."

Troy was unsure of how much to disclose. The goal wasn't to traumatize but to relay the facts. He also realized that the telling of this story–hurt. The sight of Francine strung up flashed before his mind's eye.

"Troy…" Jennifer's soft voice moved him back to the awful task at hand.

"The dress Francine wore had been slit open and she was tied up."

"Did they… ahh… f-force her?" She breathed.

"No."

"She didn't report it. Why didn't she report it?" Tears stained her face.

"There was nothing to investigate."

"These people should be locked up." She said.

"Two men–both dead."

"Dead?" she repeated.

"I killed them." Troy paused for a beat. "I took Francine home and kept her."

A stillness fell over the room, and then Jennifer's eyes widened. He expected her to start yelling, but uncharacteristic of their past encounters, she remained quiet. His sister-in-law allowed her scrutiny to bounce first to Akeel and then Levi, but his cousin never looked up from the floor. She turned her attention back to him.

"Are you here to take a second hostage, Troy?" The force of her words hit him hard. She offered him a pitying smile as Troy fumbled for control. But before he could recover, Jennifer scrambled. "You need me or you wouldn't be here; so don't think you can bully me."

Levi attempted to explain the issue further. "Sweetheart, we came—"

"Don't, Levi," Jennifer put her hand up like a traffic cop. "You been gaslighting me for months. Just, don't."

Troy braced himself as she turned back to him. Normally, everything she felt was on her face, but at this moment, he couldn't get a read. Troy knew Levi had stepped in to save him from himself, but he opted for the truth.

"Yes, Jennifer, I'm here to take a second hostage."

"How's that workin' for you?"

"You tell me," Troy countered.

"Did you force Francine, sexually?"

"No," He answered.

"But you did take her from her life–against her will? You did marry her against her will–correct?"

"Yes."

"I don't like you Troy Bryant–not one fuckin' bit."

If not for her words, he wouldn't have been able to detect her disgust with him. Jennifer's facial expressions continued to be opposite her speech. It was unnerving. He decided to press forward to get to the root of the problem.

"Francine is pregnant."

There was more rude silence, but Jennifer's face did soften with those three words. Though her response was salty. "Let me guess. Frankie doesn't want children with a man who is too stupid to see that his wife and in-laws are not hostages."

"Yeah," he acknowledged.

"My sister is alive and for that... as far as the pregnancy..." she couldn't finish a sentence.

Troy's desperation was tangible. "I think my wife needs someone other than me to speak to about this matter. As far as the baby... whatever she decides... I just want her."

"Threatenin' to kill your wife's family to get what you want–ain't love, Troy."

Levi jumped in. "Jennifer, I think you should know—"

"For months, you both made me feel like I was crazy. While you two bitches were terrorizing Frankie. You no longer gotta babysit Troy's sister-in-law, Levi. It took me some time to figure it out, but you're in love with Karyn Battle. Please feel free to pursue her because I don't want shit else to do with yo' *gaslightin' ass*."

Troy flinched and turned to look at Levi; Akeel did the same. His cousin grabbed the back of his neck; his discomfort real. But Jennifer wasn't done.

"All of you, get out."

Akeel stood and walked out the door. Levi looked as though he wanted to speak, but he didn't; instead he followed Akeel out to the breezeway. This left Troy alone to face Jennifer. There was no fear from her and there was no remorse from him. She spoke before he could, and her tone was mocking.

"Don't waste your breath–I get it. You'll kill me if I tell anyone."

"Yeah."

Jennifer glared at him, then took a menacing step forward. Troy held his hands up in surrender. He didn't dare smirk, but he said softly, "Don't waste your breath–I'm clear. You don't give a shit."

"Nope."

"Butch will be here in the morning to escort you back to the house." Troy turned and strode out the door.

6

THE END GAME

Jennifer's statement about Karyn Battle made the ride to Bryant and Associates awkward for all three men. Troy sat in the back while Levi drove; his cousin avoided the rearview mirror and all eye contact. As for Akeel, he kept his attention on anything that whizzed by the passenger window. When they pulled in front of the office building, Levi got out and Akeel maneuvered around to the driver's seat. Levi's voice was thick with emotion.

"I'm going to start working through the items on my list–catch y'all later."

Troy watched as his cousin disappeared into the lobby, then turned to Akeel. "Did you know he wanted Karyn?"

"She asked to meet you. He only did what she wanted." Akeel replied.

"Did you know?" Troy caught Akeel's eyes in the rearview. "So, you did know."

They stared at each other for a time until Akeel said, "I'll park and wait for you."

Troy nodded, popped the back door and followed Levi into the building. His cousin stood at the bank of elevators, clearly waiting for him. Levi pushed the silver call button and when the doors slid open, both men stepped inside.

They held their words until they reached Troy's office. The receptionist took one look at their faces and went back to what she was doing. When the men were alone, Troy fidgeted and grabbed the back of his neck. There was too much tension surrounding them; they didn't need this—not now. Levi broke the silence.

"Listen, man—we brothers in my eyes. Karyn wanted you, she didn't know I wanted her. You and me got no issues."

"I wouldn't have…" Troy was at a loss for what to say.

"Being a big dude works against me at times. Karyn was nervous around me. It's only been lately that she has become comfortable in my company."

"Lately?" Troy asked.

"Karyn has been to Atlanta for several medical conferences. As a favor to Keisha, she brought information to me from Sloan. We met for lunch." Levi shrugged.

Troy saw what his cousin hoped to hide. Levi didn't know how to get around the fact that he and Karyn slept together. And given what he felt for Francine, Troy understood the problem. They weren't the kind of men to discuss at any great length the women that fell into their beds. But Troy had to know.

"Jennifer?"

At the mention of his sister-in-law, Levi became guarded, slightly hostile and possessive. His cousin never dropped his gaze, the unspoken message apparent. Levi wanted him to back off, but again Troy discerned what his cousin hadn't made verbal. Their connection had caused his cousin issues with not one, but two women. Troy, unable to let go, was about to speak, but Levi beat him to it.

"I ain't been up in her because of how you met Francine. Jennifer has been consumed with worry for your wife. She has, on occasion, begged me to tell her the truth… I didn't."

Troy nodded, then turned to stare out the window. He turned back to Levi, choosing his words carefully. "I think I got us in some heavy-duty chick shit."

Levi looked relieved that he was backing off. "Yeah, man."

"I'll clock in tomorrow at 9 to prepare for my meetings. Francine and Jennifer need time together, so I'll work all day from here."

Levi shoved his hands in his pockets, fidgeting. "About Francine and the baby…"

"We good." Troy countered.

The men shook hands before Troy exited his office. He took the few moments on the elevator to gather himself. Back at the truck, he climbed in and focused on the scenery. Other than firming up plans for the next day, he and Akeel didn't converse.

It was quarter to six when they arrived at the house in Calhoun. The rain that had been threatening all day started in fat drops as they got out of the truck. Both men made a dash for shelter. Troy unlocked the door, greeted by a sweet scene. Francine and his nephew were sprawled out on the floor going through Junior's bookbag. Monica sat a few feet away writing something. When his sister looked up, Troy noted the stress on her face. Junior spoke first.

"Hey, Dad—Uncle Troy."

"What's up little man?" Troy countered.

Akeel's voice was gruff. "How was your day, Junior?"

"It was good, plus no homework." The boy spouted with glee.

Akeel chuckled. "I guess that is a good day."

Monica got to her feet and greeted them with a nod, even as she spoke softly to the boy. "Okay, Sweetheart—get your things together so we can go with your father."

Junior raced off calling over his shoulder that he'd left his shoes in the kitchen. Francine got to her feet, handing Monica the remainder of the papers from the floor.

She moved in close, pressing herself against Troy's side. At the feel of his wife's body, he was overcome by emotion. Troy almost missed his sister's reaction when Akeel reached out and touched her hair. Monica was skittish and the pulse at the base of her throat revealed her discomfort, but she didn't pull away. Junior rushed back into the living room, and his presence got everyone back on track.

"I'll pick you up after I take Junior to school in the morning." Akeel said to Troy.

"Aiight."

Francine chimed in. "I'll see you day after tomorrow, Monnie. Jennifer is coming tomorrow to hang out."

"All right. I gotta get Junior and me settled. I'll call you." Monica replied.

The rain had downgraded to a drizzle, as Troy and Francine stood with the door open until the truck pulled away. Troy closed the door and locked it.

"You wanna watch television in here or in our bedroom?" Francine cocked her head to one side, awaiting his response.

"Bedroom."

"You hungry?"

"I am, I haven't eaten all day."

"We have meatloaf, mashed potatoes and broccoli. Come, I'll make you a plate."

"Who else is here?" Troy asked.

"Just us."

Francine took him by the hand and led him into the kitchen. His wife plated their food, then sat opposite him at the table. She was dressed in black jeans with a soft yellow blouse that buttoned down the front. On her feet were a pair of blue booties with treads on the bottom. Her hair was pulled up in a ponytail, and she looked tired.

Troy finished off a second plate, noticing that Francine ate little; she mostly pushed her food around with her fork.

"Not hungry?" he asked.

"My belly is unsettled. I don't think it can take any action."

Troy stood, scraping both plates in the trash. Afterward, he reached into the refrigerator for a can of ginger ale. Francine retrieved a glass. They walked hand in hand to their bedroom. Placing the glass and the can on the nightstand, Troy undressed down to his briefs. Francine disrobed in the closet and emerged bedecked in a red pajama top with white laced panties. He pulled back the covers, allowing her in bed first. Francine fluffed the pillows, then snuggled in close to his side; she promptly fell asleep.

The television was background noise that Troy didn't care to hear. Reaching out, he gently took the remote from Francine's relaxed fingers and pressed the power button. Their bedroom was immediately submerged in darkness. The clock on the nightstand boasted the early hour of 8:00 p.m.

Careful not to wake his wife, Troy swung his legs over the side of the bed. He would pace the house to ease his tension as thoughts of Levi and Karyn came unbidden. One memory plagued him, and he was forced to examine it with new eyes. Karyn had come to Atlanta to spend the weekend. Butch had escorted her to the law office at his request. He had been seated behind his desk with Karyn on his lap. Levi had knocked, entered and found them kissing. Troy now had a different understanding of his cousin's expression.

Standing in the center of the living room, he muttered. "Shit."

There was nothing he could do about the Karyn situation, and it was obvious his cousin still wanted her. Troy was equally baffled by Levi's reaction when asked about Jennifer. Still, he was good at signal reading–he wouldn't pry again.

On his third lap through the house, Troy found himself standing in the corridor between the pool and the media room. He turned his mind away from the Levi–Karyn debacle and placed his focus on the Shirley–Darrell dilemma. As he trekked through the kitchen, he looked for the loose ends. Stepping through the events chronologically, Troy looked for the gaps and areas where he might have dropped the ball. He had chased the coincidences of the case, now he would pursue the absurd.

Once on the main hall, Troy headed for his office; his bare footsteps fell softly on the hardwood floors. Francine opened the bedroom door as he was about to stroll past. She had turned the television back on, providing a blinking, unsteady light in the space between them; no sound emitted from the screen. Behind him, the light from the kitchen bled faintly into the corridor. It was enough to see that his wife was frowning.

"What's wrong?" he asked.

"You said you wanted to watch TV with me."

He tried not to laugh. "I did want to watch television with you, but you fell asleep."

"I wasn't sleep," she snapped.

"You were sleeping, and you were snoring."

She gasped. "I don't snore."

"I turned the TV off because I couldn't hear it over your snoring."

"You are so damn rude, Troy. Do you know that?"

He threw back his head and hooted. In his life, he often had to work through controlling his anger. There were times when he had to refrain from beating the fuck out of someone. But his sweet wife was the one person who made him snort with laughter.

"I came home early to watch TV with you. You fell asleep and started snoring as soon as we got in bed. Yet, you think the impolite one in this situation is me."

"I do."

"You just not gonna be truthful, are you?"

"Nope." She smirked.

Francine turned, walked to the bed, pulled back the covers and allowed him in first. She fluffed the pillows once more, then scooted in close to him. The television remained muted. She laid her head on his chest, then wrapped her legs around one of his. His wife was pinning him in place.

"So you want to cuddle–not watch TV?" He called her out on the maneuver.

"Mmmm," she responded.

Troy stared at them in the mirrored ceiling. Even in the dimness of the room, he found their reflection stunning. What could be more beautiful than the sight of his wife and child asleep in his arms. Francine had indeed fallen right back to sleep, but he didn't try to untangle himself. Instead, he laid there working through the circumstances of Darrell Jenkins in his head.

When morning came, Troy found himself surprisingly well rested. He woke to find that he was spooning his wife and his erection was pressed firmly against her wriggling ass; he groaned. The digital clock facing them read 6:53 a.m. Francine pushed back into him once more, causing him to grip her hips to stop the slow grind that was killing him. She was still half sleep and whimpered from his bruising hold. He was going to lose his shit and shoot in his underwear.

Troy took two cleansing breaths. He wanted to sink deep inside his wife and forget everything. The need for intimacy with Francine was urgent, but Jennifer loomed large in the background. He didn't want to take from his wife, he wanted to share with her. There could be no sex until after Jennifer's visit. Francine would see his actions as selfish. Telling his sister-in-law how they met made her an accomplice and a hostage. Orgasmic bliss would have to wait until Francine finished being angry with him.

He climbed from the bed and headed for the shower. The water was cold against his skin, he needed it to cool his hunger. When he was done in the bathroom, Troy dressed in the closet. Francine was propped up on several pillows watching for him as he reentered the bedroom. The sight made him smile.

"You're up."

Francine grinned, sheepishly. "I've been a little more tired than usual. Sorry, I fell asleep on you."

Troy was concerned, but he didn't want to push her. The topic of the baby or pregnancy made him afraid to be shut out. Still, he asked, "You feel all right?"

She instantly became guarded. "I'm fine."

He changed the subject. "I have to go into the office. I'll be there until about four o'clock. If you need me, Jewel knows how to contact me. Butch will be here in my absence; he'll take you and Jennifer out if you wish."

"When will you be back?"

"I'll be back in time to have dinner and..." Troy coughed. "to watch TV with you."

Her smile was back. "Perfect."

"You hungry?" he asked.

"I'm gonna have breakfast with Jennifer."

Troy finished dressing, kissed his wife and met Akeel in front of the house. The ride to the law office took about thirty minutes longer than normal because of traffic. When they were younger, Akeel always had a joke or some anecdote he couldn't wait to tell. But post–jail Akeel didn't talk much. If you engaged him, he would converse, but he did not seek to be warm and fuzzy. Troy understood this change, so he was shocked when Akeel turned to him at the red light.

"Monica and I are sleeping in separate rooms. I fuckin' hate it."

"She's in the house with you–it's a start." Troy replied.

"It's not just sex, she's afraid of me."

"If she thought you would hurt her, she wouldn't be at your house." Troy said.

Akeel chuckled. "What you really mean is if *you* thought I would hurt her..."

"Monica is my sister... even when I'm mad at her."

"You still mad at her? Because I can tell you, she's hurt."

"I still feel some kinda way with both Francine and Monica. I ain't in the position of power." Troy explained.

Akeel laughed as he pulled into the parking lot of their destination. The men slid right back into silence as they exited the truck, strode through the lobby and rode the elevator. Denise looked up at their approach.

"Levi is in his office, gentlemen."

"Good morning, Denise." Troy said.

"Denise," Akeel parroted.

The smell of coffee assailed Troy's senses as he headed for the conference room to set up shop. Akeel disappeared in the direction of Levi's office, and Troy would have followed, but everything still felt awkward. He unpacked his briefcase and began looking through previous notes and to do lists. Denise brought him coffee and a bagel, but when she didn't walk away, he looked up to find her wringing her hands and staring at him.

"Something wrong, Denise?"

"Your first meeting is at eleven. I'm worried I did the wrong thing by scheduling this woman. She wouldn't stop calling, if I didn't answer the phone–she left message after message. When I asked the reason for the meeting, she became hostile. I don't want you to be angry with me."

Troy stared at her, while trying to think through what she was saying. "I'm not going to be angry with you, Denise. If you were having trouble, you should have come to me or Levi. Based on what you're telling me, she probably wants to complain about Shirley Jenkins."

Denise winced. "Sorry, Troy."

"No worries."

"I didn't get the feeling it was about the Jenkins lady."

It was Troy's turn to cringe. "One of the victims then…"

"She ahhh… sounded like a middle age white woman. I'm interested to see what she looks like and what she wants." Denise admitted.

"Well, it's after ten, so we won't have to wait much longer."

"Don't take the meeting alone, Troy."

He sighed and began putting his paperwork away. "Tell Levi and Akeel to get ready for this meeting."

She smiled weakly, then rushed off to do his bidding. When he had the contents of his briefcase tucked away in his office, he made some final notes before Akeel and Levi appeared.

"Denise expressed her concerns. You want to cancel this meeting?" Levi asked.

"Naw—if this is a loose cannon, we need to get a handle on it."

Akeel chimed in. "I say we see what this is about."

Troy gave Levi the once over. His cousin was dressed in jeans, unlaced work boots and a wrinkled, white button down. There was no mistaking, Levi looked as though he hadn't slept; he didn't look in any condition to take a meeting.

"Have you been home?" Troy asked, directing his question to Levi.

"No, I've been working through my list. We don't have time right now to discuss it, but the D.A. is avoiding me. If Larry was some place taking a shit, I could get him on the phone. It took me some time to recognize it, but he's got me on ice." Levi said.

Before Troy could answer, Denise appeared. "Margaret Hyde is here for her meeting with you all."

Troy stood and angled himself to the left of the table, so he could see all the way to the receptionist area. His eyes landed on a small white woman dressed in a brown pantsuit. The hair on her head was black and cut short. She was seated in one of the chairs by Denise's desk, but only the side of her face was visible.

"Give us five minutes, then escort her back." Levi said.

"All right," Denise replied.

When the door closed, Akeel said, "She looks like she can whoop your ass."

"Fuck you." Troy shot back. "We'll sit her with her back to Denise. I'll sit opposite her. Levi, you sit to her left. Akeel, you'll stand behind her on the right."

The men moved into position and when Troy looked up, Denise was walking toward them. He still couldn't see their guest clearly until the receptionist stepped aside to open the door. Margaret Hyde was a tiny woman with brown eyes that bounced around the room. Her straight black hair was laced with plenty of gray strands. She had a pointy nose with small lips that were set in a frown. On her left shoulder was a tan pocketbook and in her right hand, a manila folder.

"Can I get you something to drink?" Denise asked.

"N-no… thank you," the woman's gaze latched onto Troy.

"Good morning, Ms. Hyde. I'm Troy Bryant and this is Levi Bryant." He gestured with his right hand to the left of the room. "And that's Akeel Marshall."

"Gentlemen," She greeted. Her eyes went wide when Levi stood.

"Please have a seat," Troy offered.

But Margaret Hyde didn't sit. "I'm sure you're all wondering why I'm here, Mr. Bryant–gentlemen. I'm a forensic scientist and I work for a lab contracted by the state to process physical evidence."

Troy had to remember to close his mouth. Levi grunted, leaving Akeel to pick up the conversational thread. "Please continue, Ms. Hyde."

She nodded. "It's dangerous for me to be here, but I was out of options. The physical evidence in the case against Darrell Jenkins has gone missing."

Levi finally found his voice. "I figured as much, but were the samples ever tested?"

"Yes," she replied cautiously.

"Who's blood was it?" Levi asked.

Margaret Hyde stared at Levi for seconds before reaching for the manila folder on the table in front of her. Troy noted that her fingernails were cut short and clean, yet her skin was dry and scaly. He was certain it was from the constant handwashing given what she did for a living. Ms. Hyde slid from the folder a stack of eight by ten, glossy photos. After turning the prints so they would make sense for Levi and Troy. She looked over her shoulder and addressed Akeel.

"Please come see."

Akeel obliged and moved closer, coming to stand between himself and Levi. When Margaret had the photos laid out, she retrieved a miniature composition notebook from her purse, referring to it as she explained each photo. Troy noted her steady, confident demeanor. The woman before them was certain of her conclusions.

"This a picture of Mr. Jenkins when he was still at the crime scene. Please note the smeared blood at the bottom and around the belly of his shirt. The pattern is consistent with his trying to climb the fence behind the victim's house."

There was indeed a picture of Darrell, arms at his sides, eyes closed against the harsh flash of the camera. Margaret looked to her notes, then pointed a chapped finger at the print. She leaned in, her short hair falling over her forehead. "This one is a shot of Mr. Jenkins at the station. In this print, please note that he is wearing the same shirt with what looks like a new blood stain at the collar. Yet in the previous photo, there is no blood at the collar of this garment."

Troy kept glancing between the first and second photo, but he didn't interrupt. He was comparing the images of Darrell while trying to comprehend the truth. Ms. Hyde continued. "The next few photos will make what I'm saying easier to follow. This is a print of Mr. Jenkins' shirt after being brought to the lab. Again, the blood smears are consistent with rubbing against something. The stains at the collar appear to have come from a fresher source like the nose or lips. These stains are also circular as if the blood seeped into the fabric."

"Are you saying the smeared blood didn't come from the same source?" Levi asked.

"Correct. It's as if Mr. Jenkins attempted to stop the flow of blood by pressing the collar of his shirt to the source. The smears appear transferred from an object—not a source. The next prints further illustrate my findings. Please note the photo of Mr. Jenkins' trousers. There's blood at the crotch and on the inner thigh, also consistent with climbing the fence. I should tell you that there is trace amounts of blood at the hem that can't be seen in this print. The rest of the photos are of the fence behind."

"Ms. Hyde, who's blood is it?" Akeel asked, his exasperation obvious.

"Forgive me for rambling, gentlemen. The blood sampled from the collar matched Darrell Jenkins. The smear sample match the victim, John Unger and…"

"Spit it out," Troy snapped.

"A—a relative of Darrell Jenkins." Margaret Hyde answered in a rush. "Actually, if I didn't have a blood sample from Mr. Jenkins, the DNA mixed with the victim's would have gone unidentified."

"Relative?" Levi barked.

"Shit," Troy added. "Jarrell had me fooled."

"The brother didn't present as unstable." Akeel said, incredulously.

"Ohhh, no—gentlemen, the smear sample came from a woman—Mr. Jenkins' mother."

Troy couldn't breathe. He jumped from his seat and began pacing the conference room. Margaret Hyde gasped in terror from his sudden movements. He could hear Levi attempting to soothe their guest while he tried to reconcile the information.

"Are you sure?" Levi asked.

Margaret held her hands up, but not in surrender; the action was imploring. "Of course I'm sure... You should know that it's my fault the evidence is missing. It's why I've come."

"Your fault?" Troy countered.

"Y-yes." She replied. "I presented my results to the arresting officer, and days later, the lab suffered a power outage. Important physical evidence went missing from several cases. I think the Jenkins' case was the target. Detective Logan was involved, but I can't prove it."

"Chris Logan?" Akeel growled.

"Y-yes." She answered.

Troy tried to collect himself. "Ms. Hyde, are you saying the young man's mother killed John Unger?"

"I'm saying, if you look closely at the prints of Mr. Jenkins' at the scene and at the station, in the second photo, his nose looks a touch swollen. The skin over his upper lip has a faint laceration. I believe the blood at the collar confirms he met with manhandling by the police. But his mother was in the company of the victim when he bled. She could have cut herself trying to exit the scene and the transfer of blood happened when he climbed the fence later."

"Can we keep these prints?" Levi asked.

"Absolutely." Margaret Hyde paused, before adding. "Mr. Jenkins could be covering for his mother, but the victim's DNA presence was significantly less than that of Darrell's mother. The blood smear on his attire indicates that he wasn't present when his mother or the victim bled."

"So you don't think Darrell did it?" Akeel asked.

"No," she sighed, "but again, he could be covering for his mother."

Troy nodded. He was about to ask a question when Ms. Hyde added one more crucial point. "Mr. Jenkins' hands tested negative for gunpowder residue."

The silence that hung in the air was deafening. Troy lost his train of thought and the question he was going to ask. Levi spoke, and the exchange was jarring.

"Ms. Hyde, may I ask the name of your employer?"

"I work for Reliable Laboratories." She answered.

"I've never heard of Reliable Lab." Levi responded. "I thought the samples were placed with Sunny Labs."

"Aero Loop Tech owns Reliable Laboratories." Margaret Hyde explained.

* * *

Troy stood at the window, staring down on the expressway. He'd moved to his office because the conference room left him feeling too exposed after their meeting with Ms. Hyde. There had been no reprieve since Jasmin had shown up on time. She'd lost too much weight and worried endlessly that they'd forgotten about Darrell. But Troy assured her that nothing could be further from the truth. She'd burst into tears twice, and he had to look to Denise for help. When she calmed down, Hassan escorted her home.

Seeing the girlfriend of Darrell Jenkins in an emotional meltdown had done nothing for his mental state. A blanket of melancholy had settled over him for reasons he couldn't admit. His own mother would never have watched him twist in the wind for a crime she committed. The anguish and longing that rolled through him for his mama was at this moment acute. But it was the uncertainty of fatherhood that broke him and the knowledge that the woman he loved didn't want to carry his child. And it was all his fault.

Troy was jumbled up inside, and the appearance of Margaret Hyde with all her scientific talk had humbled him. The case of Darrell Jenkins had too many jagged edges. They now had to investigate Ms. Hyde and the moving parts that came with her because photos of blood stains do not free a man. He had also gone through his previous notes and found two tasks that had not been completed. Still, his biggest problem outside of Darrell— the murders of Sam Fields and Harold Dawson.

The connection between his shit and the Jenkins case was incestuous. Everything was cooking in the same pot and it was starting to boil. He would make some stops, then go home to face Francine. Levi's voice halted his thoughts.

"You ready?"

"Yeah," Troy replied. "I have a few errands, before we head to my house."

"I'll drive. Akeel took my car to pick Junior up–it's me and you."

"Aiight," Troy frowned. It was unlike Akeel to leave without speaking with him.

"Meet me at the elevator."

"Give me five," Troy answered.

He had his briefcase packed and was striding down the hall to the meet Levi in under four minutes. They rode the elevator in a fog of tension. Once in the truck, Levi asked, "Where to first?"

"College Park."

Troy was quiet as Levi moved the truck onto the expressway. It was just past the lunch hour, so traffic was still thick. The sun had pushed through the clouds, shaping up to be a beautiful day. He kept his eyes on the road ahead and the weather helped lift some of the sadness that had taken hold of him back at the office. They hadn't discussed at any length what to do with the information from Ms. Hyde. Troy still didn't know what to think, but Levi, it seemed, had a plan.

"I'll draft and file a motion to dismiss."

Troy nodded. "How confident are you that the case will be dismissed?"

"I'm not sure, but it seems to be the next step. The physical evidence is missing, which means the chain of evidence was compromised."

"I'll investigate Margaret Hyde, in case shit don't happen the way we anticipate. Me and the men will stay the course."

"We may need to have a press conference," Levi countered.

"I figured as much."

The conversation lulled until the Washington Road exit came into view. "Where you tryna go?" Levi asked.

"I want to swing by Mr. Mitchell's house. Tyrell and I never got back with him. I would also like to knock on Ms. Montgomery's door. We were told she went to stay with her daughter for a while, maybe she's back. She may offer something insightful."

"Have you figured out what to do about Darrell's mother?" Levi asked as if unwilling to say her name.

"Shirley–no. What I have figured out is that the Sam Fields and Harold Dawson matter were deliberately linked with this case. It was meant to publicly control me. I just haven't decided if Shirley is a tool or the mastermind."

"You worried about being locked up?" Levi pressed.

"Naw… I would off myself," Troy said.

He felt Levi abruptly turn to look at him, but he didn't return the contact. The key was to ride this out, see where it took him. He would help get Darrell free while getting his will in order. The latter had moved up on his list of priorities. Troy would make certain Francine was cared for.

"I see ya thought this through." Levi's words were thick.

"I did."

The only sound in the truck was the rapid clicking of the signal as they made a right off the exit ramp. Godby Road had a traffic light out, but once they were past the jam of vehicles, they turned onto Rose Street. There was no one out and about, but Troy knew once he was spotted, they might end up with a small crowd of onlookers. As soon as they parked in front of the Mitchell house, Troy felt something was wrong. He popped his door and got out after Levi. His cousin was the first up the walk way.

At the end of the street, a school bus stopped, brakes screeched, and children could be heard in the distance. Laughing, chatting and yelling, it was the sound of young people moving closer. Troy turned his back to Levi and gazed across the street at the Montgomery house. The grass was freshly cut, and he took it as a good sign. They wouldn't leave without trying to meet Ms. Montgomery.

It occurred to him that based on his only other encounter with Mr. Mitchell–they shouldn't have reached the front steps. The old man should have stepped from his house at their approach. Levi rang the bell but couldn't tell if it worked. He watched as his cousin tried the storm door. When it gave, he banged on the front door twice.

Troy looked to the bottom of the driveway where a sea of young brown faces moved as one along Rose Street. The colorful bookbags, jeans, sneakers and bright shirts reminded him of a more innocent time. A girl stopped, her eyes curious, her skin dark. She wore two big pom-poms on her head.

"Mr. Mitchell ain't home."

"Do you know when he'll be back?" Troy raised his voice a tad.

"My mother don't think he's coming back." A boy wearing green jogging pants and a black short sleeved shirt chimed in. He was light skinned with fat braids all over his head.

Troy was about to ask another question, but the door opened behind him. The kids scurried off. He turned in time to face a woman who looked to be in her mid-thirties. She was holding tightly to a cane, and her hair was flat on one side as though she had been resting. She was eggplant dark and the smile she offered was weak, but polite. Her blonde sew-in was matted and poorly done.

The woman before them was thin of frame with warm brown eyes that radiated pain. Her nose crinkled, and her eyes narrowed as she tried to place Troy. Her voice was soft, and her whisper sounded more like a plea. "Are you the Silent Activist?"

"I'm Troy Bryant, and this is my cousin, Levi Bryant."

"Ohhh," she sobbed. "Did someone tell you that my father is missing? Is that why ya come?"

"Missing?" Troy chanced a quick look at Levi. "Are we speaking about Mr. Mitchell?"

"Yes, sir. I'm Danielle Mitchell, his daughter."

"Please call me Troy. I came to speak with your father about the Darrell Jenkins case. I was unaware that he had gone missing. Are the police involved?" Troy asked.

"How long has your father been missing?" Levi added.

"We don't live together, and Dad hates talking on the phone. He's been missing about three weeks or at least that's when I noticed something was wrong and called the police." Her voice trembled with emotion. "Forgive me, please come in."

They were about to accept her invitation when a blue Honda parked at a sharp angle in front of the house. The driver's side opened and out stepped Shirley Jenkins. As she walked up the driveway, Troy could feel the venom secreting from her. She was dressed in a navy blue skirt with a light blue blouse. Her natural hair was pinned back from her face; her brown eyes angry. She addressed Mitchell's daughter first.

"Hey, Danielle, how you feeling?"

"I'm fine, Shirley." The words fell from Danielle's lips like ice chips. "I'm busy, we'll have to speak another time."

Shirley ignored the other woman's rudeness and directed her next statement at Troy. "Jasmin tells me ya still working Darrell's case. I haven't gotten an update."

"Good afternoon, Ms. Jenkins." Troy countered.

Levi didn't speak, instead he followed Ms. Mitchell into the house. Troy stepped over the threshold last. Danielle, quietly shut the door in her face.

"This way, gentlemen."

They walked down a long hall that led into the large kitchen. The place reeked as if the house hadn't been aired out in quite some time. Stale-old, yet not unclean. A beige round table with four matching chairs sat to the left of a chrome, double sink. The white stove bragged of a silver pot with food stains around the sides; the pot sat on the back burner. At the edge of the kitchen was a matching refrigerator and to the right of the towering appliance was a small dining room.

"Can I get you all something to drink?" Danielle asked.

"I'm good." Levi and Troy responded in unison.

"I apologize that you had to see me actin' rude and ill-mannered. Shirley works my last nerve."

Troy asked. "Why don't you like Shirley?"

Danielle looked away, embarrassment clear on her face. "I know it's petty, my mother has been gone for some time, but Shirley was seeing my father. I came over unannounced one afternoon and found them…"

Troy nodded, then looked away to give her a moment. The window over the sink held a huge potted plant that obstructed the view. He changed the subject. "What kind of plant is that?"

"I'm not sure. It was from my mom's funeral. We've cut it back, but we couldn't get rid of it. My father said he feels better having it in the window." Danielle's eyes watered.

"How did you get the news that your father was missing?" Levi asked.

Danielle grabbed a napkin from the holder in the center of the table.

She looked close to collapsing. "I came to take him shopping. His keys and wallet were here, but not him. The front door was unlocked yet pulled tight. I called the police; a Detective Hernandez is working the case. He's keeps me updated, but it doesn't look good."

Troy's thoughts raced as he listen to Danielle. He never looked away from the plant in the window. His own voice almost wobbled. "Is Ms. Montgomery home or is she still with her daughter?"

It was that question that caused Danielle Mitchell to pitch forward and cry uncontrollably. Troy didn't look at Levi as he waited patiently for her to gather herself. Finally, she whispered, "Ms. Montgomery doesn't have children. Cordelia's been missing since June."

Troy remained pokerfaced when he repeated. "Missing since June— no daughter."

"The body of an elderly woman was found down by the airport—a week ago. They think…" Danielle breathed.

"I see," Troy responded because he couldn't make himself stay quiet.

BOOK 4

Position of Power

1

SEPTEMBER 1995

After promising Danielle they would make subtle inquiries into the disappearance of her father, they left College Park. Once on the expressway, Troy issued several orders. "Let the men know we'll meet at my house tomorrow at 7 a.m. Unless there's an emergency, I'm not to be disturbed tonight. I'll be dealing with my wife and sister-in-law. I've also updated my will–I'll give it to you in the morning."

"I was gonna come home with you," Levi said.

Troy turned, locking eyes with him. "No."

The men stared at each other for seconds until Levi relented. Troy gave no explanation of his decision to go it alone with Francine and Jennifer. Forty minutes later, he took over driving the Yukon after leaving Levi in front of the office building. The time had pressed on to early evening and rush hour traffic offered the right amount of delay as he headed for Calhoun, Georgia.

Troy wanted a moment to decompress. He needed to make certain this interaction with Francine wasn't tainted by the life he led outside of her. The only way to separate this problem from the rest was to admit that he was feeling homicidal.

As he sat in bumper to bumper traffic, he consoled himself with the knowledge that in the coming days he would do violence. But this evening, he would bend to his wife and her sister. He would be firm when needed, manhandle when necessary and coerce to get his way. Still, they would remain in charge. Troy was prepared to give them glimpses of the real him and the thought made him laugh. As traffic loosened, propelling him swiftly toward home, he understood that for the next few hours–he would be the hostage. Troy appreciated this distraction, for without it, he would scorch everything in his path.

When he finally turned onto his gravelly driveway, his blood was thrumming. The sun had shifted in the sky and the receding light bled through the autumn leaves. The dirt road leading to the house caused the truck to rock from side to side. He brought the Yukon to a stop, and the house door swung open. Butch stepped onto the tiny porch. The old man's face was unreadable, which said much.

Troy got out, rounded the front end and leaned back against the truck. He crossed his feet at the ankles and folded his arms over his chest. It wasn't sweltering, but it was hot in Calhoun. Butch was agitated–Levi had called ahead.

"You blocking me, old man?" Troy asked.

"No."

Butch was surefooted in violence, but at this moment he was strung tight. He had placed his loyalty with Francine, and Troy almost smiled. "It sure feels like you tryna stop me from entering my own home."

"Wanted to make sure..." A muscle ticked in the old man's jaw. "She been upset all day."

"You checking me?" Troy clipped out.

Butch jammed his hands in the pockets of his worn jeans. His black skin gleamed with sweat and the red t-shirt he sported was stained at the armpits. He looked hurt. "She said her stomach was unsettled–thought you should know."

Troy's voice was thick. "Francine hasn't decided if she wants to continue with the pregnancy."

Butch nodded. He looked like Troy felt. "You told Jennifer."

"I did."

The old man stared out past him into the trees. Troy stood to his full height. "Consider me checked."

Butch didn't attempt more eye contact; instead he stepped down off the porch and walked away. Troy pushed away from the truck, ambling into the living room. He stood in the center of the colorful carpet, pulling his shirttails from his trousers. His undershirt was exposed as he pushed the button down out of the way to shove his hands in his pockets.

Troy listened for sound, but he heard nothing. He strode to the entrance that connected the hall to the living room and overheard the clinking of dishes. The kitchen would be the first point of contact for the three of them. He walked the long corridor, allowing his footfalls to echo. When he reached the entrance of the kitchen, both women were seated at the table staring intently at him.

He stopped at the island, then leaned against it. Troy was trying not to loom over them as he gauged them individually. Jennifer looked wrung out, her hair, which was loosely curled, framed her face. His sister-in-law's eyes were red from crying, and because her skin tone was lighter than Francine's, her nose appeared rosy as well. She wore a black blouse, which made her pallor even more off-putting. Jennifer dropped her gaze.

Next to Jennifer, his wife looked stricken. Francine wore an orange blouse, which added to the sadness in her eyes. He didn't think it possible, but his wife was even more beautiful than usual; his heart squeezed at the sight of her. It looked as though she had curled her hair, then pulled it into a messy ponytail when she got tired of it. Thin tendrils framed her face, and Troy wanted to kiss her. She spoke first and there was bite, which made the confrontation severe.

"You told my sister that I'm in love with my abductor."

"I told your sister how we met." He countered.

Jennifer was in his periphery, but he saw her flinch at the harshness of Francine's words. He waited for her next outburst as pain settled between the three of them.

"This doesn't make me want children with you," Francine hissed.

His sister-in-law gasped, but he nodded conceding to her feelings. Tears spilled from Jennifer's eyes, but Francine's remained dry. A weight formed in his stomach, but he controlled his hurt. He didn't lash out, which would have been so easy to do.

"Did you take my sister hostage, Ernest?"

"Yes."

"Did you threaten my sister?"

"Yeah, I threatened Jennifer."

Francine's voice caught. "Why would you do this? I gave in to you on every front except about the baby."

The rustiness of his speech reverberated around the kitchen. "You needed someone to talk to about this other than me. I can't let you go to your mother... I can't let go."

Jennifer placed her hand over Francine's, and it caused him to look at her. When his eyes locked with his sister-in-law, she spoke. "Frankie tells me you were asked to help find the men who did this to her. She says she met a few of their victims. I understand they're dead, but you're not involved with this media circus, right?"

"No," he answered.

"Good," Jennifer shot back. "Cause fuck them."

His eyes widened; he would have laughed, but Francine said, "I want out of this—"

"This is your fuckin' life. You will not leave me." Troy stood tall, unfolding himself from the island and glared at his wife.

Francine snatched her hand away from Jennifer and pushed her chair back from the table all in one motion. He had never seen her so angry, and fuck–he was turned on. There was an urgency to yank her against him. She wasn't leaving–he wasn't playing.

When his wife tried to step past him, he moved to block her. At the opposite end of the kitchen came Butch's warning. "Troy–that's enough for now."

He didn't turn to look at the old man; he kept his eyes glued to Francine's face. She looked away, trying to shut him out. Jennifer was wide eyed; his wife was trembling, and behind him, he could feel Butch vibrating. They were all waiting for his next move. He stepped back, allowing her to pass. Francine ran off down the hall, and when he heard their bedroom door slam shut, he faced Butch. His voice was even-calm.

"Back off."

Jennifer stood and stepped into the space between them. Butch folded his arms over his chest, unfazed. Jewel appeared behind her husband, looking stressed. The older woman wore a floral dress with yellow slippers on her feet. She moved around her husband and smiled up at him.

"Jennifer and I are gonna cook. You two go take a break," Jewel instructed.

Troy turned to walk away, but before he could step into the hall, Butch spoke. "You can thank me later."

"Yeah," Troy answered.

He headed for his office, flipping on the light. When he rounded the desk, he looked up to find Jennifer in the doorway. He hadn't known she was following him; her voice broke.

"Hearing the story from Frankie… thank you for saving her."

He nodded, but words escaped him. Francine was shutting him out; it was all he could focus on. Jennifer must've read his mind because she smiled weakly. "You're the hostage, Troy."

Blowing out a shaky breath, he replied, "Yeah."

When the office door closed behind Jennifer, Troy sagged in his chair. The need to keep his hands busy was strong. He unpacked his briefcase, but he didn't go through the contents. What he did was ponder the last several months–minus his wife. Where was the connection? Who would dare to exploit his fixation with the former Detective Chris Logan? He didn't know if the other men saw the problem, but he did. And while he wasn't uncertain about many things, he knew where to start.

As the hour grew late, his thoughts turned to his wife. He felt choked by his insecurities, causing him to obsess over the first statement she made when he entered the kitchen: *You told my sister that I'm in love with my abductor.*

* * *

Francine lay in bed seething at herself for loving him so much and at Troy for his need to control everything. She'd been prepared to discuss being pregnant with Jennifer. Talking about a possible baby and her feelings concerning the pregnancy would have softened the hardness between them. But when they sat at the table to eat breakfast, Jennifer had blindsided her with one whispered sentence.

"Troy told me how you two met."

Francine froze, unsure that Troy would have told Jennifer such a thing. Still, the loud tick of the clock on the wall at the entrance of kitchen, the low hum of the refrigerator and the birds chirping outside the bay windows muted her senses. She stared blindly at Jennifer.

"What did my husband tell you?"

"He told me that you were abducted and that he killed the men who took you. Troy told me he kept you against your will." Tears spilled from Jennifer's eyes.

Francine looked away trying to hide from the vision of herself strung up, dress slit open—exposed. She was so far into her own thoughts, she almost missed the softness of her sister's next question.

"Do you want me to help you get away from him?"

"What... n-no," Francine answered. "I love him."

"I thought so, but I had to offer," Jennifer replied. "Will you tell me what happened?"

Francine took in a breath, readying herself to decline her sister's request. But the whole story fell out of her. How the Tonya—woman had crashed her date with Jalal. The way she had run from the restaurant like a coward, and if that wasn't bad enough—the way she paid no attention to her surroundings. She told how the white van had screeched to a halt in front of her; how the door shot open before she could understand what was happening. The way Sam Fields had beat her while the other man drove. She spoke about how they discussed stringing her up before they actually did it. Lastly, she talked about feeling faint with relief when Troy showed up, then realizing this wasn't the rescue she had hoped for.

She paused before explaining being forced to marry. Francine exhaled sharply when she admitted to feeling safe with him, finding him attractive and needing to be with him. When she discussed being jealous of Karyn Battle, she closed her eyes. She confessed to hoping that he would never let her go, while trying to comprehend—her new self. In the end, she owned up to not wanting children but needing Troy. Jennifer cried and so did she.

As the hours whittled away, Francine had set aside her embarrassment in favor of anger. Troy had told their secret, threatened Jennifer and left her in the dark about his intentions. This situation had her feeling like her dog had gotten off the leash and was trotting the neighborhood biting folks. When Troy stepped into the kitchen to face them, he had resigned himself to her anger. He was docile with his answers, being ever truthful to sidestep a fight. It caused her to lash out and coerce a reaction from him.

When he stepped into her path, she wanted to punch him and then fall into him. The bedroom had grown dark, but the hour was still early. There was a knock on the door, and Francine thought it was Troy, but Jennifer popped her head in. The light from the hall illuminated the room in a slice of clarity.

"You up?" Jennifer asked, like she did when they were children.

"Yes."

There was no invitation that Francine could recall, but Jennifer entered the room and climbed into the bed on Troy's side.

"How you feeling?"

"Mad," Francine gritted out.

Jennifer giggled, causing Francine to snap. "What's so damn funny?"

"You like to control everything, now you're married to a control freak. Me and mom couldn't wait for you get a husband, so you'd stop bossing us around."

Francine sucked her teeth. "I think this is different."

"The circumstance is horrific, but you're still standing. I was just trying ... I'm sorry I didn't mean to make light of the situation."

"I love you, Jennifer."

Her sister moved in close and hugged her. "I love you too, Frankie. This is prolly inappropriate, but I'm excited about the baby."

"I was starting to feel that way too, until he did this." Francine gestured between them.

"There's more to it... why don't you want the baby?"

"It was Levi," Francine answered.

She told of her first interaction with him and how she wanted to shit herself. Her words were honest when she admitted to still fearing Levi. Jennifer was quiet for a few heartbeats before she spoke.

"Troy wouldn't let anyone hurt you—not even Levi."

"I know."

"Levi loves Troy," Jennifer said.

"And you love Levi."

The conversation lulled until Jennifer said, "Yeah, I did, but that's over."

They didn't push each other any further. Francine was still awake when her sister finally dozed. She was aware when Troy opened the bedroom door and walked up to the bed. Upon seeing Jennifer, he turned, leaving as quietly as he had come. He lingered in the doorway, his back to the room and she was sure he believed himself exiled from their personal space. Francine changed clothes, donning one of his t-shirts. She brushed her hair and teeth before going in search of her husband.

Troy's office was dark, and at the opposite end of the hall, the light over the kitchen sink flickered. All the doors along the corridor were open except one, and she knew he had chosen the third room on the left. She knocked gently and waited. His voice was rusty.

"Come in."

The room was lit by the spill of light coming from the bathroom. Troy stood at the window, his back to her. Francine stepped into the room, closing the door with a soft click. He turned acknowledging her, half his face shadowed. He wore only his underwear, the muscles in his chest bunched as he moved to cross his arms. She was trying to think through articulating her pain when Troy beat her to it.

"No."

"No?" she replied, confused.

"This is your life–here with me. I can't... *I won't* let you go."

He didn't wait for a response, instead he turned away. Francine moved in close enough to lean her forehead against his back. Her anger had dissolved some, still it was present.

"You told Jennifer in order to manipulate me."

"I told your sister, so you could speak freely with her about the baby–about me." He sighed. "I think you need the friendship you had with her."

Francine abruptly stepped back from him, her attitude beginning to burn hot once more. "You can't take my sister hostage, Troy."

"I can, Francine–I did. Please remember that your sister and mother were already at my mercy. Jennifer is just aware of it, now."

His tone was nonchalant but resolute, and it made her shake with a newfound annoyance. She turned swiftly on her bare feet, her intention to escape; but when she reached for the doorknob, he was there crowding her–pressing into her. She felt his erection against her rear, while over her head, he placed his palm to the door. His voice was a mixture of arousal and hazard.

"You're pushing me for a reaction–please don't."

Francine's breath caught at his ability to read her. "This was our business… you shouldn't have."

Troy moved in, laying his other palm to the wood to keep her locked in place. "The decision about the baby is still yours. I'm trying to give back some of the shit I stole from you."

He nuzzled her neck; the bristles of his goatee caused her to moan involuntarily. His masculinity laced with Egyptian Musk oil wrapped about them in a plume of erotic need. She dropped her head and shuddered as he ground his hard body into her. His speech was both coaxing and demanding.

"Take off these clothes," he snapped, before adding softly, "Please, baby."

Francine didn't get a chance to answer; he grabbed the hem of her shirt and tugged. The garment landed on the floor as he shoved at her panties until they were pooled at her feet. When she was naked, Troy gave more instructions.

"Put your hands against the door and don't move until I tell you… please."

He took hold of her hands to position her–palms flat to the door. Roughly, he kicked her feet apart making her stance wide. When he stepped back from her, cool air assaulted her hot skin. In her sideview, she saw his swift movements, and then felt his naked heat. His leaking hard-on left streaks of pre-cum on her hip and ass cheeks.

"I'm trying to compromise, Francine. I know what we are, but I am attempting to offer some normal." He didn't evade conversation, speaking truth between them in his velvety voice.

"Troy…"

"Shh–I'm talkin' not you." He brushed his dick along the cleft in her ass. "Damn, Frankie."

She was swallowed up by his presence–all of her person submerged in him. Troy was hard where she was soft; the coarse hairs on his legs, chest and arms made her body sing. Francine's taste buds overlapped with her sense of smell allowing Egyptian Musk oil to collect in her throat. His voice dripped sex as he spoke into her ear. She was faced away from him; her sight subdued.

"Jennifer won't speak about this because she loves you. I did threaten, but she didn't care."

He brought his large hands around her body, cupping her breasts. He rolled her nipples with his thumbs and forefingers, causing her to pant and cry out. Troy dropped his right hand to her belly, splaying his fingers wide–where their child rested within her. Finally, his touch dipped lower and his knowing digits danced over her clit.

"Ohhh, Troy."

She was trembling at his touch. Placing his feet outside of hers, he pushed her thighs closer together. Troy didn't enter her, but he did rub his tip against her core.

"Fuck, that's magic." He groaned.

And it was magic, Francine thought. The roughness of his hands made her realize it had been a long time for them. She was strung tight, her need gigantic. He asked a question and she found it difficult to focus.

"You want to be free of me, Francine?"

"No," she breathed.

"Oh, baby." He whispered, sinking his teeth into the sensitive flesh at her nape.

She was close to bliss and still so far away. Delight skittered around her navel, her limbs were weak from the promise of pleasure, but he didn't take her over the edge. She started fucking his fingers in earnest trying for more traction–more friction; but he asked another question. She whimpered at his filthy conversation.

"Can I have some pussy, Francine?"

"Y-yes, Troy."

He grunted. "Can I fuck you from behind?"

"Yesss."

His words almost got her where she needed to be, but he suddenly withdrew from her and stepped back. She sagged against the door, disappointment blanketing her. Francine was about to beg when he abruptly picked her up and carried her to the bed.

"On your knees," he said, "hold on to the headboard."

She scrambled to do his bidding, clutching the wooden frame. Francine braced herself as her husband moved in behind her; his chest to her back–his big fingers spanking her clit. He placed the blunt head of his erection at her opening and yanked at her hips, easing into her. They both groaned.

"Want to fuck you slow." His voice shook. "Don't wanna hurt you."

He twined his fingers with hers and helped her play with herself. Francine was enthralled. She fell into a sharp orgasm, her body stiffening as she gasped his name. He pulled her to him, turning her face so he could kiss her from the side. His range of motion was limited, making the contact electric. They swallowed each other's cries until her tremors ebbed.

Troy helped her reach for the headboard, steadying her hands with his own. He angled her hips, while pushing into her and withdrawing on a rhythm. The sex was indeed slow and perfect. She rocked with him, hating his retreat. He hit a spot up inside her that made her drop a hand to her clit with no urging from him. He strained against her–Troy was throbbing inside her.

He added more of his weight, his thrust becoming erratic. His speech was gravelly, as he leaned over to press open-mouthed kisses along her spine. "Gonna cum… gonna cum… fuck, I'm…"

Francine was shocked when her body began to spasm and ecstasy seized her once more. Behind her, Troy was still stroking her. "Tight… hot… shit, Francine."

She gave into the beauty of frenzy with him, allowing her head to fall back against his shoulder as satisfaction overtook them. Francine's voice broke. "Ohhh… love you."

They collapsed in a heap, their labored breathing filling the room. Troy went to the bathroom and came back with a warm cloth. Francine lay with one arm thrown over her eyes, but she opened her legs for him. When he finally climbed in bed, he pulled her close. She lay with her head on his chest and wept.

"You still mad at me?" he asked.

"I still see myself strung up, telling Jennifer wasn't easy."

"You have nothing to be embarrassed about." His hand rubbed lazy circles on her back.

"I can't function without you."

Francine couldn't stop crying, it was the shame of needing him so much. Admitting that she couldn't function in her day to day life made the humiliation too great to stomach. Troy understood the meaning of her confession because she felt him tense.

"I can't function without you, either," he replied.

"You can go out without me—you can still handle everyday life without me. There is no weakness holding you back."

"I could see why you would think this way, but you are my strength. Before you, I had stopped interacting with the men and the organization. I was losing it. I need you, Frankie." His breath caught on the last two sentences.

Francine sat up, thankful for the light spilling from the bathroom. Troy never called her Frankie and he had done so twice. She studied his face, noticing the stress around his eyes and the pain he tried to cover. Reaching out, she touched his lips and then his goatee. She even fingered the gray patch in his chin hair. She leaned in and kissed him deeply. He gasped.

"I didn't want you at the literacy program. I hated that you wanted me to back off. The shit at the law office was a distraction, but when I thought you were trying to get an abortion..."

"I don't want to talk about the baby." She said without anger.

Francine buried her face in his neck as if to hide, but Troy kept pushing. "Levi is—"

She shoved her tongue in his mouth to stop the conversation. When she pulled back, it was his turn to scrutinize her. Francine tried to look away, but he grabbed her chin.

"You made a decision, didn't you? Baby, please... tell me."

"I was hoping my mother could stay with us for a while after the baby comes. Between my mom and sister, they'll keep me from fucking this up." She breathed.

He pushed her onto her back and eased into her. Francine wrapped her arms and legs about him, holding on tight through the ride. Troy speared her with his tongue and his dick; still, he remained gentle. Against her lips, he told her how weak he was without her and he promised to love her always. And when she felt his stride falter, she heard him whisper absently.

"Sweet pussy... sweet."

2

BRING IT

Troy looked about his office where the men had reconvened. Only Butch held eye contact. Everyone else was flipping through the pages of small notebooks and tablets. All the men looked exhausted except Akeel, who appeared preoccupied. The goal of this meeting was to listen and process the information brought back. He would break down this fiasco in two parts, then address by measure of threat.

What he had right now were puzzle pieces with no corner. There was nothing to connect the facts other than absurdities and wild ass coincidences. Troy didn't understand how all the fragments fit together, but he was clear about how the next few hours would go, and it made him smile.

Hassan spoke first, his annoyance evident. Troy figured it was because of the early hour. Since his release from prison, Hassan made it a point to sleep in, and it was 7 a.m.

"You assigned Shirley Jenkins to me because Tyrell woulda been shitty."

Troy chuckled. "What ya got?"

Hassan flipped through his notebook. "Shirley Jenkins grew up in foster care. The only family she has is her sons, an estranged sister and one nephew. She preys on older men to sustain her and her children. I didn't see where she had any friends. She moved back into her house with her two sons after the safe house incident. The older son spends most of his time with his boyfriend."

"Jerrell calls the law office every other day to check on our progress. Denise says he always asks for Troy," Levi said.

"The people Troy and I interviewed didn't want Jerrell present," Tyrell explained. "They wanted to bitch about his no good mother."

Hassan reached down beside his chair and pulled out a manila folder. He spilled the contents onto Troy's desk. There were pictures of Shirley Jenkins shopping, eating out with her youngest son and standing in line at the bank. The last set of prints showed her in a restaurant with Larry Wright, the D.A. Troy's head popped up.

"I followed her all the way to Ludowici, Georgia, for that pic. After that encounter, I never saw them together again. But they did drive four hours to meet in private. I think that says much."

Troy looked to Levi who said, "I still haven't heard back from the D.A., Larry is definitely avoiding me. We're going to have to force his hand."

"Yeah," Tyrell agreed.

"I did some digging into Aero Loop Tech, Margaret Hyde and Reliable Lab," Levi offered. "Margaret Hyde is telling the truth; Aero Loop Tech dabbles in all kinds of shit from airplanes to commercial real estate. Richard Unger, the nephew of our murder victim, works for the company. Aero Loop Tech has been trying to buy up some land in College Park. It seems they set their sights on John Unger's property."

Jesse chimed in; Troy watched as he fumbled with his notes, his palms almost as dark as the backs of his hands. When he lifted his mean eyes, Troy cocked a brow.

"Yo' ex-cop been spending all his time with some lady cop. It's hard to keep an eye on 'im wit' 'im being followed by the po-leece. The woman Logan fuckin'—can't tell if she wit' him or against him."

Butch nodded as if to say he agreed with Jesse. Akeel stared out the window, offering nothing. Troy made a mental note to speak with him after the meeting. His thoughts were wandering when Tyrell spoke up.

"John Unger led an uneventful life. He grew up rich and white with a yen for black women. This didn't bode well for a relationship with his family. Still, he inherited from his grandfather. Unger owned a lot of property in Atlanta. He had no children, and apparently his nephew thought shit should go to him, but Shirley Jenkins happened."

Troy gave an accounting of the meeting with Margaret Hyde. But it was his telling of the encounter with Danielle Mitchell that made Tyrell ask incredulously. "Are you telling me Mr. Mitchell lied to us and now he's missing? You think the body found in the field is Ms. Montgomery?"

He didn't know how to respond to Tyrell's questions. Troy felt a way about the fact that the elderly were being preyed upon right under his nose. When he gave the situation real thought, he wondered how much of Mr. Mitchell's disappearance was a direct result of his inability to follow up. He hated to admit it, but even he had become a pawn in this game. Worst yet, the damn plot kept thickening, and the more answers he uncovered, the more confused he felt.

Troy's brain itched with the knowledge that he had been played. He pondered the nerve of the person who orchestrated such a thing and shook his head as he gazed around his office. All eyes were on him.

"Next move?" Levi prompted.

"We'll start where I'm most comfortable." Troy responded.

"When?" Tyrell asked.

"Now," Troy replied, and everyone stood.

Akeel, Butch and Levi hung back as the men filed out of the office. They were waiting for instruction, but Troy directed his words to Akeel.

"You aiight, man?"

His friend looked to the window. "Just seems like we're chasing our tails. The old man was murdered, I get it. But to steal evidence and falsely accuse... Logan needs to be smoked. Why are we chasing this next thing?"

"We have two problems," Troy explained. "One is my naivete and the other... How long will it take before Logan figures out that I can't apply pressure to him because someone is applying it to me?"

Akeel stared at him, then nodded. "I'll ride with you."

Troy changed the subject. "Francine has decided to keep the baby."

Butch stepped forward and clapped him on the back. Akeel's eyes were bright, but Levi looked away, his relief tangible. Troy stepped forward and clapped his cousin on the back. When the moment passed, his next thoughts were for Butch.

"You and Levi will stay with the women."

Levi tried to protest. "Listen… Francine–Jennifer, ahhh they don't want…"

"Work from my office," Troy ignored his cousin's doubts. He almost smiled at how the women intimidated Levi.

"Monica is here," Akeel grinned at Levi. "She won't let anything happen to you."

"Fuck both of ya," Levi countered.

Troy stepped into the hall. He could hear the women in the kitchen, but he avoided any interaction with them this morning. He had kissed Francine awake and made love to her again, now he was about the business of keeping her. Troy turned his mind to the players and the game.

Akeel and Butch left the office, giving Troy a moment alone with Levi. "Force the D.A.'s hand."

Levi nodded as Troy walked away to meet the men out front. Hassan rode with Jesse in the Benz, while he rode with Akeel and Tyrell in the Yukon. As they rolled toward College Park, Troy tossed over in his head the words of Margaret Hyde and the common sense she had applied to dumb down her explanation. Today, thoughts of what she did for a living gave him pause, but it didn't stop the show.

Traffic was thick when they reached Sparks. The place had the appeal of a nightclub rather than a gas station. In the light of day, it was dreary, even though the morning sun shone brightly over Georgia. And while the sign in the window flashed "Open," Sparks didn't appear to be attracting patrons. Tyrell pulled the truck to the front of the store and parked. Troy got out and made for the entrance with Akeel on his heels.

Tyrell posted up at the front door while Jesse and Hassan approached the building from the back. Troy noted his reflection in the glass door before stepping in from the heat. He wore blue jeans with a hole in one knee, a black t-shirt and black work boots, and on his hands were a pair of surgical gloves. Akeel was dressed a bit neater, but still in jeans, a t-shirt and work boots–surgical gloves in place.

At the counter and behind the bulletproof glass stood Justice himself. He was stoned, yet alert, and there was no fear in him. Akeel kept on until he was at the door that led behind the counter and kicked it in without hesitation. Two young black men stepped into view with their weapons drawn; the standoff was clear.

The squealing of a heavy door from somewhere in the back of the store made the men with Justice turn back–involuntarily. But Jesse was a rough dude; he slammed the guy in front of him in the head repeatedly with the butt of his gun until he was out. The man in front of Tyrell, raised his hands and his gun to the ceiling in a gesture of surrender.

Behind the counter, Justice and Akeel stood, guns trained on each other. Jesse stepped up, his weapon and his words pointed at Justice.

"Come on, talk to us, son. If ya shoot him, Imma shoot you in the dick."

"What the fuck, Troy?" Justice gritted out.

"Took me some time to realize it, but I'm closer to the truth by being in the same room with you, Justice. We need to talk."

"Go head. Talk–den." Justice growled, but he didn't lower his weapon.

"We ain't playing," Troy's voice and demeanor–calm. As if on cue, the guy Jesse beat in the head moaned.

Akeel let off a shot, causing Justice to duck. "Next one gon be in yo ass."

Troy watched the scene before him unfold, and one thing was apparent. Justice wanted to live, and the notion would be his demise. If he had gone for broke, he might have been the only one to survive this exchange, but the bitch in him was on display so Troy pounced.

"You and Jasmin set me up."

"What? No, man, Jasmin is a sweet girl. She ain't in this shit." Justice said.

"We have her–you wanna talk or no?" Troy countered.

"Fuck–man, where is Jasmin?"

Troy and Justice stood suspended for a time, sizing each other up. Abruptly, Justice laid the gun on the counter. Jesse moved in, taking his weapon, but Akeel offered direction. "This way."

Hassan called his name, silently asking what was to be done with the other two. Troy turned his attention to the men, studying them for the first time. The man on the floor was out, and quite frankly appeared near death from where Troy stood. His skin was dark, and his hair was cornrowed.

Troy's eyes bounced to the guy standing next to Hassan, who gazed nervously at Jesse. He wore jeans, a green t-shirt and green sneakers. Dude looked to be about twenty-six with bright skin, black hair and light brown eyes. He stood just under six feet, his frame formidable.

Jesse was speaking to Akeel about tying Justice up, causing Troy's attention to slip back to the real matter at hand. When Justice's hands were secured behind him, Tyrell stepped in and led him out to the truck. Akeel fell into step with them, headed for the parking lot. Troy turned to speak with Hassan and got an eye full of why this venture went so well. Jesse walked up to the other hostage, grabbing him by the nape of his neck. The act established dominance as Jesse shook green t-shirt guy, firmly but not without affection. When the younger man looked up, Jesse leaned in whispering something in his ear. Green t-shirt guy nodded, and Jesse stepped in kissing him hard on the mouth.

Troy watched as Jesse whispered for a second time in the guy's ear; the man never spoke, but he did turn and walk toward the back of the store. Hassan gestured to the guy on the floor, bringing them back to business.

"What do you want done with him?"

"Dump his ass by the flea market on Old Nat."

And with those words the men separated to work through the day and the task at hand. In the back seat of the Yukon, Troy and Akeel sat with Justice between them—Tyrell drove. The ride back to Calhoun was silent, except for the one question asked by their prisoner.

"Where is Jasmin?"

Troy didn't answer, he kept his eyes glued to the back of Tyrell's head not even daring to gaze out the window for a distraction. The commute was less than swift on the way into Fulton County, but heading toward Calhoun, there was almost no one on the road. Tyrell moved the truck off the highway as soon as he could, taking the back way for discretion. Each mile drew them closer to the truth—to full disclosure, and Troy was giddy.

When Tyrell turned onto the long drive of his property, Justice tensed beside him. He parked the truck alongside where Butch and Jewel entered their apartment. Akeel popped his door and turned to get Justice out. Their hostage immediately started bucking and yelling.

"Where the fuck is Jasmin, man?"

Troy popped his door, then yanked Justice backwards by the collar, causing him to fall from the vehicle upside down. Tyrell put hands to him to get his screaming ass right, then he and Akeel subdued him while Troy held the door open to the raised corridor that led to Butch's humble abode. At the top of the stairs stood Jewel dressed in beige slacks and a black, short sleeved shirt; her hair was combed to cover the scar around her eye. She pulled the door wide when they reached the landing, and Tyrell carried a dazed Justice over the threshold.

The small apartment had a living room to the left and to the right, a bedroom which couldn't be seen if the front door were open. Across from the entrance was a bathroom, the color scheme, sky blue. The kitchen had a yellow swinging door that was propped open, inside was a small round table with two chairs. On the counter was a coffeemaker and a loaf of bread. The sink was an old fashion double that was deeper on one side. Beyond the living room with its brown couch and matching loveseat was a sunroom. There were lots of beautiful plants. Troy had never ventured into Butch's space, but now he understood where all the plants in his house came from.

After Tyrell and Akeel tied a woozy Justice to one of the kitchen chairs, they left to handle the rest of the day. There was nothing left to do, so Troy sat opposite his hostage in the black, wood framed chair with the red leather seat. He leaned in, elbows to knees, waiting for signs of lucidity. Troy needed confirmation of what he had already figured out.

Justice's hair was cut close, his dark skin was bruised under his right eye where Tyrell had punched him. He also sported a split lip, but there wasn't much blood from his exchange with Tyrell and Akeel. His hostage groaned, then eyed him. The *confused and out of it look* was disappearing–in its place was the *angry if I get loose look.*

Troy ignored the silent threat. "Why did you pull me into this shit?"

"Listen, we both know you can't kill me–you a public figure now. Jasmin ain't in this."

"Did you think you could use me because I'm a public figure?" Troy almost laughed out loud. Justice had gauged him wrong. Still, he would give his prisoner some power, so he could get at the truth. "You offer the truth, and I might offer a truce."

"Where Jasmin, Troy?" Justice's tone was less hostile.

"Where she is, and her well-being depends on your answers. I'm waiting." Troy knew Jasmin was innocent, but he found it interesting the lengths

Justice was willing to go to for her safety. His concern for the girl was his downfall. There wasn't a smug bone in Troy's body because Francine was his weakness.

Justice sighed. "What is it ya wanna know?"

"Everything."

"I know I ain't the one that pulled you into this shit, the D.A. asked you first. If I had known that he asked for yo' help, I wouldn't have come to you."

"So you and Larry Wright are friends then?"

"I ain't no friend of the fuckin' D.A." Justice sneered. "Why would I have expected his help? He ain't never helped before wit' shit."

The last part was an afterthought not really directed at Troy, but he followed the thread pressing Justice. "Why don't you like the D.A.? The shit with you and Larry sounds personal."

"Larry Wright is my father; he left my moms when I was about three for Shirley. He ain't never acknowledged me—named myself Justice to fuck wit' 'im."

Blindsided—Troy hadn't seen that coming, and he was afraid to ask his next question. "Why *did* Larry help?"

"Shit—maybe he felt sorry for Darrell. How the fuck should I know? Shirley is my mother's younger sister. The D.A. don't want nobody to know he got four sons."

"Are you telling me that you and Darrell are brothers?" Troy was incredulous.

"I know we're brothers—shit, and cousins too, but the three of them don't know. They don't know about Larry either."

"You stepped in because ya know who killed John Unger—don't you? Darrell is innocent, and it bothers you."

Troy leaned back in his chair. They stared at each other for moments and though he felt he knew the answer, he asked flat out. "Who killed John Unger?"

Justice shook his head. "Mr. Mitchell shot Unger; he was jealous over Shirley. She played the old man 'til she offed his friend."

Troy's mind jumped to Margaret Hyde, and he frowned. He had

deduced everything incorrectly. The silence must have troubled Justice because he started rambling.

"When Mitchell shot Unger, the bullet nicked Shirley. She bled like a stuck pig–the old man's hand wasn't steady. Guilt started screwin' wit' his ass, and she worried he would tell someone. Plus, Shirley wasn't sure what Ms. Montgomery saw from one of the windows at the back of her house; everything was a damn mess."

"The body found in the field by the airport is Ms. Montgomery, correct?"

"Yeah."

"Did Shirley kill the old lady?" Troy pressed.

Justice looked away, and Troy's blood ran cold. "I broke into her house and... I smothered her. Shirley said if she were implicated, Darrell would never be free again."

"Who killed Mr. Mitchell?"

"She promised me money if I helped clean shit up. I did the old man too."

"Where is Mitchell's body?"

"In the field behind Sparks."

The men fell silent once more as Troy tried to process the facts against the truth. Where did Richard Unger and Chris Logan fit into this catastrophe? There was obviously two plots on John Unger's life and money. His mind tossed over Justice's statements: *I broke into her house and... I smothered her. I did the old man too.* While he replayed the conversation, Justice asked again.

"Where is Jasmin?"

Troy shrugged as his eyes locked on the other man. "I'm not sure where Jasmin is; she's probably at school."

"I thought you said Jasmin was here."

"Why would she be here?"

"You fuckin' played me..." Justice growled.

Troy remained unfazed. "It's about time I played somebody–instead of being played for the damn fool."

"Fuck you," Justice fired back, his words aggressive.

Troy leaned in–elbows to knees once more, never taking his eyes off

Justice. "What should be done with a man that would smother a defenseless old woman?"

Justice had the grace to look away, but Troy couldn't get past the events that had taken place. More awkward quiet ensued as he stared at Justice. Troy worked out in his head what should be done and stood, moving about the kitchen. He rummaged through the two drawers to the right of the sink and then the pantry until he found what he needed.

He turned to Justice, items in hand and felt no shame regarding his actions. The industrial size green plastic bag Troy held made a snapping sound before he yanked it down over Justice's head, torso and the back of the chair. He pulled silver duct tape tightly around his victim's neck to close off all air. And when Justice began to violently thrash about, Troy pushed the chair against the wall to keep it upright.

"Troy… please, man! Please!" Justice's pleas were muffled.

A detachment fell over Troy as he listened to the other man beg for his life. The movement of the plastic around Justice's head slowed, then stopped and still Troy waited; he leaned in again, placing elbows to knees. His victim wasn't breathing. Troy sat for an hour facing the green plastic bag. After a time he felt and heard the trickle of liquid. He gazed down to find that Justice was pissing on his boot.

Troy offered no emotion, as he shook the urine from his right foot before standing. He left Justice and headed outside. When he stepped into the sunlight, he noted the time to be two in the afternoon. He lit a cigarette, inhaled deeply and exhaled sharply. The men appeared.

"What you want done with him?" Butch inquired.

"Drop his ass in the parking lot of one of the tittie bars downtown," Troy replied.

3

MEETING OF THE MINDS

The hour was late and the house quiet as Troy stood at the bedroom window staring into the darkness. Behind him were his wife and the muted television. He hadn't left the room to pace because he wanted to be near Francine. Her presence hushed the unreasonable. Guilt rode him about Ms. Montgomery, though she was already dead when he became entangled in this mess. Troy even felt bad for not following up with Mr. Mitchell.

What turned his stomach most was the fact that he had been incorrect about damn near everything. Shirley may have provoked jealousy, but it was Mitchell who shot and killed his friend. And still, after all that had been revealed, the question of who knew about his crimes was still a mystery. He had the power of deduction on his side–there was only one place left to go at this point. The case for Darrell had been solved, but how they would get him out of jail remained to be seen. The last people standing in this tragedy had something to lose. He–himself had committed homicide and Shirley...

Troy waited for his conscience to kick in, but it never did. He had gone about his day secure in the knowledge that not another person would encounter Justice. Plans and strategies were discussed with the men. He ate dinner with his wife and sister-in-law. Later, he and Francine propped up in bed to watch television. When she fell asleep, he paced the room.

His mind turned to Chris Logan. He realized that Richard Unger and Logan had plans for John Unger, but Shirley beat them to it. Still, Logan couldn't have been aware of how lost he had been. If the ex-cop had detected even the smallest weakness, he would have used it already. The same could be said for Shirley. In dealing with the mystery of Sam Fields and Harold Dawson, Troy would have to set everything else aside and face the puppet master himself–Larry Wright.

He continued to match Justice's words against the facts piled in his head. While he contemplated his next step, his wife spoke into the quietness.

"Troy."

There was a rustling behind him, and then a soft shuffling of feet against the floor. He wasn't aware of his nakedness until Francine hugged him from behind. She caressed his chest before one hand slid down to his dick. His breath caught as she gave him a firm squeeze and then a tug. She kissed his back and whispered.

"What is troubling you?"

He would share none of what was in his head. She carried his child, and that's all he wanted her to worry about. "I'm placing my schedule so I can be available for you–no worries."

She nuzzled his back. "So, you're not going to tell me."

"I promise nothing is troubling me. You know I don't sleep well."

The muted television brightened, as he turned to face her. Troy saw the skepticism in her eyes, but she didn't push. "Come lay with me," she requested.

He allowed himself to be led back to bed. Francine climbed in first and when he was settled next to her, she perched on her knees to maintain eye contact. Troy thought she would sleep, but she began chatting him up.

"Is this about Sam and Harold?" her voice shook when she said their names.

"No."

He didn't look away in an effort to reassure. She smiled weakly, the action was short of calling him a liar. His wife leaned in and kissed him. At first it was a chaste joining of their lips, but he grabbed the back of her neck to deepen the exchange. Francine moaned, then abruptly broke away. Troy was concerned he was too rough, but she shocked him, moving in for another kiss—one that she controlled.

His wife backed away once more and began placing open mouthed smooches along his jaw, neck and bare chest. When she reached his stomach, he propped on his elbows to witness the beauty of her touch. She pulled back the light sheet that covered him from the hips down. His erection bobbed free, and without preamble, Francine took him between her lips. Troy's head fell back in sheer delight.

"Woman," he groaned.

The feel of her hot mouth was torture as she licked him from base to tip. She sucked him deeper after each skim of her tongue. He felt his balls tighten, a signal he was getting close to release. Troy thought opening his eyes would stop the earth-shaking orgasm threatening to consume him, but it wasn't so. The lighting from the television flickered and changed making the scene before him even more erotic.

"Ah, Francine," he gritted. "Easy, baby, I don't want to cum yet."

She moaned around his dick and began sucking him harder–sloppily. The sight of her enjoying blowing him, the noises of appreciation and vibration of her sounds sent him to the edge. He had to fight to not snap his hips while shoving her head down further onto him.

"Shit, baby, I'm gonna cum–back up." Troy was panting, but Francine doubled down, sucking him with purpose. "Fuck, I'm cumming."

And still, she didn't back away from pleasuring him. Troy grunted, growled and cursed his way through the mind-blowing sensations that rocked him. When she squeezed the last drops of his seed from him, Troy collapsed back on the bed. He was vaguely aware of Francine pulling the sheet over them. She kissed him, and he tasted himself on her tongue.

"I love you," he murmured.

It was his last thought before sleep claimed him. He awoke to sunlight spilling through the window and Francine curled up beside him. Troy lay staring at their reflection in the mirrored ceiling, and the sight took his breath away. Francine stirred before meeting his gaze in the mirror; she smiled then rolled to the edge of the bed. He watched as she tiptoed into the bathroom. When he heard the shower, he followed suit.

She was already lathering up he when joined her. Francine smiled wickedly as she began washing him with her strawberry soap. He kissed her, tasting mint.

"No one will take me seriously today smelling like damn strawberries."

"Everyone takes you seriously," she countered.

"You feeling all right?" he asked.

"I feel fine–just hungry."

"You want me to cook for you?" he offered.

"Can you cook?"

"Good point," he answered, causing his wife to giggle.

Troy shut off the water, and they toweled each other dry. Back in the bedroom, Francine sat in her favorite chair, tending to her toilette. He was digging through the drawer for underwear when his wife unmuted the television. She switched channels until the voice of an unfamiliar news anchor flowed into their bedroom. Troy was pulling on his briefs as a middle age white man began speaking. His eyes flashed to the clock near the bedside. It was 8:00 a.m.

"David Marsh here for channel 77 News. In local news this morning, we have another tragedy that is all too common in this part of downtown Atlanta. Behind me is the adult entertainment club, T and A. The body of Lawrence Jenkins was discovered as patrons and employees were leaving in the wee hours."

The screen split showing another clean-cut, middle age white man. His brown hair was swept to the side, and he wore wire frame glasses that sat high on his nose. "David, what do we know about the victim?"

"Here's what we know, Brandon. The victim, Lawrence Jenkins, also known as Justice, was a career criminal who had frequent brushes with the law. Authorities believe his death is gang related. There was an eerie message left with the body. *'Bring it'* was scribbled across the victim's forehead."

The news anchor at the station fondled the papers in his hands. "You're right, David, the message is unnerving."

"The owners of the establishment could not be reached for comment. Patrons and employees refused to be interviewed for fear of retribution. Lawrence Jenkins is also the cousin of Darrell Jenkins, the man implicated in the College Park murder of longtime resident John Unger–back to you, Brandon."

* * *

It was ten in the morning, when Troy stepped from his house to find Levi,

Akeel and Jesse waiting for him. Beyond them sat the idling limo. The men didn't speak as they climbed into the vehicle headed to the only place left to go. They arrived at an upscale subdivision off Fulton Industrial at five minutes to eleven. The grounds were well-kept and manicured throughout the neighborhood. Magnolia Hills contained mansions and oversized homes that were gaudy to Troy's way of thinking.

Jesse pulled up a steep incline, leading to a house at the end of Genteel Street. The structure was beige brick with traces of brown stone. The windows were large and uncovered but smoked, so one couldn't see in from the outside.

"Are you two, ready?" Levi asked.

"Yeah," Akeel replied.

Troy nodded. Levi gave a curt shake of his head, then opened the door and got out. Akeel climbed out behind him, but he didn't venture away from the limo. In the front seat, Jesse checked his weapon, then followed Levi to the front door. Troy could see Levi ring the bell and after a time speak to the person who answered the door. But he couldn't see who stood in the doorway.

More time elapsed before Levi began speaking again. He gestured with his hands toward the limo, and then Larry Wright appeared on the walkway. Through the window, Troy witnessed Jesse roughly patting down the District Attorney before opening the car door. The brightness of the day spilled into the vehicle as Larry climbed in followed by Akeel. The opposite door opened, and Levi slid in sandwiching the D.A. between he and Akeel. Troy sat facing them.

Larry was dressed in dark slacks, and a light blue vest with a white collar sticking out. A gamut of emotions splayed across his face–but his fear was palpable. Troy waited until they started moving to address his guest verbally.

"Good afternoon, Larry. You're a hard man to connect with."

The D.A. coughed. "I've been busy."

"Too busy to follow up on the case you gave us to investigate–too busy to inquire after your son?"

"What the fuck do you want, Troy?" Larry spit out.

"Let's not waste each other's time, you know why I'm here."

"I know what you are, Troy… keep that in mind," Larry sneered.

Troy leaned in, his tone flat. "You threatening me, Larry?"

The District Attorney held eye contact, his voice was cold. "Yes, Troy, I am threatening you."

"Well that just makes shit all the more interesting, my friend."

"I guess it does," Larry shot back.

The atmosphere in the limo stalled as each man sized the other up. Troy chuckled. "You don't want it with me, Larry."

"What I got could put your ass back in jail, Ernest. If something happens to me, you'll be exposed for who you are and that sweet wife of yours will be visiting you in prison. Hell, maybe she'll testify against you about crimes that happened before she became your wife."

Troy smiled. "Larry you would be doing my lovely wife a favor by having me locked up. I love her enough to understand that about our relationship. It's for that reason that the possibility of dying doesn't shake me. She will be set no matter how this plays out. I'll kill you, Larry—I don't give a fuck about exposure."

The District Attorney looked faint, and Troy thought that was good. The older man needed to understand the game and the players. While he wanted a life with Francine and would do whatever he could to protect his time with her, he was willing to leave her and the child to a life without him. She would be well off, and his child would want for nothing. In life, he couldn't let her go—but in death, there were no choices to make. Still, he would try for Francine.

Larry tried to barter. "Listen, let's make peace instead of war."

"Truce is for the man who approaches me from the front not from the back." Troy said, then nodded to Levi.

"You will hold a press conference to drop the charges against Darrell by morning. If we get to noon and you have not done so, Troy will hold a press conference of his own letting the people of College Park know that the D.A.'s oldest son killed two elderly people to cover the crimes of Shirley Jenkins. We will also let the city know that you fathered Shirley's sons—the people will recognize abuse of power when they see it." Levi explained.

"Shirley didn't physically kill anyone." Larry countered, defensively.

Akeel chimed in, his annoyance was visible. "She coerced your eldest son into killing Mr. Mitchell and Ms. Montgomery. Mitchell was willing to confess, but she had him silenced by Justice. Your younger son is paying for crimes he didn't commit."

"Yo' bitch ass still loves Shirley—don't you?" Levi barked. "Why involve us if you didn't really want to help Darrell?"

"I wanted to help him," Larry snapped. "The shit got bigger than me. It always does when Shirley is involved. When I brought you in, I thought Logan was the problem."

"What happened?" Levi pressed.

Larry sighed, then directed his words at Troy. "Shirley called me right after you and she held the press conference. She wanted you all gone. I chose the case of Sam and Harold because I knew it would make you stay... At least long enough to find out who knew about you."

"How long did you know about Sam and Harold?" Akeel countered.

"Rudy Wilson, one of our investigators was following Sam Fields and Harold Dawson. He believed them responsible for several rapes and two murders. The victims' families believed the same, but lack of evidence kept them on the street. Rudy was following them the day Francine was stolen off the street."

"So, when Jalal Dorsey got picked up?" Levi asked, incredulous.

"I wasn't aware when it first happened," Larry's voice tight. "Rudy died in a car accident this past June. He left his confidential material to me—Troy's file was marked *public service*. Rudy had decided not to turn him in."

"Where do we go from here?" Akeel asked.

"I want to be part of your organization." Larry shot back.

Levi and Akeel looked to Troy. They wanted him to accept the truce, so they could be done with this thing. But when Troy opened his mouth, malice fell from his lips like stone, so heavy were his words.

"I won't do business with a man who seeks to control me."

"You got shit on me, and I got shit on you. We're even." Larry answered.

"The way I see it, Larry, you owe me for taking care of Sam and Harold. Their victims were women of color, so I'm clear why they weren't stopped. You owe me for Justice, who victimized the elderly in a black neighborhood and it never made the news—not like John Unger. You will stop Shirley Jenkins, or you will wake up one night to find me standing over you. You owe me, Larry, because you're still alive."

The limo came to a complete stop once again in front of Larry's home. Jesse pulled in front of the house on the street, making the D.A. have to walk the steep driveway. Akeel got out and held the door. Larry looked as though he had more to say but thought better of it; he got out and walked away.

On the ride back to Calhoun, Troy went over everything in his mind. He had been bested by Larry Wright, but an enemy seen was better than an enemy unseen. While he was working through how to kill the District Attorney, Akeel broke the silence.

"So this is it? We're going to forget all that Chris Logan did to us?"

Troy's eyes collided with Akeel's hard stare, there was a wildness that had not been present before. Troy understood his friend's plight, he finally had Monica in his home, but she was distant and afraid. It was a constant reminder of the price they paid. Junior was the measurement of time. Troy didn't answer Akeel–he couldn't.

Levi made the attempt. "Let's focus on getting Darrell out."

The car fell quiet once more, and when they made it back to the house, Troy thought to speak with Akeel alone. His friend, however, didn't venture inside. Akeel took his leave as soon as Jesse parked the limo.

As Troy watched Akeel drive away in the Yukon, he turned to Jesse. "Don't let him out of your sight–change the car you work from. Call me day or night."

4

THE BEGINNING

A television had been rolled into the conference room at 7:55 a.m. Denise pressed a hot cup of coffee into Troy's hands as he stood at the far end of the long table. Tyrell, Hassan and Jesse were in early to help coordinate getting Jasmin and the Jenkins family to the prison. Akeel was not in attendance. Troy had decided to steer clear of Shirley for fear of strangling her. While he sipped the black brew, Denise set the TV to channel 55.

Levi received official word from the District Attorney's office yesterday evening. Due to lack of evidence, Darrell Jenkins would be released as soon as he could be processed out. The men stood, speaking with one another about what needed to be addressed for the day. Troy kept his eyes glued to the television. Tyrell asked him a question, which brought his attention back to the conversation.

"Jerrell wants to speak with you. Do you want me to bring him by the office?"

"About what?" Troy replied.

"The kid is distraught about Mr. Mitchell."

Troy's head popped up. "What is talking to me going to do? I can't change that he's missing."

Tyrell stared at him, offering nothing verbal. Troy sighed. "Bring him by when you finish with Darrell."

Tyrell nodded, then walked away. The men filed out of the conference room leaving Troy by himself, and seconds later the music for the local newscast began. Thom Flint started his morning monologue, his tone dry, face serious. His silver hair made him look distinguished.

"Good morning and happy Thursday. In the news at the top of the hour—a live conference with the District Attorney's office. Our own Lacey Bowers is onsite."

The screen switched to Lacey dressed in a dark pants suit and peach blouse—blonde hair flowing about her shoulders; a microphone in her right hand. The conference, it seemed, was already underway.

"Good morning, Lacey Bowers here for channel 55 Action News. We're live at the District Attorney's office where Larry Wright has announced that due to lack of evidence the case against Darrell Jenkins has been dropped."

The screen cut away to show an exhausted Larry speaking. "The charges against Darrell Jenkins have been dropped due to lack of evidence. I will not answer questions at this time as the investigation is ongoing."

There were lots of camera flashes and questions being hurled at the D.A., but his entourage covered him as he left the stage through a side door. Lacey's voice and image came back into focus. "That was a clip from the live conference, which lasted only moments. Darrell Jenkins is free, and the investigation into John Unger's murder is ongoing. Back to you, Thom."

Troy picked up the remote and turned the television off. He went back to his office, shut the door and began pacing. Francine and the baby popped into his mind; he bought more time with them by pinning Larry down, but the peace wouldn't last. Although he had gotten rid of the Darrell Jenkins' issue, he now had the added bonus of dealing with Larry Wright, Chris Logan and Akeel, who was losing his shit.

There was a knock at the door. "Come in," Troy barked.

Levi stepped in and behind him stood Jesse. His cousin shut the door. Jesse broke the silence. "Akeel is following Logan—the problem is that Logan is being followed by the cops. I got a friend watching him for now, but Akeel ain't thinking clearly."

"I'll talk to him." It was all Troy could offer—he wasn't in a position to promise more.

* * *

Across town Chris Logan stood in his kitchen drinking coffee and watching the live newscast from the District Attorney's office. Darrell Jenkins was being released and Chris' hands shook from all it implied. Time had run out on him. Troy Bryant was controlling every damn thing. His life had become tight, but he would shake Richard's ass down in order to loosen things up. There could be no more delay, he would start tonight.

He couldn't call Unger, he was sure his phone was tapped. When they last met, he had given Richard until the following Sunday to come up with his money. But at three in the morning the Saturday before payment was due, Richard had shown up with twenty thousand in cash, asking for more time. Chris had given him till the end of the month. The money had been a show of good faith and a dumbass move on his part.

Chris was also frustrated about Amanda. She loved him, that much was clear, but would she leave with him? He didn't think so, and it pained him to see the regret in her eyes. She was sorry she loved him, but powerless to stop it. Sexually, she opened to him like a flower in the morning sun. He took his time when she allowed him into her sweet body. Chris tried to love away her misgivings, but he couldn't be different. This was who he would always be, and she understood that even if she didn't verbalize it.

Amanda limited their time together, and Chris tolerated her behavior. He suspected she told those in charge that she couldn't lock him down. And so, to the tail that was placed on her—they appeared to be fuck buddies. But he couldn't get enough of her and was desperate with thoughts of leaving her behind. He would see her tonight, but when the hour grew late and she had gone for the evening, he would reach out to Unger.

* * *

Troy had called Akeel several times and got Monica each time. His sister informed him that Akeel had not been home all day. The man Jesse had tailing Akeel lost sight of him around noon. It was now 7:30, and the fact that he kept calling caused Monica concern.

"Is something wrong, Ernest?"

"No."

"All right, I'll tell him you called."

Akeel wouldn't do anything without talking to him first. He wouldn't jeopardize a life with his son and Monica by going in with no backup—would he? That was just it, Troy couldn't say. He went through the motions with Francine. They ate dinner and were watching television when she dozed on the couch. At 9:30, Troy picked her up and was carrying her to their bedroom when he spied Butch standing in the doorway of the kitchen.

Francine mumbled something, and he kissed her forehead. She never noticed the old man. He walked into their bedroom, and she murmured, "Do you wanna watch television in bed?"

"Butch is in the kitchen waiting to speak with me. I'll be right back."

Francine nodded, then rolled over to get comfortable. Troy shut the bedroom door quietly behind him before heading to the kitchen. He found the old man leaned against the island. Butch got right down to business.

"Jesse been waitin' outside of Akeel's all day. He finally came home, stayed for thirty minutes and is on the move again. Jesse says he thinks Akeel might go to Logan's house. It's where he was last night."

Troy stared at the ground as Butch went on. "Jesse thinks you should meet him there. Take the old Honda. I'll watch over Francine. Levi is going to Akeel's house to watch over Monnie and the boy."

Troy nodded, his voice rusty, when he replied. "Yeah."

He backtracked to his office and retrieved his nine millimeter. Butch left the keys for the car on the counter in the kitchen. Troy exited the house through the side door.

* * *

At 11:19 p.m., Chris heard the hinges of the back door creak ever so slightly. Amanda had just fallen asleep and it looked like she was going to stay through the night. The plan was to wait until she left for the evening to seek out Richard Unger. But Amanda was still in his bed, and Chris suspected it was because Darrell Jenkins had been released from prison earlier that day. She was trying to offer comfort in the face of the storm that was brewing.

Chris wouldn't ask Amanda to leave—he was too weak. Judging by the sound of the back door squeaking, Richard must be aware of Darrell Jenkins' release as well. Chris would bet his left nut that Richard had come to kill him rather than pay him. He was up in a flash pulling on his jeans while reaching for his gun. Next to him, Amanda, who was also law enforcement, did the same. When she reached for her weapon, they stared at each other for moments until she nodded.

They stepped into the hall as one, each covering the other. Briefly, Chris entertained thoughts of Troy Bryant coming for him, but tossed the notion out because the Silent Activist was far too cunning for a move like this. The more he thought about the boldness of the situation, he realized it was Unger come to pay him a visit. Still, Richard was the type of man who believed others should do the dirt and he should reap the benefit. This incident had to be paid for by Richard.

Chris moved down the stairs with stealth, settling on each step with both feet for seconds, so as not to make the wood groan. His back against the wall, he saw Amanda's murky figure at the top of the staircase covering him. Chris always left the light on over the kitchen sink, so that he didn't step blindly into his house after a long day. But tonight, he was met with darkness.

At the bottom of the stairs, Chris worked off instinct and memory. He crossed the hallway, before pressing his back firmly against the wall. Behind him, Amanda followed the same path making not a sound—gun drawn. He caught sight of the dining room and a spill of light from the window. The curtains were parted emitting the dregs of the neighbor's floodlights in the distance. Next to the window stood a shadow about six feet in stature. Chris took aim, but he never got off the shot.

The sound of glass shattering came from the direction of the living room. Smoke immediately filled the house, and Chris vaguely registered tear gas. The figure by the curtains disappeared into the fog, and Chris gave chase. He heard the back door open swiftly—clumsily, his lungs burned causing him to burst frantically into the backyard. A hail of rapid gunfire erupted, he crouched behind a chair on the small patio and watched in horror as Amanda went down after clearing the doorway.

"Shit—Mandy." Chris yelled as he dragged her behind the chair.

"Logan," she mumbled.

Chris let off several shots, then heard a definite howl of pain. More gunfire and, in the background, sirens—then quiet ensued. His arm and chest burned.

Troy had parked his car at the all-night pharmacy on the corner of Powder Springs Road and South Marietta Parkway. The night was mild, but he was sweating. He hustled toward Whitlock Avenue, unable to stick to the shadows because Powder Springs Road was alive with too many fast-food joints and well-lit. When he turned down Whitlock, darkness enveloped him.

The street was lined with large oak trees and on a soft breeze, the leaves rustled. Troy turned down a side street with no directional sign and kept moving until he heard a faint bird call. He crouched near a huge bush and called back; seconds later, Jesse appeared at his side. The house behind them was dim, but a hall light burned somewhere within. The drapes were pulled back without a care for privacy–historical Marietta spoke of money and power.

"What do we got?" Troy asked, not really wanting an answer.

"Logan's house is on the next street over. The gray house, three doors down on the opposite side of the street is being used by the cops. The woman is with Logan tonight, and Akeel is in his backyard. He knows I'm here, but I have not approached."

"Shit," Troy hissed.

They cut through the yard of a big Victorian style home and moved quietly into Logan's yard. Trees of all sizes dotted the two acres of land and the swell of the earth elevated them above the house. The hill was slight, but it gave an advantage to anyone standing in the thicket. In the yard diagonal from Logan's was a bright floodlight that offered more shadows and undiscerning figures. Troy was certain of one thing–Akeel was not in the backyard. It was his last thought before everything got hectic.

The sound of glass breaking was followed by the back door being swung violently open. Based on the dim lighting, it appeared Richard Unger was trying to get away. Hot on his heels, Chris Logan stumbled from the house, gun drawn and moving quickly to take cover. Unger turned in time to let off several shots taking down a woman who was exiting the house. Troy looked to Jesse who stood still as a statue while the drama unfolded. He peeked around the tree to witness the woman being dragged behind a chair–then more gunfire.

Akeel rounded the house from the left, gun drawn and stepped right into a hail of bullets. When Akeel went down, Jesse covered him as Troy ventured from his hiding place to drag his friend to safety. The siren was getting louder, and Troy knew a moment of panic.

"What are you doing here?" Akeel asked, his voice weak.

"Shit, man, are you hit?" Troy countered.

"We out of time–gotta get to the car." Jesse said, as if trying to keep them on track.

"My car is too far away," Troy answered.

"Can he walk?" Jesse asked.

"Yeah," Akeel replied.

Troy was sure Jesse didn't hear him. "Aiight–we following you."

There were no more words. Jesse led them through a few backyards, and just when Troy thought he would collapse under Akeel's weight, a small car came into view. Troy pulled open the back door and fell into the car on top of Akeel–who grunted. Jesse started the engine and drove the opposite way from commotion.

As Troy lay on top of Akeel, he felt wet and sticky; he knew his friend was bleeding profusely. "We need to head to a hospital."

"No... no," Akeel said.

"They gonna report it. Gunshots get questioned–hang tight." Jesse said.

"Monica..." Akeel moaned before passing out.

Laying in the backseat with Akeel cradled in his arms, Troy was disoriented. After about ten minutes, Jesse stopped at a pay phone. Troy could see a sign for Jona's Coin Laundry from his position, and soon they were traveling again. He stared up at the sky as lightning began to flash. It started raining in earnest by the time they pulled into Akeel's garage. Troy didn't move until the automatic door slid back into place, shielding them from prying eyes. Butch and Monica were waiting; his sister was frantic.

* * *

The need to be transparent to the press kept Troy in his routine. When he arrived home after helping Monica and Butch stabilize Akeel, he was exhausted. Levi was sprawled out on the couch; his cousin had switched places with Butch and brought Junior with him. Francine was in the kitchen with Jewel, and Troy could hear the light murmurings of their conversation. He had been about to shower to get the grime and blood off when Junior stepped into view from a room further up the hall. He was thankful he had changed his bloodstained shirt.

"Is everything all right, Uncle Troy?" Junior's anxiety was visible.

"Yeah, little man. Your mom and dad had some business to handle. I'll get you to school."

Junior stared at him as if gauging his honesty. "All right, I'll be ready soon."

When his nephew turned to go back inside his room, Troy noticed Francine at the far end of the hall. She looked troubled but didn't speak. He nodded curtly toward their room, and she rushed forward. Closing the door softly behind them, he took a shaking Francine into his arms.

"Are you all right?" she whispered.

"Yeah... I'm good. Akeel was shot last night—in both legs and his right shoulder. He's going to be in pain, but he'll live."

Francine stepped back from him, her eyes shiny with tears. "Monica?"

"Monnie is good, she's with him. We'll keep the boy until she comes for him."

His wife nodded, and his eyes drifted over to the clock on the night stand, 6:15 a.m. He needed to dress. "I'm going to drop Junior at school and stay at the office until it's time to pick him up."

"You want me to come to the office with you?" she asked.

"No."

He kissed her forehead, then turned and walked into the bathroom. When he emerged from his shower, he found a cup of coffee on the nightstand next to the remote. Troy decided against the morning news. He dressed and stepped into the living room where his nephew sat on the couch next to Levi.

"You ready, little man?"

"Yeah... Will my mom be here after school?" Junior asked.

"We'll see."

Troy never looked at Levi, but he knew his cousin's thoughts were the same. They would stay in routine while Hassan and Tyrell remained out of sight, covering the question of Akeel's absence. Jesse was out front leaning against the Yukon smoking a cigarette. When he noticed them, he opened the back door, and Junior scrambled in first.

Levi rode in the front with Jesse, and Junior kept his attention on the swiftly moving scenery. There was no music or radio, and fifty-five minutes later, they pulled into the parking lot of the George Washington Carver charter school. They were in line behind several vehicles waiting for drop off. The children were all dressed in khaki bottoms and blue shirts. Along the stairs of the small red-bricked building, several teachers stood greeting the students as they leapt from the cars.

Troy turned to his nephew. "Have a good day. I'll be back for you when school is over."

"Yes, sir." Junior climbed out of the truck and disappeared into the throng of children.

Once they were back in traffic, Levi spoke. "The female cop isn't expected to make it. Richard Unger is dead… Chris Logan is expected to make a full recovery."

"Shit," Troy countered.

"The news is saying Unger attempted to kill Logan because his uncle's murderer went free," Levi paused, then breathed in deeply. "They believe Richard Unger's accomplice got away."

Troy didn't comment. If not for Jesse, he and Akeel would have been caught at Logan's house. He was pondering the last few hours when Jesse chimed in.

"Akeel is weak, but no fever."

They pulled into the parking lot of the law office and witnessed a crowd of reporters shoving at each other to get to the vehicle. Troy sighed, and Levi advised. "No comments."

The minute Troy stepped down from the truck, he was blinded by the camera flashes. When the truck door closed behind, he found himself in a semicircle of reporters, microphones and cameramen. Levi pushed his way into the crowd and yelled.

"Back off!" But no one gave him a second glance, firing question after question.

"Troy, what are your feelings about the shooting that took place at Chris Logan's home last evening?"

"Troy, do you think Chris Logan framed Darrell Jenkins?"

"Troy, we noticed that the D.A. stated they didn't have the proper evidence—not that Darrell Jenkins was believed to be innocent. Have you helped a murderer go free?"

"Troy is the aggressive attitude you've had toward the justice system and former detective Chris Logan getting better for you?"

On and on went the insults, but it was the last question that caused him angst. He had started for the lobby when he heard the word *aggressive*. Troy stopped, faced the cameras, and in a voice as smooth as silk—commented. "So you find me aggressive, but not Chris Logan—the man who stole my life and my family by using a system that has exploited black life since 1866. At this moment, ladies and gentlemen, my hostility is for the news media outlets that knowingly continue to misrepresent people of color."

Turning toward the lobby, Ernest Stephen Bryant walked away, leaving the questions and flashing lights behind.

Coming Soon

INSEPARABLE

PROLOGUE

SEPTEMBER 1995
DALLAS, GEORGIA

Akeel was awake, but he hadn't opened his eyes. And though pain wracked his body, he remained perfectly still. Disoriented, the silence was unnerving as he tried to recollect the last the few hours. Something warm pressed against his right hip, and when he dared to open his eyes, the white ceiling fan in his bedroom came into view. He turned his head ever so slightly in both directions, gaining two pieces of information. He was hooked up to an IV on the left and Monica lay snuggled at his right, near the bottom of the mattress.

A wave of nausea rocked his being, causing his eyes to drift shut. He braced himself against the discomfort as flashes of light exploded behind his lids. Along with the sparks came the memory of the last few hours–days. Akeel had shot Logan and he had been shot by Logan. And while the ache in his body made sense, confusion settled over him like a thick mist.

Monica gave a small sigh, burrowing closer into him and he allowed his fingers to curl into her untamed hair. She stiffened at his touch, but he didn't let go. Akeel knew she had awakened, but like him, she said nothing. He was exhausted and unable to fight the fatigue claiming him; there would be time to sort shit out later–Monica was in his bed.

***

A week and a half passed with Akeel only offering polite words–the disconnect between them growing. In the face of Akeel's quiet, Monica looked to Troy for an explanation, but her brother was evasive on all fronts. Butch came daily to help with Akeel's care, but he was even more closed off than her son's father. She was essentially left in the dark until she flipped on the television one evening to find that Chris Logan's house had been shot up.

The early weeks of living with Akeel had been awkward after the situation with Francine. Junior was the highlight of both their days, and Monica was thankful for the time father and son were spending together. Things seem to flow well with them. She caught glimpses of the man she fell in love with when their son told an animated story about school. But Junior's absence submerged them into an emotionally strained state that could be felt all the way to the ends of her hair. She should have stayed in New Jersey with Malik, everything with him had been simple.

Monica stood in the tiny kitchen; her hands shook as she reached for her favorite yellow mug. In the background, she could hear Akeel maneuvering the stairs. Far from steady on his feet, his steps were slow, labored and deliberate. She reached for another mug to pour him some coffee and waited. He shuffled down the hall until he stood behind her.

"Good morning."

"Morning–how are you feeling?" she countered.

"I'm fine."

It was the same exchange every morning and then nothing for hours. He moved to open the back door where he sat to take his coffee, but she stopped him.

"Troy will bring Junior home today."

He turned to stare at her before offering an indifferent response. "Yeah."

"If you're not ready, Junior and I can stay with Troy."

Akeel stepped away from the back door, placing his mug on the table. He was dressed in blue jeans and a black t-shirt, on his feet were black work boots–unlaced. Monica met his glare and the urge to take a step back was real, but she maintained her stance under his scrutiny. He had dark smudges under his eyes, and he hadn't shaved. She braced herself for who he was now as his lips pulled into a sneer. The tone he offered was threatening, dangerous and promising.

"Why the fuck did you come back to Georgia?"

She looked to the window, the kitchen consisted of a sink and Formica countertops diagonally placed to the right of the white stove; behind her stood the matching refrigerator. The tiny space led to an equally small dining room dominated by a large oak table with six chairs. Against the back wall was a large window and next to it, the back door. When she could no longer ignore him, she returned his stare.

"I wanted Junior to get to know his father and uncle."

"I stayed away so you wouldn't have to deal with this…" and to himself, he muttered. "Fuck."

Since they were in the conversation, and this was most feeling he had shown, Monica spoke of her plans as they pertained to their son. "I'm moving back to New Jersey. Junior is comfortable with you–that was my goal. He can begin seeing you summers and holidays."

Akeel had been shot three times. Once in the right shoulder and in the right thigh with the bullet lodging in his left leg–flesh wounds. Still, the scars were nasty. He tried to hide his pain, but his pallor told a different story. At her statement, his light skin became bloodless. He stepped right up to her, his gait aggressive.

"You tryna go back to him?"

She didn't respond to the question about Malik. And though she was terrified, again, she managed not to step back. Monica willed her voice to remain steady. "Your only business with me is our son."

"Oh, Monnie, you are so wrong. You are mine–the boy is mine and you will not take my son to another man. I backed away and you came to me. Your chance to be free of me is gone."

"I'm not afraid of you," she whispered to his chest.

Akeel leaned down and spoke softly in her ear. "Perfect–you're not afraid and I don't mind breaking you."

The doorbell chimed. Monica knew it was Troy bringing Junior home. Akeel moved back but blocked her way out of the kitchen. Apparently, he wasn't done with his words of warning.

"No man will dictate how it will be with you and me. Troy can't help you, do you understand me?"

Only after she looked up into his face, acknowledging his anger did he step back and allow her to pass. The center of the front door was made of decorative glass and she could see a distorted image of Troy, Butch and Junior. She opened the door and her son pressed himself against her. Monica felt his worry.

"Mom, I got stuff for you to sign in my bookbag." He looked around. "Is Dad here?"

Monica smiled. "Dad is in the kitchen, let's put your things in your room first."

She gazed at her brother and then Butch before backing up to allow them entry. It was Troy that asked, "You all right, Monnie?"

"Yes," she nodded, before turning to follow Junior up to his room.

* * *

Akeel stood propped against the counter listening to the exchange between Monica and Troy. She had followed their son to his room. Butch and Troy appeared at the archway where the hall and the kitchen met. The old man spoke first.

"Feeling any pain?"

"Naw." Akeel shook his head. But it was a lie, his heart ached.

Troy stood behind Butch, eyeing him. They hadn't talked business because Monica was always around, and now Junior was home.

"You wanna go for ride?" Troy asked.

"No."

"We need to discuss Logan." Troy replied.

"What's to discuss—the mafucka lived." Akeel's voice was tight.

Troy sighed. "You have Monica and the boy to think about. You can't do this again—not this way."

Akeel's insides warred with his cool exterior; his tone was matter of fact when he offered his thoughts about all that belonged to him. "Monica and my son are not your damn business. Your fuckin' thoughts and feelings are not welcome here."

Troy smiled as he folded his arms over his chest. Akeel stood to his full height moving away from the counter. He saw the challenge in Troy's eyes, and he was prepared to meet it head on. The Silent Activist would not run his life.

Akeel dropped his arms and Troy spoke. "If she doesn't think the boy is safe in your presence, you will lose her. I'm not trying to run yo' shit, and while I won't make offers against you, if Monica comes to me–I won't turn her away."

"You didn't stick to the fuckin' plan." Akeel hissed.

"No, I didn't stick to the plan because Francine happened."

"Logan stole from us." Akeel gritted out.

"The rest you're giving away with both hands."

"Dad!" Junior yelled from the top of house, the rushed sound of foot-falls could be heard as he made his way.

"Stop running–walk." Monica chided.

Troy didn't break eye contact until Junior came running down the hall and threw himself against Akeel. Closing his arms around his son, he watched as Troy turned and walked away. Butch nodded, then followed suit. Monica appeared in the archway, her gaze glassy with unshed tears. In the distance, he heard the front door open and close.

As he stared at the mother of his child, Akeel contemplated Troy's words. He would take heed and disengage from the reckless thoughts that plagued him. What he would not do is step away from his plan to kill Chris Logan.

Made in the USA
Columbia, SC
08 May 2020